Blurring Reality

R. D. Chapman

This is a work of fiction. Characters, names, places, and events have all evolved from the author's imagination and/or used fictitiously. Any resemblance to any person, place or event in the real world, dead or alive, is entirely coincidental.

Editor: Ray Rhamey
Cover Design: SelfPubBookCovers.com/thrillerauthor

ISBN: 978-1-7371741-0-3

Warm hugs to my family for their patience and help. A very warm thank you to my editor, Ray Rhamey, who showed how to make Jem's story so much better. Lastly, a very special thank you to the readers who are willing to give a new author a chance.

CHAPTER 1

"Emergency! Emergency!"

Jem Wilmont rolled her eyes at the idiot screaming over the loudspeakers. What? He didn't think sirens deafening everyone in the Folsum spaceport wasn't a clue?

"Inbound shuttle—engines failing!"

Transparent blast shields snapped over the fifth-floor observation window. For Pete's sake, she grumbled, glaring out the blue-tinted glass panes. The Delmark Three colony was old enough to have weathered real emergencies. Three out of five engines were enough—

"Two engines dead, third failing! Find the nearest shelter. NOW!"

What? Jem's head jerked upward as people and vehicles bolted in every direction. Two! She'd only tampered with two! But the super-heated glow around the growing bright speck testified to a too-swift descent. She grasped the window frame with a white-knuckled grip.

Voices babbled around her. Someone recited a prayer for the hundreds onboard as the shuttle became visible, its engines a thunderous roar in the distance. The shuttle began pitching backward. Screams turned to loud gasps when it stopped, the nose pointed up and the shuttle coming straight down.

"Sonofabitch, they're riding their fire!"

The surging throng crushed Jem against the thick window as everyone tried to see. Be enough…be enough, she chanted silently.

Down…down…the delta-wing's left stream sputtering flames, its right one trailing only smoke. Streams of hell-fire from the two over-taxed rear engines struggled to slow their descent.

Four hundred meters—they're going to make it!

1

Slower…slower…

Two hun—oh SHIT!

The observation room made a collective inhale as the left sputter flared in a multi-colored burst, then died.

The shuttle wobbled. Dropped. The remaining engines snapped off and the flare of thrusters flipped the ship back to horizontal right before it plunged behind a low ridge.

The room fell silent. Emergency vehicles raced toward the billowing smoke and dust.

"The screen," someone yelled. The mass of watchers wheeled as one. A ten-foot viewscreen had flickered to life, displaying the lead vehicle's bouncing video. They waited.

One minute. Two minutes.

Sounds filtered through Jem's numbed senses. A broken-off sob. A woman shushing a young girl. An elderly man collapsing on her left as someone called for medical assistance.

Three minutes.

The video steadied in a final swirl of dust. Out past the vehicle's nose lay the smoldering ruins of a charred cornfield. The shuttle was tilted off center, its crumpled undercarriage exposed. A large crack spiraled up and around from the rear door to the pitted engine base. The cracked tail fin tilted precariously to one side. It was broken and blackened but, mostly, in one piece.

Jem shuddered in relief even as the tail fin gave up and tumbled to the ground.

There was a burst of white light and a hatch flew up and away. A figure appeared in the opening and the observation dome erupted into screams and back-thumping hugs.

Jem slid to the floor in overwhelming relief. She was not touching another engine. Ever.

***

Inspection has discovered all three of the Hermes Ion Engines failed without warning. The three hundred and sixty-one shuttle occupants, plus any ground fatalities, would have made it the Republic's worst accident in twenty-two years, the newscaster intoned solemnly. *On close review, the Federal Safety Commission has determined yesterday's incident was only the latest in a series of similar, although minor, events scattered throughout the Republic over the past eight months. An FSC team of experts is being dispatched to the Hermes System to investigate the situation at the manufacturing facilities.*

"Finally," Jem said, toasting the screen with her glass.

She'd been fidgeting in her room all day, watching replay after replay of the shuttle's near-disastrous flight. All the multitude of interviewees had offered were possibilities and speculations. And now that the official announcement had come? Perfect.

Due to the seriousness of these events, the FSC is also taking the unprecedented action of ordering all transports—I repeat, ALL transports— using the Hermes Ion Engines grounded until they receive a thorough inspection by a qualified safety team. The disruption and uproar from all sectors of the public and business world are unparalleled.

A grin split her face. Hah! That beats a huge fine. If Kurzvall had been furious after the Orion trouble she'd caused him, this should have the bastard spitting titanium chips.

The newscaster's image faded, replaced by those of the shuttle pilots—a husband and wife team. The narrator recounted their earlier careers with Survey and how their skill, experience, and unorthodox use of the shuttle's engines and docking thrusters had prevented a major tragedy. The next image was of the shuttle's smoldering, cracked frame. The video zoomed in close to its undercarriage, revealing how far the mangled structure was pushed up into the cargo area. The inherent strength of jagtin, used in the shuttle's construction, had kept it from being worse.

Swallowing hard, Jem snatched up the control and jabbed the off button.

Shit, damn, crap. She'd never even considered another engine failing in conjunction with her tampered ones. Didn't matter now. Goal achieved. Time to leave. He'd know she was here, and his thugs were probably already on their way. She tossed back the last of her wine, remembering when she hadn't moved fast enough.

CHAPTER 2

"The Bright Star Tour Line has cancelled all thirty-one orders for Hermes Ion Engines," McNeil reported, his voice neutral.

Reginald Kurzvall's jaw tightened. He was down millions of dollars, and it was only the first item on his aide's list. The fallout from last month's fiasco on Folsum was only getting worse, thanks to the unmitigated gall of the Federal Safety Commission.

First, they grounded *every* transport using his engines across the *entire* Republic until inspected by their so-called experts. Then the FSC inspectors not only derided his claims of sabotage, the fools slapped him with an unbelievable fine. Maybe there had been a few accidents in the plant over the years. No one had died. And if they had, it would've been their own fault for not paying attention to the machinery.

As if the disruption and bad publicity weren't bad enough, the ongoing loss of business was going to crash the company. A growing number weren't waiting for inspections. They were simply yanking out the Hermes and installing his competitor's engines. At this rate, he might as well close the assembly plant down.

And he knew exactly who to blame for all of it.

McNeil's listing of several inquiries from the Janus Legacy Foundation briefly caught Kurzvall's attention. Now that was a well-named institution. The current bastards managing it were just as two-faced as their founding father. He drummed his fingers on his desk top, only half listening to McNeil's litany of news and updates.

Jem Wilmont undoubtedly was also the cause of that Orion mess. The anonymous source exposing his business arrangements with the System Senator had provided Law Enforcers with an incredible amount of information. Detailed *confidential* information that could only be learned by someone with a unique way to eavesdrop like the freak she was. He now conducted private business only in specialized rooms containing very sensitive motion and weight sensors.

McNeil's droning faded even more as he continued cataloging the damages.

The Orion Sys-Senator had lost his job. So what? All Kurzvall Industry companies were now banned from doing business with any Orion System-based company for the next twenty years. *Twenty years.* Anger bubbled up anew. The edict not only hobbled several business ventures, it had forced him to pull completely out of one contract and had cost him another million-plus in penalty. Closing the Hermes engine plant would seriously impact several other contracts but… He paused, thought it through. *It might not be a bad idea.*

Let the idiotic emotionalism die down. Promise significant discounts for delayed deliveries. Make a few updates to keep the FSC morons happy, then reopen in six, seven months with great fanfare for the improved and retooled factory. Yes, it should—

"…Universal Postal and Messaging Service has opted out of their contracts."

Kurzvall jolted back to full attention. "What did you say?"

McNeil cleared his throat. "Universal Postal and Messaging Service has canceled all Hermes Ion Engine contracts. As their services are so extensive and vital, UPMS insists on an escape clause in all their contracts allowing them to cancel, without penalty, if it's deemed continuation may impact their performance." He cleared his throat again. "The key phrase in their lawyer's message was: 'Unreliable engines present a negative and potentially deadly state.' They listed all the incidents from this past year as evidence. Sir."

UPMS mail and courier pods were the glue which kept the Republic together. Averaging seven meters long from engine base to electronic nose, the autonomous Class One drones transported their cargos to even the farthest systems in hours instead of the days and weeks larger ships required. Messages and packages, news and information, data and financial transfers: all carried in either physical or electronic form. Compartments could be reconfigured as needed for specialized cargos, from people to produce: anything needing to get somewhere fast.

"Where's that Tracker?" Kurzvall snapped. Faced with nothing but apologies from his so-called security specialists and a growing financial drain, he'd been forced to hire someone outside his normal business connections.

McNeil flipped his reader to a new screen. "Baron reported two weeks ago from Bellar, Sagious One. He's found evidence Wilmont was there three months ago and was—"

"Wilmont was on Folsom three *weeks* ago. Contact him. If he's so damn good he should be able to track her from there."

That bitch. That interfering, meddling *bitch*.

Rage coursed through Kurzvall as his aide slipped out of the office. Wilmont would pay for all her meddling when he got his hands on her.

There would be no escape this time.

CHAPTER 3

The assassin-ghost poured a mean glass of Aspric whisky.

Thane Baron inhaled slowly through his teeth and lowered his glass to the tabletop. *Breathe, lungs, breathe. In. Out.* Wow. Talk about getting your landing gear kicked out from under you. Served him right, forgetting miners on the edge of nowhere expected drinks as tough as they were.

Thane studied his quarry while taking a second, more cautious sip. Would the men sitting at the counter still flirt if they knew she could kill them just as politely as she served their drinks? She didn't look like someone who blew up research labs and crashed shuttles. Nope. More like a dancer. He watched her graceful stretch for a glass above her head, the tip of a light-brown braid swinging just above her waist. His free-gravity dance-loving aunt moved similarly, but Wilmont's fluidity more likely came from martial arts training.

Okay, Jem Seaborne Wilmont of Sol, I found you. Now what?

His client's orders were simple: find and report her location. If possible, he was also to keep her from leaving while arrangements were made. Originally that last directive had made him laugh. He'd quit laughing months ago. It was unbelievable how the woman just vanished, a ghost slipping in and out of buildings, cities—hell, Thane snorted, entire solar systems.

Poof. Gone. Not a trace.

He scowled down at his drink. He had twelve years of experience and a reputation for finding anybody this side of the incinerator. Yet this woman had left him floundering like a trainee sniffing out his first trail. It had taken eight months and a lot of systems to track her from the fiasco on Delmark Three to Minos Four. Then he had lost her. Again.

He'd hate to admit it, but finally learning about the contract she'd signed with the Euphrates Mining Company had been pure luck. *I'd have found it ...eventually,* he consoled himself. But this isolated mining colony on the Republic's rim had been a major and completely unexpected move. After all, her port-drifter cover was perfect for someone who needed to slide in and out of an area without needing a reason. So why commit to a year on Pappia and its rigidly controlled access through a single spaceport?

A commitment, Thane acknowledged irritably, which was the only reason he'd caught up with her. *Stop grousing and think. The woman must have a reason.* Was there some connection here to his client? He'd have his ship's comp brain research the possibility. Decide to get lost for a year, take a vacation while—nope, scratch that. She didn't need to come to Pappia to get lost. Not with that disappearing trick of hers.

He studied her again over the glass rim. At least she shouldn't go poof for the foreseeable future. Too risky. EMC contracts were lawyer-proof and the company took an aggressive stand against contract jumpers. He'd done a few retrievals for them himself.

She must be targeting someone on EMC's payroll and, yeah, a work contract was her only means of access. Pappia didn't allow drifters of any kind. Except for those visiting for some reason, like him, everyone was either a company employee or a registered Independent. After months in a mining site rich with possibilities, had she already hit her target? Was she now biding her time till her EMC contract was up? Nobody the wiser and bankrolled by two employers? Not like the woman needed her EMC paychecks. Her assassin fee must be huge.

Huge? That was an understatement, considering how much she'd accumulated in just a few years. Wilmont could buy a huge chunk of some planet and live gracefully with her obscene Earth account. Yet here she was. On an Earth-sized moon wobbling around its giant host like a drunken marine on first-leave, living in a company dorm, and working her nice ass off on a retrograde night-shrouded dust ball.

Hmmm. Maybe she was on vacation. An assassin-ghost might feel right at home here.

He watched her pour a dark-colored drink into a steaming glass, her movements quick and competent. Nothing wasted. Not even the deft twist removing her hand from a miner's grasp. The guy should count himself lucky his cheek wasn't getting a harder pat than his arm currently was. But then, management probably frowned on hard swats to a customer's anywhere.

He took another sip and swished the whisky around for several seconds before swallowing. It was actually pretty good. Or everything between his teeth and guts was numb.

Thane rubbed his jaw and gave his neck a couple of twists. He should be the one thinking of a vacation. He'd been tracking Wilmont for almost a year and before that…the Engle and Johansson cases, about seven months total. He scowled, thinking about the museum job prior to them. It had only lasted four weeks but ended with him fighting off a bunch of crazy cultists. Yep, once this job was completed…

Wilmont glanced in his direction. Her gaze paused briefly before moving on.

Thane's lips curved slightly, realizing he'd just been assessed and dismissed. Her mistake. Downing the final swallow, he exited the Pounding J with a casual stride, relaxed from both whisky and another successful hunt.

CHAPTER 4

Mr. Mystery was missing.

The black-haired stranger had first shown up three nights ago. The man always came in about her mid-shift, sat at a table along the back wall and nursed a drink or two before leaving. Always drinking Aspric whisky and always paying upfront. Quiet. Non-threatening. Yet Jem found herself on edge as soon as he walked in the door.

Speaking of missing, *about frigging time* she fumed as Margo came hurrying in behind the counter.

"Sorry." Margo moved quickly to the bar comp and logged in.

Jem shot an annoyed glance at the tall blond as she filled another order. "Jansom's going to say something if you keep this up. Or fire you."

Two months ago, Margo had opted to remain as an Independent after completing her EMC contract. Company policy forced her to move out of the modest-but-free employee accommodations and into a modest not-so-free rental. She'd started coming in late shortly after moving her boyfriend in three weeks ago. It'd been almost half an hour tonight.

"I know, I know. I sometimes wonder why I let him move in."

"Shared costs and great sex, if I remember correctly," Jem replied testily.

"So true, so true. He's got a great—"

Jem waved a hand over her shoulder "Don't want to hear it."

"Yeah, but he's got this trick that—"

"Margaret Tonelli!"

"*Fine*. No need to get insulting. Can I at least tell you he's a slob?" Margo pouted, looping a hand towel around her belt.

Jem sighed, turned. She liked Margo, even if the woman had absolutely no filter on what came out of her mouth. Margo had managed to drag her out for shopping, even successfully overridden her protests for a spa day. "Okay."

Margo's face lit up. "SLOB. All capitals. Just getting a snack turns the kitchen into a disaster area. The apartment is a hazard zone five minutes after he walks in the door. He doesn't like taking a shower unless I'm in it, and he wants—"

This time Jem waved both hands before Margo went any further. "Enough and *yuck!*" She shuddered. "Give Alicia all the details, nitty, gritty and *dirty*."

Margo gave an impish grin. "Don't worry. I make sure he stays clean." She started reviewing the waiting orders. "How long did the mystery hot-hunk-of-silence stay tonight?"

Hot hunk? "Didn't show up at all. Maybe he left. I think table three is having a contest."

The waitress unloading empty glasses from her tray to the countertop looked up. "No. The Tracker's ship is still here."

Margo snorted. "Got a date scheduled?"

"No," Alicia replied, leaning against the counter.

When the over-endowed brunette with low-cut tunics started at Pounding J six weeks ago, she had readily admitted her intention of leaving Pappia with as many credits as possible. Jem was willing to bet she was making as much on the side as she was at J. Was the company women hired for that brand of entertainment aware of the competition?

"How do you know he's a Tracker?" Jem asked. Rampant speculation had guesses ranging from mercenary, her personal favorite, to some type of Enforcer.

"Lisa told me. She works in the port office."

"Lisa?" Jem asked as a second waitress started unloading her tray next to them.

"Lisa Calhoun Travis. My sig-ner."

Both bartenders stared. Melissa froze, two glasses still clutched in her hand.

"We signed up together," Alicia continued.

"Does your significant *partner* know about your after-work *dates?*" Margo snapped.

"Of course," she said, apparently unfazed by their reactions.

Jem's mouth dropped open again.

"That's messed up." Melissa plopped the glasses down and unloaded the rest.

"Lisa is okay with you f—ouch!" Margo yanked her foot out from under Jem's and shot her a glare.

"Lisa knows I'm only interested in their money. We'll be buying a ranch and going into horse breeding when we return home," Alicia told them. "Expenses will be high for years until we have stock to sell. Table three looks to be getting impatient."

***

Jem stepped out of Pounding J's back door into the dimly lit service way. She scanned what passed for a sky as she pulled gloves on. Nope. Still no stars. Even after four months, some part of her still hoped for a miraculous glimpse of them. But starlight was too weak to penetrate Pappia's dense atmosphere. Sunlight just barely made it through the swirling brown stuff outside the transparent dome. High noon here most planets would call twilight. What weak solar radiation that did make it was absorbed by the dome, keeping the colony reasonably warm during the day. The warmth bled off quickly after sunset, making nights chilly as well as dark. Away from the colony's well-lit primary business hub—which never shut down—streetlights and individual buildings provided the only illumination.

What in the frigging universe had she been thinking?

This was almost as bad as living on a space station. Something she'd done just once. The scar on her ribs testified it had been a disaster in more ways than one. And she still had eight months, three weeks *aaaannnnnd*…some frigging days left on a frigging contract she'd been a frigging idiot to sign. The worse part? Being sober when she signed it. She hunched deeper into her jacket and flipped her twenty-minute walk home to autopilot. Navigating across streets and around obstacles, her aching feet punished her for staying and helping Margo catch up on the orders stacking up during Alicia's bombshell explanation.

Bombshells. Plural.

Alicia held a Master's degree in Agriculture Sciences, specializing in Animal Husbandry. Lisa, her partner for over eight years, had a Doctoral in Biological Sciences with a genetics specialty. It was her Master's degree in Business Management which landed her in the Port Authority office. They planned to breed a new strain of horse, one able to function in at least two full Earth gravities, since that was the range of most settled planets. The current limit was of one and a quarter E-g, which most breeds could barely tolerate.

Jem shook her head. She should know better than to trust first impressions. She had shrugged off Alicia's behavior as just more of what she'd seen in countless Port Circles from both sexes. But these two women had long-term goals and were working, uh, diligently toward them. Her lips twitched, remembering some of Margo's colorful and innovative comments. Still, there was no way she would ever consent the same for her partner or spouse.

Something I'll probably never have to worry about. Regret simmered briefly.

Rotating her neck, then following through with a shoulder twist, rewarded her with several small pops. Pappia's gravity might only be two decimal points higher than Earth-standard but, really, eleven hours on her feet in any gravity was just too long. Especially since tonight had been absolutely one of the worst she'd had since leaving Earth. In fact, she'd rank it as second, right behind that cesspit on Mandoria.

There had been two shoving matches, four down-and-dirty brawls—one in the employee locker room—and a puke-fest at table three. She'd heard some interesting side bets as the hair-pulling catfight rolled across the floor. The three jerks at table eight tried to slip out without paying while attention was on the employee brawl. Lizzy, waitress and unknown-till-now martial arts expert, caught them. The resulting broken arm, broken nose and dislocated shoulder— theirs, one each—generated a visit from the Law Enforcers and all open tabs paid up promptly.

Last and most annoying were the two lecherous new arrivals parked at the counter who just wouldn't believe she really did want them to keep their hands to themselves. Saul-the-bouncer's patience was worn pretty thin by then and had thrown them out into the street. Literally, judging from the shouts and hissing air brakes.

Shit, damn, crap. What a night.

Maybe things wouldn't have been so bad if Mr. Mystery had dropped in. No one bothered him. No one tried to start up a conversation. Even the tables around him were the last to fill up. A lot of subtle glances were flicked his way, as if everyone kept a wary eye on him. Heck, she'd flicked more than a few herself. The whole bar would probably freeze if he ever made a sudden move. It was amazing how a bar full of rough, tough, ego-pecking-order miners had, by unspoken consensus, granted the man a wary respect others usually had to win with their fists. *Then again, maybe not,* Jem mused. Even across the room there was an aura of danger around him that—

A pair of legs sticking out of a doorway brought her to a wary halt. Crime wasn't common on Pappia, but it wasn't unheard of either. She leaned over the dark mass, only to reel back as an exhaled toxic blast of Ore Hammer preceded a loud snore. *Oh my God.* Jem spun around, sucking in fresh night air and blinking hard to clear watery eyes.

Her anger spiked when another look revealed shiny new boots and pants. A newcomer. She sidled carefully around the legs. With her nose tucked safely behind a glove, she determined there was no blood or other obvious injury. At least, nothing external. Dammit. The sadists could have at least dumped their victim back in his dorm room where he could be miserable in private.

Some of the old-timers enjoyed a cruel game. The last time the idiotic 'initiation' was tried at Pounding J, Jem also served the potent drink, on the house, to the two assholes hosting it. When both refused the second round and had drunk very little of the first, the well-muscled newcomer got the message. They got knocked out of their chairs. Simultaneously. The guy didn't even come out of his seat to register his two-fisted irritation. He simply leaned forward and *POW!*

Her boss had also admired the comet-fast punches. The newbie had readily accepted Jansom's employment offer, more than happy to switch his contract out of the mines. With two other Sauls already on J's payroll, everyone had started tacking on adjectives to keep a conversation straight. Even better, Jansom instructed all his workers to limit Ore Hammer orders to one per person and to warn about its time-delayed potency.

Giving the prone figure a last pitying glance, Jem continued on home. Night patrol would pick the poor guy up when they swept through here. They'd probably take him to the MedCenter for a checkup. Maybe a transfusion. She hoped the guy wasn't too hardheaded or proud to say who fed him the drinks. Those assholes were the ones responsible for the loss of work and should be getting the company reprimand. *Skip the frigging reprimand.* Jem jammed her hands into her pockets. Force them to drink the same number of rounds they tricked their victim into. See how they liked two or three days of head-pounding, gut-puking, piss-burning misery nothing but time solved. It might even get the practice stopped once word got around.

Jem turned onto Newburg Avenue, her thoughts settling back on the black-haired mystery. A Tracker, huh? Made sense, since everyone agreed he appeared to be watching and waiting. Her shoulders hunched. Could Kurzvall—*no, he wouldn't.* She let out a sigh of relief and relaxed. He'd keep the hunt to his personal thugs. Taking it outside his circle would risk having someone else made aware of some things. Of her. At least her goal of being Kurzvall's number one pain was working. Her last successful score had focused FSC on his ion engine company and cost him millions in lost income and penalties. *Yay.*

Her grin slid away as she remembered the shuttle's cracked frame. Thank God both pilots had been ex-Survey. No deaths. Even the elderly relative watching from the observation room had recovered from his heart attack.

What's next? How to twist the knife deeper? She had plenty of time to plan out—

A hand closed around her arm.

Jem wrenched herself free, twisting to deliver a defensive blow. It was blocked. So was the next one. Her third attempt was simply turned against her, her back forced up against a building and arms locked beside her. Her assailant's effective hip movement also thwarted a knee-strike. She froze. The shadows were too deep to see his features clearly, but she had no trouble recognizing the *eau de Dangerous* permeating the air around him.

"Why are you following me?" Mr. Mystery asked.

Jem blinked. Blinked again. "What?"

"Following me. Why?"

"Not me."

"Someone is."

"Do I look like an idiot?"

"You look like a Pounding J bartender."

"You got a thing against bartenders?" Wary of his silent scrutiny, she shifted to indignation. "Do you always attack first and ask questions later?"

"You attacked first."

"Un-un. Pouncing from behind? In the dark?" Accosting her in a section with burned out streetlights was no accident. "*You* attacked. I simply responded." Fat lot of good it had done her. He'd swatted her to the wall with little effort. Jem tried to flex her arms. There was no give whatsoever in the two steel bands pinning her. Her pulse dropped to a normal beat as her brain kicked in. She wasn't hurt or cuffed. Maybe this was just a misunderstanding.

"I don't pounce."

This close up, she could understand why the miners didn't mess with him. He was taller than she had thought. Her five-foot-nine would tuck nicely under that shadowed chin. Sure, his shoulders were broad, but there were miners with wider ones. It was the impressive, rock-hard chest pushing against hers that made one's survival instincts sit up and wave flags. And his arms were thick and powerful, without the bulky biceps many of the miners sported. The guy either grew up working hard or in Earth-plus gravity. Maybe both.

She took a deep breath as he released her, checking the street in both directions as he stepped backward. Okay, she could see a little better. *Yep, verrry nice chest.*

"You pounced," Jem said.

"I did not."

"That was definitely a pounce." *Bet his shirts are specially made.*

"I don't *pounce*."

The irritated growl was a hard mental smack. What was she doing? Fumes from the sidewalk sleeper must have muddled her brain. She tilted her head slightly, still unable to see his face clearly. She crossed her arms and dredged up her best glare.

"It's been a long night and I'd like to get home and off my feet. Which is where I was headed when you…waylaid me." He didn't like that term either.

"Don't like the grav-level?"

"Don't like ten-plus hours on my feet."

After a pause he said, "I'll walk you to your place."

She watched him give the area another quick scan. "No thanks. I'd prefer not to be anywhere near when you take care of whatever issues you're having."

His gaze zeroed back to her. "I have issues?"

"Obviously."

"What if I needed help taking care of them?"

Like getting them to the MedCenter afterward? "Besides, I don't allow strangers to—"

"Thane Stohlass Baron of Midgard, Wotan Two. And you are?"

"Annoyed and pissed." She was pretty sure one of his eyebrows moved upward. "A name doesn't make you any less strange," she told him. Wow. What formality. One's full name plus home *and* galactic system names wasn't usually heard in bars or on dark streets.

"Especially with one as unusual as yours." He tipped his head slightly. "May I escort you to your dorm, Miss Pissed?"

Jem eyed him suspiciously.

"Weren't you in a hurry to get off your feet?" he asked. "You were going this way, I believe." His arm swept out as he moved back several more paces.

Jem seethed quietly. She started off at a fast clip, ignoring the pain-in-the-butt keeping silent pace beside her. Reaching her building's well-lit entrance, she whipped around. And nearly tripped over her own feet.

This fully explained the miners' reticence to engage him.

His was a narrow face filled with sharp angles and prominent cheekbones, leaving no room for extraneous flesh. The square jaw she could tuck under probably wouldn't notice any thumps below jackhammer level. His eyebrows were a blend of black and silver, a thin scar over the left one making a forty-five-degree beeline for parts unknown in his hair. And his eyes. Eyes that sucked in everything around him and gave nothing back. Icy fingers walked their way up Jem's spine as his hard gaze held hers. A gaze which said *try me; you'll regret it.*

Clearing her throat, she waved her hand vaguely behind her. "Dorm Twelve, fourth floor." Forget a disdainful putdown, Jem was just glad her voice wasn't doing the same quivering dance her insides were doing. *Calm, stay calm* she chanted to herself. *He's not after you. I hope.* "Satisfied?" He contemplated the building as she waited silently; a rabbit hunched down in the weeds as a hawk circled lazily above.

She almost jumped when he turned those deep-set eyes—gray?—back to her.

"Room number?"

Jem's smile was a brief flash of teeth. "Four-oh-four."

CHAPTER 5

Thane exited the rail system inside the spaceport dome snuggled against its larger parent. Retrieving gear from his rented locker, he thoroughly checked it while waiting for a ride to the long-term parking ramp. A near-fatal attempt early in his career had demonstrated locks were no hindrance to determined individuals. On-the-fringe Pappia was a perfect hiding spot for those types. With near-standard pressure and no hazardous bacteria, he'd opted for the minimum gear needed in the moon's environment.

His weldmet, the offspring of a welding mask and space helmet, and a well-zipped bodysuit were adequate protection from the perpetual sandstorms generated by its eccentric orbit. Zipped, buckled, and air tank connected, he was fully geared up by the time a shuttle arrived. His belt even held the high-powered light highly recommended *for those who want to see where they're going and be seen before a miner's rig flattens them,* as the Company's info-site bluntly put it. Being prepared was another lesson learned early in his career. He didn't plan on wandering around outside, but circumstances could change quickly. Rarely for the better.

Dropped off only a couple of meters from his ship, Thane waited until darkness swallowed the shuttle before activating his ship's remote and accessing Thor, its computer brain. The landing lights came on, creating a bright pocket in the swirling soup. Thor reported no activity around it since he left and released the locks to the airlock in the lower level.

The Class Two Globe, named for the old-fashioned snow globe it resembled, had been his home-away-from-home for nearly a decade. It was over eleven meters in diameter at its widest and slightly over twelve meters tall, including the inclined base housing both sets of engines and a built-in staircase.

The main ship consisted of two primary levels with electronics and miscellaneous equipment in the rounded top. The *Lone Tracker* was large enough to be comfortable and small enough to offset the inconvenience caused by the Otanak Drive's transit quirk. It wasn't unusual for him to beat a quarry on a larger ship to their destination.

They were usually less than thrilled by the surprise.

Thane paused in the airlock as Thor applied a five-second blast of air to remove Pappia's grit. He stepped into the plazo, the large open area taking up a full third of the lower level. Loosening his throat straps, he stripped off the weldmet and stowed it neatly in the small environment locker. He set his tank on the bench, a reminder to refill it before putting it away. He stripped off the bodysuit and dropped it next to his tank.

A long spine-stretch later, he climbed the ladder rungs to the main deck.

Starting to fix coffee, he reached for whisky instead. His lips smacked at the first swallow, its gentle heat unsatisfying after several days of Pounding J's version. He leaned back against the navigation console and evaluated his first face-to-face with Wilmont. He was confident the woman was unaware she'd been targeted.

His client, however, would not be happy. The man had stated explicitly— at least four times by his recollection—about not making any contact. But a small, relatively speaking, closed colony did not breed the same anonymity as a large urban city or Port Circle. Hanging around for no obvious reason already had rumor and speculation flowing.

They'd even given him a nickname.

Besides, he was curious. Could she really be responsible for all those engine failures? He'd posed the question to his mechanical genius cousin and gotten a long-winded reply back. Andi had not only insisted it was physically impossible but had described, in detail, all the technical reasons why. Yet Wilmont's presence in the vicinity of so many similar failures simply could not be written off as coincidence. And just how did someone vanish so completely?

People thought *he* was a mystery? Not even close.

On top of that, for a supposedly top-line assassin, none of his contacts in that murky profession knew anything about her. Not even a rumor. In fact, he thought wryly, from their interest he might even have drummed up some business for her. The only incident where he could positively place her nearby—*more coincidence?*—was the lab explosion on Earth.

Thane shifted uneasily. That edgy, something-didn't-feel-right feeling was back again.

Was one of Kurzvall's competitors seeking to ruin him, as the man claimed? Or was it something else? It wouldn't be the first time a client had left out embarrassing or unflattering information. Or, in this instance, the real reason for being targeted. Like maybe a private vendetta of some kind? Thor had retrieved some very unflattering information about Kurzvall, including a nasty scandal in the Orion System.

He only had Kurzvall's word she was responsible for the deaths at Myerstone.

But what else could explain those two mind-blowing cash deposits? Irritation flared anew at how casually the man had provided her bank information. Had Kurzvall pulled the illegal flags on Wilmont's account as he'd advised? Probably not. People like him didn't bother with pesky little rules.

He hadn't needed Kurzvall to give him her account details. The auxiliary law enforcement clause in his Tracker license authorized him to request financial and Port Authority information. It was the most effective way of tracking a person between systems.

"Thor. Anything back from my inquiry to Sol Archives?" He'd added a search for any and all information available on Jem Seaborne Wilmont to Thor's to-do list.

"No. Resend with higher priority?"

"No." He didn't want to raise a flag somewhere. Flag? One look at all those holes in her background and it would be upgraded to solar flare in a heartbeat.

He thought about those gaps as he sipped his drink. More than bothersome, they were confusing. Why didn't she maintain the poor-drifter image? What factors determined going poof over buying a ticket or working as crew? What was hidden in those black holes?

Who did she become? What did she do?

Sure, people with lots of money could disappear if they wanted to. Undocumented ship passage and alternate identities from nefarious sources could always be bought. But if that was the answer, where did the funds come from? That Earth account had been dormant for two years and Thor's search hadn't found even a hint of another one.

His comp brain had also compared lists of all outgoing vessels from the places where he'd lost her trail. There were no unexplained duplicates for ships, passengers or crew. Ad hoc bribery? Are there that many individuals willing to risk their license and livelihood? Again, with what funds? From where?

Thane shook his head. His list of questions was turning into a book.

This job was going to drive him crazy. Rubbing his neck, he downed the last of his drink. Ugh. Definitely wimpy. He made a mental note to stock up with several cases of Pounding J's brand before leaving.

He was shaking the bottle's last drops into his glass when Thor informed him of three incoming messages from Port Control. He'd changed his Midgard postbox from 'Hold" to 'Forward' when he sent his report to Kurzvall confirming Wilmont's location.

"Type and sender of the first one?"

"An audio message forwarded from Helga Perlman Baron, Romanique Three."

Thane's jaw set. "Delete it. Second one?"

"A text message forwarded from Patricia Ford Keegan, Saltusa One."

"Read it."

"Mr. Baron. I would like to utilize your services in retrieving a missing item. I'll pay double your rate. Please let me know when you are available for a contract. End."

Utilize my services at double rate? Somebody had swiped something important and she didn't want to involve Law Enforcement. Most likely because it was a family member or a disgruntled ex-partner.

"Send the Unavailable Response to—no, cancel." Depending on how fast Kurzvall's men moved, he should be done here in another week or so. Technically, his contract was completed once he'd found her. Keeping an eye on her was extra. "Send the Will Contact Response to the Keegan message, time frame within thirty E-days." She could contact someone else if it was too long. "File message and contact information under Jobs Pending. Third message?"

"A text message from Pappia Port Authority."

"Read it."

"Greetings from the Port Authority, Comptroller office. Will you be filing a flight plan tomorrow as specified in your initial reservation or staying longer? Please respond. End."

As inquiries went, it was one of the nicer ones. Usually, it was along the line of 'pay up or leave.' "Response to Pappia Port Authority. Text only, start: No. *Lone Tracker* will be extending. End."

"Message sent."

Thane shoved away from the console. "Transfer payment to the Comptroller office for two week's stay, local time." Any unused days would be refunded.

"Transfer completed," the comp brain informed him after a couple of seconds. "Receipt acknowledged and recorded."

Settling at the small table separating the compact kitchen and command area, Thane brought up Wilmont's file on the small computer terminal. He entered the date and method of contact in his report and why he'd chosen to ignore his employer's...advice. Typed *Observations*, then paused. What had he learned? Leaning back, he tapped his drink lightly against his forearm.

He'd definitely caught her off guard. It probably didn't happen too often. Thane's brows drew in slightly as he mentally replayed her reaction. Though fast, her responses had been more of a general street-based defense, not the controlled martial arts moves he'd been prepared for. Still, those blows would have been pretty effective if they had connected. Especially that knee. Were there a few nasty tricks up her sleeve? A small grin curled his lip. That was okay. He had a few lurking there himself.

Most surprising of all had been her reaction to him.

At various points, she had displayed irritation, anger and caution. But no fear. Not even when she finally got a good look at him at her building. It'd been startled surprise—*dare he think awe?*—widening those incredible eyes. Late night, accosted by a stranger with the impression he knew he made would have most women shaking in their boots.

But then, she's an assassin-ghost, not a woman.

No, he amended, maybe not a *normal* woman, but most definitely a woman. She was a good head shorter than him with a narrow waist. Her height was a bit tall by Earth standards, but average by Midgard's. And were those firmly toned arms acquired from slinging liquor cases or bodies? There'd also been an interesting squish of full breasts when he pinned her against the wall.

Nope. Not putting *that* in his report.

He'd gotten his first good look at her eyes there in the dorm's illumination. The picture in her file did not do them justice, especially the way they stood out against her fair skin. He'd met a few people with bi-colored eyes, but none with Wilmont's combination of deep green and soft golden brown. Emerald and amber: no wonder her parents named her Jem. Incredible eyes that—

Thane swore softly, realizing how far his thoughts had drifted. He was not getting bushwhacked by a pair of eyes, no matter how remarkable they were.

Bushwhacked.

Grinning, he took another swallow before setting the glass aside. His grandfather's old-fashioned term would probably be very appropriate if he showed up at door four-oh-four, Dorm Twelve. Thane was pretty sure it wasn't hers.

Devious. Yeah, it definitely fit under observations.

CHAPTER 6

"Looking for something?"

Jem's head snapped down. Mr. Mystery. Propped against the wall at the service way's entrance. Waiting for her? She'd struggled to not think about last night, but as soon as her attention wandered her mind slingshot right back to him. To the hard eyes in the hard face.

Take a deep breath and fake it. She was good at faking. She excelled at faking.

"I'm an optimist. I keep hoping to see stars." Gathering both coat and courage tighter around her, she moved briskly toward the street and the safety the open sidewalk offered. Starting to swing around him, she stopped instead and gave him a frown.

He tilted his head inquiringly.

"Do you always do that?" she asked in annoyance.

"Do what?"

"The bug treatment."

"The what?"

"First you swat me against the wall like one and now you're studying me like an interesting specimen under a microscope."

"Sorry." He straightened in a single fluid motion. "Can I buy you a late dinner? Consider it an apology for last night's swat. How are you tonight, Miss Pissed?"

"Annoyed," she snapped.

"First name basis? Okay. Mine's Thane."

She walked right into that one. "It's Jem, Jem Wilmont," she said, her lips curving upward. He couldn't be too bad if he's got a sense of humor.

"Jem," he acknowledged. "Dinner?"

What could it hurt? "Apology accepted. The Grub Stake is a couple of blocks over. It's always open and the food's good. I often stop in after work. Sometimes before, too."

"I ate there a couple of nights ago," Thane said as they began moving down the sidewalk. "First decent bowl of Earth-style chili I've had since I sampled the real stuff."

"Oh?" She flicked a quick glance sideways. "How long ago?"

He thought it over. "A job took me there…about a year ago. It was my first visit, and I took time off to be a tourist. Toured some of the old ruins in Europe and South America. Green. I couldn't believe how green it was."

"Ireland?" Jem grinned.

"It was," he acknowledged. "Wandered around Australia—we still haven't found anything to match kangaroos, and I had to visit the Scandinavian region. It topped my list."

"Why?"

"Curiosity and ancestry. My great-something grandparents' whole village emigrated to Midgard from there when the sea-level rise started flooding them out. A lot of our cities and the three and a half continents are named—"

"Wait. How do you get half a continent?"

Thane grinned. "Copenhagen is either the smallest continent or largest island, depending on your viewpoint."

"Viewpoint being whether or not you're from Copenhagen, I assume?"

"Or a snob from Stockholm, which is the largest. Mostly we just ignore the issue."

Jem's grin turned mischievous. "Pounced on anyone lately?"

"No." He shot her an irritated look.

The rest of their journey was in a companionable silence. His stride was casual, yet Jem would bet he was aware of everything and everyone around them.

Located on a quiet side street, the Grub Stake could be found by asking directions or following one's nose. Selections ranged from vegetarian to carnivorous and were served in generous quantities. It boasted compact booths with individual sound suppression systems instead of tables, welcoming tired miners with a quiet meal or private conversation. The service was quick, the tables clean, and prices reasonable. It was a working person's oasis.

This time of night, the restaurant was busy without being overly crowded. Thane threaded his way toward an open booth in a back corner. Trailing behind him, Jem passed several of Pounding J's regulars. Their expressions ranged from startled to nonplussed. She settled into her seat with resignation. She'd be fielding more than drink orders next shift.

Thane glanced at the booth's automated menu. "I'm going to have some more of the chili. Spicy hot. And a beer," he added, punching in his selections.

Jem chose a milder version and a glass of water. She also selected a serving of Corrate bread to go with it. Thane said that was a good idea and updated his order to match.

He leaned forward on his forearms. "Suspicion and wariness I'm used to. Even outright hostility. Why am I getting a bunch of confused looks from a number of our co-diners?"

"Probably because of all the other dinner offers I've turned down. But this is an apology, not a date. I'm hungry *aaaannd*...you're Mr. Mystery." Jem cleared her throat. "It's what, ah, some of us at Pounding J call you."

Thane leaned back and flashed her his first full smile. She almost fell out of her seat at the transformation to his face.

"Beats some of the things I've been called. So, who would actually answer four-oh-four's door if I knocked on it?"

Jem gave a sheepish grin. "Name's Boyd. Just Boyd. Most of us can't pronounce the rest of it. He's on his fourth contract with EMC and has appointed himself as the unofficial protector for everyone living on our floor."

She studied the man lounging across from her, an arm slung negligently over his seat's top and fingers lightly stroking the wall behind it. She'd become fluent in reading personality types since leaving Earth. Thane would be one of the hard ones, she decided, but found no sign of meanness in that formidable face. Ruthless? Yep, but not indiscriminately or without a good reason. Of course, she thought wryly, their idea of what constituted a good reason was probably a galaxy apart.

Thane's lips twitched. "Now who's doing the microscopic inspection?"

She felt her cheeks warm. "Sorry." Desperate for a topic, she blurted out the first thing that came to mind. "Your eyebrows don't match your hair."

One of those flecked brows tilted upward.

"Usually the hair goes first." There weren't any light-colored strands in his dark hair and he didn't seem like the type to hide it. He could be anywhere from a hardened thirtysomething to a well maintained fifty something. "How old— sorry." Jem blushed. "I'm getting personal."

Thane's shoulder lifted a fraction. "I turned thirty a couple of months ago, in both Midgard and Earth years as they're a close match. The silvered brows are a family trait that usually shows up in the mid-to-late twenties regardless of hair color. My mother is the only one in her generation who doesn't have it." He grinned. "Both my aunts have threatened numerous times to shave hers off in retaliation."

Jem grinned with him. His family sounded close and there was affection in his voice. "I hear you're a Tracker." He nodded. "Isn't your family worried about the risks?"

"Not really. True, sometimes my quarry objects to being found," he added when her gaze flicked to his scar. "But I'm careful and not all jobs are tracking people, criminal or otherwise. I once had a job for a museum to locate a statue. It went missing the same time as one of the employees."

"Did you find him? It?"

"Of course," he said, an eyebrow arched regally. "Got the statue and gave him my client's two-worded message: you're fired."

"You didn't take the thief back?"

Thane shook his head. "The museum just wanted its statue. He became the local Law Enforcers' problem after I informed them they had a nutcase starting up his own cult. He'd been using it as a focus in his new religion."

"Which are you hunting now, person or object?"

"Neither."

Jem's brow furrowed. "Then why are you way out here?"

The Tracker tilted his head, his face an impassive mask.

Her mouth opened, closed, reopened. "Sorry, that was rude. It just…popped out."

"No." His gaze was unwavering. "You're nervous. Any particular reason why?"

"You make a lot of people nervous," she said defensively. His answering grin was sharp enough to split the table top in two.

"Yeah? Well, there are undoubtedly three or four—dozen—people on Pappia who are probably wondering if their past has caught up with them. I could probably make quite a bit in bonus if Thor ran some deep checks on EMC's payroll. A mining moon on the Republic's edge would be a great place to hide, wouldn't it?"

Would Kurzvall think to look here? Panic and fear shot through her. Jem swallowed, striving to push the emotions down. "I guess it would be," she agreed, dropping her eyes. Too late, she knew. *How much had that penetrating gaze seen?*

Thane released a sharp breath. "Sorry. You're not the first to ask. The others have just been more subtle." He held up a finger; she closed her mouth. "Don't apologize again. I find your directness refreshing, so you'll be the first to get my boring answer. I just finished a job and I'm waiting to meet someone. The why and what for is my business."

She hid the uneasiness his words caused. The meeting wouldn't be here unless it concerned someone on Pappia. One of those dozens? Her? Could she be wrong about Kurzvall? Who the hell was Thor? About to ask that, she was sidetracked by the arrival of their food. She gave the waiter a bright smile. He was a talkative, friendly guy who liked to wind down at J on his nights off.

"Hi, Aaron, I didn't know if you'd still be serving."

The waiter flipped an assessing glance over Thane before returning her smile. "Welcome back, Jem. I bet you're the mild with water."

"Yep."

The chili deposited in front of them was a deep, rich red, its flavor-filled steam rising in lazy swirls. The honey-brown bread was soft and slightly tart, the perfect complement for soaking up broth. Jem inhaled deeply, the scent making her realize just how famished she was.

"When's the kitchen promotion?" she asked.

"Soon. Charlie's contract is up in a couple of weeks and he can't wait to leave. The head chef told me I'll be—"

"Getting a glass for my beer," Thane interjected.

"Of course," Aaron said stiffly. "Chilled or warmed?"

"Chilled."

"Anything else? Jem? No?" His eyes flicked at Thane and back. "Take care."

Jem waited until Aaron vanished through the kitchen door. "Now *that* was rude."

Thane simply started in on his chili. Several bites later, a frost-coated glass plopped down in front of him and Aaron returned to the kitchen without a word.

They ate in silence: Thane with apparent gusto, Jem with growing annoyance.

She used the last of her bread to sop up the last of her chili. Thane had already finished and was sipping on his beer. Two more minutes and she was gone. *Mr. Thane Baron can keep himself company,* she fumed. *He could also—* a soft buzzing sound interrupted her silent litany.

Thane leaned back. A frown came and went quickly as he read his phone display. "I have to leave."

"No problem. I'm done."

He pulled out his cash card and slid it into the auto-biller in the base of the menu and tapped *Accept* for both options. Upending his glass, he finished his beer. Jem was sliding her jacket on as the auto-biller flashed green. They slid out of the booth together. As soon as they were out the front door Jem swung around, prepared to give Mister Tracker a frostily polite thank you. She was startled to see him already several long strides down the sidewalk.

No good-by. No wave over the shoulder. Nothing.

Those long legs had him vanishing around a corner in practically no time. Jem didn't know whether to be irritated or relieved, which promptly added annoyance to the mix. She headed toward her dorm, acutely aware of three things. Mr. Mystery was dangerous, unpredictable, and rude with a capital R. Okay, make it four, she thought wryly. He also had a Class Ten rear view.

**

No, no, no… Jem struggled, but the nightmare had her in its grip.

She was inside the rear mail pod section, configuring it for the courier Dani was flirting with. Screams. A black hell grabbing her. Twisting her inside out. It ended as abruptly as it hit.

She was lying in the ripped remnants of the mail pod and other debris. Everything hurt. Her head spun like a carnival ride, and when she turned her head she almost lost the battle with her stomach. There…sticking up out of the debris. She recognized the ring, despite the blurred and double vision.

Had a shuttle crashed into the hanger? Was Dani alive? Dimly she heard voices. Shouts.

Inching sideways slowly, carefully, she reached out and grasped the bloody hand. Gave it a tug. "Dani? Are you…"

She was holding a hand. Just a hand. It ended just past the wrist: white bone showing among the tattered strips of skin and—

Jem slung it away. Rolling on her side, she let her stomach have its way.

Soaked in sweat, she bolted for the bathroom as bile clawed its way up her throat. She barely made it before losing her supper's remnants. She leaned back against the cool tile, trying to swallow past the raw burning in her throat. It took a couple of minutes before she could pull herself up and wash her face. She rinsed her mouth. Twice.

She collapsed back on her bed.

The arm flung across her eyes only shut out the dim light slipping past the curtains. Not the screams. Not the images. Dani's mutilated hand always hit her the worst. She shuddered, bile threatening to erupt again. Finally, mercifully, the past faded away. If only it'd be permanent.

At least she didn't have to go to work tonight.

Jem swung her feet to the floor and went to look down at the street. She inched the window open. Four stories below her, the off-duty colors and styles from dozens of star systems blended with EMC's simple uniform in a slow, flowing river of humanity. Their babble was voiced in a multitude of accents and even a couple of the old languages.

She watched a foursome laughing and gesturing at each other as they walked away. Just normal, everyday people working toward a future. Longing, envy, and regret swamped her. She'd wanted that too, in her naïve days on Earth. *Someday* she'd told herself, letting yet another opportunity pass. *Plenty of time yet. I'm young.* Then time ran out when any chance of normalcy was ripped away. Now she was a tool, a weapon others fought and killed for. She clung to the shadows now, hidden and alone. Afraid to trust. Afraid of endangering others.

Her head dropped against the window pane. *Is that why I came to Pappia, a place buried in darkness?* A place her subconscious felt she could safely pretend, even if only for a year, to be like everyone else? Able to call a compact apartment home? Able to call people, however tentatively, friends?

No, Jem thought wearily, that mail pod hadn't protected her from the worst. Surviving had been worse.

CHAPTER 7

"That was awesome."

The black-haired woman held the door open as several others followed her out. None of them noticed the lone figure lounging in the shadows between the spa and its neighbor.

"Yeah, most of the kinks are gone," agreed the tall, stoutly built brunette. "At least until next shift. I've reported those shocks on my machine twice now. I think my kinks had knots."

"*Oooh!* Lyra has kinky knots." The door swung closed.

The others laughed as the brunette swatted the shorter woman's arm.

"Keep it up, Rita, and you'll have knots," a woman with multi-colored hair said.

"Go the MedCenter, Lyra," the willowy ash-blond said. "Get your problems documented and then come see me,"

"I can't afford to lose my contract, Jenny," Lyra said hastily. "I need the money."

"Not a problem. We'll just get you moved into another position, temporarily or permanently as needed, and then file for compensation due to company mismanagement or negligence." Jenny rubbed her hands. "My law firm just loves those cases."

"I think I liked the Hot Rock Spa over in the Hub better," black-headed Rita said as they began meandering down the sidewalk.

"Why?" the blond lawyer asked. "The only real difference I saw was the number of credits I paid there."

The woman with black, blond and green streaked hair, agreed. "I can't see spending the extra just for a slightly better décor."

Rita made a noise in her throat. "There's décor, then there's *décor*. Did any of you notice the new masseur working in Hot Rock's Jovian Room?"

"*OOOOOOH, YEAAAH*," the other three chorused.

Thane's eyebrows made several more trips upward at the raunchy banter before their chatter faded in the distance. Did his mother and aunts talk like that when no menfolk were around? Probably, he thought, grinning. They were vocal enough when—*finally!* Thane's focus shifted to the woman entering the restaurant directly across from him. Several more of the dinner crowd followed in behind her.

Perfect. It would soon be full.

He'd replayed their previous dinner numerous times. Wilmont alternated between two personas. Sometimes quietly shy, other times boldly forward. Wary intelligence watched him from those fabulous eyes. When she wasn't guarding every word, a humorous imp peeked out. And that flash he'd seen in Wilmont's eyes before she hid them? Fear.

He'd met hardened killers of all types over the years. They were a cautious, emotionless group who simply saw themselves as business people. Hot-blooded, cold-blooded, psychotic, demented, or just plain warped, they all shared one trait: lack of fear. Fear, one memorable female had told him, was a death knell. It slowed reflexes and clouded the brain.

Yeah, Kurzvall had definitely left a few things out. Like what the exact hell was going on. What would a killer fear? Not that he could ask her…even if he'd been able to.

He was still kicking himself for not realizing she'd started her weekend. Pappia's thirty-hour rotation was split into three ten-hour shifts and employees worked a four-on-two-off cycle. He'd been watching the Grub Stake tonight, hoping she'd eat there prior to work after spending two days nesting in her apartment.

At least, he thought sourly, it's what he had to assume she'd been doing.

Had the woman really stayed there the whole weekend? Had she slipped out for some shopping or assassin mayhem? Who the hell knew? He sure didn't. He couldn't get in the damn building and she hadn't answered his calls. He couldn't watch all four exits and he didn't dare install any covert surveillance.

If she didn't detect it, company security would and the Port Authority's next inquiry wouldn't be automated or polite.

Thane pushed away from the wall, casually glancing up and down the street as he crossed over. There it was again. He'd lost count of the number of times his tingling neck told him he was being watched. He'd even been tailed a couple of times. Was it the same person or just everyone taking their turn? When Wilmont said he was making people nervous, he didn't realize she meant half the dome's population.

Where was Kurzvall's men? The urgent message Thor had interrupted their dinner with said he was sending two men. They would take over and complete whatever arrangements necessary with the local Enforcers. He was not to contact them on his own.

They wanted the credit? Fine. He just wanted done and off this dark rock.

Stepping inside, he paused and scanned. There. Against the left wall, staring into the empty seat across from her. Thane slid into it seconds later, freezing as her eyes shifted upward to his. A heartbeat later, the bleak gaze vanished. It was replaced with irritation.

"I don't recall inviting you to sit."

"Place is plenty busy. Seating's tight." He scanned the menu. "What'd you order?"

"Food." She looked around.

"Anything else?" He selected a large order of pasta and a bottle of red wine.

"Something to drink."

Hitting the *Place Order* button, he folded his arms on the tabletop. Studied her for several moments. She looked...drawn. Tired. "They can't fire you because you're on contract. It wasn't a bad night at work because you haven't been there for the past two nights. So, it leaves what? Bad weekend? Fight with your lover? Find a gray hair?"

"I don't have a lover. A gray hair?"

"My mother became real, uh, unsociable when she got one. Actually, it was silver. Didn't help the situation any when it was one of my uncles who pointed it out at a family dinner. Adding fuel to the fire, he joked about the family trait probably popping up in, uh, other places. Next day Mom took an unscheduled week-long vacation at one of those fancy resorts."

He watched the battle across her face. Curiosity won.

"What happened when she came back?"

Thane gave her a sly grin. "Nothing. Said uncle and his wife had just left on *their* week-long vacation, cruising down the Langford River. No sign of a light-colored hair on Mom either."

Her lips tilted slightly. "Your mother has a bit of a temper?"

"She has a way with words, Wilmont. She can slice, dice and fillet you without raising her voice."

"How do you know I've not been to work for two days?"

Thane's brow arched at the suspicious tone. "I've been there, you haven't. And I asked. Coupled with the gossip about our dinner the other night, I'm afraid there have been some assumptions generated among your co-workers."

Wilmont groaned and dropped her chin on her chest.

"Sorry. Just ignore them."

She gave a deep sigh then asked, "What about your father? Does he have any gray or silver hairs?"

"We lost my father when I was ten." Caught off guard, his terse response held too many undercurrents for her not to hear them. From the way she was eyeing him, she had. "What about your parents?" he asked, trying to lose the stiffness in his voice.

"Both died in a shuttle accident when I was thirteen. Granny took me in, raised me. I think that's our food headed this way."

At least the server wasn't chatty Aaron.

A large salad piled high with vegetables was placed in front of Wilmont. Her dinner came with a side dish of creamy dressing, a basket of warm bread and a dark beverage. Thane inhaled deeply as he received his own large platter. The pasta was topped with a generous amount of meat sauce and ringed with sliced dark-red sausages. His side dishes included a bowl of shredded cheese and his own basket of bread. The wine was wrapped in a chilled sleeve and he declined to have the first glass poured for him.

He watched her make a hole in the center of her salad and place the dressing in it. She swirled a forkful of vegetables and lettuce in it before popping it into her mouth.

"Most people spread the dressing on the salad and mix it in," he said.

She munched a couple of times before swallowing. "It's a large salad. It'll be soggy by the time I get to the bottom." She took another mouthful.

Huh. "You know, the waiter didn't ask who had what. I could have ordered the salad." She stopped chewing and gave him a strange look. "What?"

"You don't look like a salad-type of guy," she replied dryly.

"Really?" He filled his wine glass.

"Really."

Thane dumped a handful of cheese on top of the pasta and mixed it all up. He filled his fork, speared a sausage to hold it all in place, and took a bite. The burst of flavor on his tongue immediately ranked the dish right up there with the chili.

They concentrated on their meal, the conversation kept simple and light. Thane learned she was drinking moon ale and didn't have any gray hairs. He admitted to still waiting for his contact and they had yet to find a second silver hair on his mother's head. Not that anyone was looking very hard, Thane confided, both of them laughing. They swapped her last slice of bread for the last of his cheese.

She leaned back. Stretching her legs under the table, she bumped Thane's leg. "Sorry. Just trying to see if I can make room for these last bites."

"Did it work?"

Wilmont contemplated her plate sadly. "No."

He reached over. Her plate was empty when he returned it. She blinked in amazement. "Do you always eat this much?"

"Uh-huh." He upended the last of the wine into his glass. "I've learned to take advantage of good cooking when I find it." He shifted around until comfortably slouched in the corner on his side of the booth, one long leg cocked on the seat and the other one stretched out beside it. One hand wrapped around his wine glass. "Feeling better?"

"Feeling stuffed."

She set the small condiment tray back beside the menu. After wiping the tabletop with her napkin, she slid it back under her drink. She glanced around the room. Tucked a stray hair behind her ear.

Stop fidgeting. How often had his grandmother told him that? Sometimes with a bop on the head.

"You called my apartment several times," she blurted out.

"I got your number from the company directory. Why didn't you answer?"

"Why'd you call?"

"If you had returned one of them, you'd know."

"I didn't feel like it."

A server materialized with a tray and collected their empty dishes. They kept their glasses but declined refills.

Thane reached over and flipped on the sound suppression switch located above the menu. "Okay," he said quietly, facing her across the table. "Guess it was a bad couple of days."

Those enigmatic eyes searched his face. "Why do you care?"

"Because I know what it's like to sit alone in a crowded room. I know what it's like to *be* alone. Sometimes you need something other than a wall to talk to." He swallowed some wine, uncomfortable. He'd never admitted that to anyone else. Why now?

"I talked to Der Bear."

Who? "Who's Derbear?" He'd researched her background thoroughly. That person hadn't popped up anywhere.

Her smile was weak. "D-E-R Bear. Two words." The smile faded. "I went through a rather...volatile stage after my parents died."

That was obvious from her school records.

"One day Granny handed me this large, stuffed grizzly bear, saying she would only accept civility from then on. I had been kind of, uh, sarcastic and temperamental to her."

Thane coughed. Twice.

"When she told me the bear would handle everything else, I said, 'So, *Der Bear* can handle me?'" Her eyes lost focus. "'It'll take your anger and your tears.

It'll keep your secrets and your fears. It'll never complain, no matter how tight you squeeze or hard your aim.'"

Thane realized she was quoting the older woman, the words having stayed with her through the years. "She taught you control, yet gave you an outlet." Wilmont's ninety-plus great-grandmother had held her own with the sullen teenager. Thane wished he could have met the feisty woman one neighbor remembered fondly as a force of nature.

"Granny taught me a lot. She died shortly after my graduation." Jem looked down for a moment, then back up. "You heard about the mining accident day before yesterday?"

"No way not to." He'd even wondered if she was behind it. If one of the dead had been her target. "It was a major bad day for over a dozen of them," he continued, "including the idiot who tried to hold up the mountain with a front loader."

She stiffened. "Fourteen died. The loader driver's name was Gloria. I knew her."

Foot-in-mouth for dessert.

"Gloria usually worked outside the tunnel. When she realized what was happening, she rammed her machine in as far as she could underneath the collapsing walls. Her cab..." Jem looked away, her voice dropping, "the cab was crushed, but it kept a large enough opening for most of them to get out. I won't say we were friends, but she sat at the counter whenever she came into Pounding J and we'd talk." She paused, shook her head. "Unfortunately, it was history repeating itself. Her husband was killed in a mining accident three years ago on some planet elsewhere. Don't remember which."

"Then she was aware of the dangers and risks associated with the job." He slid his glass aside and leaned on his forearms. "They get paid, and paid well, to take those risks. Grandiose extras, if they survive, do not get a bonus."

"She wasn't *planning* on any grandiose *extras*." Anger coated her words. "She was *planning* to go home in another three months and open her own business to support herself and her two sons. They're calling her a hero."

"She's a dead hero and her sons are orphans," Thane said flatly.

"Over thirty miners are alive because of her!"

"Do you think her sons will care?" he snapped. "Don't you think they'd rather have *her*? Who's going to tuck them into bed, read them stories? Who's going to help with their homework or answer their questions? Who's going to hold them when—" Thane ground to a halt.

"Fortunately, there are two sets of grandparents and umpteen aunts and uncles. There'll be plenty of arms for tucking and holding. You still had one parent as well as a whole table full of relatives. I was nowhere near that lucky."

"You're right," Thane said, his voice as icy as hers.

He fumbled in his pocket for his card. He jammed it in the machine, stabbed the accept button beneath his order. Yanked it out at the green light. Grabbing his jacket, he bolted from the restaurant and stalked toward the docks. He'd had to get out of there before saying something else he shouldn't. Dammit. He was supposed to be getting past her guard, but she had barreled right through his instead.

He stopped and ran a hand through his hair. When was the last time he'd blown up like that? Cousin Nicky, naturally. The irritating idiot had made several sarcastic insinuations about his family without ensuring he wasn't nearby. It only underscored the incompetency which got him fired from the family business in the first place. That was what...six, seven years ago? He blew out a breath. Thank God he was only a cousin-by-marriage and those genes weren't swimming in his pool.

He needed a drink. Not the wimpy stuff in his ship either. He wheeled around, heading for Pounding J. Wrapped up in his thoughts, he made his second mistake of the night. He failed to stay alert.

Two men hiding in the alley struck silently.

CHAPTER 8

It was a slow, painful climb back to consciousness. Concussion, he thought groggily, recognizing the pounding pain. He tried to move his arms, not surprised to find them tied. And legs. It felt as if he'd been trussed up like a duckbill for dinner. He pushed the pain away and focused on his surroundings.

Hard floor. Cold. Dark. No sounds, not even distant ones. One of the warehouses on the city's edge, most likely.

He must have made some betraying movement because a low voice ordered him to open his eyes. A voice Thane was pretty sure he recognized. A small light flicked on. Yep. It was Wilmont, although the hard-eyed look was new. So was the wickedly efficient knife in one hand. Damn, just how many mistakes could he make in one night?

"Can you walk?" she asked softly.

"Sure, I practice the duckbill waddle just for times like this."

She flashed a quick grin. "So, you get thumped, lumped and dumped a lot?"

Thane shot her a dirty look. "No. You caught me off guard."

"Me?"

"I pissed you off pretty bad. Now you're here. With that." The knife hovering over his chest got a pointed look.

"I was following you to apologize, you idiot," she said. "Knowing about your father—"

"What about my father?"

"He died when you were a kid and it's obvious you still aren't over it. I should have realized how Gloria's situation would stomp on your sore spot. I shouldn't have pushed."

Great. "I don't need pity."

"That's for damn sure. How about some sympathy? Or just plain empathy? Now, shall we continue this *fas-ci-na-ting* conversation or would you like to get out of here?"

"Fine. Leaving w—*oomph.*"

Clamping her hand over his mouth, Jem's attention shifted to the door on his right. Male voices were muffled, but the *slit his throat* part of the conversation came through quite clearly.

Thane cautiously eyed the blade hanging about an inch above his left eye. "Cuz me loofse, kick," he mumbled around her hand.

A chain rattled. Jem's light cut off.

"No time," she whispered, closing his eyes. He felt her move away. Got it. Pretend unconsciousness while she did…what? There were at least two and both bound to be armed. Hide, then jump them? There better be a lot more room behind him than what he'd seen in front.

A bolt scraped. The door swung open. A light flashed over his eyelids.

"Think he's still out?" someone asked in a surly tone.

A hard boot pressed down on Thane's groin. There wasn't a man, alive and conscious, who wouldn't react to that poke.

"Nope," a different voice replied cheerfully.

Thane squinted up at the guy with the inquiring foot. "I take it this isn't just an opportunistic mugging." No shouting or pointing. Good. Jem found a hidey-hole.

"Nope," Cheerful said again.

"Just slit his throat," Surly said. The light in one hand glistened off the knife he raised with his other one.

He and Wilmont must shop at the same place. "Okay, we'll start with the obvious. Where am I and what's going on?"

"You're making somebody nervous," Cheerful replied.

"So I've been told. People with large knives make me nervous. We all have our little idiosyncrasies."

Surly's scowl deepened. "You calling me an idiot?"

He'd laugh if it wouldn't hurt. He sighed instead. "I'm waiting to meet someone."

Cheerful snorted. "Everyone knows that. It's what you're going to do when they get here that has some people concerned."

Thane shrugged and instantly regretted it. A painful lightning bolt told him Zeus had joined Thor's hammer party. "I don't know," he said between clenched teeth. "I'm to get the details when he arrives. And no, I don't know why he hasn't shown up yet."

"The Boss doesn't want to take any chances." Cheerful shot a hard look at his partner. "And he doesn't want a murder investigation."

Could this night's debacle get any worse? "So? Accident or just missing?"

"Missing would still create an investigation. You're going to go poking around supply crates and trigger a defective explosive."

"Defective explosives are called that because they don't."

"This defect will be in the safety." Cheerful double-checked Thane's restraints before moving behind him. "Jimse, go make sure no one's around while I drag him out."

Surly, aka Jimse, looked disappointed.

"Don't worry. You can whack him again before we untie him."

That sure cheered the guy up, Thane thought sourly. Any head wounds would be contributed to the explosion. It also explained the soft cloths they'd tied him with. No telling wrist or ankle abrasions, assuming any limbs survived intact. Grabbed under the armpits, it set off a different type of explosion in his head.

Thane kept his jaws locked as he was dragged out into the main part of the building. Definitely a concussion, which wouldn't matter if he didn't come up with something real quick. Considering the circumstances, his life was in the hands of a pissed off assassin.

Cheerful dropped him. Even though he hit soft packing, Thane still swirled toward unconsciousness. He fought the blackness back, refusing to make this any easier for them. He forced his eyes open. A miner's lamp lit about a five-meter area. His assailant was leaning over something, the metallic scraping sounds probably last-minute adjustments to the pseudo-defective explosive. No sign of the other one.

Wilmont was out there somewhere. Waiting for a chance. *Needs a diversion.*

Taking a deep breath, he focused his wavering vision on his captor. Rolling forward, Thane knocked his legs out from under him but the bastard flipped away before he could pin him with his weight. The guy wasn't so cheerful now, spitting out a long string of curses as he jumped to his feet. Teetering on the brink of blackness, Thane watched his foot swing backward. *That's going to hurt.*

THUNK. The curses cut off in mid-word. The man dropped like a kinetic missile beside him. Wilmont stood with a raised pipe in one hand.

"Hi," Thane told the wavering figure. "I was…you…" he blinked several times as she knelt beside him, "not too p-p-mad."

"I got over it." Pulling her knife from its sheath she began cutting his bindings.

Thane tried to focus on the two figures wavering into view behind her. Both of them looked like— *"Jem!"*

Throwing herself sideways, the ripping sound in her jacket told him just how close it had been. Two more quick rolls and she came up on her knees.

Damn good throw was Thane's last thought as the blackness took him.

* * * * *

Her feet would be as flat as Saul-the-waiter's before she got off this rock. Only another hour to go and Margo had better not be late. Every frigging miner was apparently thirsty tonight and Saul-the-bartender had left early due to a bad case of backroom trots. She hadn't had a chance to trot there herself since her mid-shift break. Jem finally motioned Jansom over and told him she had to go—*now*.

Thane was sitting at the counter when she returned.

It was the first time she'd seen him since his attack three nights ago. Watching from hidden safety, her anonymous call brought Enforcers swooping down on the warehouse. Emergency vehicles of all types followed quickly, blocking the surrounding streets until the rigged explosive was safely disarmed. Being late to work hadn't even required an excuse as several coworkers and half their customers had been in the curious crowd.

News of Thane's assault had spread like wildfire. Law Enforcement and Euphrates management were asking the unknown person who helped to step forward, both in recognition for their assistance and as a witness. Not that additional testimony was needed. The surviving attacker, one Phillip Kramer Rosen, was trying to minimize his penal time by cooperating with the authorities.

The theft ring exposed was still the number one gossip item.

EMC was reeling after learning one of their long-term managers had apparently been recruited by someone to steal raw ore. It had gone undetected for almost two years because the quantities received by the processing plants matched the doctored invoices. He was unable to provide them with his contact's identity. Just a shadowy figure he only met once. Contact was maintained afterwards by text messages through one of Palmyra Two's anonymous postboxes.

 Ore wasn't the only thing the crooked manger had siphoned off. An audit found chunks of funds missing from Pappia's various operating accounts. Arrested, he had handed over his hidden account numbers in a move to minimize his own penal time. Unfortunately for everyone involved, the company was not feeling generous. Not only because it'd lost billions, but because of the potential damage to the dome if the warehouse had blown up.

Jem studied Thane as she moved toward him. He appeared outwardly unaffected by his recent experience. Still…something was different. She found it when she looked into his eyes. They were empty, devoid of any emotion. She'd seen him cold, angry, or indifferent. Even menacing. Tonight, it was as if he had pulled everything inside himself and bolted the hatch.

"Have you ordered yet, Mr. Baron," she asked.

"No."

"What would you like?"

"Aspric whisky, iced. And," Thane's voice dropped, "to say thank you."

She dipped her head in silent acknowledgement and turned to fill his order. She froze for half a beat before continuing on. He was at the counter. Her hindbrain frantically waved its neurons at her: this was a deliberate move. Her pulse kicked up several notches. Something was going to happen.

Nothing happened.

Unless everyone watching furtively as he wordlessly sipped his one—
one!—drink counted. Jem closed out her last orders, ignoring Margo's pointed
looks between her and the individual slipping out the door. She logged off the
computer and flung her towel into the wash bucket. Not finding him outside J's
back door only wound her tighter.

Halfway home, she jolted to a halt when Thane stepped out in front of her.

"Jem Seaborne Wilmont of Sol, you're in trouble," he said without
preamble.

"Someone found out I was the one who killed him?" It had been deemed as
justified defense, but the Enforcers still wanted to do reports and other stuff.
And it hadn't made sleeping the last couple of nights any easier. She could still
hear the thud, see her knife sink deep into his chest. She'd also spent hours
wondering why he'd kept her identity secret.

"Myerstone Research Laboratory."

She went statue still. "Myerstone?" she echoed.

"On Earth. It blew up. Took its science team with it. Did you tamper with
its power generator? Are you responsible for their deaths?"

Her chin lifted and her eyes met his. "No."

Something flickered in his eyes. "Have you tampered with shuttle engines,
like the ones on Folsum, Delmark Three? That's a yes," he added when she
looked away.

"Who told you about Myerstone?" Jem folded her arms to hide their
tremors. She leaned against the Muddy Sky Caterers storefront for support as a
group of arguing miners swept past.

"Does it matter?" Thane asked, waiting until the miners moved out of
earshot.

"Yes." His voice was flat and unemotional, just like his eyes. "Who?" she
repeated.

"The man who hired me to find you."

"Kurzvall." That explained his silence on her identity. Wouldn't want
anything to interfere with his job. Or complicate her retrieval. She stared off into
the dark. "How long ago?"

46

"A year." He glanced irritably at another group coming down the sidewalk. Jem gave a small nod. A year. "Your visit to Earth?"

"Informational research."

Of course. "What did he tell you?"

"You're an assassin hired to destroy him and his company. You started with blowing up his pet project—that would be Myerstone—and then moved outward."

Jem gave a harsh laugh. "And naturally you believed him."

"He's a well-known venture-cap who was funding the lab's research. You're a drifter with a background full of holes and a bank account most people would happily retire on."

"And I just told you, I didn't do it." Jem matched his angry glare. "The money came from something else."

"Something else? What else pays that well—*in cash?* Not to mention, your account's astronomical growth occurred in the months between the explosion and you leaving Earth."

Her shoulders drooped. Yeah, that did look bad. Her word against Kurzvall's. A drifter versus an ultra-wealthy powerhouse. Who'd believe her?

"Jem, everything okay?" The man stopping beside her gave Thane a suspicious glare.

Boyd was well past middle age, his five-foot chunk as solid as the ore they pulled from Pappia's crust. His fifth generation high-gravity bones and muscles shifted cargo crates and surly miners with ease. She could easily add a narrow-eyed tracker to that list. Tempting, but it would only cause additional problems.

She faked a smile. "Just a little disagreement, Boyd. That's all, but thanks."

The two men exchanged glares. Giving a growly *watch-it*, Boyd headed after his companions. Sending a final warning glare, he disappeared around the corner.

The silence stretched. People dodged around them, the rising tension sensed by anyone below the well-lit stage.

"We need to go somewhere private to talk." Thane glanced meaningfully at yet more people coming their way.

"Wouldn't that be dangerous for one of us? I'm reputed to be an assassin and you certainly look like one." Her sarcastic jab zinged right past him.

"The Grub Stake okay?"

She couldn't just walk off. He'd either alert EMC Enforcers or try to take her in himself. He was a Tracker. She'd let herself forget it. No, she admitted honestly, pushing away from the wall, she had overlooked it. They moved wordlessly down the sidewalk, a wall between them neither made an effort to break.

Jem's thoughts veered wildly. Leaving Pappia was a given. Fast. She hastily assessed the items in her room. What to take, what to leave. Where to hide until there was a ship leaving she could sneak onto. This was a disaster. Breaking contract would have more than just Kurzvall's men after her. Or a certain Tracker. EMC would have her image posted in every Law Enforcement office.

Shit, damn, crap.

Maybe they could work this out. Remind him about saving his life. If nothing else, maybe Thane would give her a few days head start before reporting back to—no, he already had. It must be Kurzvall's people he was waiting for.

Shit, damn, crap.

She eyed him sideways. He wasn't moving quite as gracefully. Was he impeded by injuries? Could she outrun those long legs? "You've recovered from the other night?" Once out of sight she could shift. *Hah. Let's see him track me then.*

"The local MedCenter is well staffed and I heal fast. A headache and some stiffness are all."

Scratch running. Two more storefronts were passed in silence as she planned. She'd take the first chance she got, even if it meant tripping him. Then shift. Risky, but she had no choice. Would he see her? Would someone else?

Jem's shoulders moved restlessly. "You've been hunting me for a year?"

"Yes. You hide your trail pretty well."

"Evidently not well enough," she grumbled. Thane steered them into a different side street from the one she usually took.

"Well enough to dent a twelve-year reputation with that disappearing trick of yours."

Jem stumbled. "Disappearing trick?"

"You're somewhere, then you're not. No connection between where you were and where I finally pick up your trail again." Thane looked over. "How does one go *poof*?"

Poof? She waved her hand dismissively. "Sorry. Professional secret."

"You're a professional ghost?"

"Ghost?" She smirked, thinking it was fairly close to the truth. Before she could say anything else, a man stepped out of an alley and shot her.

CHAPTER 9

Thane caught her collapsing body and swung her limp form into his arms. The man was alone. "Where's Law Enforcement, Dougson?" He yanked the dart out of her neck and waved it at him. "Was this necessary?" He stuffed it into a pocket.

"What took you so long? In the alley. Quick," Dougson ordered.

Dougson had been present at his one and only meeting with Kurzvall. Thane had disliked him on sight. Current events weren't improving his opinion.

"Hurry." Dougson shoved him forward.

Thane twisted, planting his back against the wall as a second man stepped into view. "Why the *hell* is Branigan here?" he asked, tense.

Thane had crossed paths with the extremely volatile and deadly mercenary once before. The laz-gun centered squarely on his chest would be illegally modified for a full stream instead of the normal half-second pulse. He'd learned the man's personal preference the painful way.

Dougson grabbed Thane's arm and shoved again. Hard. "Move it."

No alternative. Branigan's eyes told Thane the merc would be more than happy to even the score between them. Careful to keep him in his peripheral vision, Thane followed Dougson and climbed into a cargo hauler. He cast a furtive glance around the narrow street at this end of the alley, wishing a few of those earlier bodies would wander this way.

There was no one. He had chosen the ambush site well.

***

Thane found himself in a dimly lit office in a poorly lit supply warehouse. Jem's unconscious body lay behind him. Branigan leaned against the doorframe, his hand resting ominously on his holstered weapon.

"Why isn't she being turned over to the authorities?" Thane faced the two men, his feet automatically spread in a battle-ready stance. "Why did you drug her, where are the Enforcers, and why the hell did we *sneak* in here?"

"No Enforcers. We're sneaking around because the bitch usually bribes some of them. The drug is the only way to control her until we meet up with Mr. Kurzvall. He has a special anklet to keep her contained until we can deliver her to the Earth authorities."

Thane did not like the man's too-smooth explanation or his condescending attitude. He didn't like the way Branigan watched him. He most definitely did not like the suspicion he had just made the biggest mistake of his life.

"Why not bring in the local authorities?" he asked.

"Did you miss the part about bribery?" Dougson sneered.

"Can't be all of them."

"No time to find which and I'm not taking a chance."

"What about my bonus?" Let them think he was buying this load of crap.

"Once I've assured Mr. Kurzvall we have the woman, the money will be transferred to your account on Midgard. In the meantime, you're to return home immediately and not mention this to anyone."

"Why?" Thane said bluntly. "Wouldn't Kurzvall be happy to announce you caught a mass murderer?" *She'd said no.*

"Kurzvall has his reasons," Dougson snapped. "You're paid to follow them."

Wrong, asshole. He'd completed what he'd been paid to do. He was on his own time now. "Fine," Thane said, "anything else before I go?"

"No. Yes. Mr. Kurzvall said to tell you how pleased he is and you should expect more work in the future. Have a safe trip home."

Several tense seconds passed before Branigan slid to one side. His stare never left Thane.

Giving the merc a contemptuous look in passing, Thane stormed out of the warehouse. More work, his ass. He wouldn't take another job from Kurzvall if the SOB offered triple wages. Branigan shadowing behind him only stoked his anger.

The merc followed him all the way to the spaceport. They evidently wanted to ensure he left. Thane looked forward to disappointing them. He wasn't going anywhere until he got some answers. By the time he'd collected his gear and boarded a shuttle, the big-mistake suspicion in the pit of his stomach had morphed into I-really-screwed-up certainty.

Dropped in front of his ship, Thor reported there'd been activity: a single person arriving and departing on foot. The sensor readings the comp brain relayed had Thane spitting out a nasty Dantos Two phrase that would send both his grandfather's eyebrows winging upward. The person had accessed the external engine bay and messed around inside for over twenty minutes. Damage unknown. Not even his cousin had come up with engine-bay survivable sensors.

It took him eight minutes to find what had been done, two and a half minutes to stop cussing and thirty minutes to safely remove the bomb and make repairs. Thane stomped onboard and ordered Thor to run a full system diagnostic.

Thor had been unable to get a good reading on the figure, not even gender, as the individual had worn a full environment suit. But add in the skill needed for the delicate sabotage and Branigan floated to the top like the scum he was. Had he done it under Dougson's orders or arranged his own payback? Thane was betting on the former, remembering the barely hid smirk when told to have a safe trip home. All the talk about bonus and future work was only meant to placate him, right up until his ship exploded on activating his Otanak engine.

Bastards. Both of them. All of them. Kurzvall had to have given the order. As for why? He was the link between Jem and them. *Jem,* not Wilmont. Somewhere in the past few days he'd stopped thinking of her as just a job. Just a quarry.

Thane stared at the bulkhead as he coldly sorted, shifted, and reevaluated the situation. Jem was aware of the SOB and his hunt for her. Kurzvall was after something, and it wasn't the justice the spash had spouted. Branigan had probably tailed him to ensure he didn't make any unwanted stops. The merc probably would've shot him at the first sign of deviating and ensured his body wasn't found until after they blasted off.

The drug they used had been fast—oh! Thane patted his pocket and pulled out the dart. Opening an access panel, he ordered a full analysis.

He fixed a cup of coffee and checked over the control console. Everything still green there. Wandered over to a locker, opened it and stared unseeing at the contents for a minute. Closed it. Went back to the table and sat down. He checked for messages. His lip curled in disdain on finding another one from Helga Baron. He deleted it, as he had been for months. Was the woman daft? She should have gotten his unspoken message by now.

His father and mother had been 'love at first argument,' according to family lore. How Gregory Perlman Baron had managed to turn out so different from Helga Baron—who he refused to call grandmother—was a miracle Thane's whole family rejoiced in. The woman personified everything he abhorred in a person. Now, for some insane reason, she expected him to ignore the years of no contact as readily as she had ignored them for all those years.

"System diagnostics complete, no anomalies found," Thor announced. "Substance analysis in progress."

Still? That was some chemical cocktail. What had Dougson said? Something about it being the only way to control her? Control her for what? Why was Kurzvall really after her? Twice he switched the table comp to communication mode. Twice, he switched it back. Regardless of Jem's background or profession, this was a kidnapping. He should be contacting Law Enforcement. Why was he hesitating?

Because you've already betrayed her once tonight, his conscience informed him.

He was in the middle of something bad. Very bad. Something worth kidnapping and murder. Kurzvall's involvement, with all the power and resources it implied, signaled it was also complicated. He hadn't gotten the real story—just enough to find and hand the sonofabitch Jem.

The manipulative asshole. Bastard. Spash.

Thane ran through a few more creative and well-deserved descriptions. It helped to drain off his frustration, leaving deep-seated anger and resolve behind.

This mess was his fault and he'd get her out of it. He also needed to hear Jem's side of whatever was going on. Assuming she'd talk to him. Guilt punched hard on remembering the look in her eyes before they closed.

"Analysis complete. Item matches controlled substance 'Fire and Ice.'"

Thane had the information displayed on the table comp. Hmm…a fairly new drug, Earth origin but not from the Myerstone lab. Used exclusively by Law Enforcement—*yeah, right*—for controlling prisoners, rioters, and other dangerous situations. He scrolled down to the description.

Stage One is immediate debilitation, caused by an acute disruption of the autonomic nervous system. …often described as molten fire…unconsciousness …allows time for Stage Two…muscular paralysis…

Thane's guts were churning by the end of the section. How many times had she gone through that? "Thor, is there a counteragent available?"

"None listed locally."

"Can one be created using our supplies?"

There was a pause. "Counteragent possible, but not all required components are available."

"Can the non-available ingredients be obtained locally?"

There was another, longer pause as the comp brain accessed local inventories. Thane didn't realize he was holding his breath until Thor answered in the affirmative.

"Begin immediate analysis and construction of counteragent for drug called Fire and Ice. Top priority. Copy a list of missing components and the amounts required of each to a text file," he ordered, hurrying over to the weapon locker. His hand hovered briefly over the laz-pistol before pulling out a stunner. His Tracker license authorized both, but the stunner would cause less problems if LE did become involved.

"Display listing of Euphrates Mining Company's local personnel and their contact numbers on the table comp."

Twenty-eight minutes later, Thane left the *Lone Tracker* locked tight and all sensors engaged. He jogged in the darkness toward the space dome using Thor's navigation signal to his remote. He spent several minutes fuming when blocked by a towed train of heavily loaded ore containers. The lights of a shuttle swirled around him when he was over halfway there, the driver almost running him over before slamming to a halt. Two hundred dollars stopped the lecture in mid-sentence and got Thane dropped off at a maintenance entrance on the main dome.

Ten minutes later, his gear hidden under a bench in a supply closet, Thane was moving swiftly back toward the warehouse section, armed and furious.

CHAPTER 10

Thane slipped inside the room, closing the door quietly behind him. Jem lay where he'd last seen her. Was she conscious? Kneeling, he rolled her over gently. His jaw set at the faint whimper. Pain-filled eyes met his.

"What do you want now?" It was a ragged whisper.

He pulled out the injector Thor had prepared. "To get you out of here. I'll apologize later." He pressed the needle against her arm.

Her eyes popped wide. "Wh-what's that?"

"Pain killer. Has either one of those pieces of spash hurt you?"

"Spash?"

"Space trash," he spit out.

"Oh. Well. No, just—*oh, wow*—Dougson's disgusting hand search. He took my knife. *Ooooh*. This stuff is good. Is it legal? Do you always carry it around?"

Thane leaned in close. "Listen carefully. Dougson and his hired merc are emptying a shipping crate out in the warehouse. Probably your ride onboard their ship. We're going to sneak past them."

"I can't move."

Thane allowed a small grin at the petulant tone. She also sounded a little high. Unsure of her system specifics, Thor had set the dose slightly high for an equally-sized Midgard woman. "I'll carry you. What I need is for you to be quiet. Don't speak."

"Can I sing? I like singing."

"No." Yep, she was high. "You have to be as quiet as a Mollari wisp."

"A what? Is that an animal?"

"Never mind." Thane settled her gently on his shoulder.

"On Earth we'd say 'quiet as a mouse.'"

"Jem?" Thane stopped at the door. "Quiet as a mouse. Now."

"You've got a great looking ass."

"*Jem!*" Thane didn't know whether to laugh or strangle her.

"Okay, okay. Got it. Mouse."

Thane eased the door open and listened. Nothing. Eased the door closed behind them. Settling Jem more comfortably, he pulled his stunner from his holster. Hesitated. He wouldn't be able to hang on to both if things went to hell. *If?* Snorting, he slipped the safety off and re-holstered it. Edging to the office corridor's entrance, he scanned the large warehouse.

Cargo crates, pallets and other loose items were stacked randomly across the open floor. The door he'd snuck in was to his right. Unfortunately, it was almost at the other end of the warehouse and in plain view. They needed to make it before the bastards knew she was gone.

Now that was a tempting target.

Branigan's ass hung over the edge of a medium sized container on his left, packing foam dumped haphazardly around his feet. Several more chunks flew out to join the piles. Where was Doug—a muffled sound from behind had him pressing against the wall. The bathroom. A taunt grin lifted his lips. Little shit having a big shit? He wouldn't get a better chance than this.

Moving swiftly, he kept as many stacks between him and Branigan as he could. They were almost there when—.

"*Branigan!*" Dougson yelled. "Baron's got the girl!"

Thane darted behind a stack of large pipes just ahead of the *z-ping* of a stunner blast. This was not good. Too open. They could come at him from two directions. Branigan would already be angling around for a clear shot.

"We're in trouble," Jem mumbled.

No shit. He gauged the distance to a pile of mechanical parts.

"Put the woman down and we'll let you walk away," Dougson yelled.

Yeah, right. Gripping Jem tighter, he darted out. Keeping low, he slid into the pallet's shadow just ahead of several more pings. Propping Jem against a weird-looking valve assembly, he pulled his weapon and reevaluated their situation.

Twenty-plus feet to the door. Open floor all the way. Screwed.

Two expert shooters waiting to lay down a crossfire? Doubly screwed.

"Door," Jem said.

He shook his head. "Too far, too open," he said, scanning the area around them.

"Go poof."

"That would be nice," he muttered absently.

A mixed stack of crates and coils of rope slightly to his left would take them further from the door, but the L-shaped pile offered better protection. A couple of the smaller crates could be shifted to form an enclosure. Maybe he could take one of them out. Maybe hold off until day shift arrived. Or someone else. The call he had placed—

"Thane, will you trust me?"

He looked down into slightly unfocused but steady eyes. She may or may not be the galaxy's best assassin but right here, right now, he didn't give a damn. "Yes."

"Baron! Leave now! Go out the door with hands up."

Did Dougson really think—Thane ducked as two stunner shots pinged off something. Both came from his right. Dammit. Dougson was the distraction and keeping him pinned down. Which meant Branigan was sneaking around on the left.

"I'm not in the best shape to do this," Jem whispered. Worry laced her voice. "It's a huge risk for you."

"Do what?" Something metallic fell loudly on their left. "No choice." Whatever it was.

"Hold me as tight as you can against your chest. Both arms."

Thane scowled down at her. Do what? That would impede any shooting.

"Press my hands as tight between us as you can," she continued.

"The fireman's carry will—"

"No. Trust me," she whispered. "Please?"

He couldn't ignore the pleading in her eyes. Giving a quick glance around, he reluctantly holstered his weapon. He pressed her and her hands against him as she'd asked. Jem gave him a slightly muddled smile before eyeing the door.

"When I say *go*, run for the door. Ignore any strange sensations," she said.

Strange sensations? Was she expecting him to outrun a stun shot? Could he? His arm muscles rippled as he shifted for a better grip. Scanning the area again, he froze. Branigan's smug face was hanging ten feet up on cargo netting. He had a clear shot.

"Knew I'd get the drop on you someday," the mercenary taunted.

The warehouse door opened just then and a technician with a tool box stepped in. His mouth dropped open when he spotted Branigan hanging like a spider.

"Hey! What are—"

Z-ping-ping!

"Go!"

Z-ping!

A stinging numbness hit Thane's thigh as he surged forward. Simultaneously his vision blurred and a wave of nausea struck. He didn't stop, the leg pain gone as fast as it hit. Behind him, Branigan was cursing as Thane raced past the crumpled worker. His vision cleared as they barreled through the open doorway.

Momentum carried them across the alley to a door opposite the one they'd just exited. He whipped around, his back taking most of the jarring impact. His left leg buckled but he managed to catch himself against the wall without dropping Jem. Wow, they actually made it.

"Where are we?" asked a muffled voice from his chest.

He sucked in a fast breath, blew it out. "Service alley. Dead end. Left leg took a stun." No way could he move fast enough to get them away. "There's a dumpster—"

"No. Away from the dumpster. Hurry."

"What good will that do?" Thane demanded, even as he slid deeper into the alley. He pulled his stunner.

"No! Don't!"

Don't what? Fire? Was she serious? They weren't about to just let them go.

Jem told him to hold tight again and not move. He gritted his teeth as the nausea flared even stronger, accompanied this time by a stinging, crawling sensation over his entire body. *What the hell is this?*

A bright light shot out and into the alley. Thane tightened his grip on his stunner when it flashed into his face. Only...he wasn't blinded and Branigan continued to swing the light past him. He stared at the merc. Dumbfounded. Branigan played the light around carefully before stepping out into the alley. Dougson was a cautious shadow behind him. They circled, illuminating every corner of the alley.

His mouth hung slightly agape. *Was this real? They didn't see him and Jem?* He looked down at her tightly closed eyes. *Holy shit! Ghost is right. How—who cares?* It was working. Whatever it was. He hugged her a little tighter.

The more Dougson muttered and swore, the bigger Thane's grin grew. When the SOB didn't find anyone in, under or behind the dumpster near the alley's entrance, he rattled the other service door, the one they'd slammed into. *Yeah, it's bolted from the inside.*

"You're sure you zinged him?" Dougson said.

"In the leg."

"Then he couldn't have gotten far carrying her."

"I've learned to never underestimate Baron." The mercenary watched Dougson with a fixed, speculative gaze as the man repeated his kicking motions around the dumpster.

"Then you should have known he'd come back," Dougson snapped.

"How about you explain how they made it out of the building."

Thane heard the controlled fury in Branigan's voice, despite their oddly flat and slightly muffled speech. Evidently Dougson didn't because the idiot sneered, "Not your business."

"They fucking *vanished*. Right in front of me. How?"

"If Mr. Kurzvall wanted you to know, he'd have told you."

It was like watching one of those very old movies in black and white. No color and fuzzy around the edges. *Another by-product of whatever Jem is doing?*

"That lack of information just cost us. I won't ask again." Branigan's voice was cold.

"Some type of device," Dougson said grudgingly. "It lets her—"

Branigan pulled a second weapon from his belt. "You're a lying piece of shit. You wouldn't have left it on her."

Thane smirked. Merc, one. Idiot, zero.

Even idiots know when death stares at them since his second weapon wasn't a stunner. "Okay, okay," Dougson muttered. "She's some kind of mutant freak. She can make herself invisible. Like an Earth chameleon or a Tardon rock spider."

The emotions flashing across Branigan's face went from disbelief to speculation. "That's why you were kicking around the dumpster." The grip on his laz-gun tightened. "Baron could be standing two feet away and fixing to zing us?"

"Ah…" Dougson swallowed, looked around. "He'll probably need to keep contact with her to maintain the…the cloak. And he's only got a stunner."

"Baron can shoot just fine with one hand," Branigan said, his voice contemptuous. "And depending on where it's aimed, an up-close stun can be extremely painful."

Thane smirked at Dougson's twitch. Tempting thought, but it would give away their position and why she warned him not to fire.

"How long will the drug last?" The mercenary's voice turned brusque.

"The dose I gave her should last about eight hours for full effect." Dougson stomped toward the warehouse door. "Another hour or so as it gradually wears off."

"How long can she hold the cloaking?"

"Hell, I don't know," he threw back over his shoulder. "We didn't even know the bitch could do it with another person. That might shorten it." He stomped back inside.

Branigan shined his light around the alley as he slowly backed toward the open door. One final mutter and the door shut firmly. A bolt slammed home.

Thane agreed with Branigan's opinion of Dougson. 'Deaf corpse' was lingo in certain quarters for someone who didn't have the instincts to keep them from becoming one. The mercenary had undoubtedly sensed what Dougson hadn't: the being-watched feeling which raised neck hairs. He had known they were there. Somewhere.

"Whatever you're doing, hold—" His lips were moving but no sound was coming out. Just how many 'strange sensations' did this whatever have? He issued his warning instead with a raised finger to her lips, repeated it against his when her eyes flickered open. He also made the same request to his stomach.

Sure enough, a couple of minutes later a bright light blazed around the corner from the street. Branigan once again played his light over the wall, around the dumpster, and tried both doors. Dougson watched him from the entrance.

"Will Baron go to the Enforcers?" Branigan asked.

"Wilmont won't let him." Dougson glanced nervously down the sidewalk. "She doesn't want what she is to get out any more than the boss does."

"Understood," Branigan said softly, switching off his light.

Yeah, Thane thought sourly, watching them leave. He just bet he did. Dougson was truly a deaf corpse if he thought Branigan would let someone else have Jem and her obvious potential. And that there, he realized grimly, was Kurzvall's real reason for hunting her.

Jem kept them cloaked for several long minutes more before finally letting it slide away.

This time Thane felt the flicker, like a wave, passing through him. He managed to control the retching but couldn't suppress the shiver racing upward from his toes. He took a relieved breath as the weird crawly-ants sensation and nausea faded away. *Was that normal?* Stupid question. Normal got jettisoned in the warehouse.

His mind whirled. This explained her disappearing trail. It was how she'd hid in the storeroom. Jem must have followed and slipped in behind them before they locked it. "He's right…you camouflaged us somehow," Thane said in a low voice. He watched the alley's entrance, his weapon held ready. Visible equaled vulnerable.

"Yeah," she said, exhaustion in her reply.

Thane glanced down. "Are you all right?" Was the paleness from the drug or her hiding them?

"No," she admitted. "Tapped out. Need to get somewhere safe until this wears off. You?"

"Wobbly, but it was just a side nick. Feeling is already coming back." His eyes flicked between Jem and the alley entrance. "What, exactly, did we do? The nausea and other stuff weren't from being stunned." He'd been hit enough times to know.

"I promise to answer questions later. Can we, just, get out of here first?"

Good idea. This alley would be a death trap if she couldn't hide them again. "My ship is the safest." He moved slowly, testing his leg. It was tingly and shaky but holding up. He stretched it a couple more times. His stomach had also settled.

"No, they'll anticipate that," Jem warned. "My apartment—"

"Un-un. How would it look with you slung over my shoulder?"

A position she found herself in once again, held in place with his hand wrapped around the back of her knees. He grinned at the muttered "like the catch of the evening."

She cleared her throat. "Umm. Did I really say…what I think I said…about your ass?"

"Uh-huh."

"Sorry. It was the drugs."

Reaching the entrance, Thane peered cautiously in both directions. A late-night transport zipped past them, turning left at the intersection at the far end of the street.

"I don't have a great looking ass?" Did she just growl at him?

"Just find us someplace to hide until this stuff wears off."

"Heading there, Miss Catch-of-the-Evening."

"Other than your ship" was the annoyed response.

He slid cautiously out of the alley. "It'll take a lot of effort to break into my ship. I don't think they'll risk alerting the port officials or enforcers." Plus, Thor was working on the antidote. His eyes roamed, watching for the slightest movement.

"We can sneak in through Twelve's maintenance entrance."

"Security cameras."

"Oh. Right. We could—"

"Quiet." Thane crossed over into a narrow side street stretching through more warehouses. "Mouse, remember?"

"I can—*Dammit!*"

A hard tap on the firm rear next to his ear produced a furious silence. Oh well. She wasn't the first pissed-off woman on his shoulder, but they usually wore restraints. Thane breathed a little easier as he turned into the first cross street. Hopefully those two spash were several blocks away by now.

Except they weren't. He froze in mid-step as Dougson stepped out in front of them.

Grinning broadly, he aimed a laz-gun at Thane's chest. "Figured she couldn't hold it too long and you'd head for your ship. Lucky for you, you came my way."

"How's that lucky?" Thane asked sourly.

"I just plan on killing you. I believe Branigan plans on separating various body parts first. Drop your weapon. Good." He kicked it somewhere out into the dark. "Put her down."

Thane carefully lowered into a crouch. Sliding Jem off his shoulder he lunged forward, using her body as a battering ram to knock the other man off his feet. Two quick punches—okay, three—to the head and the bastard was out. Grabbing Dougson's weapon, he slung Jem back over his shoulder.

"Sorry about that," he apologized.

An irritated *"told you so"* drifted up from his waistline.

Pausing at the next corner, he scanned the area carefully. Branigan was out there somewhere. The warehouse district took up this whole side of the dome, its lighting sporadic. Plenty of ambush opportunities.

Thane moved quickly through the mostly silent streets, staying in the shadows as much as possible. He paused, checked his bearings. Almost there. Just a couple of more blocks to where he'd left his gear and an extra weld—

"Down!"

Jem's yell almost came too late. Thane let his body fall forward as a laser stream sliced into a wall, taking singed hair and scalp cells with it. He lay face down, motionless, listening to cautious footsteps as they came closer. Paused.

Moved closer. The boot in his ribs almost exposed him. Jaw locked, he absorbed the blow, remaining limber and unmoving.

Waiting until he felt Jem being pulled away, he whipped sideways and fired from the chest. Branigan toppled backwards, a blackened hole where his right eye used to be. Sitting up, he winced at the pain burning a line just above his left ear. That could not have been any closer.

"Jem? Aw, shit." The knot already rising on her temple was not good.

Pushing himself to his feet brought another streak of pain. He sucked in a sharp breath, let it out slowly as he ran a hand over his side. Nothing felt broken. Hopefully Branigan's heavy boot had only left bruises. He carefully cradled Jem's unconscious body. Turned. *Dammit to hell. Was anything going to go right tonight?* Dougson stood with legs braced, bruises blooming, expression pissed, and holding that damned dart gun. He eyed it warily.

"Yeah, it's loaded. Drop it."

Reluctantly, Thane let the laz-gun fall before obeying the motion to move aside. Eyes and weapon trained on Thane, the man knelt to pick it up, then shoved the dart gun into a small holster at his waist. He fumbled through Branigan's pockets, pulling out a cash card and shoving it into his own pocket.

Thane's lip curled. "Bonus, right?"

Dougson stood, took several steps back. "Lay her down. Slowly."

Thane ignored him. "You think you'll get away with this?"

"Yeah, I do," he said with a smirk. "The tech will be out for a couple of hours after a double stun, and he only saw Branigan. Works out great since we used one of his ships."

"Night patrol will find Branigan before long." He kept his gaze off the compact form creeping up behind Dougson.

"So? It will look like you and Branigan took each other out. The ship's ready to go. I'll swipe a shuttle and be gone before they find your bodies. As for Wilmont, they won't know she's missing for two days. Thanks, by the way, for that great timing."

Dougson elevated his gun. "Now. Put her—" A hand closed lightning fast around his. There was a loud *CRUNCH,* followed by a choked gasp as he collapsed to his knees, his mangled hand still in Boyd's fist.

Boyd's hard eyes traveled from Branigan's body to the one in Thane's arms.

Thane nodded. "She's okay. You get the items?"

"Yes."

"How'd you find me?"

Boyd jerked his head. "I had Skinny following you." There was a steady stream of violent cursing and one final yelp as he pried the gun from the crushed hand.

Thane's lips pursed in a soundless whistle when he spotted the aptly named young man wearing all black behind Boyd. Even if he'd known someone was tailing him, the guy wouldn't have been easy to spot. With his matching skin tone and hair, Skinny wouldn't be more than a small lump pressed up against a wall.

"I need the dart gun on his belt."

Boyd unclipped the holster from Dougson's waist. Handing it to Thane, he then turned to his employee. "You saw nothing and heard even less."

Skinny's head bobbed. "Right, boss." He handed Thane his stunner, which he must have scooped up behind them. "Haul the dead nothing to the waste dump?"

"Acid wash," Boyd said.

Thane shifted uneasily, aware of just how far out of legal bounds this night had gone.

"Change your mind? Want Law Enforcement involved now?" Boyd asked.

Thane squared his shoulders. "No. Not till Jem tells me what's going on."

"Us."

"Us," he agreed, having involved Boyd now.

"Then the body has to disappear."

Boyd was right, and he'd committed to this action when he left his ship. Well, maybe not this particular one, he thought, watching Boyd sling the body onto Skinny's thin shoulders. The young man took off with his burden, surprising Thane with his near jog. More strength there than he would have figured. In another couple of hours, even Branigan's DNA would be gone.

"What about him?" Boyd toed the man at his feet.

Thane gently transferred Jem to Boyd, then carefully squatted down in front of a pale Dougson. Hate outweighed pain in the eyes meeting his. "I have some questions."

"You expect answers?" Dougson sneered, his maimed hand tucked under an armpit.

"Yep. Courtesy of Boyd here and a slow," Thane leaned forward, ignoring his side's protest as his eyes drilled into Dougson's, "dip in an acid wash. Starting with the feet."

Dougson swallowed. "You're bluffing."

Yes, he was. He leaned back. "Answer my questions to my *complete* satisfaction, and I'll send you back to Kurzvall alive and without the bath."

"I say he gets it anyway, up to his knees." Boyd looked down at Jem and back up. "Think I'm bluffing?"

Dougson took one look at Boyd and his face slowly went white as the blood drained south of his collarbone.

CHAPTER 11

Jem kept her eyes closed and her breathing steady. Memories of a dark doorway, a man, and a weapon did not bode well. A small test showed her arms and legs moved freely and without pain. The throbbing in her right temple probably came from being dropped. Yeah, she remembered that. Barely cracking her eyelids, she peered cautiously through her eyelashes. Seeing no one, she opened her eyes fully.

It was a ship's sleeping compartment.

Panic hit. *Where was*—wait. There was no irritating throb at the base of her neck, so the O-engine wasn't running. No vibrations from the ions either. Relief hit. Unless they were just hanging in space, she was still on Pappia. Since she wasn't tied or drugged or locked in, this wasn't Dougson's ship. Whatever had happened, Thane had won.

She swung her legs to the floor and surveyed her surroundings. A med-kit sat on the built-in desk and various medical supplies were in the open cabinet above it. Looking up, she spotted the medical scanner embedded above her.

He kept a med-room? Just what kind of jobs did he take?

She peeked under the door, which was slid two thirds upward in its track, and into a short hallway. A storeroom opened directly across from her. A lift filled the hallway's end on the right. Well, that was convenient. But if it wasn't locked, the hatch somewhere below would be. And running was no longer an option.

Looking left, the hallway ran past two more doorways before opening into a large open area. Lights blinked on a panel against the far wall. That would make it the main command center. *Clank.* She jerked back at the sound of a locker door shutting. When Thane didn't appear after multiple heartbeats, she peeked back out. He sat in front of a comp screen against the far wall, oblivious to the glare stabbing between his shoulder blades.

Inching down the hallway she paused at the doors. The room on the right was definitely Thane's bedroom. Left? Her bladder immediately signaled *Hallelujah* as she dashed inside and pulled the door down. Minutes later and feeling a lot better, she entered the main area warily.

A navigation console with two pilot chairs stretched along the bulkhead opposite her. Above it hung a large viewscreen, with three digital clocks displaying different times above that. Lockers lined the wall on her right all the way to a stairwell. A compact kitchen filled the left side. The comp Thane had been working on sat on the short leg of an L-shaped table. The longer, wider leg visually divided the two functional areas.

Her side trip must have taken longer than she thought. He'd rotated his seat around and had two steaming cups beside him. His gaze flicked over her before snapping back up.

Their eyes locked: his cool and appraising, hers cold and suspicious.

"We need to talk." He pushed one of the cups across the table.

"It didn't turn out so well for me last time, did it?"

He acknowledged that with a slight head dip. "I own you an apology and we both have some explaining to do."

"Yeah, well…" Her gaze locked on a thin, *fresh* laser burn on the side of his head.

"Boyd's on his way. I let him know you were awake while you were in the bathroom."

She jerked her gaze back to his. "He knows I'm here?"

"He helped get you here."

Her supply friend would not have been happy, especially if the bruises she'd seen in the bathroom mirror had already started blooming. Sinking warily into the chair opposite Thane, she slid the cup closer and inhaled deeply. Coffee. "Earth?"

"Tellmark. It's sweeter."

Jem didn't know what to make of him. He'd participated in the ambush, then risked his life rescuing her. She flicked another quick glance at the burn.

How was he still alive? Despite the anger still churning inside, she asked how badly he was hurt. Other than the obvious.

"I've had worse," came the nonchalant reply. "As mentioned, I heal fast."

Yeah, right. "What's worse than a carved skull?"

"Carved chest."

Jem blinked. He wasn't kidding. *Good thing that med-room is next to the lift.*

"Besides the laser burn, I have some bruised ribs. Nothing major," he said. "You have a minor concussion with various scrapes and bruises. Sorry does not begin to describe how I feel, Jem, for what happened last night and my part in it. I didn't have all the facts. The real facts."

Last night? "How long have I been out?"

"Thirteen hours, roughly."

No wonder her bladder had been on overload.

"In case you're wondering, Margo got you the clean clothes."

"Well, who the frigging hell else knows about this?"

"Would you have preferred me or Boyd changed you?"

Flushing, she hid her face with her cup. *She thought Thane had.* She'd noticed the different clothes in the bathroom, along with the rainbow of colors running from her ear down to her collarbone.

"She only knows we were attacked," Thane continued after swallowing some coffee. "She believes it was another attempt on me and you were simply caught up in it. Drugged. Boyd and I convinced her neither of us was seriously hurt and didn't need to go to the MedCenter. *I*," he emphasized, "needed to keep the incident quiet."

"Margo? Keep quiet?" *He'd directed the attention away from her again. What was the reason this time?*

His lips lifted in a faint grin. "I think you'll be surprised. After losing the argument about taking you to the MedCenter, Margo provided a distraction while Boyd sneaked all of us into a maintenance shuttle. She left me a—call it a strong warning about not taking any advantages. There is more to that woman than meets the eye. Especially her vocabulary."

70

Jem propped an elbow on the table. There'd still be plenty of questions about her colorful neck. Good thing she'd just started her weekend. She still had a day to come up with an explanation that wouldn't have Jansom forcing her to the MedCenter or calling the Enforcers. Her eyes flicked back to his burn.

"What happened? Last I remember is a guy in a doorway and being dropped."

He cleared his throat. "Yeah. Sorry about that. Anyway, we were lucky." Thane summarized the events after dumping her on her head. He finished up with Margo and Boyd's help in smuggling her aboard the *Lone Tracker*.

"Why did Boyd have you followed?"

"Because he knew what I was doing. No, not that," he said quickly when her eyes widened in shock. "Afterwards. I called him, told him you were in trouble and I was going after you. He doesn't know I got you into it."

"Did you have to involve them?"

"Besides needing help?" Thane said, plainly irritated. "Boyd picked up the ingredients Thor needed to make the counteragent for the drug they used on you. I was kind of busy."

"Counteragent?" Jem asked sharply. Thor again. Just who was this guy?

"It took a couple of hours to completely flush your system. You've been out mostly from the concussion and exhaustion. Remember, you'd just gotten off shift."

Her stomach chose to emphasize it with a loud rumble.

Thane's lips twitched. "It has been a while since you ate. Any dietary restrictions?" he asked, walking to the food carousel with stiff, careful steps. The carousel's internal light clicked on when he started its rotation.

She glanced over the rest of his kitchen. A standard freezer-cooler combination butted against the carousel with two stacked microwaves on the other side. Cabinets stretched from the micros to the hallway, both above and below the miniature sink in the middle. A trash compactor and recycler would be tucked in the lower ones.

"You really are a ghost, aren't you?" he said quietly, watching the dishes cycling past the transparent window.

She bit her lip, wary and unsure. Not like she could deny it now.

"Can anyone else in your family do it?"

"No." She gave a bitter laugh. "Like Dougson said, I'm a freak."

"Unique," Thane corrected over his shoulder.

She stared at his back. *Unique?* How could she stay angry after that?

He stopped and started the carrousel several times before he finally pulled out a frozen meal. "Stew," he told her, starting to strip off the outer wrapping. Remembering his Grub Stake selections, she hoped it wasn't too spicy.

He set the upper micro's timer. Settling back into his seat, he speared her with a determined look. "Natural born ability?"

"No." She played with her cup handle. What should she tell him? How much would he believe? Or accept? She liked being thought of as unique. No, not everything then. He'd already had his universe tilted sideways, but the tech opening the door had saved her biggest secret. The rest…she'd keep it to bare facts as much as possible.

"I was in between jobs and just sort of roaming." Until she stopped to help a friend. "I got caught up in one of Myerstone's experiments when it flared out of control. It made a mess of both me and the lab."

His eyes narrowed. "I included the lab in my background research. There was only one other report of an explosion and having to replace a power generator. But that was about seven, eight months before you went to work there."

She cleared her throat. "Well…"

"It's also about the same time as your first poof. There's no trace of you for months. *Including* at Myerstone."

"And now you know why. No one but the lab team knew about me. After they dragged me out of the debris, I was kept hidden from the rest of the estate workers at Christine's place—a team member who lived about a kilometer from the lab." How would he take the rest? "I'm, uh, changed…at the cellular level. And my nervous system. Stunners only tingle."

"That explains their using drugs. How bad did it mess you up?" Thane asked quietly.

"Physically, I didn't have a scratch. Otherwise?" Her laugh was hollow. "Hallucinations, vertigo, nausea, muscle spasms, jangly just-coming-alive nerve sensations. Double, even triple vision. You name it, I probably experienced it sometime during that first month. Spells of flickering on and off like a neon sign in a bar window lasted about two months. No set pattern and I'd...wander. During one of them, I ended up at a duck pond. They weren't friendly."

She laughed with Thane. Yeah, it was funny now.

"So, one or two of them always stayed with me. The team protected me and kept me sane during the months it took to stabilize." Months filled with panic and fear. And anger. At them. At the Universe. Why her? "They helped me learn how to deal with it, especially after it became obvious I had a new...skill. Marion—Dr. Bluethon—told me I blurred the lines of reality."

His intense study made her nervous. She could almost see his brain churning.

"I needed to re-enter the normal world and they wanted to monitor me a little while longer...side effects, problems...whatever might pop up. That's when I 'hired on' for several months, working as general labor and fine-tuning my control."

Her stomach knotted. She was not going to like what was behind that scrunched brow.

"Dougson called you a chameleon, but a chameleon's ability only affects itself. You shouldn't have been able to include me by simply maintaining a close contact. What did you actually do?"

Shit, damn, crap. Shit, damn, crap.

"I have no clue," she said. Lie number three million and ten, she thought wearily. "I concentrate and the shift happens. Holding onto something does let me, um, take it with me. Your tight hold, with my hands pressed between us, worked the same." *Thank God.*

"Why was our vision and speech affected?"

Jem made a helpless gesture, hoping he'd interpret it as another 'no clue.' "Thane, I don't understand it either and there's no one I can ask." Now that was nothing but truth. Her stomach knotted at the way he was eyeing her. He knew she was holding back. *Please, please let it go.* She gave a small mental *yay* when he did.

73

"You held it last night for a total of, what, twenty, thirty minutes? It wiped you out."

"Yes, and my system was already compromised from the drug." She glanced at the clocks above the auxiliary console.

Thane noticed. "One on the right is local time. Boyd should be here soon. I haven't told him anything. For what it's worth," he said bluntly, "I think he needs to know. Margo, too. You'll need someone to watch your back in case others come looking."

A well-modulated voice floated out from nowhere. "An EMC vehicle has stopped inside the ship's perimeter."

Jem leaned forward. "Is someone else here?"

Thane shook his head as the same voice said, "Mr. Boyd is requesting entry."

"Release the locks. That's Thor." He rose, giving a vague, circular hand wave. "The comp brain that runs my ship."

Jem's eyes widened. A comp brain? In a ship this size? Might as well use a fusion plant to power one city block. They were more than a computer but not quite an AI. It also explained why Thor lacked the digital undertones she could hear in most computer-generated voices.

"*Wow*," was all she managed.

"Thor came with the ship," Thane said grudgingly. "My father had it installed when he purchased the ship for my mother, who isn't a licensed pilot. Its full auto-nav systems allowed us to visit and spend time with him when he was on Survey expeditions. She gave it to me after I started freelancing."

"You're rich and work as a Tracker?"

"Beats being a port drifter," he shot back, pouring coffee into a sturdy-looking cup.

Boyd popped nimbly out of the stairwell. "How's the head?" he asked Jem, seating himself between them at the table's end. He accepted the cup from Thane as his sharp-eyed gaze roamed over Jem's facial scrapes and bruises.

"Um...sore, a little." What story could she come up with? A mugger? A run-in with a shuttle? No, both of those would have LE reports. How about the classic trip down a stairwell? Yeah, it might—she jumped when Boyd set his empty cup down with a sharp *thunk*.

"Good coffee." He looked between the two of them. "What the hell's going on?"

The micro pinged.

Jem jumped out of her seat. "I'll get it."

"Silverware is in the drawer under the micros." Thane met Boyd's gaze. "I'll talk while she eats."

Jem listened as she dug hungrily into the rich mixture of chunky meat and vegetables. Thane's report was concise and straightforward, detailing Kurzvall's false claims and his hunt for her. He made no attempt to soften or excuse his role in her abduction, which had Boyd's eyes promising pain. That promise faded at Thane's description, minus the details, of her rescue.

"That's the guy you were questioning Dougson about," Boyd said, after giving Thane's new scar several seconds of study.

"Which was a waste of time. His boss evidently doesn't trust him with very much."

Boyd crossed his arms. Looked at Jem. "Exactly who is this Kurzvall?"

"Reginald Salazar Kurzvall is a fine, law-abiding, *respected* member of the mega-rich society." Jem's sarcasm was on par with an acid wash. "He's also an ambitious megalomaniac who uses whatever means necessary to get what he wants. As demonstrated. What changed, Thane? Why did you decide to help me?"

"Other than them trying to kill me? I was already suspicious more was going on than I had been told. Thor found enough information that I was beginning to wonder..." His voice trailed off at the resentful look he was receiving.

"Didn't stop you from helping them."

"I'm a Tracker." Thane's chin lifted, his gaze steady. "I'm hired to locate and/or apprehend and return. It's for the legal system to determine one's guilt or innocence. Yes, you denied being responsible for Myerstone but wouldn't offer the same for the shuttle engines. Tampering with them and endangering lives is called sabotage. Last I checked, it's still illegal."

Pink tinged Jem's cheeks, aware of Boyd's narrow-eyed scrutiny. "I never intended for anyone to get hurt. The event on Folsum was...unexpected."

"Regardless of intent, your actions were still illegal."

She sighed, gave her spoon one final lick. Yeah. Sooner or later, that was going to be a problem.

"Okay, back to this mega-asshole. Why is he really after you?" Boyd asked.

"Data," she said. While not the whole truth, it was the safest piece of misdirection she could give. Even to Thane. "Myerstone's research data is on a hand comp. It wasn't destroyed with the lab."

Thane's brow furrowed. "The Otanak TVS problem?"

Boyd's fingers were doing a cup dance. "Which isn't exactly a unique topic. They've been trying to figure out what slows down the larger ships since we began using the drive. So," he said bluntly, "what is worth killing and chasing you all over the galaxy?"

"The time-versus-size research was camouflage," Jem said. "Their real goal was to adapt the Principles so that when two points on a planet's surface were linked together it would provide near instantaneous travel between them. They even postulated it might be possible to eventually extend it between planets within a star system." Should she tell them it had worked? That she had been sucked to the lab from the hanger she'd been working in? Over two hundred kilometers distant? She mentally shook her head. It would lead to other questions. Other revelations and, eventually, to more dangerous truths.

Thane gave a low whistle. "It would completely revolutionize travel and planetary planning. And be extremely profitable if someone could maintain control of it."

"Which is Kurzvall's goal," Jem said.

"All right, I can understand why you don't want him to have it," Boyd said, nodding. "Pick someone. Anyone. Give it to them."

"Can't. I don't have it. Kurzvall does."

"Ooookay," Boyd drawled. "Why is he chasing you for something he already has?"

She sighed. "Because I passcoded the damn thing."

Thane laughed. "To have the data, and yet not. Perfect."

"Well, then, give him the wrong passcode," Boyd said, shrugging.

Turn everything into a mess of unsalvageable electrons? "No."

Boyd frowned. "The Republic works just fine now as it is, and you won't have to worry about him anymore."

"No." She pushed her empty tray away.

"Why?"

"It's my friends' legacy!" Jem's voice pitched higher. "Theories. Equations. Equipment modifications. All their work, all their ponderings on the Otanak Principles; all their conclusions from first to last experiments. Even a year's worth of private correspondence and notes from their personal accounts. Grathen siphoned off *everything*."

"A useless legacy if it's kept locked up. Who's Grathen?"

Jem recoiled as if she'd been slapped. That was brusque, even for Boyd. She swallowed. "The lab technician who was selling the data to Kurzvall and blew up the lab to hide his theft."

"If you believe it's that important, let Kurzvall and his people work with it."

"No." Jem returned Boyd's glare, her jaw set at a stubborn angle. Thane was silent, watchful.

Boyd leaned forward. "Destroy it or let him have it," he said, each word enunciated as if she were an addle-brained teenager.

"*No!*"

"The bastard will stop chasing you."

"No, he won't!"

"Why the hell not?" Boyd roared.

"Because Kurzvall intends to wield me like a weapon," she yelled back. Then vanished.

CHAPTER 12

Thane stuck a finger in his ear and waggled it a couple of times. "No yelling." A large metal ball had top-notch acoustics.

Boyd ignored him. He was staring slack-jawed at Jem's empty chair.

Poof was definitely the right word, Thane thought. There one second, then not. Or the reverse, he though drily as she reappeared behind Boyd.

Jem tapped Boyd on his shoulder. His head whipped around. "*Jasper's Balls!* You teleported!"

"No. Invisibility. I call it shifting. Although," she shot Thane a sideways look as she retook her seat, "I like his ghosting analogy."

"What would an amoral sociopath with access to *that* do?" Thane asked. She wasn't going to tell him. If Boyd hadn't pushed, he still wouldn't know.

"Nothing good," Boyd said. Jem snorted. "Right. Damn. Invisibility. That's how you two escaped the warehouse."

"Yes. I extended it to Thane."

"We'd have been seen if we'd moved?" Thane asked, remembering her warnings.

"Probably not—it was dark, but I didn't want to take a chance. With good eyesight and that bright light, they might have seen a rippling…like a heat wave. I was more worried about holding it. The deeper—crap." She scratched behind an ear. "The harder, longer I push, the more energy needed. Stressed and drugged as I was, I couldn't be sure we were, uh, deep enough to hide the ripple."

"So, it's not just an on-or-off thing?" Thane said.

He gaped along with Boyd as Jem faded into a transparent apparition. Holy frigging hell. He gave a long, appraising look as she gave them a ghostly wave.

Just how was she doing it? That was not a chameleon-like talent. She literally became an actual ghost. Impossible.

Jem solidified back to full human. "It's more like a variable dimmer switch. Going poof, as Thane puts it, requires a hard yank."

"If I hadn't seen it—" Boyd muttered, then gave her a piercing look. "Were you born able to do it?"

Thane listened as Jem gave him the same—and incomplete—story about Myerstone's disastrous experiment as he'd gotten. He could fly the *Lone Tracker* through some of those holes. What was she leaving out and why? Something linked to that ghosting?

"What?" Boyd said when she finished. "Those geniuses didn't remember to take precautions?"

"They did...the accident just kind of exceeded their expectations. They didn't expect their equipment to be fried, much less have a ten-foot hole blown in the lab wall by the industrial-sized generator out back. The O-field—"

"Wait. They were using O-engines? No wonder things blew up," Thane said, disgusted. "Everyone knows Otanak engines don't like gravity fields."

"No, not engines. Supposedly, they were only simulating fields *similar* to what the engines generate and only on a small scale. I don't understand the difference either," she added when Thane's mouth opened. "Everything was in scientist-speak and usually made my eyes glaze over. Even when translated into non-genius, most of it still zipped right past me."

"Fine. They helped you after messing you up," Boyd growled. "How does this Kurzvall fit in?"

"He was providing the lab's primary funding. Once it was repaired and operational again, he began pressuring them to restart their experiments. They resisted, in favor of evaluation and more research into O-fields."

"Well, darn," Thane said. "Now why would they do something sensible like that?"

Jem flashed him a brief smile before turning somber. "That's when things fell apart."

Thane frowned as Boyd asked, "What happened?"

"Mega-sized hissy fits."

* * * * *

Jem grinned at their blank stares. "Temper tantrums. First one was when the team leaders, Drs. Lammstein and Bluethon, got tired of Kurzvall's constant demands and terminated their association. Second one was when they told him Myerstone's data wasn't his to take and they had no intention of giving it to him. He planned to start up another lab somewhere else using their data. Kurzvall went livid—I didn't realize someone could literally turn purple.

"Anyway, I left right after that scene, moving into town and job hunting. Kurzvall had been pressuring me too, wanting me to work for him. I didn't like him or the vague answers about *what* kind of work. Grathen had told him about my invisibility." Fortunately, only Dr. L and Marion had known the full extent of her mutation.

"Grathen…Grathen lured me back one night with a phony text message using Dr. Bluethon's phone. I found the entire team in the lab's control booth, unconscious. Dougson's dart gun? It was Grathen's. He used it on all of us." She'd never forget Grathen's malicious glee or the punch of his drug-filled dart in her shoulder.

"You didn't go invisible?" Boyd asked.

"He caught me off guard and I still wasn't used to—call it the hard side of life."

"There was, uh, evidence showing *all* of the team died," Thane said tactfully.

"Yes…" Jem's eyes unfocused as she pulled on memory fragments. "I came to briefly, slung over his shoulder. We were outside somewhere…the parking area, I'm pretty sure. There's a high-pitched whine—the power generator reaching critical. He'd set it to overload. He's arguing with someone. It's Dougson, although I didn't know the voice at the time. Then yelling. Someone pulled me off his shoulder. I blacked out again."

"Grathen became a liability as soon as they got what they wanted. Probably stunned him and tossed him back in the building before bolting," Boyd said. "The SOB deserved it, and not just for your friends. The drug he used, Fire and Ice? It's cruel, and Thane said it kills."

"It's only dangerous in high doses. They wouldn't..." her voice trailed off as Thane's head shook.

"Thor says getting hit with two of Dougson's darts would cause massive organ paralysis followed by failure. The bastard said the high dose was to keep you safely incapacitated until they met up with Kurzvall."

Had they been aware of that, or just didn't care? She ran her hand through her loose hair, automatically braiding it. "Hair tie?" she asked.

"Med-room somewhere," Thane replied, stacking their coffee cups in the sink.

Thane had three glasses filled with whisky by the time she returned, her braid hanging neatly down her back. *Just what the medic ordered.* Accepting hers gratefully, she took a long sip. It only generated a soft warmth.

Boyd was looking at his glass. They both looked at Thane.

He held up a hand. "Yes, I know. Wimpy. It's my last bottle. I plan on restocking with Pounding J's version before I leave. Okay, what happened after being kidnapped?"

"Due to those hallucinatory wanderings, Dr. L had borrowed a tracking bracelet from a doctor he knew who worked in a psychiatric hospital. A signal from a remote dispensed both a knockout drug and activated a locator beacon. I wore it for months, until we were sure I could control it."

"Zap bands," Thane said, nodding. "Law Enforcement uses them, mainly when transporting prisoners. Habitually troublesome Fed-Pen prisoners can end up with a permanent one. I've never had a need for them."

"Grathen stole it too. I was wearing it when I woke in Kurzvall's plush suite, still paralyzed. His welcome-to-the-team speech was pretty blunt: I worked for him and would do what I was told. Kurzvall took great pleasure in informing me Dr. L's benign drug had been replaced with the same drug in Grathen's darts. Fire and Ice. The locator was my leash. If I tried to slip it, pain would be both penalty and punishment. Along with helpless humiliation." She took a large swallow of whisky. "I can still feel Dougson's hands roaming over me."

Crack! Whisky dripped from Boyd's fist. He set the fractured glass down and shook his hand. He shot Thane a frigid look. "You should have let me dip the bastard."

"Dip him?" Jem repeated, reaching for his hand. There was only one thin cut across two fingers. She grabbed a handful of paper napkins.

"How did you get away?" Boyd wadded one napkin in his fist as a bandage.

"Low dose," she said, wiping the table. "Grathen wasn't sure of the drug's strength or how my weird system would handle it."

"It wore off quicker than they were expecting." Thane nodded. "That's why Dougson pumped up the dose this time."

"Probably." She set the ruined glass in the sink. Returning to the table, she refilled her glass and slid it over in front of Boyd, figuring he needed it more than she did.

"I went searching for the remote controller as soon as I could manage a shuffle. Without it, I'd have to stay put and wait for another chance. I'd just started searching a backpack, which turned out to be Grathen's, when Kurzvall returned. I shifted, planning on slipping back and pretending." Her eyes took on a gleam. "Then I spotted the remote in his hand.

"I, uh, popped in behind him and gave him a well-deserved kick in the ass...hard...sent him flying into a side table." Both men's expressions radiated approval. "I grabbed up the remote, tossed it into the backpack, gave him the finger, shifted, and got the hell out. I knew someone who would cut the band off my ankle without asking questions."

That got a narrow-eyed look from Thane. Right. Tracker and auxiliary enforcer.

"I didn't go to the authorities because," she sighed, "because of so many things. Like the contents in Grathen's backpack. The hand comp appeared to hold all of Myerstone's data, as well as the team's personal files. Even more shocking were the two cash cards. Both were unbelievably high and undoubtedly his payment. Having both data and cash put me in a spot. Kurzvall could accuse me of what Grathen actually did and of extorting money from him. To tell the truth, I'm not sure why he didn't."

"Can't use you if you're locked up in a Fed-Pen cell," Boyd said.

Wish she'd thought of that. "After a couple of tense weeks, I finally deposited most of the cash. There was still the potential problem of the hand comp. By then, I was working retail in a flower shop and dodging his watchers. Then I got this fantastic idea. The comp and the data were two different things. I could give him one, without the other. To doubly protect the data, I encrypted it as well. Then I switched to ghost-mode" that got her a couple of chuckles "and snuck into his hotel room to leave it."

"Well done," Thane said. Boyd nodded in agreement.

"It turned out to be a very enlightening visit. I caught his end of a comp call where he was chewing out someone for not getting something done in the Federal Senate he wanted. Following that," she looked between the two men, "he received a call confirming completion of an assignment in the Meridan System by one of his assassins."

"His *what?*" Boyd sputtered. Thane's eyebrows shot upward.

"Assassins." Her eyes flashed. "This one took out a Planetary Representative named Webley. Kurzvall ordered his assistant to pull the merc's final payment from their *special* account; Dougson was to arrange delivery of the cash card. I, uh, peaked over the guy's shoulder to get the account information and then completely emptied it the next morning. It took *three* cash cards. That was the second large deposit you found, Thane. There was no way I was keeping that much on me."

"What is the bastard up to?" Thane said.

"No idea but, from the pieces I overheard, he definitely has a long-term goal. Something which includes manipulating and killing people to get it." Maybe she should have eavesdropped a bit longer.

"Something he wants to use you for though." Boyd rubbed his jaw. "Can we link the bastard to that account?"

"No. It's closed."

"You should have left it alone," Thane said, shaking his head.

Boyd scowled at him. "I've no problem with her draining the killer account."

Thane's jaw set. "Authorities could have traced it, maybe linked it to something. He's undoubtedly opened another one somewhere else and that option is now gone."

"Do you think the Enforcers would have paid her any attention? Believed her over him without proof?" Boyd waved a hand in Jem's direction. "She'd have probably been arrested for hacking."

"She probably will be and not for hacking. Linking that account now to even one act only leads back to Jem," Thane said, irritated. "With the timeline on those deposits and her questionable background, most people *would* conclude she blew up Myerstone."

Jem cupped her chin. Listening. While neither action might have been her smartest move, it certainly wasn't worth a snipe-fest between two supposedly grown men. "Let me know when you're done. I'll finish up then." That shut them up, but the glares? *Hooo, boy.*

"The last thing I overheard pertained to some under-the-table contract fixing with an Orion Sys-Senator."

"You're the anonymous tipster?" Thane pointed a finger at her. "It caused quite an uproar."

"Yeah, especially for Kurzvall. Creating financial disasters is the way I've been getting back at him. Anyway, his goons made a grab for me a couple of days later. It didn't succeed, but I knew he'd keep trying." She flashed them a satisfied smirk. "But I had him worried."

"Little bit jumpy, was he?" Boyd said, grinning. "Wondering where you were, or might be?"

Thane snorted. "That would explain his paranoia. When I interviewed about the job at his home on Hebros, I saw sensors all over the place. I'm willing to bet there were others I didn't detect. Heat, weight and motion sensors, right?"

Jem nodded, not about to explain why they wouldn't do any good.

"Nowhere was safe, not with his resources. I left Earth and just drifted, not staying long anywhere and hid my eyes with colored contacts—I hate those things. I kept to Port Circles or small colony towns as much as possible, taking low-level jobs that didn't require a lot of paperwork or questions. I kept everything as random as possible so they couldn't guess where I was or might be heading."

"You also muddled things up by occasionally ghosting aboard ships. Right? No wonder I kept losing your trail. There wasn't one. You nearly lost me when you signed on with EMC."

Curious, she asked how he did find her.

"Best Tracker around." Thane shrugged when two sets of brows shot north. "It also helps when you're drowning your frustrations and the table next to you is filled with EMC recruiters discussing their latest quotas and recruits. I was still sober enough to recognize the importance of one guy's remark about a two-eyed bartender he hired for Pappia from that very same bar. The place I *had* tracked you to, I'd like to point out."

Jem rested her chin in her hand and gave a long, exaggerated sigh. What were the odds? The place, the people, a random comment? "I thought Pappia was far enough out it'd be safe enough to just stop for a while. Thought I was being careful." She gave Thane a resigned smile. "But it didn't fool the galaxy's best Tracker" —he shot her a grin— "with the damnedest luck."

Boyd chuckled when Thane's expression reversed into a scowl.

A companionable silence settled, everyone lost in their thoughts.

Boyd looked over at Thane. "I take it we're still not going to Law Enforcement."

Thane rubbed the back of his neck. "Is there *any* way to prove Kurzvall was behind Myerstone's destruction? Assassinations or any other illegal activity?" Jem shook her head. "So it's still our word against his then."

"Yep, and he keeps himself well-buffered from questionable activities. Enforcers would get the same story he gave you. At the time, authorities assumed it was another experiment that got out of hand. Now, as you pointed out, my bank account's growth will stand out."

Thane sighed. "It's a good thing you held off depositing those cash cards."

Boyd flexed his hand. Finding the bleeding stopped, he dropped the napkin on the table. "This ghosting is why you haven't gone to the authorities. Making a complaint about Kurzvall stalking you risks him revealing it in retaliation. Every crook, SOB and spy agency out there would be hunting you."

His expression grim, Thane said, "Unfortunately for Jem, secrets have a way of sneaking out. It's always going to be a risk."

Jem slumped back in her seat. No, there'd never be an end to it. Always looking over her shoulder. Always paranoid about mistakes and waiting for betrayal. What kind of life was that?

"I'm either a tool to use or a threat to eliminate," she said tiredly. "How can anyone truly trust someone who can silently listen to their secrets and watch access codes? Or poison their drinks?"

"You're kidding, right?" Boyd said. "That someone would be the most successful, wealthiest mercenary-thief in the galaxy, not serving drinks to miners in a Rim bar."

"You've saved my life twice for no reason other than it was the right thing to do. Even when pissed," Thane said. "You could have gone down the same path as Grathen, Dougson or Branigan. Many would have. You didn't."

"I don't want to be like them. To steal. To be a killer." She bit her lip.

"Forced to kill in self-defense or in defense of others is not the same as *being* a killer." Thane's voice softened. "Sometimes one has no choice, but to do what is necessary…as I did last night. As you did the other night. Jem, your life has been turned inside out. You could take out Kurzvall and Dougson at any time to make it a whole lot easier."

Boyd's hand shot up. "I vote for poisoning their drinks." That earned him a snicker from Jem and an exasperated look from Thane.

"Instead," Thane continued, "I've heard a number of intriguing stories floating around the various systems I chased you through."

Jem gave him a blank look. "Stories?"

"An elderly couple on Sagious One were somehow miraculously rescued from a raging inferno by an unknown person. Authorities on Kettleman Three received an anonymous tip on where to find a kidnapped child and his neatly tied up captors. Another unknown protector on Minos Four thwarted the assault on two young girls who sneaked out of their parents' hotel suite and got more excitement than they planned on."

"Oh. Those stories." Jem took a sudden interest in her hands. "I've heard a few myself."

Thane nodded when Boyd inclined his head questioningly toward Jem.

"There are others, and probably even more that didn't make the news or gossip circuits. In each case, a woman appears out of nowhere and leaves the same way. She collects no rewards, no thanks. She keeps her face hidden, but the kidnapped boy thought the long braid was pretty. So, Jem, I'd say you are as far opposite of those spash and their like as possible."

A sudden worry hit Jem. "Where's Dougson now? And who was the other man—Branigan?" At their exchanged looks, she said "Never mind." It might be better if she didn't know.

Thane's lip curled. "Branigan was an extremely bad SOB, a full-blown sociopath with psychopathic tendencies. He led a group that's more Fed-Pen candidates than mercenaries. There was no way he'd let Kurzvall have you after he witnessed what you can do."

"Dougson is alive. His ship left about," Boyd glanced at the local time display, "ten hours ago."

"I have to leave." Jem bolted up. Boyd grabbed her wrist and pulled her back into her seat. She popped back up. "Kurzvall will have—*oomph*." She glared at Boyd when the second chair plop was a lot harder.

"No need," Boyd said.

"We sent a message back with Dougson." Thane propped himself on his elbows, winced and leaned back again.

"Message?" she asked warily.

"It will be in his best interest to leave you alone and to *not* go looking for you again, especially since the galaxy's best Tracker—I'm glad you agree—will not be available."

"We implied you're paying off the remainder of your contract and leaving," Boyd added.

Jem nodded in agreement. "That would be accurate. I can afford eight months—"

A cash card landed in the center of the table.

"Branigan doesn't need his anymore." Thane tossed a second one on top of the first. "Dougson, uh, donated his as compensation for undue hardship and aggravation."

"Uh-huh. Did you also get my knife back?"

"Yep."

"Well? Can I have it?"

"Sure. Now I know I'm safe. *Annnyway*," Thane said over their snickers. "We took him back to his ship. Safe and sound." His head rocked sideways a couple of times. "Mostly."

Boyd stirred. "Well, he did have a little trouble handing things over. With the condition his hands were in, I had to get the cards out his pocket."

"Both of them? I thought only the one got crunched?"

Thane rubbed his ear. "Margo sort of accidently stepped on the other one."

"Accidentally?"

"Yeah. She even apologized."

"*Riiiiight*," Jem said. *That's a sucker's smile if I ever saw one.* "Anything else?"

"We certainly didn't dip him in the acid wash like Boyd wanted to."

"You were the one talking about cutting off his third leg."

"It's kind of useless right now with his hands messed up, don't you think?"

Boyd grinned wickedly. "Then maybe it's the part we should've dipped."

Jem bit her lower lip.

"Hmm, didn't think of that." Thane scratched his chin. "Too bad we can't go back and get him."

"Don't worry," Boyd assured her. "All we did was toss the bastard inside his ship. It was already prepped for departure. Thane activated the autopilot so his comp brain could link in and do the final clearance. Port Control thought they were communicating with Dougson." He slid a glance sideways. "Something I didn't know comp brains could do."

"Then," Thane said smugly, "before we locked the hatch, he got a taste of his own darts."

Jem lost the battle. Throwing back her head, she had the first good laugh in a long time.

CHAPTER 13

"She was over an hour late this time. When is Jansom going to do something?"

Jem's eyes rolled. Sheesh. Like she needed another Boyd. "Margo has taken care of it herself."

Thane paused, quickly scanning the street and building fronts before he'd let her step out onto the sidewalk. "Got rid of the boyfriend?"

"Yep. She came in tonight with a black eye." Thane shot her a sharp look as she laughed. "We made quite a colorful pair behind the counter during turnover." Her own bruises were still healing.

Thane paced silently beside her.

Her smile slid away. Wary stiffness had filled the silences between them since the attack. Tonight, he'd added brooding. Fine. She could brood too.

As an Independent, she had two weeks to leave or find a job and move into a new apartment. She'd initially planned on going with Thane on his galactic shell game. After several quick stops in various systems, her opponents wouldn't know where to start looking. But the others had convinced her leaving later would be better. She'd be pouring drinks at Pounding J while they'd be looking everywhere else for her.

Or, according to Margo, trying to pull ideas from their asses.

No problem getting an apartment, Jem thought grumpily. Assassination and other mayhem paid well. Branigan's cash card still held a large balance after using it and all of Dougson's to pay off her contract. His card would be doubly handy now she knew about Kurzvall's flags on her Earth account. No wonder his thugs had nearly caught her a couple of times by tracking her credit withdrawals. It was a good thing she'd switched to just using her cash earnings.

"Have you told Margo yet?" Thane abruptly asked.

"Tomorrow. She'll be starting her weekend and was to come to my place. But she doesn't have a roommate now, so maybe we'll talk there." She'd agreed to give Margo all but her ghosting secret. *Will the knowledge cost her? Has she endangered Boyd?*

As if Thane had heard her thoughts, he pulled her into a darkened doorway. "You've been really hesitant about things. Why?" he asked, his voice suspicious.

Scowling, she fisted her hands on her hips. "Has it not occurred to you— any of you—I want to protect all of you as much as you do me? I don't know if they meant to kill him, but Mr. Petrov, my last landlord on Earth, tried to help when they came after me. He called the Enforcers before barreling out of his house with an old-fashioned shotgun." Her mouth set in a hard line. "The Enforcers were quick but not fast enough. It was reported as an attempted robbery gone badly."

She brushed past him and continued on toward her dorm.

Thane fell in step beside her, his silence throbbing with anger. He slowed when her building's brightly lit entrance came into view. He stopped in the shadows between two streetlights. "Where will you go? What will you do?" he asked, keeping his eyes on the bright glow ahead.

"I don't know." Jem looked up at the impenetrable darkness beyond the dome. "Somewhere I can see stars and a real sky again, that's for sure. I don't care what color it is. Just drift again, I guess. It'll be safer," she said softly. Pappia had proven it was too dangerous for her to stay anywhere for long. She glanced over, curious. "What's your world like?"

"Midgard?" He paused. "It's one of the few worlds almost identical to Earth, astrophysically speaking. The years are a few days shorter; the days a few hours longer. It's a little larger so the gravity is about the same as Pappia's, maybe just a little more." His lips tilted upward as their eyes met. "Stars fill the night sky, even when Embla and Ask are up. Two moons," he added at her questioning look. "And the day sky is a gorgeous blue-green. Well, when it's not foggy or raining."

"Get a lot of that?"

"It pretty much describes our fall and winter."

Jem looked at her dorm, then back at Thane. "Would another bowl of Earth-style chili get me more info? My treat."

He flashed a grin. "Bribe accepted."

Jem's questions started immediately. By the time they arrived at the Grub Stake, she could easily visualize his beautiful world. Like Earth, it had lots of water and was littered with land masses ranging from barely-there islands to those three-and-a-half continents. Sailing vessels of all sizes gracefully unfurled sails to capture the constant breeze. Decorative grillwork protected turbines inside discreetly placed wind pylons that provided most of their power. She could image the huge forests towering above serene rivers, both fed by the moist, rainy climate.

Thane, Jem marveled as they slid into one of the booths, didn't just spit out facts, he spun out descriptions. She quickly punched in her menu selection

Thane studied the menu. "That pasta dish was fantastic, maybe…no, I'll go with the chili again." He punched in his order and slouched back into a comfortable spot on his side of the booth.

"Where does your family call home?"

"The Stohlass family home and corporate headquarters are in Azusa on Oslo, which is the largest city on the third-largest continent."

She got a few more questions in before their food arrived and the conversation drifted to general topics, although she was able to glean a few more interesting tidbits about his family. Jem sipped her Moon Ale and thought about the CEO, the dancer, the family clown, twin surprises, and a migraine that wouldn't go away named Cousin Nicky. His cousin Andi was the gifted engineer who'd designed several of the sensors on his ship. Evidently his mother had inherited her way with words from *her* mother.

An empty ache stirred. "When was the last time you were home?" she asked quietly.

Thane stopped chewing, his gaze somewhere over her shoulder. "Nineteen months. Gram's memorial. She was Grandmother's mother."

"I'm sorry."

"So were we. She was only a hundred and nine. Mom thinks she just missed Gramp too much. He passed on about eight months earlier, but he was older: a hundred and twenty-four."

"You have a wonderful home, a family with close bonds. You should spend time with them more often."

* * * * *

Her undisguised wistfulness smacked Thane in the chest.

Here he was, going on about his large family, and she had no one. What was it like to have no family? No friends? No one who cared? His family could be a pain in the ass, but he wouldn't trade them for anything. Well, no, not true. There were a couple of cousins he wouldn't mind upgrading to more personable models. Feeling guilty, he asked about her parents. After learning they were deceased, he'd simply slid them into the 'doesn't matter' category.

Jem grew quiet for several moments. "My father was six-foot-three and full of laughter and jokes. My mom was a full foot shorter than him, but she was the dominant factor in our family. She was our center. Both were university teachers, the typical quiet, bookish type...except when Mom was poking Dad in the stomach during one of their conversations." Jem's smile flashed and was gone. "Dad taught mathematics and Mom taught European history and literature, with a specialization in Earth myths and legends."

No wonder he hadn't needed to explain a lot of Midgard names and such to her.

"Waving at me from the shuttle steps is my last memory of them," Jem said. "They were going to a conference. Mom stood a step higher than Dad so they'd be even. Their arms were around each other. Waving together. They were killed coming back when their shuttle went down in a massive thunderstorm over the ocean."

"No other family, besides your grandmother?"

"There's a couple of distant cousins on my mother's side, according to Granny, but I never met them."

"I know it's been years, but I'm sorry for your loss. I wish there'd been others to help you through it."

Jem smiled. "Well…Granny, who was actually my great-grandmother on Mom's side, more than made up for it. She was outgoing, plainspoken, and loved sports." She laughed. "Boy, did she love sports. Mom and Dad eventually stopped going to games with her. She'd gotten into the habit of informing the players, the coach—anyone she felt needed to know—what they were doing wrong and how to fix it. She *obviously* knew what to do, since she *obviously* had more years of experience than they did."

Jem leaned toward him, her eyes dancing with mirth. "Mom told me once you haven't been truly embarrassed until you had an entire sports team glaring at you from the field, along with everyone in the nearby bleacher seats giving you both glares and single-finger salutes. Which, by the way, was when they called it quits."

Thane threw back his head and laughed. "I thought parents were supposed to be embarrassed by their children, not the other way around."

"You didn't know my Granny," Jem replied dryly. She propped her chin in her hand.

"That last incident I had to get from Dad because Mom refused, *ab-so-lute-ly* refused to discuss it. It seems Granny not only returned all those, um, sentiments, but being ambidextrous, she did them *one* better. Then she was going eyeball-to-chest—shortness ran in Mom's family—with the people around them and—how did Dad put it? Oh, right, comparing ancestry options and exchanging nicknames." Her brow wrinkled. "Or was it familial descriptions?"

Thane was laughing hard by this time.

"They would yank her down and away from one person and she'd start in with someone else while they were still trying to apologize to the first one. Dad said he wasn't sure how he got them out of the stadium without blows also being exchanged. Personally, I always figured it was her white hair."

Thane wiped his eyes and looked over at his booth partner. Big mistake. It wasn't the laughing eyes that set him off again. It was the mental video of her mortified parents trying to hustle out a short, white-haired, dirty-mouthed matron giving dual single-fingered gestures.

It took several minutes before they finally managed some semblance of control. Thane wiped his eyes again. Force of nature? Hell, yes. Granny had been a hurricane.

Jem wiped her face with a napkin. "Then there was an incident with—"

Thane held up a hand. "Please, don't get me going again. Surely you had some friends." He was surprised at her sudden stillness, her gaze and thoughts going elsewhere.

"One," she said softly. "Dani Ballou. We met in high school. She died in an UPMS hanger accident."

She'd lost everyone. "Up-ums hanger?"

She returned to the present and gave him an apologetic smile. "Sorry. U-P-M-S hanger. I have a tendency to vocalize acronyms."

"Why don't you come for a visit?" he said, not fighting the impulse. "My family would love to meet you. They'll love hearing your stories and," he added ruefully, "rib me about you saving my butt."

"And dropping me?"

He winced. "You're not supposed to remember things right around concussion time."

Jem waved her spoon. "I've decided to forgive and forget."

"I don't usually stay away this long, but I had several jobs stacked on top of each other, not counting Kurzvall's." Thane scraped one last bite from his bowl. "I'll be heading back soon, though. Mom sent a message letting me know GG had called for a family reunion."

Jem swallowed. "GG?"

"Family name for Granddad and Grandmother, whose names also just happen to be Gordon and Gwendolyn. They normally call for one, oh, about every three or four years. The last one was five years ago, so we're overdue. They give plenty of notice—about seven months this time. You had better be dead or similarly indisposed if you don't show up."

Jem laughed at the face he made and quickly finished up her meal, paying as promised. The meal and conversation had burned away the last remaining stiffness between them, although he couldn't help sinking into silence again.

Escorting her back to her building, Thane nodded and turned to leave. He stopped. "Kurzvall won't stop looking, you know," he told the darkness surrounding them.

"I know. Is that what you've been brooding about tonight?"

He took a couple more steps, then pivoted. "I can swing this way again in a couple of months. If you decide to wait, I'll take you to wherever you want to go," he offered.

She nodded. "If I'm still here, I'd like that."

His chin dipped in acknowledgement and then he was gone.

CHAPTER 14

"Why didn't it explode?"

"How the hell would I know? Try it again."

The guy with the controller pressed the button several more times.

"Is it working?" the shaggy blond asked.

The brunette pointed the controller at his partner. Pressed. "See a light? Then it's working. Did you wire it up correctly?"

The blond glared. "It's not my first bomb."

"It might be your last one. Boss wants him and his family gone as an example." He held the remote out at arm's length, pointed it at the house, and pressed the button several more times. His arm dropped. "Why won't it go off?"

The two stared at the house they were trying to demolish.

Because I have it safely isolated in ghost-mode.

Jem glowered at the two would-be bombers from about ten feet away. *There are toys on the back porch, you...you...splash!* They were going to blow up kids. She ought to just drop the box behind them and hope they tried the button again. Except she'd be sacrificing the small stand of trees they were standing in. She liked trees.

She'd caught sight of the two men slinking around the house on her way back to the spaceport. Late night slinking was never a good sign. It was reinforced when a closer look revealed what they were doing. Jem made a fast call to Law Enforcement's universal emergency number, grabbed the box they'd positioned against the back door, and shifted. Hopefully the two people she could see hugging the shadows along the buildings as they moved quietly up the street were Enforcers.

If they weren't...well, she had a bomb.

"Still nothing," the brunette muttered.

"Stop pressing the damn button. I'm going to go check—"

The door on the house flew open and three people ran out. A woman and young girl in night clothes and a man wearing only pants.

"Shit," the brunette said. "What spooked them?"

Excellent, Jem thought. LE must have tracked the address she'd given to a phone number and alerted the family. The woman and young girl pelted down the street; the man stopped a short way away and looked around. He had a weapon.

"*Run*," the blond hissed.

Too late. The two Enforcers she'd spotted surged forward, blocking their path and shouting for them to halt. The idiots dodged between two houses instead and promptly ran into three more Enforcers. The brunette went down in a tangle with one of them while the blond was gently restrained—*slammed*—against a wall. The bare-chested man from the house barreled into the fray.

"Is that them?" he demanded, pulling back a fist.

An Enforcer stopped the punch aimed at the blond. "Check the house," he said sharply to another one. "This is a remote detonator."

Oops! Jem darted back across the street. No bomb, no charges. No way were the two SOBs going free. The box materialized as soon as she let go, just seconds ahead of an enforcer warily shining a light around the corner.

"There's a large box leaning against the back door," he called back. "And I smell accelerant on the wall."

***

Jem leaned against a fence, just another face in the crowd that had gathered. The bomb had been deactivated and carted away; the bombers were at the local Law Enforcement Center being interrogated by Lieutenant Glen Curtis. The same lieutenant they had targeted. She watched the fire department hosing down the house and mulled over the information she'd heard while eavesdropping on the officials swarming around the lieutenant's house.

Tardon was in the process of upgrading its status from colony to full membership. One Navere Manis had decided this entitled him to upgrade his status from smuggler to kingpin of Tallon, Tardon's capital city. He was doing so in a manner both aggressive and ruthless. Lieutenant Curtis was spearheading the effort to break his budding empire apart. They were having difficulty getting proof of the organization's activities and keeping witnesses alive.

Déjà vu.

A vehicle pulled up as the horizon began to lighten. The lieutenant's wife and daughter stepped out as another one screeched to a halt behind them. An older couple exited that vehicle and immediately launched into an argument with the wife. The girl was plastered tight against her mother. Jem couldn't hear them but guessed from gestures the older couple were wanting the two to go with them.

The woman shook her head, took the girl's hand and walked toward her home.

"You're not safe with him," the older man screamed.

Did anyone on the block miss that?

The woman ignored him, entered and shut the door. The hostile man started toward the house but the older woman—*her parents?*—grabbed his arm. Another argument ensued with the Fire Captain joining in. Finger-poking joined arm-waving. The woman finally got the man stuffed back into their vehicle and drove them away. The captain stomped toward his vehicle, shaking his head and probably muttering things she was grateful not to hear.

Jem stared at the home. Safe. Was anyone truly safe? Or was it simply belief in an illusion that kept people from becoming quivering masses of fear and indecision? Her faith had certainly been shattered. This family just had their veil ripped off. Instead of sleeping tonight, would they prowl through the house? Tomorrow night? Would others, fearing the same?

Movement three houses away caught her eye as someone dodged behind bushes as the Fire Captain drove by. Jem squinted, trying to make out the person watching the lieutenant's house. Male? Female? Whoever it was, they disappeared back into the shadows.

Jem pushed away from the fence. No. Frigging hell, no. They were not going to be an example. The Universe did not need another Kurzvall.

Her debate of whether to stay or continue on had just been settled.

She had been extra careful since leaving Pappia. She'd moved constantly, never more than two or three days somewhere. Living off her cash cards allowed her to use false names for renting rooms, or she'd just find an empty one. She even wore those hated contacts regularly. She'd ghosted aboard the supply ship heading for Tardon on a last-minute whim, despite having planned to go elsewhere earlier.

Curiosity, she'd told herself, on seeing the posting on the departure board. This system was one of the few containing only a single planet. *Had the same Fate that brought Thane to Pappia brought her here? Was the Universe sentient?*

Jem headed back toward the Port Circle. She snorted. Triangle would be more accurate. But round, square, trapezoid, or octagon, it didn't matter. For some weird reason, they always called the spaceport support areas a Circle. Stopping at a comm kiosk, she extended her phone's temporary number before renting a room as Sadie Longstrate. The irritating contacts were plucked out as soon as she was inside. She'd need to hunt up a part-time job since just hanging around would make her stand out to the locals. She yawned and rolled her neck. Nap first. Plopping down on the bed, she bounced a couple of times. Not too bad.

Taking Kurzvall down would be a long-term effort, assuming they even could. But Manis? The ceiling witnessed a slow growing, self-satisfied smile. Her curse was about to become someone else's.

CHAPTER 15

"Jem's not here."

Not for three weeks, according to Pappia's port manifest. Thane had checked it as soon as the *Lone Tracker* landed. Then he'd dragged his grandfather to Warehouse Eight, only to find Boyd was gone. He'd left five days ago for some kind of family thing on his home world, according to his skinny employee. Which was why Thane was here, trying to talk to the Queen of Bluntness. Jem had moved in with Margo right after he left.

"Shouldn't you be in the Hub with the rest of the snotty CEO's?" Margo added.

"Turned it down. Where did she go?"

Margo spotted Saul-the-bartender waving and pointing to a comp screen full of orders. "Stay put," she ordered before hurrying away.

Thane looked around the packed room. He managed to hang on to his patience for fifteen minutes. When Margo zipped past him for another order, Thane reached over, grabbed both arms and dragged her across the counter until they were nose-to-nose.

"Where. Did. Jem. Go?"

"I. Don't. Know."

He dropped her back on her feet. Margo shook her head at the bouncer starting in their direction, and tugged her tunic back into place. "She left a message, assuming you'd show up sometime. Not that I expected you to. You actually turned down Baron Financials?"

"Yes. What's the message?"

"What, is CEO too much effort? Not enough perks? Or perky assistants?"

"Message?" Thane managed between gritted teeth.

Margo leaned forward and smiled much too sweetly. "Order coming up." She bustled back a minute later and slapped two glasses of Aspric whisky down in front of them.

"*Margo*—" His grandfather's leg-bump cut him off.

Gordon Stohlass lifted an eyebrow. "Is that supposed to be a glare? It doesn't even rate a four against some I've received in or out of the courtroom. Your mother has a couple of good ones she should teach you."

Taking a large swallow of whisky, Thane silently ran through every swear word he could think of. Keeping his family ignorant of his current problems was impossible now. Something he could thank Patricia Keegan for, whoever the woman really was. She'd vanished, her mail account closed.

His arrest on Random Two had left him reeling.

He'd met with the supposed thief and handed over Keegan's cash card after verifying the case held her property. How was he supposed to know there was a large cache of highly illegal drugs underneath the statue's padding? That comment had elicited snorts from every Law Enforcer surrounding him outside the *Lone Tracker*. Naturally, their tip about his 'drug buy' had been anonymous. Considering the setup, it'd probably been the thief and explained why he'd arranged the meeting with Thane on the other side of the city. It gave time for LE to act after his call. The SOB had now disappeared as completely as Keegan. Everything Thane knew about the two of them was false.

Running out of options and facing decades of prison food and terraforming labor, he'd had no choice but to send for the craftiest legal expert he knew of. It'd still taken over three weeks for the truth to come out and another three days before the Enforcer Commander grudgingly gave him his ship back. The man had filed paperwork to take possession of it. *Personal* possession.

His grandfather had insisted on staying with him afterwards. Cool silence had met his offer to take the older man home before heading here. The odds of getting off Pappia without him smelling stink weren't good.

Another hour passed before the orders slowed down and the two bartenders weren't brownish-green streaks behind the counter. His grandfather survived his first jolt of Pounding J's specialty with a wide-eyed deep breath and 'damn fine whisky.' He was sipping on his second one while Thane still nursed his first.

The bouncer kept eyeing him, only leaving his end of the bar to stop a couple of arguing miners before they escalated.

Being dangled a foot off the floor de-escalated most people.

Margo stopped in front of the bouncer, setting a fresh glass of water in front of him. Her murmur was too low to hear but Thane recognized the message their body positions gave away. He also fully comprehended the message the cold hazel eyes flashed at him over her head. *Don't touch.*

Message loud and clear he telegraphed back with a slight nod.

Margo briefly touched her guy's arm before moving toward them. Giving a stretch and shoulder roll, she leaned on the counter in front of them and drew in a deep breath. "That was fun. We haven't had a rush like that in months." Her gaze locked on Thane. "Popping in for a visit?"

"Not exactly. I owed her passage to wherever she wanted to go."

"Damn straight you did."

He shifted uncomfortably under his grandfather's curious look. "Can I please have Jem's message?" Hadn't she tortured him enough?

"Well, the congratulations on your CEO-ness are evidently wasted. She thanks you for everything—well maybe not *everything*—and to consider the debt paid." Margo's grin turned mischievous. "Then she suggests being a bit more careful since she won't always be around to save your Class Ten ass. Can't blame her as I happen to agree with her rating."

Heat crept up Thane's neck. His grandfather's grin sent it all the way to the tips.

"Don't worry, honey," she crooned to the bouncer glaring at Thane. "Yours is a perfect twelve with a perfect *size*." She winked at him.

Gordon's grin faded. "Just how many times did she save my grandson's good-looking butt?"

"Three." Margo eyed Thane shrewdly and then added, "That I know of." She pursed her lips. "The newscast indicated you'd already accepted CEO from your grandmother."

"It's a pre-emptive strike by Helga Baron and I refuse to call her that."

Margo's gaze flipped to the older man.

"Other side. I'm Gordon Larrs Stohlass."

Margo flipped back to Thane.

"She expected to coerce me into agreeing to it in exchange for resolving some legal issues I was having. I refused. I'll set the record straight as soon as I get home."

Helga Baron's lawyer had arrived five days before his grandfather. The arrogant little snot had assured Thane he could negotiate—meaning buy—his freedom, but only if Thane agreed to become part of the Baron corporate family. They were so sure he was desperate enough to accept, the twit had a signature-ready contract and Baron Financials's PR had made the announcement.

"What's your problem with her?"

"The woman never accepted us and she's ignored our existence for twenty years," Thane said flatly. "She went after everything Dad had as soon as they officially declared his ship and all aboard lost. Called them company assets." His mom hadn't cared then and still didn't. "She couldn't touch the ship he'd deeded to Mom or Dad's personal Survey account. Granddad successfully argued her wedding ring was a gift."

Margo reared back. "The bitch wanted her *ring*?"

"Yep."

"And this lunatic asshole actually thinks you'll just do what she wants?"

"The lunatic asshole expected him to heel to her commands," Gordon said, contempt sharpening his voice. "She expected disassociation from *my* family since we're beneath her orbit. And, of course, he is to marry someone of a suitable pedigree to continue the Baron name. Probably has the poor girl picked out already."

Thane shot an annoyed glance sideways.

"Love the growly voice," Margo told Gordon before switching her attention back to Thane. "Need to work on yours. What changed?"

"My uncle, his wife, and their two children all died in an accident about a year ago, leaving me the last in her line. Her lawyers contacted me about a month later. Apparently, I was to trot on over and joyfully take my place in the Baron family and business. I joyfully told them what they could do with it."

"She crazy?"

"Arrogant. Egotistical. Conceited."

"Opinionated, self-centered, self-serving piranha," Gordon added succinctly.

Margo snorted. "That should cover it. You butt heads often?"

"Every time we talked," Gordon said, his jaw set. "Last time would've been at my son-in-law's memorial. The woman demanded Reyna give her the Survey flag she'd received. 'It belongs to the Baron family. Of which you are not.' were her exact words."

Margo's mouth pursed. "Wow. Now that is a space-cold bitch."

Thane shook his head. "I didn't know that. Bet Mom went off on her."

"No, she didn't. Your mother simply pointed to where you stood with your Grandmother. The ceremony. The flag. That's when it truly hit you." Gordon's voice turned somber. "Up until then, you were probably hoping it wasn't true. Hoping Greg would walk into the room and flash that wide grin of his. You were hugging the flag so hard and the look on your face was just...lost. Baron walked away and never mentioned it again."

"The bitch did something decent?" Margo said.

"Shocking, isn't it," Gordon said sourly.

"She showed up at my hatch."

Gordon's head pivoted sharply. "Where and when?"

"Umm, Minos Four...four, five months ago? I've been deleting all her messages. Unread. I guess she believed gracing me with her personal presence would make a difference." Both listeners snorted *Hah!* "I told her to go hug a black hole."

The woman had left furious, her two aides in shock, when he refused to even let them onboard. Actually, Thane thought sourly, he owed her. It was anger on top of frustration that drove him to the bar and the table next to the EMC recruiters.

Well, what do you know; Fate really is a Bitch.

"Aren't there other Barons somewhere this piranha asshole can annoy?" Margo asked.

"Oh, yes. Her brother died twelve years ago from a rare blood disorder, but he left three daughters." Gordon smirked. "Then there's a younger sister who managed to marry someone the family disapproved of even more than my daughter. She has four kids, two of each."

Thane grunted in surprise, unaware of that piece of family gossip.

"Valeria left the family. Literally. She took a huge settlement in lieu of any inheritance. She used it to establish her and her veterinarian husband in a new colony as far away from them as possible. Even worse, the children aren't *Barons*. Valeria and her husband—Travis Dupre Holtzclaw—went with the standard naming convention of given, maternal, paternal."

Thane was surprised by how much his grandfather knew about his father's family. Not like he'd made any effort to. Turning back, he found Margo eyeing him.

"The bitch reversed it for your Dad and uncle? Why is she so hung up on a name?"

Switching the maternal name to last wasn't unheard of, but Thane doubted Helga Baron's reason was the usual one. "Ego. Family politics. Who knows? Do you have any idea where Jem might have gone after Euphrates?"

"Nope. Every time I asked, she just shrugged and said something about throwing a dart."

Thane's eyes closed in resignation. The Euphrates System was a major hub, with a hundred ports scattered throughout the overpopulated system. It was the perfect place to lose a trail, even for non-ghosts. Finding where she disembarked wouldn't be a problem. She'd left Pappia with a ticket to Riviera, Euphrates One. Finding which ship she left on from there? When she probably ghosted aboard to stay off the port lists?

Gordon polished off the last of his drink. "So? You're a hotshot Tracker. Go find her."

"Took me a year last time," Thane muttered, not missing his grandfather's sharp look.

"That was one long job?"

"Pretty much." But he had broken away to do a couple of quick retrievals for law enforcement. Usually during one of the frustrating post-poof searches. "Have there been any problems?" he asked Margo.

She glanced around before leaning closer and lowering her voice. "Nope. Nothing since you two nearly got killed. Are you having any? People like him don't give up easily."

"It's why I couldn't make it back sooner," Thane returned just as quietly. He was pretty sure who masterminded the nine weeks of hell on Random Two. Keegan had just been the front, probably Kurzvall's backup plan if Dougson and Branigan failed to kill him.

"Think he'll try again?"

Thane's shrug pretty much said it all. With no reason to stay any longer, he rotated his seat toward his grandfather. *Uh-oh.*

His grandfather's hard-eyed gaze wasn't speculative now, it was calculating. Appraising. It belonged to the lawyer who had taken on three of the largest interstellar corporations existing at the time in a two-year, no-dirty-trick-untried lawsuit and won.

"Did this *him* have something to do with the quagmire on Random? Those weren't just trumped-up charges against a convenient scapegoat. You were targeted, son. Lured there with intent to frame. And it was a damn good one, too."

Thane finished his drink in a single gulp. Yeah, he knew. If it hadn't been for a vindictive woman pissed because her stingy boyfriend wouldn't share his payoff, he doubted even his grandfather's expertise would have gotten him cleared. Even the snotty lawyer had proved useless. He'd been sent packing back to Helga Baron, briefcase tucked between his legs and under threat of attempted bribery charges.

"Let's go, Granddad."

"What about grand-bitch?" Margo called out as they left the counter.

Thane turned back, his smile wolfish. "I'm compiling a list of black holes."

* * * * *

Gordon followed his grandson up the *Lone Tracker's* sloped steps. He hadn't pressed him about what happened on Random. Thane would talk about whatever mess he'd stepped into when he was ready. But two plus two was adding up to an extremely nasty four.

"What's going on, Thane?" he asked as soon as he got his weldmet off.

Thane slotted the equipment into their assigned places, closed and stared at the locker door for a long moment. "It's a long story, Granddad."

"It's a long trip home."

CHAPTER 16

GG's family reunions celebrated everything of interest since the last family fling. The giant wall board overflowed with five-plus years of information, from the latest batch of births to Thane's liberation from jail. That last item, discretely tucked at the bottom of the board, had spiced up quite a few conversations. So had his CEO denouncement two weeks ago, with opinions ranging from understanding to Cousin Nicky's long-winded diatribe which could be summed up in three words: *are you crazy?*

The annoying little shit didn't realize how close his puffed-up tirade came to being cut short. If Katrina hadn't noticed and drawn the idiot off into another conversation...

Had it been the white-knuckled grip on his glass that tipped his sister off?

Thane found a quiet corner and propped against one of the Grecian styled columns to people-watch and sip his tart punch. Most of the family wouldn't have been offended by a brawl—especially a short-lived one—considering the source. There'd be some eye-rolls, maybe even a few discrete thumbs-up. But as satisfying as it would've felt, he didn't want to cause the family any embarrassment. The room was packed with people.

Looking out over the crowd, there were very few outside of the family he recognized. This, the gathering's third and final night, was always an open celebration. The family had rented the entire first floor of the Branson Hotel's South Wing and turned it into an old-fashioned ballroom. Family friends. Business and political relations. Getting an invite was considered a social and political coup.

A few last-minute grazers were hurriedly filling plates as caterers began clearing the buffet. His mother and several of her siblings were in deep conversation with GG. If he wasn't the current subject of their discussion, he'd probably be the next item on the agenda. He gave the group a brief scowl before surrendering with a sigh. He'd be banging on his sister's door if Kat was having problems. Did he really expect the family not to jump in after hearing about his?

Thane's face split into a wide grin when his Aunt Jane, Uncle Dane and their spouses joined the family huddle. He was two years older than the family's twin surprise. Two plus years ago they married another set of fraternal twins and both women were now very pregnant with, not surprisingly, twins.

He spotted Andrea in conversation with another cousin next to a set of opened terrace doors. Aunt Gilida's youngest and only daughter was the biggest jaw-dropping surprise of this visit. The green-eyed, fiery-red pig-tailed, only-interested-in-engines genius-tomboy had been the bane of her three older brothers and most of her male cousins. Including him. He'd come home to find Andi morphed into a stunning six-foot-plus Valkyrie.

The transformation was attributed to the *seven*-foot-plus pillar of muscle towering possessively beside her. Thane was willing to lay odds the man could even take Boyd down. He and Andi had been another Stohlass sunk-at-first-sight engagement. He'd liked Nicholas O'Daniel as soon as they were introduced. Respect quickly followed when it became apparent the man's impressive biceps weren't what got him appointed as head of Stohlass Security.

He was trying to find his sister in the throng when GG's favorite slow waltz started up. He watched as his grandfather swept his wife into his arms and they swung gracefully around their multitude of descendants and guests. Envy stirred. GG. Gordon and Gwendolyn. Granddad and Grandmother. However you thought of them, you couldn't think of one without the other. They were a matched pair in every way that mattered and a lot that didn't.

A rustle of silk and the soft scent of his mother's perfume preceded the hand sliding around his arm.

"Any word yet?" she asked.

Thane shook his head.

He'd made the announcement about the Baron Financials 'misunderstanding' in front of the family's corporate office. Finished, he closed with a final statement made straight into the camera. *Anyone needing to contact me, with questions or concerns, can reach me through the family offices of Stohlass Enterprises here on Midgard, Wotan Two. They will ensure I receive it.*

He'd received several job requests, two sig-ner proposals and a reply to the message he'd left with Skinny. Boyd's response had been exactly as he'd expected: short and rude. Not only had he not known Jem's plans, Boyd was as annoyed and concerned about it as Thane was. But no word from the one person they were all hoping for.

"Not that there's any real reason she has to," he said. "I did hope to get word she was okay and somewhere safe." He'd given the family the same version of events Margo got, his well-rehearsed explanation flowing smoothly. The story of a powerful amoral megalomaniac and his pursuit of critical data contained no mention of a disastrous experiment or special skills.

"Bastard."

"Bastard spash," his grandmother clarified, joining the conversation.

One of Thane's brows quirked up. The women in his family believed a person should communicate clearly, honestly, and with no misunderstanding. Some of their legendary communications were highly descriptive. His grandmother had incinerated several political ambitions without raising her voice. Quite a number of his mother's pithy comments hung framed on executive suite walls, usually by those who had been seared by them.

Gwendolyn Williams patted her grandson's arm. "Don't worry, dear. Sometimes only certain expressions adequately convey one's feelings."

"Can I convey my feelings right now?" Thane flashed her a wide smile.

"No," his mother replied calmly, "too many young ears." She leaned back to peer around a thick stand of plant foliage. "Marcus Taft Stohlass, I'm sure the caterers can provide you with plenty of conversation and things needing to be washed in the kitchen."

Startled, Thane watched Uncle Clint's youngest bolt for the other side of the room.

Gordon materialized at his wife's elbow with three drinks. He handed two off to his wife and daughter. "That boy is becoming a first-class sneak. Marcus is either going to be a FLEA or a family embarrassment."

"Having a Federal Law Enforcement Agent in the family would be a first, I believe," Gwen replied, her face thoughtful. The other option wouldn't be. Martin Myers Stohlass, GG's nephew sitting in a cell on the Federal Penitentiary planet Skewed, had been a shocking, family-rending first. No one in Gordon's brother's family had spoken to anyone on this side of the tree since he refused to represent Martin on the grounds of 'the boy is a menace and getting what he deserves.'

"Maybe you should consider taking him on as an apprentice, Thane."

Thane mock-scowled at his grandmother. "I only sneak when I'm on a job and use only the methods you taught me." Laughter and chuckles surrounded him. On impulse, he leaned over to lightly kiss his mother's cheek.

"I can't help but feel sorry for Jem. She's got no one."

Reyna patted his arm gently. "She has us now. We'll find some way to help her."

"What you've told us about that young woman and what's happened to her…it's just incredible."

Thane's back straightened as his grandmother switched into what he privately called her don't-give-me-shit voice. With the exception, maybe, of his granddad, no one dared to.

"That man already has more money than any one person should ever have. Yet what he did…for more money? For power?" Gwendolyn huffed indignantly. "For Odin's sake, if they were that good, why didn't the man just let the Myerstone people finish out their research, get the instantaneous transfer working, and *then* argue the legalities? Him or his heirs, depending on how long it took. Why did he push it? Why is he still pushing it? And why did those lab people feel such a powerful need to keep the data out of Kurzvall's hands?"

He'd wondered about that last question himself. Jem was entitled to her secrets, but why that one? Why had she encrypted *and* passcoded the data? Thane didn't need to look over at his grandfather to feel his intense study.

"You said it," he said, trying for nonchalance. "Greed and power. Kurzvall faced losing control, not to mention profits, once it was in the public domain. I doubt he expected the team leaders to terminate their association."

"Self-entitled people like him don't like being told no, much less dumped," Gordon said. "Usually, they're the ones doing it."

Reyna eyed her son. "I keep wondering about how Jem knew about their research. How she was able to save it."

Gordon nodded. "I've had a few wonderings about that myself. How did a temporary, odd-job employee become so knowledgeable of their work? One that had *just* moved on? And *just* happened to show back up that night, which *wasn't* in the official report? Which I've read."

Trust Granddad to find the weak links. "Jem doesn't understand the data any more than I would. She got caught up in what happened when she went back to visit. She recognized the file contents on the stolen comp from conversations she'd heard while working there and managed to..." His voice trailed off at the circle of furrowed brows and narrow-eyed stares.

"Son, would you like me to point out all the holes in your scenario?"

"No, I wouldn't." *Dammit, I just yelled at my granddad.*

"That's enough, Thane," his mother said firmly. "We realize you feel an obligation to protect her, but we want to hear what—"

"Here comes Andi and Nicholas, with Katrina," his grandmother interrupted in a low voice. GG had insisted on keeping Thane's immediate problems at the family's highest level. It had translated to the top two generations.

"Don't mind us," Andi said, waving her hand. "Go right on with your plotting."

"Plotting?" Gordon arched an eyebrow.

"Plotting, scheming, planning. All the stuff you do when you don't want any of us young folks to know what you're up to."

"We are not scheming about anything." Reyna made a tossing motion. "We were merely discussing one of Thane's recent adventures."

"Which one?" Kat asked, looping her arm through Andi's. "Where he was framed on Random Two, harassed by grand-bitch Baron on Minos Four, or nearly killed on Pappia?"

"Young lady, have you been eavesdropping?"

She certainly had, Thane fumed, if she'd heard him using Margo's phrase.

"Sure. How else would a young lady learn anything of interest, Mom?" Kat flipped her wrist toward Thane. "Especially when her one-and-only brother comes home under less-than-ideal conditions and with a fresh laser scar hidden under his hair."

All eyes swiveled to Thane.

Well, hell. His hair had grown during his time on Random and he'd been wearing it down. Evidently his nosy sister had still spotted the scar.

"Thane?"

"Above his left ear, Mom."

His sister got a will-get-even glare as his mother reached up, smoothing the hair back behind his ear. The scar could be seen, starting just above his ear and moving in a slightly tilted line backward. Reyna's fingers traced its full length before letting her hand slid slowly down his ear. Her eyes locked with his.

"It wasn't so much hid—*ow! Dammm*—Mom! I'm not fifteen. *Owww!*"

Reyna hung onto the earlobe. "It's not nice to keep things from Mother Reyna. And you'll always be fifteen." She gave it one more pinch before releasing him.

Thane rubbed his ear, shooting his sister another glare.

"I'm the one who spotted it and asked Katrina about it."

Thane switched his glare to Nicholas, who merely lifted an eyebrow. Well, it was the guy's job to notice the small details. "Fine," he said sullenly. "I wasn't hiding it so much as just covering it up."

"There's a difference?" asked his grandmother.

"Really?" said his mother.

"If you had asked, I would have told you," he said, still sullen. "I just didn't want people staring at it and constantly asking questions." He was getting enough as it was.

"I requested copies of the official reports from Pappia detailing the assault and attempted murder," Nicholas said. "There was no mention of a laser burn. Only a concussion with minor bruises and scrapes."

Thane took a quick step sideways from his mom. "The burn came later during a, um, later event." The only difference in the glares he was getting was the coloring of said glares.

"Just how many 'events' did you have on Pappia?" Nicholas asked.

"Two." Thane scowled at the circle around him. "I didn't bring it up because it didn't have anything to do with...the other thing." That was a lie. If they heard about Branigan and Dougson, they'd know he was hiding something a lot more complicated. As if that boat hadn't just sailed, he thought crossly.

Gordon cocked his head. "I believe three was the number the bartender gave."

Thane gave his grandfather an exasperated look. "Two sort of go together."

"Would any of those be the reason your ship is being watched?" Nicholas asked.

"You're sure?" he asked sharply.

"It started about five days ago. Considering the troubles you've had recently, Mr. Stohlass asked me to keep an eye on the *Lone Tracker* while you're here."

Thane clenched his jaw in frustration. Dammit, he'd wanted to keep the SOB and his problems away from the family. "It's a possibility. Why am I only hearing about it now?"

"It's being handled," Nicholas said calmly, "but I need that information so as to properly assess our security needs."

Glancing around their small circle, he gave up. The family just wasn't going to keep their noses out of it. "Okay, but we need to take this conversation somewhere more private. Granddad's library?" Thane asked, glancing over at the older man. He received a nod. "I'll meet you there as soon as possible."

"At twenty-six hundred."

Thane gave his mother a sharp look.

Her father nodded in agreement. "We can't all suddenly leave. Everyone would wonder what's going on. There's several newsmen sprinkled throughout here, two of which have been flashing curious glances this way." He took his wife's arm and gave Thane a warm smile. "The watchers are being watched. Your ship is locked tight and you're safe. See you at midnight."

They moved off. His grandmother whispered something in his ear, causing his grandfather to throw back his head and roar with laughter.

***

Thane slipped through the mostly silent house. The guest rooms were full and the few snippets of conversation and laughter he passed indicated not everyone was in bed. He paused outside the library to run a hand gently down the thick-paneled double doors. This had been his haven after his father's loss.

We've lost him, Thane.

His mother's tears echoed down through the years. He'd escaped into the printed words and worlds of long-dead authors. But the respite was only temporary, and the pain struck anew when he had emerged. *We've lost him.*

The door opened, jarring him back to the present.

Reyna stood before him, understanding softening both her smile and her eyes. She ran a comforting hand up her son's arm before stepping back. "You're late."

"Sorry, Mom. I was just trying to figure out—"

Thane stumbled to a halt and gaped at the roomful of people. Was his whole family here? It looked like they'd decided to add everyone of legal age. His grandfather sat behind his desk, his grandmother in her usual place on his left. His two pregnant aunts had commandeered the small sofa, their husbands hovering behind them. Everyone else was spread out in chairs or propped against bookshelves and furniture.

"Figure out what to tell us?" Erik said, arms folded across his chest. At sixty, his oldest uncle mirrored his father in appearance and attitude.

"And what to leave out?" Seth Sullivan said. Aunt Gilida's oldest son had taken after his father in appearance and their grandfather in profession.

"Thane won't leave anything out this time, will you?" At Thane's silence, Gordon's fingers began a slow tap-tap on the desktop.

"One targeted family member makes all members susceptible, either as bait or cannon fodder," Janice said.

"Thank you, Commander," Thane said. "I see you've fully embraced your recent promotion." Uncle Clint's oldest daughter had just been assigned to a Border Patrol ship.

"Sarcasm is unwarranted," his grandmother snapped. "She also has a valid point."

"I didn't want to involve the family," he replied in a more subdued tone. "I wanted to keep it—keep him away from the family. I didn't want to worry anyone."

"We're not worried." Kat strode to a halt in front of him. Slamming her hands on her hips, the green eyes she inherited from their father blazed hotly. "We're *pissed*. Pissed some spash is after you and doubly *pissed"* she finger-poked his chest "about you not telling us."

He took her hand, squeezed it. "I didn't want to endanger you."

"I'm afraid that boat sailed yesterday, son." Gordon looked around the room. "Thane has landed feet-first in the middle of something that's already proven to be dangerous. He's a real psychopathic nutcase."

"But Thane is *soooo* likeable."

Thane's lips twitched as laughter broke out around the room. "Thanks, Uncle Clint. I really like you, too."

He looked slowly around the room as the laughter died. No, he hadn't wanted to involve them. But as he absorbed the strength in their set shoulders and firm gazes, he knew his grandfather was right. More, he needed that strength and everything that went with it. He gave his sister a quick hug before walking over to where his grandparents sat.

He leaned back against the antique desk. Gripping the edges, he took time to meet each person's gaze. Taking a deep breath, he spoke the opening lines of his newly modified version somberly. It provided more of the what, but not the how. He would not betray Jem again.

"For those who don't already know it, the bastard's name is Reginald Salazar Kurzvall of Hermes."

* * * * *

Gordon listened closely to Thane's new information.

So, Jem is a threat to Kurzvall. It definitely put his focus on her in a new light. Attacked, kidnapped, overheard damning conversations: the woman had firsthand knowledge of his dealings. It also explained his grandson's determination to help, apart from his fury at being used to hunt and trap her.

Kurzvall was a blight on both the Republic and humanity. *The bastard will end up in a Fed-Pen cell if I have anything to say about it.*

As for her capability for bypassing security systems? No wonder Thane was reluctant to share that. If it got out…the galaxy was full of SOBs that would make her life hell. Just as the current SOB was doing now. His lips twitched. *It's not making Nicholas too happy either.*

"They spotted me sneaking Jem out of the warehouse and came after us."

As Thane began calmly revealing the events behind his scar, he felt Gwen's fingers curl around his. He patted her hand more confidently than he felt and smiled into her worried eyes. She nodded and returned his smile. Yes, the family would stand together, a solid shield against anyone who would hurt one of their own.

Gordon gazed at his grandson, pride and regret mingling equally. Greg would be proud of the man his son had become.

CHAPTER 17

"Do it again, Dad! Again!"

Laughing, Kurzvall swung his daughter around him, rotating her so her legs drew lazy eights around them. He finally set the giggling girl down. "Guess I won't get to do that anymore after next week."

The giggles instantly transformed into a pout. "Why?"

"Well, you are getting bigger. It would also be undignified. After all," he replied, grinning, "you're going to be *twelve*. Your mother—"

"I don't want to be a lady." Brown eyes flashed and a small foot stamped. "You said I could be anything I wanted."

"And I meant it. But it doesn't mean you can't be a lady. In fact, *being* a lady means knowing how to handle whatever comes your way. Quickly and decisively." He tousled her blond hair before glancing at the middle-aged man waiting silently several feet away.

"McNeil?"

"I have several reports for you, sir."

"DAAAAD! You promised to spend the afternoon with me."

"I am." He tapped her nose lightly. "Why don't you go have Firestorm and Pepperspray saddled while I hear what he has?"

With a squeal only a young girl can make, she shot off toward the stables.

"How are the party arrangements going, McNeil?"

"Everything is complete except the menu, sir. Your wife is with the caterer now. Sys-Senator Stevenson was killed on Tylander when a rock slide pushed his vehicle into a ravine."

Kurzvall waved that away. "What about the special present I ordered?"

McNeil tapped this notepad, scrolled to an entry. "The current owners still refuse to sell."

"Make them change their minds. I want it purchased and shipped in time for Cassandra's birthday party." He turned toward the stable.

"Yes, sir." McNeil made an entry. "There's been a complication."

He swung back. "What kind of complication?"

"Stevenson's wife and children accompanied him at the last minute. All killed."

"Their bad luck is not a complication."

McNeil cleared his throat. "Dougson reports the, ah, expert who engineered the rock slide is unhappy about the children. The man refused his final payment and demanded to know who hired him. Dougson immediately terminated contact."

The engineer threw away a hundred thousand dollars? And wanted to know who hired him? That wasn't a complication; that was a major problem. At least there was no immediate threat as Dougson kept all contact with outside contractors anonymous. Still, the man was getting sloppy and having trouble adapting to the unexpected. The number of failed or incomplete assignments had crept upward over the past year, the most notable being the fiasco on Pappia.

With that Tracker involved now, the unexpected was to be expected. It was time to find a more suitable replacement. Too bad that mercenary hadn't made it back. He looked over his shoulder as two horses exited the stable. A groom held the reins of a prancing roan stallion. His daughter was mounted on a white mare with black dots scattered across the hindquarters and back legs.

"Where's Baron?"

McNeil checked his notes. "He's still at his parent's home on Midgard. There was a large family gathering two weeks ago. No contact of interest reported."

"Maintain surveillance on Baron. Tell Dougson to acquire all available information on the engineer. Contact the mercenary group we hired the last guy from and arrange a meeting with whoever replaced him. Anything else?"

"No sir."

Kurzvall joined his daughter on horseback. She giggled out a comment and he laughed in response. They cantered toward the woods.

CHAPTER 18

"You're making a big mistake."

Navere Manis yanked to a stop in front of the two enforcers, fury boiling off of him.

Lieutenant Curtis raised an eyebrow. "No, you did when you killed Manuel Walker and Janice Balzer in front of witnesses. Then you ordered those same two witnesses to dispose of the bodies. We met them outside Granger Crematorium."

"Then you have your murderers."

"Don't think so. *They* called us. Neither had laz-guns and one was having trouble with his stomach—you burned off half of Walker's face. They wanted nothing to do with it, you, or the possibility of being next."

"Liars!" Manis shouted, shaking his cuffed hands in their faces. His two escorts each grabbed an arm. "This is harassment! I'll be out before supper. My lawyer will file charges against the city and *you* in particular."

Curtis jerked his head sideways. The two officers pulled the swearing man away.

"I'll have your fucking job, you fucking bastard," Manis screamed before being shoved into a police van.

Detective Andre Kahn crossed his arms. "Think we'll ever hear a different exit line?"

Curtis shrugged, watching one of his detectives jog out of the house and toward them.

"It was right where the informant said it would be. And Lieutenant," Detective Ortiz Weil said, handing it over with a huge grin, "it's one of those new crystal recorders."

Kahn whooped.

Curtis whistled. "That informant has some great connections."

Yep. Helps to have friends in supply, Jem agreed, an invisible member of their small group. She'd risked contacting Boyd. If he could get her one, she'd reimburse him. Two had shown up in her alias's postbox. They were accompanied by a Boyd-rude message that had her grinning even as her ears burned.

They keyed it on and three heads bent over the video.

"Look at the clarity," Weil said, his tone reverent. "It has *two* days of recordings?"

Manis had become increasing volatile and paranoid by the constant eroding of his organization. Three days ago, a raid's arrests had dismantled his original smuggling enterprise. Hoping the man was about to do something irrational or stupid—murdering with witnesses qualified as both—she'd hidden a recorder in his office yesterday. She had planned on retrieving it tomorrow night after it reached capacity. Happy to see an arrest in progress when she came down the street, she'd sent a text with its location to the lieutenant.

Her hunch had paid off.

Jem watched as they started and stopped it whenever something or someone caught their attention. Her grin grew wider with each comment, like "*shit, that's Judge Winterson*" and "*yep, knew Charles MacCarthy was dirty.*" A tense silence wrapped around the enforcers, telling her they'd reached the murder scene.

"Manis wasn't even sure one of them was the leak," Kahn said disgustedly as the lieutenant halted the video. "Granted, it just about has to be someone on the inside. But still, you would think he'd want to be sure."

"Might not be an insider," the lieutenant said. "If our informant got one recorder in, there could have been others."

"Either way, at least being told where to find it lets us know the person is still alive. Our hidden ally deserves more than a laser bolt for all the help we've received."

"Agreed," Curtis said brusquely. He ordered all of Manis's men currently encircled by officers arrested as accessories to murder. "We'll individualize any additional charges at the Enforcement Center. I want a warrant for the rest of Manis's home. I want warrants for everyone on this recording. Their homes, their places of business, their backyard sheds."

"Winterson's kids have a treehouse."

Curtis rolled his eyes. "We'll skip that for now." He handed the recorder to Weil. "Judge Martha Bloomburg—she hates Manis and this evidence will expedite the warrants. Go."

He took off at a run.

"Manis is going in a Fed-Pen cell," Kahn practically sang. "There's no way anything in that video, especially the murders, can be argued away as manufactured."

The expensive crystal recorders were a one-time use. Whatever they recorded was permanently embedded into them. No deleting, tweaking or overwriting parts. With no transmission capability, they were invisible to electronic sweeps. Perfect for clandestine monitoring.

"I didn't even know they had crystal recorders that size," Kahn continued. "She definitely has some serious resources."

"She?" the lieutenant said, tilting his head.

Jem echoed the question silently.

Kahn hunched in a bit. "I've been studying the security tapes of places around where we've raided on the informant's info. There's a hooded figure in several of them; sometimes not long before we get there. Never a long glimpse. It's hard to tell the gender, but the walk and a quick flash of a hand says female to me. Think she'll come forward now we've got Manis locked tight? We owe her a lot. One of those bombs we got to in time? My sig-ner's aunt would've been one of the causalities."

"And I owe her for my family. Let's hope she does. All we've got is the untraceable temp number assigned from a Circle kiosk." Curtis shook his head. "Damn, I can't believe Judge Winterson took bribes."

Jem turned away as the two men continued discussing the video. Nothing she could do about a city full of security cameras, other than being more careful. Ghost-mode had to be used sparingly. Thirty, thirty-five minutes was the most she could do at one time…which her flagging energy was about to reach. Safely concealed behind a fence, she released the shift and rubbed her eyes. She was tired. Bone tired. This had taken weeks longer than she'd expected. Between her day job and nighttime sleuthing, she'd only gotten a few hours of sleep most nights.

At least she could look forward to a full night's sleep now.

She stayed for another eight days: waitressing, sleeping, and listening. The list of people taking bribes, kickbacks, and payoffs revealed in seized documents had shocked conversations buzzing. It reminded her of Pappia after Thane's assault.

Now, backpack dangling in hand, Jem examined the departure board in the spaceport's concourse. *Dancing Girl...Jamie's Swat*—boy, she'd love to know the history behind that name. *Wisteria Dream...Ajax Three*...there. The *Honeysuckle Rose*. Destination: Orion Two, leaving in two hours and forty-six minutes. She could take another ship from there to Hebros. She had no idea what she'd do there, but spying and sleuthing had worked here. Maybe she could find real, tangible proof of *something* Law Enforcement could use against Kurzvall.

Jem purchased a ticket under her alias, then headed for the port cafeteria. She'd just sat down with her sandwich and drink when her phone vibrated. Oh, right. She still needed to dump the temp number. She grinned as she read the text message from Lieutenant Curtis.

"Your present was a big hit. Will you come forward? I'm at the head of a long line of people wanting to thank you personally. For everything."

She'd left the second crystal recorder on his doorstep yesterday with a note: *Had a spare. No sense wasting it.* It held three days' worth of video from a major Port Circle drug den. It'd captured dozens of dealers and distributors doing business. She hoped the dealer forcing desktop sex with a minor was number one on their hit list.

Taking a bite, she chewed and texted. *"No need. I owe the Universe a favor or two."* She was about to disconnect when his reply shot back.

"I owe you two."

Jem shook her head and disconnected the number. The kiosk computer would process the signal and move the number to the bottom of its available list. The lieutenant would get a *Not in Service* message if he tried it again.

She took another bite of her sandwich and pondered Thane's message. Boyd had forwarded it to her postbox a couple of weeks ago.

Contact me if you need anything, or any of my family through Stohlass Enterprises. They are determined to help. My family's resources are not as vast as Kurzvall's, but they aren't insignificant either. Stay safe. Thane

Surely Thane had told his family what they were getting into? What Kurzvall could do in retaliation? She let out an exasperated sigh, knowing it wouldn't have mattered. Not as close-knit as they were.

She'd head to Midgard after her trip to Hebros. Hopefully she'd have some useful information to share by then. She grinned into her drink cup. The news clip of him on the family corporate steps had worked its way across all the news services. Shocking, right? How many would turn down a plum job like that? But his CEO disclaimer hadn't surprised her. Thane would be bored if grounded to a desk.

Finished, she tossed her trash into a recycler. Hefting her backpack, she headed for the ramp.

CHAPTER 19

"If I were a desk pilot escaping on a three-month sabbatical from a boss who didn't understand the main purpose of a vacation, I'd disappear too."

The man calling himself William Smith Jamison remained silent.

"And instead of just waiting until he returns," Thane continued, "you want to hire an independent, *expensive* tracker to find him?"

"I can't wait another two months. I have my reasons."

Yeah, and he'd heard most of them. Thane seriously doubted this man's would be among them. He leaned back to better study the enigma sitting across from him.

He had just completed a find-my-credit-squandering-ass-of-a-child job when an incoming message requested an immediate appointment. The pouting, squandering ass was on her way home to Taurus Two and he planned on chasing down an interesting rumor he'd heard. He politely turned down the request and the insistent response that followed.

Then the guy was knocking on his hatch.

Thane ignored him, figuring he would finally get the message and go away. Fifteen hull-pounding minutes later, he was fighting the temptation to fire up his ions beneath the guy's feet. He'd slung open the hatch to very impolitely get him the hell off his ship. That intent had morphed into wariness as soon as he locked eyes with the conservatively dressed man standing with his fist still raised.

The man had promised to leave quietly if Thane was still uninterested after hearing him out. Caution, curiosity and neck tingles convinced Thane to let him onboard. The man sat calmly now, his gaze steady beneath Thane's study.

The name was undoubtedly as fake as the corporate-businessman image.

His unwanted guest had tackled the ladder rungs with a dexterity few corporate types could manage. Alert obsidian-black eyes had cataloged and assessed his ship's contents, right down to his discarded jacket tossed across the pilot's chair. He sat relaxed, but Thane was willing to bet his next month's fuel quota that any sudden or unexpected move on his part would have the weapon tucked discreetly up a coat sleeve pointed at his mid-section.

He reached for the cash card laying in the center of the table and activated the readout. It was substantial. Anonymity was the only reason to risk carrying that large a pilferable amount. Just ask Dougson.

He tossed it back across the table. "No."

"Not enough?"

"Not interested. Not interested in the real story or your real name. Go find someone else to pass your bullshit to."

"Will my real name make a difference? Or my reasons? You're a Tracker, I'm a client. I pay well and want the best."

Thane ignored the compliment. "You're some kind of flea." No reaction at the detested acronym pronouncement. "A cash card ensures neither you nor this BS can be traced. You and your associates undoubtedly have numerous resources, so secretly hiring someone from the outside does not bode well. You've evidently got an internal problem which only an idiot would tackle blind. I'm not an idiot and still not interested."

That made the man blink. Thane rose. "I believe you said you'd leave quietly."

"I lied." The man held up a hand, palm out as Thane reached across the table. "Straight. Jason's dead, not missing. Odds are I'll end up the same."

Thane sat back down. That was unexpected. "Real name and affiliation?"

"Special Agent Leroy Jamison Twobears, FBI, Earth, Sol System. I'm based out of the city of Philadelphia. Jason was based in our Madrid office."

"Why the bullshit?"

"A test. I needed to get a feel for you," the agent said, his tone clipped. "As per your succinct and correct analysis of my situation, I cannot count on my usual resources. I do need outside help but, given recent events, I'm finding it hard to trust anyone."

127

Thane glanced at the local time chronometer. "Decide fast. My exit window is coming up. Why me?"

"Your name came up as an interesting sideline in another investigation. That, plus your reputation and Jason's endorsement."

"Interesting sideline?" Thane echoed. Hope flickered. Where they investigating Kurzvall? Had the man finally made a mistake?

"Want to tell me first why there are a number of flags on you and your ship?"

"No. You came to me. I have trust issues myself."

They shared a polite silence. Twobears finally gave an amused grunt. "Fine. We're a couple of paranoid assholes."

Thane glanced at the clock again. "You've got—" he tensed when the agent reached into a pocket.

He withdrew a T-drive. "I received this twelve days ago. It will explain my situation and should alleviate some of the distrust. The vid-message isn't encrypted."

Thane inserted it into the table comp and activated the video. The man who flickered onscreen certainly looked in need of a vacation. His brown hair was disheveled, his eyes lined with dark circles in a thin face. He gave a weary smile.

Hello Lee. You're right. Everyone makes a mistake. I was careful but still tripped a flag. I hate leaving all this on you, but you're the one person I'm sure hasn't been corrupted. Trusting someone can get you killed. That includes our lofty co-workers, he said bitterly. He rubbed his hands across his face before staring grimly into the camera.

Rawlins's death just didn't sit right. I knew the driver. He wouldn't have panicked or lost control. He'd hit whatever was in the road before risking a steep embankment. I started digging. Deep. It's a conspiracy, Lee. A huge one. The deaths and political manipulation all tie back to a consortium in Sector Three. It's mostly confined to their home systems and Earth, but there are tentacles in a lot of unexpected places. It's what snagged me. Everything I've uncovered is in the encrypted file. Use the Toronto key.

One small ray of hope. It looks like there's a couple of people out there the Consortium is wary of. One or both of them may have information that can help you. There are flags against them—ports, his ship, her Earth account—reporting back just to the group, no Federal office. Yeah, I know, that shouldn't be possible. It shows just how deep and widespread the corruption is. The Tracker has a solid reputation and, I think, can be trusted. Use your judgement. More details on both of them in the file.

He stared downward. When he looked back up, his face was bleak.

Given the message I'm sending tomorrow, they'll know I plan to pass my info on. They're monitoring my communications—yours, too, after my blithering performance. They'll scramble to get my file. Unfortunately, to keep the ruse going, it has to be complete and the original. Well, almost complete. This will make it harder for you as they'll know what to eliminate or bury even deeper. Sorry. At least you'll have the names and starting points. Besides the info on those two people, your copy also has additional names and information I suspect but hadn't gotten to yet. Hopefully, those avenues don't disappear.

I'm passing all of this tonight to a civilian contact I trust implicitly. She's to wait three weeks from whatever happens to me before getting the T-drive to you. I'm hoping—praying—my subterfuge and your natural behavior keeps you safe. If not, he shrugged, *she's to use her best judgement.*

I've enclosed another, personal file for Lissa when you feel it's safe.

Be paranoid, my friend. Be safe. Screw them hard and with extreme prejudice for me.

* * * * *

"He set himself up," the tracker said, handing him back the T-drive.

"Yes," Twobears said, returning Baron's scrutiny. Had he just made his own mistake? He couldn't tell as the man gave up absolutely nothing. But he needed the brawn and experience the scars testified to. He needed the brain that had deduced his situation from practically nothing. And sitting here, staring at each other wasn't getting them anywhere. Yes, he'd come to him.

He laid the T-drive next to the cash card. Stared at it for a moment.

"Jason Smithe Noble was a researcher and analyst. One of the best. His specialty was discerning patterns and finding links. I first met him about ten years ago when we paired for a case. He's—was—twenty years younger, but we hit it off and stayed in touch outside of work. What he dug up…what he found…" he took a deep breath. "I would never have believed it possible. He broke up with Lissa, his sig-ner, about four months ago. I'm pretty sure it was to protect her once he realized the danger."

"Who was Rawlins?"

"Federal Senator Rawlins, Tricast System," Twobears said. "Roughly nine months ago he and his driver were killed in a single car accident on a rural mountain road on Earth. Evidence indicates the driver swerved to avoid something and they went down an embankment."

"Nothing to indicate anything other than an accident?"

"No. The area bordered a national forest and—while this was an extreme case—animal-caused mishaps weren't uncommon. Jason and I were discussing a case when he veered off topic. Asked if I'd heard about Senator Rawlins's death the previous week. I told him I was sorry to hear it as he was well liked and respected. Jason made a comment about how the driver shouldn't have lost control of the vehicle."

Twobears's laugh was bitter. "That's when I told him everyone makes a mistake."

"We finished our discussion. He mentioned looking forward to his upcoming sabbatical. I received his report and analysis file about a week later. That was the last time we spoke. Then, thirty-four days ago, I received a vid-message. After some lame-brain chatting—totally out of character—he said he'd be in Philadelphia in a couple of days. Said he wanted to start his sabbatical with the expensive winning-bet dinner I owed him."

"Which you didn't," Baron said shrewdly.

Twobears gestured with his hands. "Confused? You bet. I mean, we both had serious encryption on our communications. Yet Jason was alerting me in a very subtle way something was wrong. Seriously wrong. Trusting he'd give me a full brief, I went ahead and made reservations at a fancy restaurant to maintain whatever cover he needed." His jaw flexed. "He never made it, killed in an apparent home robbery fourteen hours later. All his top-of-the-line electronics and a few other expensive items were gone. His home ransacked."

Baron nodded. "They made sure to find everything he might have. Your friend made a smart move by having your contact wait three weeks. Surveillance would probably be relaxed by then, thinking they'd succeeded. Can you summarize the file's crucial points for me?"

"You and your family both have a solid reputation. You've been tracking for thirteen years, considered to be the best, and have brought in a number of violent cases for the Enforcers. Wealth isn't your primary drive as shown by your turndown of a lucrative CEO position.

"Jem Seaborne Wilmont is an unremarkable person." He paused for a beat. "Except for the size of her bank account and being hard to track. Must be why there are a lot more flags on her than you. About a year ago Wilmont took a job with EMC and landed on a mining moon in the Latvia system. Several interesting things happen when you show up four months later."

Cold gray eyes bored into his. *Don't think I want this guy for an enemy.*

"You're ambushed and nearly killed. She pays off her contract—cash. Wilmont leaves Pappia about two months after you do and disappears. No trace, despite all the flags that have gone up. At the same time, you're sitting in jail on Random Two for what proves to be framed charges. You return home—Midgard—gaining a number of flags yourself."

Baron folded his arms across his chest. "That's not critical information."

"It is to me. I don't know you and her spotty information is suspicious at best. Why the flags? Why the Consortium's interest? What are you two involved in? Are you working with a Federal agency?" He leaned forward and tapped the table top when Baron remained silent. "I've put my cards on the table, it's time for you to do the same."

"I was used once to entrap Jem," Baron said flatly. "I won't be so again. I need to know who and what this Consortium is before I say anything more."

Entrap? "All right. The Consortium is comprised of five large conglomerates based in four of Sector Three's better-established systems." The Tracker's shoulders stiffened. *Hmmm.* "It's an ambitious group of bastards with unlimited funds and an 'anything goes' motto who have apparently worked deep behind the scenes for over a decade. Objective is unknown."

"Participants?" Baron asked, his voice tense.

He knows something; he's waiting for confirmation. "The Webster Financial Group from the Intervalic System. Burkhart-Devney Security Services and the legal firm of Abrahams, Hier, Taylor, Bair and Gaspers, both out of Tricast. Kurzvall Industries of Hermes, and Meridan Securities and Investments of Meridan. Bullseye?" Twobears added, seeing the fire ignite in those hard eyes.

"Kurzvall. He's an amoral control freak who uses whatever means necessary, up to and including assassination, to get whatever he wants. If the whole group is warped the same," Baron stood, shaking his head, "you've inherited some very nasty enemies."

Baron ordered his comp brain—*how did he get that in a ship this size?*—to contact Port Control and request a slot in the next transit-out window. He returned to his seat with two glasses and a bottle of whisky. Shoving one filled-to-the-brim glass at him, the tracker reduced his own contents by a third in two large swallows.

"Kurzvall is actively hunting Jem. To say he wants her badly is a gross understatement. Among other things, she has first-hand knowledge about some of his illegal activities."

Twobears nodded, his eyes watering. "What is this?" he wheezed. He thumped his chest a couple of times to make sure his lungs weren't paralyzed.

"Aspric whisky."

"Not like any I've had." He sucked air in through his teeth.

"Special blend." Baron's grin faded. "What evidence did your friend find?"

"In the—" Twobears coughed, set his glass down. "In the last decade, fourteen of their Federal Senators and over two-thirds of their system politicians are in office thanks to support and large donations linking back to the same consortium. Control of their System Senators and Planetary Representatives will only affect internal policies of those four systems. The five Senators they each have in the Republic's Federal Senate is a different issue."

"That's only twenty Fed-Senators out of—how many now? Close to nine hundred?"

Twobears snorted. "You don't follow politics, do you? Depending on the committees they sit on and the influence and outright pressures they could bring to bear on others, twenty politicians could finagle the outcome and direction of numerous things."

"That doesn't seem right," Baron said, frowning.

Twobears felt the same, but politics hadn't changed in centuries and probably never would. "A number of others in both strategic and Federal positions—again mostly in their home systems and on Earth—have received large cash deposits from an unnamed and untraceable source. Undoubtedly from the same group and buried for obvious reasons. Odds are those others in Jason's file did also. They're probably providing manipulation and information behind the scenes. That's not the worst part."

Baron gave him a blank look. "What could be worse?"

"Thirty-one of those previously mentioned politicians succeeded individuals who suffered fatal accidents. Rawlins was the fourth Fed-Senator. The last Sys-Senator replaced with a consortium mouthpiece was killed on Tylander, Intervalic One, in an unexpected rock slide. Unfortunately," Twobears said grimly, "his wife and three small children were with him. Local geologists still swear the area is stable and what happened was an anomaly. You have proof these were assassinations? Some of them at least?"

"Verbal only. Jem overheard them talking about one."

Twobears rubbed his neck. "All this can't be just for political control. There has to be something major going on with that sector."

"That's what Jem and I have been trying to find out."

"Just who is she? Jason is *damn* good, but what he found barely covers one page."

"Someone who can slip pass security systems without leaving a trail."

Twobears blinked. "All of them?"

"That I know of. Consider her a ghost."

He frowned at the tracker's tone and half-smile. There was nothing amusing about a skill set like that. "Guess that explains her huge bank account."

"Jem is not a criminal," Baron snapped, "but Kurzvall wants to use her as one. It's the other reason he's after her. What do you think he and his buddies would do if in control of her and her skills?"

Twobears winced. "The port flags. They're counting on an alert and intercepting her there before she leaves."

"Which is why she stays hard to find," Baron said. "I don't even know where she is or how to contact her."

Twobears took a small sip of his drink. *Damn.* At least he didn't embarrass himself this time. "How does she tie in with Kurzvall? Did she work for him at one time?"

"No." Baron explained about Myerstone, his search, and her entrapment on Pappia.

Twobears's eyebrows worked their way upward as the tracker spoke of helping her escape, forced to kill and dispose of one body, and sending Kurzvall's man back empty-handed.

"Her side of the story carried a lot more weight after they tried to kill me." Baron pointed to his laser scar. "I've learned a number of things since and how he operates. Nothing as world-shattering as your friend discovered, but it does add credence to what he found."

Twobears's fingers drummed on the table as he absorbed the new information. "You truly don't know where she is or how to contact her?"

"She could be anywhere, and no. I'm hoping she'll contact me soon." He took a drink. "He's keeping tabs on me. Maybe he hopes we'll meet up somewhere."

Twobears snorted. "That would be stupid on both your parts."

"Uh-huh. But I'm a threat he can't ignore. Eventually he'll move to eliminate me." Baron flashed him a very non-friendly smile. "I can't wait for him to try."

And he'd love to be there when it happens. His jaw set. "I want them. I want them all. We've got to find this woman, Baron. Taking down Kurzvall will break open their organization. If he cooperates—"

"No concessions," the tracker interjected coldly. "No deals. Not for any of them and *especially* not Kurzvall. They all go down and as hard as possible."

Twobears thought of Rawlins, of three dead kids and his friend. *With extreme prejudice for me.* They were right. The bastards deserved no quarter. He switched his gaze from midair to Baron. "No concessions," he agreed.

* * * * *

Thane watched the Fed rise and move restlessly about the ship. He accepted Twobears's story at face value for now, but reserved final judgement. A lingering piece of mistrust had him giving the agent only the bare bones of his situation. The dead analyst's information could be both true and a trap. Seems the man had already misjudged some of his FLEA coworkers.

Twobears swung around to face him. "This is going to take more than the three of us." He raked a hand through his hair. "Something this huge requires a team and a network. We need a base, a secure central point for coordination of actions and consolidation of information. And we have to be absolutely sure of someone before we can trust them."

Thane lifted his glass and stared thoughtfully into its red-gold depths. He took a sip and met Twobears's eyes over the rim. "Not a problem."

His family was already involved. If the flea betrayed them, he'd be at the head of the ass-stomping line. He was still hoping to hear from Jem. A month ago he'd sent Boyd a request and a message, gambling Boyd knew how to contact her. Not getting a rude response back told him he'd guessed right and his message had been passed on. He'd included his personal contact information in it. So far…nothing. Not even an acknowledgement from her.

"Think they're hunting you?" Thane asked, burying his disquiet.

"Probably. I slipped off Earth five days ago. Even with relaxed surveillance, they have to know by now I'm missing and my personal account emptied. Also about my hefty advance."

Thane's glass *thunked* on the table. "Tell me you used your cash card."

"Yes, and my alias." The agent heaved a heavy sigh and dropped back down in his chair. "But I had to run an inquiry for your current location. With your ship flagged…"

Yeah, right. "Thor, how long until our exit slot?"

"Four hours, forty-two minutes and twenty-eight seconds."

Twobears grimaced.

Thane waved his hand. "Go. Collect your things. The *Lone Tracker* is safer."

CHAPTER 20

Twobears was acutely aware of his surroundings as he made his way back to his hotel, his eyes roaming and his senses on alert. Even without a looming threat, a well-dressed man walking alone through the Port Circle was a prime target. The late afternoon light wouldn't be much of a deterrent.

Like the seaports of ancient days, the areas springing up immediately around a spaceport catered primarily to those who worked there or on its ships. Hard, often dangerous places, unwary travelers could lose more than their cash cards. Those with the funds and the inclination could obtain almost any legal and not-so-legal service or product.

He was passing a service alley when he heard someone screaming *"Mine, it's mine!"* A short, gray-haired man bolted out of a door ahead of him and down the sidewalk in his direction. He was hunched over, protecting whatever he had his arms wrapped around and screaming, *"Mine, mine, mine!"* Two large men charged out of the same doorway, coming fast with their eyes fixed on their quarry. Twobears hesitated. Should he intervene?

The older man passed him; the younger men's focus shifted to him.

Instincts flared too late. *Crack!* Gray Hair's hidden pipe slammed into his ribcage.

Twobears fumbled for his weapon. *Crack!* The man's backhand return disrupted his aim and his shot went wild. The largest man grabbed Twobears, yanked him into the alley and then pivoted, slamming him face first into a wall. Twobears staggered backward, blood flowing down the side of his face. *Crack!* His gun tumbled from his useless hand.

A blow across his shoulders dropped Twobears to his knees. Dazed. Fighting blackness. *Not giving me a chance.* A kick sent him sprawling. He rolled over onto his back. It took a few seconds to focus on his attackers. "Scum. Cowards," he said, dredging up as much contempt as he could. He curled into a fetal position, arms protecting his head as blows and kicks hammered him. *Hope Baron can make good use of Jason's file.*

Z-ping. Z-ping.

Stunner, a still conscious part of him identified. Weight fell across his legs. The sound of feet pounding away. *Z-ping.* There was a metal clang and then a crashing thud.

* * * * *

Thane shoved the unconscious thug off Twobears's legs. Turning the Fed on his back, he let out several curses. He felt for a neck pulse. Was he too late?

He'd spotted the watcher on his monitor, talking on a phone and gesturing in the direction Twobears had taken. The agent was walking into trouble. Thane had ambled out of his ship in the opposite direction, then snuck back and double zapped the bastard before setting off in a jog.

Twobears's eyes flickered, opened. "Thanks." It was a hoarse whisper.

"I'll get an ambulance."

"No." Twobears winced. "Risky." His eyes closed.

The man was right. As if fighting Kurzvall's and the Consortium's resources weren't enough, now he had to worry about renegade Feds flashing their badges. They'd be able to access anything. Thane felt Twobears over carefully. Watched where he flinched. He set back on his heels. Now what? He couldn't do a shoulder carry with those broken ribs.

"We have a sled."

Thane surged to his feet, drawing his weapon as he spun around. Two children stood in the alley's entrance. The girl looked to be about ten years old, the boy thirteen or so. Neither of them gave the bloody mess at his feet a second look. He let his stunner drop, but didn't holster it.

"A sled?" Thane repeated.

"We can take you and your friend anywhere you need to go. Five hundred credits."

Thane took a couple of steps forward to peer cautiously around both corners. Clear. A motorized transport flatbed about seven feet long set at the curb.

"Yes or no," the boy said impatiently. "We have to be home by dark."

Thane holstered his stunner. Fifty dollars, huh? He ran his eyes over the unconscious assailants. Locals. Where was the one who hired them? Watching? Were there others?

"I'll make it one hundred dollars—a thousand credits—if you can get us safely, and discreetly, to the East Side short-term transit ramp," he told them.

The kids exploded into action. The girl backed the sled into the alley as the boy came over to help Thane drag the two assailants out of the way.

"My bag...hotel," Twobears ground out. "ID. Badge."

"Need to get you to my ship first." Arms under Twobears's arms, he carefully raised the agent into a sitting position.

"Not killed." Twobears's breath came in short gasps. "Discredit next."

"Using your badge. Bastards." The kids had probably heard worse. "Which hotel?"

"First Round." He started to move, stopped. His "key in pocket" was said through clenched teeth.

"Don't need to stand him," the boy instructed, as the girl lifted a side rail off. "Just lift him high enough to slip the sled under him." He grasped Twobears's legs.

Thane took a firmer grip. "Done this much?" he asked drily.

The boy just shrugged. "It's the Circle."

They got Twobears's limp form on the sled. Thane wasn't surprised he'd blacked out.

"He's an Enforcer?" the boy asked.

"Federal agent from Earth."

The boy's eyes widened. He looked at Twobears, the assailants, then back at Thane. His mouth opened, then snapped closed. Smart kid.

"First Round is not that far," the boy said, slotting the side rail back in place. "There are several connected alleys which will get you to its back door. Unseen."

***

"*Fuuuck.* Wait a minute. "

Thane halted as Twobears sagged against him. They were barely half-way up the *Lone Tracker's* steps. He was taking as much of the man's weight as he could, but just breathing would be agony right now. He really wished the boy had been taller; he'd have taken his fifty-dollar offer to help. The kid had thrown Twobears's bag inside the hatch for free.

Thane eyed the remaining steps. If he shouldered Twobears through the hips…

"Okay," Twobears said, opening his eyes. He straightened. Sort of. "Let's get this over with."

Long, drawn out minutes later, they stumbled through the inner hatch and into the ship's plazo. Thane used a foot to push the hatch closed and ordered Thor to set the locks. "Just a little bit more," he coaxed.

The shuffle onto the lift took the last of Twobears's strength. He was a comatose automaton by the time Thane laid him carefully on the med-bed. Ordering Thor to start the medical scan, he grabbed a roll of bandages and an injector from the cabinet.

Thor began listing the injuries.

Why the frigging hell didn't they just laser the man? It would've been kinder. But *nooooo*, Thane fumed, that would have brought a lot of LE attention. Especially once they learned he was a Federal agent. If they ever learned that tidbit. According to the SOB he'd caught leaving Twobears's room with the agent's badge and ID, they wanted it to look like a businessman who foolishly decided to walk to his hotel and became the victim of a not-uncommon Circle mugging which, unfortunately, went too far.

His earlier wariness of Twobears dissipated. No one would take this much of a beating to provide a cover. Roughed up a bit? Sure. Multiple broken bones and concussion? Nope. By some miracle there weren't any serious internal injuries, although the bruised left kidney might disagree. Applying a strong painkiller, Twobears revived to a groggy, half-conscious state.

The Fed was describing the ambush when Thor announced receipt of a text message forwarded from Midgard.

"Read it."

"Thane. I need to meet with you on Midgard as soon as possible. I've learned something important. I'll make contact again as soon as I arrive on-planet. Jem. End."

Twobears managed a bloody smile. "Perfect timing."

CHAPTER 21

Jem's heartbeat sped up as she watched Dougson pass a note to the Stohlass gate guard. This was not good. The bastard had been busy since their arrival from Hebros yesterday, hiring port slugs matching his low caliber and visiting unoccupied buildings on the city's edge. Whatever he was planning, it was now in motion.

She'd skulked around Kurzvall's home for over a week. Listening when she could, finding a place to hide when she reached her shifting limit. She'd almost been caught once, staggering into an empty room when a servant came around the corner. She needed to practice, to stretch out the time she could spend shifted.

All a severe case of nerves had earned her was that Kurzvall had a lot business dealings, even a private shipyard. Then she'd caught the tail end of a cryptic conversation between Dougson and Kurzvall that included passage booked to Midgard. She'd followed Dougson aboard the same overcrowded ship, spending eight days in various supply closets and sneaking food when no one was looking. She'd even managed to shower in the crew quarters once.

Jem shifted and followed Dougson half a block before turning and jogging back to the Stohlass gates. She'd find him later. Thane needed to know he was here and she needed to know what was in that note. Passing through the gate and across the yard, she headed toward the same corner of the house the guard had been. She found him talking to man who appeared to have been in a recent accident of some sort.

"...don't like it. Describe the person giving you the note," the man said, leaning heavily on a cane.

"A woman. Long braid, two different eye colors."

Jem froze. What? A car's engine had her wheeling around. Thane and another were heading out the gate.

Dammit. If she'd alerted him as soon as they arrived, he would have been on guard.

She whirled back around in time to see the man limp into the house. Jem shot the betraying guard a hostile look as he passed her. Was he the only one? Had others been bought, too? She slipped inside through the veranda doors, sparing a moment to sweep the comfy-looking room before hurrying out into a hallway. No one. Following the sound of voices around a corner, she drew up short. *Whoa. Now that's a tall guy.* They went into an office at the end of the short corridor. The sign next to the open door said 'Security.' She crept closer.

"...note said your communications were compromised," said the guy with a cane.

The giant shook his head. "Impossible. We use level seven encryption."

"Yeah? So did Jason and it didn't do him any good." He thumped his cane. "Or me."

Oh? And just who might you be? That cane thump said his accident was no accident. Another victim of Kurzvall's manipulations?

"Anyway," the shorter man continued, "Baron and his grandfather have gone to meet with Wilmont. They're—"

Jem released her shift. Stepped into the room. "No. They haven't."

* * * * *

Thane watched helplessly as two men shoved his grandfather into another room. The dust-covered sign above the door read 'Lounge.' They were in what had probably been a lobby.

"What my boss wants, he gets." Dougson's smile was cold. "And he wants Wilmont."

"I don't know where she is."

"Yeah, that was obvious. You rushed home a lot faster than we were expecting."

Understanding was a hard thump in the chest. "You sent that message."

Dougson smirked. "Didn't think you'd question it if asked to meet on your world."

Thane hadn't. He'd rushed home and spent three days waiting and fending off his family. Then an urgent message provided an address and asking him to bring a trusted lawyer. He hadn't questioned that one either. He had assumed the empty office building outside the city was a security precaution to elude any watchers. They'd been easily taken by Dougson's men.

Dumb, dumb, dumb. And last time I go anywhere unarmed.

"By the way, thanks. We figured you'd bring a family lawyer but didn't expect you to bring the old man himself. Saves us a lot of future headaches."

Thane's chest tightened. "Others know where we were going."

Dougson's laugh held a cruel note. "We won't be here long."

A broken off scream had Thane whipping around. Two laz-guns pointed at his mid-section stopped him. He lunged for Dougson's throat but crashed to the floor before he could reach him. The bastard's laughter rang in his ears as two burly men hauled him to his feet. The bolo's owner peeled it off Thane's shins and slung the three-thong weapon back across his shoulder.

"Shackle him. Make it good."

Thane's hands were twisted painfully behind him and cuffed. He gritted his teeth as several more loud thumps came from the next room. "Go ahead, kill me. I won't have to listen to your asinine gloating."

"Oh, we're not killing *you*. After they find the old man's body, we'll send word to expect more of the same until Wilmont decides to join us. As for you…"

Thane didn't think he'd seen a more evil smile.

"You get to be our guest. Accommodations won't be what you're used to, but we'll keep you up-to-date on the news. Like, who's died and how they died. Maybe even who we're going after next. You do have a large family to select from, even some new twin cousins. Hmmm." He rubbed his chin with a scarred hand. "I suppose we could provide you with videos, maybe a couple pieces, just so you know we're not lying."

Thane strained against his bonds. Hate he didn't know he was capable of drowned every other thought.

Stepping closer, Dougson dropped his voice. "After Wilmont is under our control and you know it's been all for nothing, then you'll die. As painfully as I—"

Thane's head butt sent Dougson stumbling backward. His attempted kick missed when one of his captors yanked him sideways. Dougson's backhand blow split his lip.

"You'll pay for that. Your entire family will pay." There was another thump from the other room, followed by a muffled groan. Dougson glanced over at the open door then gave Thane his evil smile. "Your grandfather's a tough old alley cat. Why don't we go see how he handles the Branigan special of losing body parts?"

Dragged to the open door, Thane reared backward but a violent shove from behind sent him flying into the room. Off-balance, he fell heavily to the floor. He had just enough time to see an empty chair, two bodies on the floor and several men plastered against the wall behind Nicholas. The thug coming through the door had just enough time to yell a warning before the fight started. A pair of strong hands gripped him under the armpits and dragged him out of the way of feet, rolling bodies, and weapon blasts.

The fight didn't last long.

His grandfather helped him to stand and tugged on the cuffs. "Which spash has the key to these things? How bad are you hurt?" he asked on seeing Thane's face.

"I landed pretty hard on my shoulder. The bolo-guy has the key. How bad did they hurt you?" He scanned the older man as he spoke. A bruise was forming on his jaw and there was blood streaked down the front of his shirt.

"Not much, thanks to rescue arriving in time. I provided a few sound effects but some of what you heard was from them." He yanked his thumb over his shoulder. The two who dragged him into the room were now being dragged out. "Blood belongs to the guy wearing a knife."

A security man brought Gordon the keys and he quickly unlocked Thane's cuffs.

"That's nine total, counting the two outside pretending to be guards," Nicholas said, coming back into the would-be torture chamber.

"Where's the head sonofabitch?" Gordon demanded.

Nicholas motioned with his chin. "Next room."

Thane trailed after his grandfather. Two thugs sat with their hands on their heads, three lay unmoving, and one was having his arm patched by a medic. Gordon stalked up to Dougson and sent him to the floor with a rage-powered punch to the jaw.

"I heard what you intended for my family. I will personally put you and your employer in the worst cell, in the worst wing, in the worst prison, on the most god-awful penitentiary planet I can find."

Dougson glared up at him. "Want to bet?"

"If Kurzvall wants a war then by God I'll give him one! Get this piece of filth out of here before I rip his head off." Fists clenched at his side, Gordon's furious gaze followed Dougson as two of Nicholas's men yanked him up and out of the room.

Thane wasn't the only one gaping in awe. This was not the man they knew; the one widely known for keeping his cool, even during the most controversial legal battles. Recovering, Nicholas ordered his team lead to call in the Azusa Enforcers.

"Think Dougson will give up Kurzvall?" Thane said, warily watching his grandfather take several deep breaths. They'd made a serious mistake in pissing off Gordon Stohlass.

Gordon frowned. "Not easily. We still have to link them—"

The loud sizzle of a laser bolt interrupted him, followed by several yells and a single scream. They raced toward the exit, skidded to a stop, and peered outside cautiously.

A quick scan showed people on the ground or huddled behind something. Two of Nicholas's men were just disappearing into the woods in a crouched run. Another was piled protectively on top of someone behind a vehicle, her hand motion signaling an injury. An uneasy silence reigned until the two came back, shaking their heads.

They raced out to the injured man. "How bad?" Nicholas said.

"Shoulder shot," Anita Laarsen replied tersely. "Through Dougson's head."

145

The medic dropped beside them as Laarsen rolled out of the way. "Ambulances on the way."

"Damn," Gordon said. "There went our best chance at Kurzvall."

Nicholas crossed over to study the body. "Downward angle." He studied the tree line carefully. "I'll have the area canvased again, but I don't believe it will do any good. It was either Dougson's backup or Kurzvall's insurance if some-thing went wrong."

One of his men walked up and handed Nicholas a knife. He hefted it a couple of times before wiping a remaining smear off on Dougson's pants.

Thane's eyebrows drew together at its familiar look. When and how did he get it?

"Nice heft and balance. Thanks for the assist," Nicholas said.

The reply of "You're welcome" came from behind.

Thane wheeled around, then continued turning, tracking Jem as she walked around them. Overwhelming relief hit him.

Jem accepted her knife back before turning to give Thane a wry grin. "Didn't Margo give you my messages? Especially the one about—*umph*."

Catcalls and laughter filled the clearing as Thane yanked her close for a fast, hard kiss. "Thanks." He released her.

"Ah, you're welcome?" Jem said, stumbling backward, eyes wide.

"Granddad, this is Jem Seaborne Wilmont of Sol."

Pulsating sirens sounded in the distance.

"Pleased to finally meet you, young lady."

Three jetters zipped over the clearing, clearly identified by their bold Azusa Law Enforcement colors. Nicholas immediately ordered all weapons put down. After a couple of evaluating circles, the oversized jetpack riders took up triangulated positions at treetop level. The weapons in the platforms beneath their feet would be trained on everyone until the ground forces rapidly approaching sorted things out.

"Nicholas, how'd you find us?" Gordon asked.

"You can thank Miss Wilmont. She let us know Bullard lied and Dougson's note was a trap. She…is gone," Nicholas said, rotating slowly. "Hanson, did she go in the building?"

The man standing next to the open door shook his head.

Nicholas rotated again, scanning the area and getting head shakes from his people. He stopped, fixing his scowl on Thane.

Thane grinned and held his hands up. "Told you she was part ghost."

CHAPTER 22

Everyone who could make it gathered in the library that evening. Gordon gave a brief synopsis of what had happed to those who had missed the excitement. Silence reigned for several minutes as it was digested and mulled over.

"Can those pieces of trash he hired be used to arrest Kurzvall?" Dane Stohlass was furious. His twin sons were two Dougson had specifically threated.

"No," Twobears said, shaking his head. "Flashing my badge got me a run down from the detective in charge. Dougson paid the locals in cash, never told them who he worked for, and was always careful to never use a name or any reference we could use."

"So, all we get is Dougson, who's dead," Thane said, frustrated that Kurzvall had slipped away yet again.

"When Kurzvall's office is contacted," Gordon said, "we'll no doubt learn Dougson was terminated from his employment and he is shocked, *shocked,* at what was attempted."

Mutters and curses bounced around the room.

"Why can't Jem just give Law Enforcement her statement?" Susi, Clint's wife asked. "She followed him here from Hebros…overheard him talking with Kurzvall."

"Sorry," Jem said, her voice holding an apology. "I never heard Kurzvall explicitly saying anything about attacking Thane. A lawyer could argue Dougson was a just-fired employee looking for some kind of revenge."

"Then we'd end up in a long legal battle for slander," Seth said. The other family lawyers murmured in agreement. "Accusing someone like Kurzvall without concrete proof would have his lawyers spinning it as a smear tactic."

"Then he gets away with it," Reyna snapped angrily.

"Did you hear me say that?" Seth snapped back.

Gordon held up a hand, stopping any further retorts. "Seth's right. We need solid, can't-squirm-out-of-it evidence or we'll wind up as the bad guys and sued for every credit he can get."

"We'll take him down," Thane said coldly. "We nip at him and the Consortium, slicing away pieces until someone makes a mistake or we find a hole."

"When do we start?" Kat asked, rubbing her hands together.

Thane nodded at Twobears. "We already have."

"I've made a list of people who are qualified to help us," Twobears said. "I've selected those who are either retired or no longer working in their previous security and law enforcement fields. They are less likely to have been approached by Kurzvall or his associates."

"I know a couple of people here who would qualify," Nicholas said.

"Good. We'll add them to the list. Everyone gets vetted no matter who they are, including Carl Childers Thaxton, Earth's FBI Director. He's at the top of my list, and what I know about him makes me seriously doubt we'll find he's been compromised. Once we verify that in truth, he needs to be alerted to what's happening in the agency and take steps to find and remove the traitors."

"Understood." Nicholas's voice was grim.

"Speaking of traitors, where's Bullard?" Thane asked. "I'd like a few words with him."

"Just words?" Blaise Sullivan asked dryly. Seth's youngest brother was still in his Sea Patrol uniform.

"Bullard is currently residing in a cell next to Dougson's men. I've already had a few words with him." There was no mistaking Nicholas's furious undertone. "He was apologetic with a sprinkling of shame. He swore he would never have taken Dougson's money if he'd known it was going to be more than a standard ransom."

"Really?" "You're kidding!" Several voices stepped on top of each other.

"What the hell did Bullard think he was hired to prevent?" Clint said, sputtering.

"Several long-term people I trust implicitly are already going over our security tapes and personnel records to see if there are any other employees who have misunderstood their job requirements."

"Good, because the vetting starts now. Who are you, Agent Leroy Jamison Twobears?" Gordon said. "Thane hauls you here, half beat to death and with a conspiracy theory that, frankly, is hard to believe. For all we know, you're actually Kurzvall's spy."

All eyes swiveled to Twobears. A couple of them winced at his mottled features.

"If I'm a spy, someone didn't get the memo." Twobears thumped his cane twice on the floor in a silent reminder. "My assailants were smart. They were aware of my training and set the ambush ahead of me—I would've detected anyone trailing me. They used a distraction, attacked aggressively, and gave me no chance to recover or escape. If Baron hadn't spotted their point man and come after me, I'd be dead," he said flatly.

"I would have liked to accompany O'Daniel today to return the favor." He shifted slightly, winced. "But I'm well aware of my current physical liabilities." Medical regenerative treatments had come a long way over the centuries, but it still had its limitations. Bones were highly susceptible to damage until the new growth hardened. Bruises and concussions insisted on still healing at their own rate.

The agent leaned forward, folding his hands on the cane's handle. "Everything I've told you is truth, as I'm sure your people have verified. I'm an investigator for the Federal Bureau of Investigations, Earth Division. Presently on a long sabbatical. The deaths and buyoffs. The conspiracy. It all exists— believe it. It's why I needed to find help from outside."

"Outside the FLEA structure," Gordon clarified.

"Yes. Jason warned they'd have me under surveillance, wondering how much I knew. Sneaking off Earth to meet with Baron confirmed their worst fears. Someone followed me and tried to make my death appear as just one of those accidents that happen to unwary travelers."

After some silent eye communication around the room, Gordon's nod signaled acceptance and for Twobears to continue.

"Once vetted, tasks will be assigned according to capabilities and contacts. Some will look into the various deaths, political donations and anything else tied to the consortium. Others will quietly look at the consortium members themselves and their background. Kurzvall appears to be handling their interests on Earth. Today's botched attack will have all of them on guard and expecting us to retaliate. If we're lucky, our obvious digging will keep our covert operations below their notice."

"Me!" Clint's hand shot up. "I've always wanted to be covert."

His wife rolled her eyes. "You're a lot of things, dear, but *covert* isn't one of them."

"Uncle Clint," Erik's oldest daughter said, laughing with the others, "you couldn't stay undercover unless tied down or Aunt Susi was with you. Or she was the one doing the tying."

"Great idea, Stacy. What do you say, Susanita?" The laughter this time had Susi blushing as Clint put his arms around her shoulders. She wacked him lightly on the arm, but he only laughed and pulled her closer. Clint looked around. "Seeing as most everyone's here, I'd like to inform the family that Jane, Dane and their spouses are bad influences."

It took a moment before their oldest boy burst out with a disgusted "Oh hell, Dad. Mom. Aren't you two too old for…" he waved his hand in front of him "you know…"

Clint laughed. "I think you're old enough to use the word *sex*, Kevin. And no, you're never too old. Ask your grandparents."

Laughter and congratulations filled the room until—

"*TRIPLETS?*"

Clint grinned broadly at Andi's surprised screech. "They were *very* bad influences."

"Dr. Barnes is hesitant to say for positive, but it looks like it." Susi added, matching her husband's grin. "Don't know if he's being cautious or just doesn't want to freak us out yet."

"Regardless of the number, there are babies on the way," Clint said. He hugged his wife. "We're going to fix up Janice's old room as a nursery."

After letting the babble continue for several more minutes, Gordon lightly tapped on his desk for attention.

"We'll have several plans active in the coming months, and some of you may be asked occasionally for help. Nicholas will also be assigning extra security. Our home here is the most secure. If you have or suspect trouble—bad feelings, gut feelings, anything—you're to come here at once. The bastard has made a direct threat against our entire family and we've just seen how far he is willing to go. Take no chances. I want everyone to stay aware, stay safe."

He looked over at Clint and Susi. "Take every precaution."

The family clown vanished behind steel-eyed resolve as Clint tugged his wife closer. His chin dipped in acknowledgement.

There were a few more questions, comments, and ribbing. People began to gradually filter out of the room until Thane, his grandparents and mother, Nicholas and their two guests were the only ones left. Nicholas closed the door and went over to stare out a window.

"This will be our core planning group," Gordon said. "No one goes off half-cocked," he said, shooting Thane a stern look. "Or traipsing down some path of their own." This time the piercing look was aimed at Jem. "That includes you, too."

* * * * *

"Me?" Jem gave the older man an innocent, wide-eyed look.

"No more messing with Kurzvall or any of his businesses."

Jem blinked. Just how much had Thane shared? She turned to the Earth agent. "Out of curiosity, Mr. Twobears, how do you plan on vetting people on Earth from here?"

Twobears's lips twisted into a frown. "I have to get back to Earth. Somehow. Once I clear Thaxton and a few others, they can help with the rest as well as start investigating."

"I'll go with you. It's going to take both our personal experiences to convince Thaxton," Thane said, forestalling any arguments. "And you're not up to one hundred percent physically. But we can't take the *Lone Tracker*, not with all those flags on it.

Jem didn't like the idea of them going to Earth. From their expressions, neither did anyone else. But the truth was, everything they did now carried danger. "Then I'll be part of the covert team. I can snoop around the Consortium undetected, and bring information back."

"How?" Nicholas swung around. "How did you get past *our* sensors and guards?"

Jem exchanged a quick glance with Thane. He'd told her about having to update her story with a security prowess.

"It doesn't matter," Thane told him. "After all, Jem is on our side."

"The hell it doesn't." Nicholas didn't take his eyes off of Jem. "You got inside the Stohlass grounds…inside the house and all the way to my office. No alarms. No visuals—actual or electronic. Effortlessly and undetected until you walked through my door."

"You have excellent security, Mr. O'Daniel, and it wasn't entirely effortless. I doubt anyone else would make it. And, no, your communications aren't compromised. That was to keep you from questioning the note."

"I don't like unknowns. I don't like having a hole in my security. I want to know where it is before someone who isn't on our side finds and exploits it."

She bit her lip and then very carefully said, "It's more a method than a hole."

"What did you use to negate the sensors?"

Silence. The faces around her ranged from Nicholas's extreme irritation through concern to none—*must be his grandfather's lawyer face.* She stood up. "I'm sure you have a lot to discuss. It was nice meeting all of you." She walked toward the massive door.

"There's no need to go," Reyna said, rising to her feet. "We have plenty of room here."

Jem declined politely. Thane rose and accompanied her out of the room. Their walk to the gates was silent, reminding her of those last nights on Pappia. Jem swung around to face him as Thane signaled for them to be opened. "How did you know Boyd could contact me?"

"It was a guess." He looked away. "You trust him."

"It's not that I don't..." Jem sighed. Yes, it would look that way. She should have sent him word after deciding to keep her alias's postbox. It was prepaid for a whole Tardon year, about fourteen Earth months. "I'll send you my contact information. Why is your family so determined to go against Kurzvall?"

"Originally, it was disgust with him and his criminal tactics. That's putting it politely. Now, after today? You need to ask?"

Kurzvall had miscalculated badly when he targeted the Stohlass family. He wouldn't recognize that or stop. "Dougson was just the beginning. It will get even more dangerous."

"We're aware of that and will take precautions."

Would Mr. O'Daniel's measures be enough? "What if I ask you to stop?"

Thane shook his head. "It's no longer just about you, me, or my family. The whole situation has gotten bigger. Nastier. You've heard Twobears's story. So many compromised; so much betrayal and death. We cannot stand by and do nothing. This Consortium needs to be exposed. Stopped. Before anyone else is hurt or used," he added in a low voice.

She saw both guilt and regret in his eyes. It still bothered him that much? "Thane, what happened on Pappia wasn't your fault."

"I'm responsible for my actions."

"You were lied to. Duped. You need to stop beating yourself up over it."

"Like you've stopped blaming yourself for the deaths at Myerstone and of Old Man Petrov?"

Jem's back stiffened. "I'll be back tomorrow to exchange information. I can't stay for long. Thanks." She marched out the gate.

CHAPTER 23

Reyna stood inside the glass doors and watched her son star-gazing on the darkened terrace. Most people would see a young, interesting-looking man leaning against one of the columns, relaxed and enjoying the night. But she knew her son. Those crossed arms and veiled eyes hid a lot of tension.

She joined him. Studying the sky herself, she said, "It is a good night for sky watching." Embla was nearly a full disk and floated serenely high above the horizon.

"I never paid much attention to the night sky before," Thane said, not dropping his gaze. "It was just there, wherever there was. But after Random…I can't help *but* seeing it. It's beautiful. I can see why Jem is drawn to it."

Reyna laid her head on his shoulder. Together they watched Ask rise above the treetops. The waning, smaller moon was only a tiny sliver tonight. After a while, Reyna asked where Jem was staying.

"At one of the transit-hotels," Thane said. "Probably somewhere in the Circle."

"She doesn't trust easily, does she?"

"No." His gaze dropped to a fountain outlined by underwater lights. Its soft splashing was just barely audible. "I can't blame her with all she's gone through. After what I did."

Reyna straightened and smacked him in the arm. "You were working under false information. You didn't betray—"

"She saved my life, Mom. Three days later I'm leading her into an ambush *I* planned and orchestrated. I should have held them off longer. Done more checking."

"Is that something you would normally do?" she said tartly.

"No." Silence. "It didn't feel right." More silence. "But I still went along with them."

"Until you didn't." She poked his chest. "You realized something was wrong; *they* were wrong." She poked his chest again. "Then you acted." Her breath hitched. "You were almost killed."

Thane's arm came around her and she leaned into his warmth. Into his strength. She closed her eyes and enjoyed the moment. There was so much of his father in him. She could almost lie to herself and believe it was Greg holding her. Twenty years and she still missed him. What would Greg think of Agent Twobears?

Her eyes popped open. *Where did that come from?*

The fountain burbled quietly. Several lights along the building's length went out as others wisely went to bed. Her mother's instinct to offer comfort wouldn't let her do the same. His arm almost vibrated with held-in emotions.

"Jem sabotaged all those ion engines."

She barely contained a snort. The whole family had already come to that conclusion. "There doesn't appear to have been either harm or profit in her actions. She sought to punish a man she saw as otherwise untouchable. Revenge is in there also. Strong emotions can blind a person and lead to questionable choices."

"Like disposing of a body?"

So that was the problem. Wondering if he was sliding down a slippery slope. "Was the choice bad? Or was it the best one for the given situation?" She felt the heaviness in his mute silence. She turned to look up at him.

"Thane, you have a tendency to see things as black or white—which you certainly didn't get from me. But life is not always so clear cut. There's a lot of gray between those two extremes. Gray is...fluid. Gray is where decisions are more apt to be tempered by human factors than legalities. They can be as simple as telling a little white lie or as complex as the reasons surrounding that body and the need to hide it."

Her poke in the ribs this time got a scowl.

"What is it with women and finger poking?" Thane demanded.

"It gets your attention. Now. Aren't you keeping something—besides those engines—to yourself because revealing it would cause an adverse effect of some kind?"

His eyes slid sideways.

Aha! There was hope for him yet. She snuggled back against him. "If it'll make you feel better, I'm more than happy to hear your confession." Soft laughter brushed her ear and the arm around her relaxed somewhat. Well, it was a start. "Jem doesn't appear to be holding a grudge."

She felt, more than heard, his deep sigh.

Thane told her about their gate conversation. "I shouldn't have thrown those deaths in her face like that."

Her heart clenched at the regret his voice held. How much of her son's heart had this woman snagged? "Both of you need to let the past go," she said firmly. "Especially Jem. Keeping it all bottled inside, with no one to talk to or commiserate with? It's a wonder she hasn't become a neurotic mess or a jaded don't-give-a-shit. You want to make it up to her? Be her friend. Listen to her. Give her a sounding board."

She rose on her toes and kissed his cheek. "Then you talk to her in return. Get a few things off *your* chest." Giving his ribs one last poke, she headed off to bed.

Alone with the night, Thane returned his attention to the panorama spread above him.

CHAPTER 24

Thane strode into Nicholas's office. "You wanted to see me?"

The O'Daniel-sized chair didn't even whimper when the man leaned back. "Close the door and have a seat."

Thane's brow creased, but he did as asked.

"Yesterday, Mr. Stohlass's ear was about to be severed. Being on-point, I was the only one in position to fire. Before I could, there's a knife sticking out of the assailant's chest and Wilmont is crouched in a doorway off to our right. She then nails his partner between the eyes with a rock. That woman has a lethal arm. I almost didn't order her back outside."

Thane flashed a quick grin. "She does, doesn't she."

"Her actions retained our element of surprise, which we'd have lost when I fired my stunner. *But.*" He crossed his arms. "No one saw her follow us in, much less make it down the hallway and around to take a position on the other side of the room. Then she used the jetters' distraction to sneak away. The man I left guarding the vehicles didn't see her go. None of the security cameras in the surrounding area—I've reviewed dozens—show her. Wilmont was polite enough to make her presence known when she walked through the gate here to wait for our return. She ex-Special Forces or something?"

How about a special something? He knew where this was heading. His silence had Nicholas's face hardening.

"Fine. Being physically stealthy is one thing. What is this 'method' she uses to blind the cameras? Where did she get it and how does it work?"

"I can't tell you."

"The woman is an extremely high security risk."

"Not to us. Twobears can tell you—"

"Very little, and that's based on an expert's research. I read Jason Noble's file. He dug up some incredible stuff on everyone he investigated *except* Jem Wilmont. He even had your five-week liaison with Ginger Mayhern. No one in the family knew about it. I asked."

Thane winced. He could hear the ribbing now. He'd been young and horny; she wanted off the space dock. She'd dumped him as soon as the *Lone Tracker* landed on Coleman Two, a planet with lots of opportunities for ambitious people. Nicholas let him have a few moments for an embarrassed squirm before continuing.

"Wilmont is fixated on Kurzvall right now. That can change. Yes, she's helped you. But you hardly know the woman or what her long-term goals are."

"Do you think I would knowingly invite a danger here, to the family?" Thane said, his gaze steady. "I may not have known her long, and I don't know all her secrets, but I *know* her. I *know* she is not a threat to any of us." He leaned forward, face intense and his voice serious. "Jem Wilmont has a code of honor we should all be grateful for. She isn't racking up the greatest theft list in history. Or hit list. Which she could. Kurzvall has been a colossal pain in her butt for over two years, but he's still alive. Even Dougson died by someone else's hand.

"Jem Wilmont is a bartender or a waitress. A clerk or a stocker. She's worked in fields, mucked out stalls, and crewed on cargo ships. She lives on the wages she earns, keeps to herself, and works hard to avoid anyone's interest. Interest of those who'd see her only as a tool to use or a threat to eliminate. Her words."

He saw disgust flicker across Nicholas's face. Yeah, like Kurzvall.

"Despite that worry, she helps people. Yes, Jem's helped others besides me. I collected some interesting information while I was tracking her."

Nicholas's shoulders had gradually lost their stiffness as he talked. After a contemplative moment he said, "You trust her. Two hundred percent. No doubts."

"None."

"Do you trust *me*?"

"Yes." Thane hesitated. Trust had to go both ways and Nicholas was the head of their security. "There's a reason why I can't tell you what you want to know. Other factors are involved. None of them endanger the family. If it changes, I promise you'll be the first to know."

"I'll hold you to that."

"Jem's more worried about us than you are of her."

An eyebrow arched. "Why?"

"Your security people are now aware of her coming and going undetected. They could spread it, mention it to family or friends or the person on the next bar stool."

Nicholas leaned forward. "Knowledge she can breach our security undetected is in itself a security risk for us and a personal risk for her. I've already briefed *all* Stohlass employees to keep quiet. They are to inform me of anyone showing an inquisitive interest in her."

"Oh." Got it. Don't tell you your job.

"I'd like to see your Jem-info collection."

CHAPTER 25

Jem stood in the shadows not reached by the light filtering in through the high windows. She watched resignedly as two men stepped into the abandoned warehouse. She'd give them the option of refusing, but she didn't think they'd take it. Which was why she'd already sent for Thane and Lee Twobears.

"This is the right address, right?" Detective Kahn asked, his skepticism echoing in the emptiness.

"Yeah." Lieutenant Curtis replied, looking around. "If Manis wasn't in prison, I'd be worried."

"Got news, LT. I am worried."

Jem grinned. Kahn was a character. Snooping on his conversations had provided some amusing moments. "Thank you for coming, gentlemen."

Both men whirled around, hands automatically falling to their weapons. She moved forward enough they could see her, but still keep her features hidden. She'd reveal herself fully once she had their formal agreement.

"You said you had information about a very serious crime," Curtis said, loudly. Neither enforcer moved closer.

"What I am about to involve you in is deadly dangerous, more so than Manis ever was. But we need your help." As a colony, Tardon and its citizens had been beneath the Consortium's notice. As a newly fledged member, they didn't yet have a Federal Bureau of Investigation office established. They were unknowns.

Kahn sucked in a breath and pointed. "It's *her*."

No further identification was needed for their mysterious ally.

Curtis strode forward until he stood only a few feet away. "We owe you many times over. Whatever you need, you've got it," he said brusquely.

"We?" Kahn said, coming up beside him.

* * * * *

Thane sat in front of his nav console, arms crossed and half amused. It was a good thing the floor was metal, else Twobears would have worn a groove by now.

"Where are these guys? We've been here for hours," Twobears said, stopping in front of Thane.

The *Lone Tracker* had been sitting on Tardon Spaceport's long-term parking ramp since mid-day, according to the local clock.

"Patience." He would have thought a seasoned federal agent would have more. "They've undoubtedly waited until dark to avoid being seen."

"That was over an hour ago. Wilmont didn't tell you anything more? Like who they are or what they do?" Twobears resumed pacing.

While they were still trying to figure out how to sneak onto Earth, Jem had already made arrangements. Just as on Pappia, she was helping him even when pissed. Or hurt. *Maybe both*, Thane thought ruefully. She'd kept a stiff distance between them during their meeting the day after the attack, not giving him a chance to apologize for his words. Then poof; gone. Five days later, he'd received her message. Disbelief, exasperation, respect, and a twinge of embarrassment had been the dominant expressions when he read it to their group. His mom had been amused.

"No. She simply said two men on Tardon—Curtis and Kahn—would be able to get us to Earth safely. They could be cargo pilots or smugglers for all we know." Thane rubbed his nose. That wasn't a good example since cargo pilots often were smugglers.

Twobears made a grumpy noise. "She's probably worked with both."

Before Thane could voice an annoyed response, Thor informed them of a male approaching on foot. He ordered the monitoring video displayed on the main screen.

"Definitely headed here. Any weapons on the approaching male, Thor?"

"One standard stunner detected."

They took the stair rungs down to the lower deck. Twobears opened the hatch while Thane stood back, his own stunner held ready.

The man stepped into the plazo with his hands held out to his sides. "Baron and Twobears? Lieutenant Glen Curtis, Tallon LE. I was told I'd be expected."

Thane holstered his weapon as Twobears closed the hatch. "We weren't expecting an Enforcer. We were only told you and one other could get us to Earth incognito."

"Miss Wilmont gave me and my partner a summary of what you're facing. I briefed my commander who is fully onboard. Officially, Detective Kahn and I are being temporarily attached to an unnamed federal task force for classified undercover work. Which is true, in a roundabout way."

"You're going with us?" Twobears said.

"Kahn and I will be your support team. He is currently making the travel arrangements. We waited until your ship landed since we didn't know when you'd be arriving."

"Is she still here?" Thane asked. Maybe he could get in that apology.

"Hell if I know. She hasn't been seen since she handed us the largest cash card I've ever seen for expenses. Now, if we can sit down somewhere, I'll lay out the plan."

* * * * *

Twobears waited beneath a red oak tree. Director Thaxton was an old-fashioned jogger. Weather permitting, he'd jog in the woods surrounding his home instead of an exercise room. He was about to be waylaid. Baron and the others were spread out as security, ensuring they weren't disturbed or overheard.

So far, Jem's plan had gone exceedingly well.

Kahn had gone ahead first, to rent quarters and to pick up the two unnamed couriers arriving in a UPMS pod. They'd vetted and cleared the top four people on his list by the time Curtis joined them five days later. The two Tardon men made all their arrangements and purchases using their civilian IDs, keeping him and Baron completely anonymous.

Twobears shook his head, amazed all over again at what Wilmont had arranged. She'd make a great Federal asset. If it wasn't for all the uncertainty—his phone pinged softly.

Inbound.

He read Kahn's text with trepidation. Now for the hardest, most unpredictable part of their plan: getting Thaxton to believe the agency had traitors taking part in a large conspiracy.

A stocky, medium-sized man came into view. Shorts, sleeveless top and running shoes. No sweat stains yet, despite the man having already jogged almost a mile. He stepped out, arms held out to his sides. One hand held his badge up for easy identification. "Director Thaxton. I'm Special Agent Leroy Jamison Twobears, based out of Philadelphia. We need to talk."

Jogging in place, Thaxton eyed his badge. Then he studied Twobears for several moments. "Meet me in my office in two hours."

"I'd rather not. It's undoubtedly bugged by the FBI traitors who tried to kill me."

Thaxton stopped jogging.

CHAPTER 26

"I'm seriously considering adding dogs to our security measures."

"Think it'll help?" came Gordon's dry response from behind him.

Nicholas released a long sigh. Despite Thane's assurances, he still wanted to know how Wilmont was slipping through their security. There was the risk she could be forced—he scowled. A tool *and* a threat. No *or* about it. It just depended on which side of the seesaw you stood.

Wilmont had stayed long enough to answer LE questions about Dougson and Bullard, corroborate parts of Twobears's information, and provide new information of her own before disappearing as stealthily as she'd arrived. He and Andi had brainstormed several possibilities, but everything had a flaw. Nothing allowed for the complete invisibility Wilmont exercised. Even his genius fiancé was stumped. She'd thrown up her hands in exasperation, saying it was probably something so simple we were overlooking it.

Like what, for Odin's sake?

He and Stuart, his second-in-command, spent days turning their security procedures inside out, upside down and topsy-turvy. They looked at everything. Gaps in the security coverage? Missed steps in checklists? Bathroom breaks? The few minor holes found and corrected would not have allowed the woman to slip past both human and electronic surveillance.

Then he'd walked into his office this morning and there she was. Waiting to talk with him. Acting as if it were perfectly normal for her to pop in whenever she wanted. Gates locked. No alarms. No sightings and no forewarning. His back teeth ground together. *Hell, yes, dogs were being added.*

"How bad was yesterday's damage?" Gordon asked.

"Minimal," Nicholas told him, studying the grounds outside the window. Frelinghutens Security Kennel in Ord provided trained dogs. He'd contact them as soon as he got back to his office. "The new security steps we've implemented paid off and the guard caught it before it got very far."

The fire at the Stohlass Arcade in Swantown, a major seaport on the other side of Oslo, was the sixth in a series of fires at Stohlass properties. There'd also been vandalism, suspicious accidents, and one bomb scare in the two and half months since Dougson's attack. They had strengthened security, adding new sensors and additional guards.

"Where's Thane?" Gordon asked.

"Finishing up a job on Dakota Two. His message said he'd be back in six, seven days."

Certain they were being watched, the family maintained as much normalcy as possible. Appointments, meetings, shopping. Thane was on his second tracking job since their return from Tardon last month. Twobears was quietly investigating the Consortium's members and its ties from the Stohlass guest suite he was staying in. Thaxton and his volunteers were tackling their Earth tentacles.

"Jem?"

"Your wife *requested* her presence on her shopping trip." Nicholas grinned over his shoulder. "From the look in her eyes, I'd say Wilmont is currently under-going an interrogation."

"How sure are we," Gordon said, "Kurzvall is behind these events? Some yes, but all of them? Branson facilities have also experienced a few incidents, although theirs have all been minor. So far."

Nicholas turned, shifting into alert at Gordon's unfocused expression. That and the gentle pencil tapping signaled his employer's brain was doing some serious work. "It would be an awful big coincidence if not. You think one of your competitors might be taking advantage of the situation?"

Gordon nodded.

"They'd have to be aware of the situation or, at least, of tensions between the Stohlass family, Kurzvall and this Consortium. I haven't blabbed," he said in an amused tone, "have you?"

"Specifics wouldn't be needed after the first few incidents. It's obvious we're having problems with someone, starting with Dougson's attack."

"I'm thinking these are diversion tactics, keeping us from concentrating on Kurzvall and whatever he's up to," Nicholas said. "We know he's stalking Thane. He could have easily hired someone from the Circle to keep us engaged here."

"Logical. Some incidents may very well have been, especially the initial ones. Still," he waved his hands at the comp terminal and papers on his desk. "It's the number of strikes...the escalation...it all seems more than just opportunistic kicks in the ass. For Kurzvall? It just doesn't feel right."

"Why?" *Just what they didn't need.*

"Because it screams to Embla someone's targeting us," Gordon said in exasperation. "The authorities have been alerted and are actively investigating it themselves. If we pointed a finger at Kurzvall now, they would take a hard look at him. It would bring Dougson's actions, his employment and convenient firing back into question. It would put a spotlight on Kurzvall and his activities I doubt the man wants. He would be more likely to wait, biding his time. His next strike will be subtle. Something that couldn't even remotely be traced back to him."

Nicholas considered Gordon's points and decided his boss was probably right. He settled into one of the deep chairs in front of the desk. Pulling out his notepad he keyed it on. "You think Branson or someone aligned with them?"

"One of the younger ones if it is, in retaliation for our supposed attacks. Maybe also someone just trying to strike back at us for some perceived slight."

"I'll check into employees—current and ex—that have had disciplinary issues or excessive complaints in the last year."

"Better make it two."

Nicholas nodded and made the note. "Who else, business or personal?"

They'd just started discussing potential suspects when Gordon's phone went off. By the time he raised it to his ear, Nicholas's phone had also gone off, its emergency tone signaling frantically. Gordon was already out the library door by the time Nicholas heard his own message about Gwen's car going over Nelson's Point. They hit the front door together.

CHAPTER 27

Welcome to Toulouse, Palmyra Two.

"The single source for all your mercenary needs," Jem muttered as she passed under the large sign and into the spaceport's main concourse. She slowed. Edgy. Uncomfortable. Did Kurzvall have flags here? Was a port employee already composing a quick message to Hebros? The other disembarking passengers funneled around her, eager to be somewhere else.

She limped slowly past the various shops, scanning right. Then left. Pretending to study something in a window, she scanned behind her then ahead. No sign of interest in her. *Yay.* She continued down the concourse. She'd left Midgard on a ticket, smiling politely at the steward as she boarded the passenger liner. Traveling this way was risky, but the best option under the circumstances. With an open accident investigation, leaving Midgard in the normal way was for the best.

Accident, her foot.

That truck had deliberately rammed them, crushing in Gwen's side of the vehicle. Everything had happened so fast. The pain and disorientation as she was flung around. When Gwen slammed into her, she'd instinctively wrapped her arms around her and shifted. As soon as the car passed them, she'd released the shift and they'd slammed into the ground. Fifteen feet from a cliff edge.

All eyes had been on the tumbling car, so no one noticed them popping into view. Everyone assumed they'd been thrown clear of the vehicle. Gwen had been in pain and too disorientated to remember anything different. *Thank you, Universe.*

A guy came rushing past her, yelling into his phone. His bag slammed into her leg. *Ow, ow, shit, damn, crap.* She collapsed against a pillar, pain pulsing from hip to knee. She didn't want to complain. Well, okay, maybe she could a little. But a bruised leg and hip socket, scraped cheek, and a headache were worth saving Thane's grandmother.

She'd been on her way here. A rumor, a small whiff of a rumor, indicated Kurzvall might have more ties on Palmyra Two than just Branigan. Made sense. Hire one merc, hire another. They were disposable short-term fixes. Her decision to stop in and update the family first had saved the Stohlass family and Midgard from losing a wonderful woman.

Okay. Hip was quiet. She looked around for a sign. *Exit.* That way.

Jem pushed herself up only to jerk back as a man stepped in front of her. *Tall, bald, stunner on hip. Steely eyed.* His Port Security patch didn't necessarily equal safety.

"I grabbed the idiot before he got far and turned his ears red. He sends his apology. Are you all right?" he asked. His eyes flicked from her leg to her scabbed cheek.

She smiled, maintaining an arm's-length distance. "Yes, thank you. The injuries are from a vehicular accident. My hip got the worst of it. The idiot just irritated it."

"Uh-huh. Do you need it checked? We have an excellent medical system."

She just bet they did. Did mercenaries have health plans? "No need, but could you recommend a good hotel? Preferably one with an in-house dining room?" She tapped her leg. "Saves the walking."

The concerned guard not only gave her directions, he called a taxi and helped her out to it. After it deposited her at the hotel, she promptly called another and went elsewhere.

CHAPTER 28

The Azusa Branson Hotel Complex was the shining star in the Branson's family empire. Its marbled stone and polished steel grandeur soared eighteen floors above the small peninsula it dominated. A glass-dome-covered restaurant on the rooftop provided the finest quality in dining surrounded by a panoramic view of sea and stars. Lush gardens filled the spaces between the four two-story wings with walkways, fountains, statuary and benches. Their matching domes and rooftops provided extensions to the main hotel itself.

The South Wing's dome shielded another lush garden, enjoyable in any weather. The East Wing was a highly regarded museum, its dome protecting the various artistic endeavors spilling over from the displays throughout it. The North Wing's dome protected two pools, landscaped as if they'd been sculpted from nature. One simulated a hot spring, the other a waterfall-fed grotto.

The West Wing was an entertainment arcade, filled with games and entertainments of all kinds and for all ages. Its unprotected rooftop held various rides, mostly for the young or those pretending to be. Half of its first floor was a theater resembling the interior of a large drone ship. It provided a tour of the Republic's diversity: cities, farms, jungles, a frozen waterfall three miles high, a nebula, or the colorful rings around a gas giant. The ever-changing simulations assured the managers of many repeat "passengers."

The movable walls of the North and South Wings' interior floors provided variable-sized spaces as needed. They had been transformed into everything from a formal ballroom to a child's birthday party. The staff's favorite so far had been the come-as-an-alien party the Azusa University's Anthropology department had thrown. With no known examples to go by, the concepts had been pretty diverse. A panel of Anthropology professors had awarded two prizes: one for the most feasible and one for the most creative but highly unlikely.

The Southwest Garden, situated between its two named wings, was hosting an old-fashioned wedding. The minister's voice was raised slightly, blending with the rainfall patter from the fountain at his back. The couple recited their traditional vows, then faced each other to give their individual pledges. She promised to overlook his absentmindedness. He promised to always be on time when it counted. With a final blessing and a broad smile, they were pronounced husband and wife.

Turning, their arms around each other, they smiled at family and friends.

People laughed and waved and mingled. Some approached the couple to give their congratulations. Others began moving toward the open doorways and the feast inside.

The first explosions shook the ground, hurling debris and people. The South Wing shuddered, then crumpled inward as more explosions sent flames leaping out windows and tearing through walls. The inferno raged, swatting away the streams of retardant desperate firemen attacked it with. Flaming fingers of red-gold lashed the blackened structure, finding handholds in exploding glass and cracking marble as it climbed the main structure.

Sounds. Images. All burned into the memories of those who stood and gaped in horror.

It was the screams that would haunt them.

* * * * *

"*How* many? And the *entire* Branson family? Five generations just...*gone*?"

The Stohlass family had packed the library waiting for news. When it came, Gwen's horror-filled voice spoke for everyone.

"Stephanie and I attended the same luncheon just last week. She was showing pictures of her baby. Ch-Charo just turned eight months old." Reyna's voice broke.

Thane gathered his mother into his arms. She buried her face in his shoulder and wept.

CHAPTER 29

"Lieutenant John Lundgren and Detective Coby Goldstein," the House Steward announced, escorting the two men into Gordon's library.

"Thank you for seeing us, Mr. Stohlass. Could you ask your grandson to join us?" Lieutenant Lundgren asked.

"Which one?"

"Thane Baron. And your Head of Security if he's available."

Gordon eyed the two Law Enforcers settling across from him. "Van, would you ask Thane and Nicholas to join us?" he asked their escort.

They waited in silence. Gordon bit his lip at the slight widening of their eyes when Nicholas arrived and took up his favorite position near a window. His height was definitely an eye opener.

The lieutenant checked his phone, sending a brief text reply to whatever the message had been. Several minutes later Thane strode in, dirt and sweat staining his clothes.

"Sorry, I was working at the back gate," he said. He plopped down in the seat beside his grandfather's desk.

Gordon winced. "You better hope that's cleaned before your grandmother sees it."

"From what Van told me I thought it best to skip the shower. What's going on, Granddad?"

"I'm sure these men are about to tell us." He introduced the two Enforcers.

Lundgren inclined his head. "My partner and I have been assigned as task leads for the investigation into the fire occurring at the Branson Hotel Complex sixteen days ago."

Gordon gave a brief nod. "You're Arson Division."

"Homicide."

Thane leaned forward, his eyes hard. "Whoever did this *should* be considered a murderer. A mass murderer. We heard the whole wing went at once. No one had a chance to get out."

"Actually, that was the intent," Detective Goldstein said grimly.

There were several seconds of startled silence. "Someone *intended* to kill three hundred people?" Gordon said, incredulously.

"No. The intended count was about four hundred," Goldstein said. "The minister for the Swatch-Jones wedding was late, caught up in a construction detour. Because of that delay, most of the wedding party was still outside instead of inside at the reception. Add that to those unlucky enough to be in the rooftop garden or nearby..." He didn't need to finish.

"The initial explosions were set at all the South Wing exit points and stairwells," Lundgren said, "collapsing them and triggering the fire suppression system. The lucky ones died in those first moments," he added quietly. Grim faced, he told them the retardant released was heavily infused with a flammable liquid that had been tapped into the system. "The next set of detonations lit it up."

Thane recoiled backwards.

Gordon whispered *My God.* His mouth opened, closed. He just couldn't process that concept. "You're positive?" he finally managed to ask.

"Confirmed by Captain Steven Lloyd, head of the Arson Division. The whole wing was engulfed well before the Fire Department arrived, despite it only being three blocks away. Flaming debris took out everything around it. Emergency doors activated on the first explosions and sealed all the wings from the main building. Even then, they were lucky to keep it contained as much as they did."

Everyone had seen the burned and blackened ruin, either in newscasts or in person. The South Wing was nothing but piles of ash and discolored stone. The West Wing, without a dome to help protect it, was twisted metal and cracked marble. The main hotel itself was a blackened, cracked shell. The other two wings were singed and discolored but their contents intact: small victories in a lost war.

"Only the South Wing's fire suppression system was contaminated or it would have been a lot worse. The West Wing lasted long enough for most of them to get out through exits. Everyone in the main complex got out safely except for some minor injuries and smoke inhalation. This was a deliberately cruel act," Lundgren said, anger sparking in his eyes. "Every law enforcement officer is dedicated to bringing the persons responsible for this to justice."

Gordon nodded. "I can't agree with you more. How can we help?"

"We've looked at a pay-up-or-expect-same extortion angle for other businesses but can't find any evidence supporting it. Not even a rumor. So, excluding a bat-crazy firebug—"

"And hoping it's not," Goldstein interjected.

"—a South Wing group was the specific target. We're going on the surmise of a group as a whole because this doesn't make sense for just one or two individuals."

Gordon felt they all agreed with Thane's mutter of "It doesn't make any sense." He also briefly wondered why they wanted Thane and Nicholas here.

"We are currently gathering information," Lundgren continued, "from prominent members in the same business and social circles as the victims. The dates for each group's events weren't secret and the entire building fairly open, which made planning and preparation simple. We believe the reason the whole wing was taken out was because it would be impossible to predict who might be where at zero hour. Bathroom breaks and such."

Gordon wrestled with that horrible theory as the enforcers keyed on their hand comps. What kind of psychopathic monster was out there?

"Did you know anyone in the Swatch or Jones families?" Lundgren asked. "Their wedding reception was on the first floor."

Gordon didn't have to think about it. He'd done nothing but since the long list of names had been released. "I didn't know the Jones in any manner and none of the Swatch family personally. Gwen and I did follow Jason Swatch's campaign last year to keep his Representative seat—the opposition fought a hard battle. I spoke briefly with him at a fundraiser and shook his hand. I heard it was his nephew's wedding."

"How did the loser take it?"

Gordon shrugged. "Unhappily, of course. He spent a lot of his own money financing it. I hear he's now gathering support and making plans for a run at Oslo's governorship."

Lundgren made a note. "The Lace and Garters Club? They were holding elections and dinner, also on the first floor."

A weary sound escaped Gordon and he nodded slowly. "I knew a good half of them, either professionally or personally. It's hard to believe so many gone in a single stroke. Gwen and I were invited to join several times but we just weren't interested."

"Any of them have enemies that you know of?"

"A number of them had family or business frictions. It would be best if you talked with the individual families for details. The only one I can speak of with any surety on is the Andersons. They are—were—in a heated land dispute with their neighbors. Powerful, ambitious people always end up with enemies, Lieutenant. It's difficult to believe someone would kill so many just to get a few for…what? I can't think of anything or anyone so deserving of this." Gordon gave a quick shake of his head. "This goes beyond vicious and well into monstrous."

"I couldn't agree more. Last group was the Branson family reunion. They had the entire second floor. Their family business, Branson Hotels and Entertainment, and yours, Stohlass Enterprises, go back for several decades. What can you tell me about them?"

"Charles Stanford Branson, the current CEO, and I had known each other for most of our lives. We met at college and ran wild together for a few years. We even chased some of the same women. Until I met Gwen, that is." The memory brought a brief smile to his face. "We married and he went into the family business, which was simply Branson Hotels at the time."

Lundgren scrolled down his notes. "He was third generation."

"Yes. His grandfather started it after immigrating to Midgard from, let's see, the Kettleman System I believe."

"He considered you an upstart."

Which snooty member of Branson's social circle said that? Probably with a malicious sneer or sniff, depending on gender. "So was his grandfather at one time. People like Charles Branson forget their family had to start out somewhere."

Lundgren looked up. When his gaze connected with Gordon's, there was a shrewdness in them he hadn't seen earlier. His instincts went on high alert.

"It was Charles Branson who convinced his father, the CEO at the time, to branch out into the entertainment field," Lundgren said. "It was about a year after you and your wife started Stohlass Arcades, the original name of your company. Your two businesses have been major competitors since."

Information gathering had just turned into an interrogation.

Gordon was annoyed with himself. He should have expected this, especially once the gossip started. They needed to find out who started those wild-ass rumors. This was the real reason for their visit. All the previous questions had been a blind, set to relax and catch them off guard. It was a courtroom tactic he'd used himself. Thane's crossed arms and Nicholas's slight shift indicated they also understood the change and their presence: they were next.

"You can take the gloves off now, gentlemen. I realize your job is to investigate all avenues, all possibilities. This one is a dead end, no pun intended."

"Gloves?" Lundgren's voice was still casual, but the watchfulness in his eyes was unmistakable.

Gordon snorted. "I've been practicing law since your father was in diapers, Lieutenant. I know an interrogation when I hear it and I'd fire any intern who missed the implication."

The two enforcers exchanged brief looks.

"Would you say the competition has been antagonistic at times?" Lundgren asked.

"Yes."

"An antagonism starting with your engagement to Gwendolyn Holmes Williams?"

"It started as soon as it became evident Logan Hagg Williams's daughter was more interested in a tree-harvester's son than someone from their fathers' club," Gordon said bluntly.

Lundgren grunted; Goldstein made a note entry.

"You spent your wedding night at one hospital and Branson at another after what witnesses described as a vicious fight after the wedding reception."

Thane cranked his neck around. "How come I've never heard that one?"

"Ask your grandmother," Gordon snapped. "He was a drunk wedding crasher. I refrained from returning the favor, drunk or sober, when he married Victoria Peterson Allman eighteen months later."

Thane grinned at him. "Bet Grandmother wouldn't let you."

Lundgren cocked his head. "The antagonism between your two families has continued in one form or another over the years. There were verbal exchanges during business or social events, insinuations and outright accusations in the press. Things of that nature. A number of these instances could be viewed as harassment. There were even a couple of court cases."

"If you'd bother checking, you'll find those totally false and/or ridiculous charges were always instigated by someone on their side and why they always lost."

"Thane." Gordon shot his grandson a warning glance. "Charles Branson was a shrewd businessman with the drive to shoot for the gold ball and an ego that absolutely hated losing at anything. As both companies grew and expanded, it was natural for our business arenas to overlap. Competition and some confrontations were inevitable."

"Confrontations," Lundgren repeated. "Yes, you had your share. So have a few among the younger generations. Some of them recent." He looked pointedly at Thane.

This time it was Gordon cranking his neck around. "Who?"

"Jeremy Branson, James and Gena's oldest," Thane muttered. "He's an asshole."

"He was being groomed as Branson's new CEO and made no secret about his plans to expand their company even further into the entertainment arena. Your area of expertise," Goldstein said.

Two identical shrugs were the only response.

"Then there's the recent problems your family and business have experienced," Lundgren resumed, his gaze shifting between the two men.

"There was an attempted kidnapping almost four months ago. It was followed by approximately three months of fires, vandalisms, and sabotage at various Stohlass properties."

"Branson properties also experienced a few incidents themselves during this same time period. Mostly minor," Goldstein added, "except for another fire a week prior to the big one."

Lundgren tapped his hand comp. "The number of injuries and scale of damage increased, culminating in a fatal accident three weeks before the fire. Your wife's driver was killed. She and a companion were thrown clear before it went over Nelson's Point and her broken arm was their single worst injury. From witness accounts and available evidence, it appears the truck driver—still missing—deliberately rammed their vehicle. Rumor has it the Branson family was considered at the top of your suspect list."

"Initially, yes," Gordon agreed. "They are our major competitor. They could have been behind some of those occurrences. But the number and sheer obviousness dropped them to the bottom of our list, even before the attack on my wife. I also couldn't see them ordering it. We are actively researching and investigating a number of avenues concerning those issues. Once we obtain sufficient evidence indicating who is responsible for our problems, it will be brought to the proper authorities' attention," he promised them.

Nicholas moved away from the window, drawing a wary glance from both Enforcers. He leaned against a bookcase.

"Approximately six days before the fire, there was another confrontation. Your daughter, Reyna Stohlass, and Charles Branson's granddaughter, Stephanie Branson, had a heated push-and-shove at a business luncheon." Lundgren scrolled down his notes. "Among other things your daughter said, and I quote: 'You think you're better than us? Not hardly, not ever. You and your family will be nothing.'" He looked up.

"Very convenient," Thane said. "Someone just happened to record it?"

"Harold Anderson, a luncheon attendee, has an eidetic memory. His parents were members of the L and G club. Ah, you might want to avoid the Anderson family for a while."

Gordon didn't bother hiding his annoyance. "Yes, Reyna mentioned seeing Stephanie there. No, she didn't mention the argument. But then, it wasn't unusual. Stephanie has—had—Charles Branson's drive and ego."

Thane snorted. "Genetic, since she wasn't the only one."

"If the event you're describing only included pushing and shoving, gentlemen, I seriously doubt my daughter was involved."

Lundgren tilted his head. "You disagree with Mr. Anderson?"

"No. I don't doubt he overheard that particular conversation. Did he supply the push-and-shove addendum?"

Both men checked their notes. "Um, no."

"Who did?"

"Not important."

"I disagree, Lieutenant, since it calls into question the attitude and memory of whoever you interviewed. If my daughter was involved in a physical altercation, it wouldn't be a pushy shove. It would be a pushy right-cross." Gordon smirked. "Gwen taught it to all the girls."

The Enforcers blinked and shared a look. Goldstein made a few more notes.

"What Anderson overheard was Reyna referring to plans we are drawing up and, yes, it is partially in response to their expansion. We discarded the genocide option," Gordon said dryly. "If you check with my management team, you'll find our plans included expanding Stohlass Enterprises outside the Wotan System. We were also looking forward to moving into *their* area of expertise: hotels."

"Shouldn't have much trouble now," Goldstein said, his lip curling slightly. "With BH&E's collapse, you'll be able to take over their existing hotels at minimum cost."

"Thane. Sit."

Gordon didn't raise his voice, but the steel in it had Thane dropping back into his seat. His grandson was going to end up arrested if he couldn't temper the furious promise in that blazing glare. Considering the direction the Enforcers were heading, he had to throttle down his own anger.

"I dislike repeating myself, Lieutenant, Detective, but considering the seriousness of your insinuations I'll make an exception. Listen carefully." It was the ice-cold, lie-ripping, alibi-stomping lawyer who folded his hands on his desk and leaned forward to pin two seasoned enforcers to their chairs with a fierce stare.

"We *did not* and still *do not* have evidence identifying the perpetrators behind Stohlass Enterprises's recent troubles. If it *had* been a Branson family member, or associate, and we had ascertained irrefutable *proof* of their complicity, we would *not* take action on our own and certainly *not* to such a heinous level."

"What about your kidnapping-assault? Three dead, right?" Lundgren tapped his comp lightly against his leg. "Wouldn't that count as taking action in your own hands? Especially since Law Enforcement wasn't alerted until afterwards?"

"Things moved too fast." Nicholas said, drawing their attention. "As it was, we were just barely in time to prevent two of them from torturing Mr. Stohlass."

"And the dead?" Goldstein asked.

"Two died from wounds received during the fighting. Dougson, the ringleader, died from a shot fired by an unknown sniper from the surrounding trees after we captured him. We assume it was to prevent him from being interrogated. My second-in-command was talking to your people when it happened."

"We've reviewed the recordings of that call. Analysis confirms one of the background noises is a high-velocity laser bolt, probably military issue," Lundgren admitted.

Goldstein looked up from his notes. "The burn angle through Artemis Dougson's head indicated it came from a point higher than him. Like a tree or …"

Thane rolled his eyes when both Enforcers looked over at Nicholas. "Really?"

Nicholas's gaze stayed steady. "I was still inside the building when it happened."

"According to your people."

"And a Federal Bureau of Investigation agent. Unless you think he lied too?"

"Would he?" Lundgren countered brusquely. "Perhaps in gratitude for whatever mess Baron fished him out of? Agent Twobears's first stop after arrival on Baron's personal ship was a thirty-eight hour stay at a medical facility. Their records cataloged three broken ribs, a fractured hip and thigh, a broken wrist, a deep scalp gash and a concussion. So many contusions, they were simply listed as 'numerous all over.'

Gordon cleared his throat loudly before Thane could reply. He still didn't trust that hot gaze. "I'll admit to being angry with Dougson." He ignored the muffled cough on his left. "But we certainly did not want him dead. Very much the opposite. We needed all the information we could get from him and were hoping to persuade him to turn on his employer. So, gentlemen, I will state categorically again no one in our family or in our employ would even think of doing something as barbaric as burning down a hotel and killing hundreds of people. Ever."

"People who wouldn't do something barbaric," Goldstein said blandly, "often find someone who will." Both Enforcers shifted and locked eyes with Thane. "Know anybody who would?"

* * * * *

Thane returned his stare. "I'm a Tracker, Detective. I've crossed paths with a lot of different types during the course of my work."

"Yes, I'm sure you have."

Thane kept his gaze steady. The Enforcer was watching him like a territorial hawk. "If you've got someone in mind, spit it out." He pretty much knew who they did.

"Jem Seaborne Wilmont of Sol has an interesting history. What we can find of it," Goldstein said. "She's been drifting since graduating public school. She pops up here and there, works briefly at some low-level job and leaves with little to no notice. You crossed paths with her about fifteen, sixteen months ago on Pappia, a moon mining colony in the Latvia system."

"So?"

"What do you know about her?"

181

"She pours a mean glass of Aspric whisky, has a great sense of humor and fascinating eyes. Oh, yeah, she has an unusual method for eating large salads."

"We'll update our notes," Lundgren deadpanned. "What we find interesting is the high ratio of unsolved murders, freak accidents—especially engine malfunctions—and other unexplained events occurring when she's in an area. You, yourself, were on Pappia when a power node that passed a safety inspection just one week prior exploded for an undetermined reason, resulting in a tunnel collapse and the deaths of over a dozen people."

"Is that high ratio across the board for everywhere she's been?" his granddad asked, arching an eyebrow regally.

Lundgren grunted. "We haven't been able to completely track all her movements."

Thane let his smirk out. *Yep, know that feeling.*

"Don't you think, as a drifter, the odds of Miss Wilmont being in a wrong-place-wrong-time scenario are higher?" Gordon asked. "And sometimes there is no explanation for something other than 'it happened.'"

"Mining is a notoriously dangerous business," Thane said. "Especially in places like Pappia, where dirt and other contaminants are constantly blowing into everything. Maybe the power node just didn't get properly sealed. Yes, detectives, I met Jem on Pappia. We shared a couple of dinners while I waited for a contact. She did me a good turn while I was there so I invited her to come visit when she got the chance. Which she did."

"At what could only be called a fortuitous time," the lieutenant said.

"Not really. She was shadowing Dougson." He shouldn't have said that.

Lundgren's eyes sharpened. "She knew about the upcoming attack and didn't warn you?"

"She only knew he was up to something but not what. She did come to warn us he was here, but it was too late. Granddad and I had already left after receiving a bogus note." He watched the two men do another silent eye exchange. Yep, he'd left out a lot.

"Don't your out-of-town guests usually stay here at your house?" Goldstein asked.

"Usually. Didn't know she was in town until the attack."

"And after you did?"

"We offered; she turned it down."

"She turned down a plush guest suite, here, for a Port Circle transit hotel?"

"Yes." Not good. They were already tracking her.

"Why?"

Thane shrugged. "You'll have to ask her."

"Could it be Wilmont was uncomfortable with anyone knowing her whereabouts?" Goldstein said. "She constantly changed her location, usually to a different place each night."

Gordon held up a finger. "That's conjecture," he stated firmly. "But probably accurate, though not for the reason you're implying. A young woman, alone, should be cautious. After all, Port Circles can be rough, dangerous places." He gave them his courtroom smile. "Hence the murders and 'other events' you've mentioned."

"Uh-huh. What good turn did she perform on Pappia?" Lundgren asked Thane.

"Personal. No bearing on current events."

"Personal, hmmm…life-saving perhaps?"

He shrugged again. Petty, yeah, but it irritated the lieutenant.

Lundgren switched his attention to Nicholas. "Mr. O'Daniel, the official report on the kidnapping-slash-assault attempt is incomplete."

Nicholas cocked his head and waited, as quickly shifting subjects was a standard interrogation technique.

"Illegal laz-guns, brass knuckles, a knife and even a bolo were confiscated from the assailants. Your people only carried standard stunners. One man's concussion was matched to a bloody rock. Did you hit him with it?"

"If I had, the guy wouldn't just have a concussion. Someone else improvised."

Thane saw the quick flash of amusement on Goldstein's face. *Yeah, kind of obvious.*

"Analysis eliminated the knife in custody," Lundgren continued, "as too narrow and short a blade to have inflicted one of the fatal wounds. Who had a large knife?"

"I'll ask around," Nicholas replied. "But everyone was focused on their own immediate situation during the fight."

"Wilmont was there, but not when the jetters arrived," Lundgren pressed on.

"Yes, she insisted on accompanying us to the site. Being a civilian, I ordered her to stay outside. She left after the fight was over and met us back here."

Thane knew Nicholas's people had done the same sidestep when questioned. *At least they can't get them for lying.* So far. And as long as they weren't asked certain specific questions. Yes, Jem's history would be interesting to any law enforcer, making her a prime suspect for a lot of things. They were just doing their job. They'd find nothing in her background indicating she could do something like the Branson Fire. Okay, fine. He could be reasonable.

"I understand your suspicions—I had them once. But Jem is exactly like she seems: a direct, unpretentious person who prefers a simple, quiet life. Like drifting. She works at undemanding jobs because she won't be there long. She usually just lives off what she makes or accumulates on her cash card. I understand she banked most of an inheritance from her parents and grandmother and only draws on it if she needs to."

Lundgren leaned back and gave him an incredulous stare. "Her bank account on Earth is more than Goldstein or I combined will ever see, most of which was deposited long after her inheritances were. It has been untouched for several years, except for a quarterly interest that would fund our department for a year. And that's one hell of a cash card because she used it to buy off the last eight months' worth of her EMC contract. Shortly after the Pappia incident I mentioned, no less. Those bartender jobs must pay a lot better than when I was working my way through college."

Screw reasonable. "Maybe she got some good tips. Maybe she's a lucky gambler. And maybe she didn't want to spend another eight months on a dark dust ball that—" Thane ground to a stop when his grandfather pressed hard on his arm.

"Bottom line, gentlemen, before I let Thane demonstrate his impressive collection of curses."

Lundgren's questions came fast and sharp.

"Was the attack on your wife the final straw? Did you believe Charles Branson's bitter antagonism had turned into hate? Did you believe his family's harassment against yours would continue to escalate? Did you take steps to protect them? To end it, once and for all?"

Gordon's eyebrows drew a hard line over a frigid mask, the furrows above it deepening with each insult. "I'd like to express my resentment, to a degree you can't imagine, for the implication—no, the outright accusation I or some member of my family is capable of condoning, much less participating in a barbaric event of this magnitude."

The tension crackling in the room would jumpstart a dynamo.

Lundgren aimed his next question at Thane. "Was having an acquaintance with a certain reputation available just too tempting?"

"Just what would that reputation be, Lieutenant?" Thane asked coldly.

"Jem Wilmont is suspected of being an accomplished assassin with an unprecedented skill for slipping past security systems and staying under Enforcement's radar. The perfect specialist with the perfect skill set needed to set up the Branson Hotel Complex job. Perhaps she approached you and made the offer. Perhaps even pro bono, seeing as how you are friends and she was nearly killed herself."

Goldstein looked up from his notepad. "We've also received evidence linking her to several other items of interest besides the mine explosion on Pappia. Specifically, a shuttle crash on Delmark Three and a lab explosion on Earth."

Degenerate-spash-of-a-disease-ridden-bastard. Kurzvall. Had to have been him. Thane's stomach curled into a hard knot. A setup. Just like on Random Two. Truth, lies and circumstances all fused together.

"Do you know where she is now?" Lundgren asked.

"No," Thane snapped. "Jem left Midgard shortly after the attempt on my grandmother. She didn't leave an itinerary."

"She came back."

"What?"

"She checked into Half Moon Rentals nine days before the fire, paying for two weeks in advance."

Thane blinked, drew back. He glanced at this grandfather, saw the slight head shake. Okay, Granddad hadn't known either.

"Fortunately for us," Lundgren continued, "the Branson Hotel's backup surveillance was kept off-site at their corporate headquarters. Records show Wilmont entering and roaming the Complex over the course of several days. Last one was on the evening before the fire. She hasn't been seen since. We're expanding our search to all establishments outside the Port Circle. She may also be staying at a private residence."

"She's not here, Lieutenant, if that was a poke," Gordon said. "And since I'm not feeling generous, you'll need a search warrant to ascertain it for yourselves."

"It was served shortly after we arrived." Neither Enforcer noticed Nicholas's reaction. "We thought to expedite matters by having them start the search while we talked."

"As Head of Security, it should have been presented to *me*."

Seven feet of pissed-off anger was suddenly very noticeable.

"It was presented to your second and Ms. Williams since both of you were occupied with us," Lundgren said warily.

"Who must have been prevented from appraising me of the situation."

Thane could have warmed his hands on the heat plume rising off Nicholas.

"Search away, Enforcers. When finished, you will apologize to my Security Chief for circumventing him," Gordon said.

"I am not apologizing for doing my job," Lundgren snapped.

Thane crossed his arms and scowled at the enforcers. "She's not on Midgard."

"Are you sure about that?" Goldstein asked.

"Someone has been impersonating Jem," Gordon said. "I don't know who is feeding you all this...this...bullshit, but my grandson is right. If Jem Wilmont was on Midgard, she would have contacted us. We can't contact her. She is assisting us in exposing who is targeting our family and business interests. We believe the root of our problems is external to Midgard, so she went to investigate. I don't micromanage. She will contact us when she has something worthwhile to report."

Gordon refolded his hands on his desk. "Have you interpreted your evidence correctly? Have you failed to consider all possibilities?"

Lundgren's face took on a cautious look. "Meaning?"

"If she was indeed this supposedly experienced assassin, with this supposedly given skill, don't you think she would make damn sure she *wasn't* seen anywhere in the vicinity of Midgard before, during, or after an attack sure to garner a veritable avalanche of attention due to its atrocity? For any incident she might instigate, for that matter, as it might raise questions by suspicious-minded Enforcers?" He gave them a bland smile. "Just because someone happens to be in the same general area at the same time doesn't automatically mean they're responsible."

"Maybe," Lundgren grudgingly replied, "but when that same person keeps popping up at similar incidents, one has to ask questions."

"Then ask questions, don't accuse," Gordon replied, his tone biting. "Work with facts, not anonymous rumors, tips, or spiteful insinuations. Look for the truth regardless of the effort, not a quick and easy scapegoat."

Lundgren turned off his comp with a sharp jab. Stood. His partner followed suit. "Keep us informed of any contact with Miss Wilmont. We'll be posting a system-wide warrant for her as wanted for questioning in the Branson Complex Fire."

"Then you've already made your minds up." Thane didn't know which emotion was stronger: anger or worry. "When you were checking out Jem's movements, did you look at everything or only those items supporting your interests? Or were pointed out to you by someone—most likely anonymously? I suggest you go back and check again, starting with Sagious One, Malver Two and Minos Four. And Tardon," he added after a brief hesitation. They had intended to keep that link quiet, but the testimony offered by an entire city of Law Enforcers would be her strongest.

Lundgren gave Thane a hard look. "Mr. Baron, regardless of what you and your family may believe, this is a very dangerous woman. She needs to be contained."

Thane's hands knotted. Contained. Controlled. It's what Kurzvall wanted, and his manipulations looked to ensure it. "Jem did *not* do this," he said vehemently.

"You've made some very serious accusations about Miss Wilmont. I want to see this evidence you've been quoting," Gordon said coldly.

"Are you her lawyer?"

Gordon's lips thinned. "Not officially."

"Then come see us when you are. The warrant being executed today is only to search for Wilmont's presence and detainment for questioning. It should go fairly quick. However, we will be interviewing members of your household over the next several days, so we'd appreciate no one going off anywhere before then. Good day, gentlemen."

Nicholas escorted them out. Thane and Gordon were still locked in their own thoughts when Gwen and Reyna scooted in through the door.

"What in Odin's name is going on?" Reyna demanded. "Enforcers are going through every part of the house looking for Jem. Even the closets and walk-in freezer."

"The freezer?" Thane sputtered

"Nicholas is about to go nova. There are a lot of nervous—*Thane!*" Gwen stared in horror at the dirty mess sitting in her seat. "Young man, for the love of—why didn't you…"

It was more the look on her husband's face than the hand wave that silenced her. She sank into the nearest chair. "Gordon?"

"Nicholas is pissed because we weren't informed of the warrant's execution until near the end of our interrogation."

"And we weren't allowed to—interrogation?" Gwen said, her eyes sharpening.

Gordon blew out a breath. "Yes. Law Enforcement has come up with both a suspect and a theory for the Branson Fire."

"They think Jem did it," Thane said bluntly.

"In retaliation for the near-fatal attack on both of you and eliminating an irritating competitor as a favor to us."

"Idiots," the two women chorused.

CHAPTER 30

Lieutenant Lundgren automatically studied sidewalk activity as Detective Goldstein eased them out the Stohlass gate and into the main traffic flow. The search had concluded like he'd expected: empty. Still, sometimes they did get lucky.

"What's your impression?" he asked his partner.

"I don't see Old Man Stohlass for this, or anyone else in their family. Their reputation is solid. Even if someone did a take a vicious left turn to hobble a competitor, they'd eliminate a couple of key individuals. Entire families? Hundreds of strangers?" Goldstein shook his head. "No. Un-un."

"Yeah, sails for me too. Less bloodshed and risk by arranging just a few accidents."

"Then they wouldn't need Wilmont," Goldstein said, shaking his head. "Just have their head of security accidently trip and fall on them. The guy was listed in the family breakdown but, still, *wow*."

"Double wow. Couldn't stop the shiver up my spine when he walked into the room."

"Mine twitched a couple of times. I thought they only came that tall from light-grav places, but his file lists him as home grown."

"Have the techs traced that text message yet?" Lundgren asked. Baron and his grandfather had guessed right about them getting an anonymous tip.

"Nope. Off-planet is all they can confirm. With the system ping-pong it went through, one tech said my guess was as good as his. All those places and incidents it listed? It sure would've been nice to get a heads-up on Wilmont before now. Talk about low profile. Even the Fed's Crime Unit reports didn't have a whisper on the wind."

"Someone has to know her. How else would anyone be able to hire her?"

"True. But if it's that limited, wouldn't she guess who snitched on her?"

"Probably why the information was sent anonymously. I wouldn't want an assassin of her rep after me. With friends like that, who needs enemies?"

"With friends like that, you wouldn't *have* enemies," Goldstein said drily.

Lundgren laughed, then grew serious again. "Someone could have felt she'd gone too far or is simply eliminating the competition. Hell, it could even be her employer trying to avoid a payoff for the fire. Had to be a big one."

"Any idea which one?' Goldstein asked, stopping for some pedestrians in a crosswalk.

"No," Lundgren grumbled, reaching for his ringing phone. "Lundgren." After a minute of silent listening, he said, "Thanks. We're on our way." He stared out the windshield for a moment, his phone forgotten in his hand. "Head for the Branson site. They've found the last victim."

***

Lundgren and Goldstein stood on the sidewalk, silently watching the small group working between the ruined South Wing and where it had been attached to the main hotel. The Arson Commander got out of his car and came to stand beside them.

"He must have been in the stairwell," Commander Lloyd said quietly. "The first explosions collapsed everything on top of him."

One of the workers stood and motioned to the orderlies waiting beside an ambulance.

Lundgren thanked every god in Odin's pantheon he didn't have to deal with what they were carefully placing in a body bag.

Every worker on the site stopped what they were doing; a few took off their hard hats. All eyes followed the grav-gurney's slow trip back to the ambulance. The black body bag stood out starkly against the white padding. It barely took up two-thirds of it.

"Mark Rutger Erikssen," Lloyd said with a hitch in his voice. "Aged nine years, three months and twelve days. Loved ice cream. Parents had a room on the eighth floor and believe he was trying to sneak into the reception to get some.

Father was here on business. Mother came to visit college friends. They're across town. Waiting. I have to go…" He turned to the two detectives as the ambulance drove off. "Find the bastards." He whipped around, stomped to his car, slammed his door, and drove off in a squeal of tires.

The site foreman approached Lundgren. "You need anything?" he asked, his voice husky. "Then we're done for the day." He began waving his arms and shouting orders. Equipment went silent; doors clanged. People streamed out. In a remarkably short time, the two detectives were alone.

Small, gray whirlwinds danced in the wind gusts.

Lundgren stared at the ruin with a heavy heart. He hoped never to experience the grief the Erikssens and many others were. Fifty-one desks throughout all grades, once filled with childish laughter and parental pride, now sat silent. Mute testimony to the horror they were still reeling from. It was the wedding party that haunted his nights. Of children who had run ahead of the adults, eager to get their promised rewards of cake and ice cream after politely sitting still through the ceremony.

"To watch, unable to help," Goldstein said softly. His balled fists and set jaw belied the calm words.

Lundgren shuddered. "I hear they've set up a group counseling," he said, his throat constricting. "Any family member or close friend affected is welcome."

"Think Captain Kelding will ever attend?"

Their captain's two children had accompanied their grandparents to their club meeting. Her husband called ten minutes before the first explosion to let her know he'd stopped in to pick them up and her parents said 'hi.' Lundgren could easily visualize the friendly mechanic taking a few minutes for chit chat. Just another five, ten minutes—God, maybe even less—and he wouldn't have witnessed his tough, no-nonsense superior melting into a puddle.

Lundgren sighed. "Maybe. Someday. She's too raw right now." He sighed again. "Who kills so many? For any reason? It just doesn't make sense."

"We aren't psychopaths" was Goldstein's succinct response.

Lundgren walked back to their car, resisting the urge to kick a tire. He leaned against the hood, his back to the hotel, and ran a hand across his face.

Their hard-nosed attitude hadn't worked with either of the Stohlass men. He'd hoped to shake something useful loose, only to find himself out hard-nosed by the old legal hawk. They'd had answers for everything, all the way back to that attempted kidnapping. *Hmmm. Something he'd said about that.*

"They wanted Dougson alive for information…to try and turn him against his employer," Lundgren muttered, playing the conversation back in his head.

Goldstein, slumped beside him, looked over. "Stohlass also said they didn't have evidence identifying the perpetrators, yet they know the root of their problem is off-planet."

Lundgren jerked upright, his pulse kicking up a notch. They had got something. "And she is assisting them in *exposing* who is targeting their family. They damn well do know who is behind it, but the hawk knows he can't make any accusations without solid proof."

"Off-planet means it wasn't the Branson family."

"But I bet they were the target. Has to be," Lundgren said, energized. "Not to minimize the other families' losses, their collective deaths have the greatest immediate and single impact. The family is wiped out, their star hotel ruined, and their company is teetering on collapse. It also removes any reason for the Stohlass family to be behind…this." He flashed a quick glance at the once grand hotel.

"Not a lot of reasons to take out a whole family. You think, maybe, a competitor looking to take over?" Goldstein rubbed his chin. "How about both of them? Framing one for the demise of the other would remove two well-established companies from the field. Then there's the general destabilization ripple caused by all the L and G deaths. Someone new would be firmly entrenched by the time everything leveled back out."

Lundgren's brain danced from one fact to another. That made an obscene sense and he'd learned to respect his partner's crazy theories. They'd netted a high closure rate due to them.

"Not to mention," Goldstein continued, "the frame redirects our focus. They had to know we'd go after the ones responsible with a vengeance."

Vengeance didn't even begin to cover it. He tapped a rapid beat against the car hood. "Manipulation…escalation of a decades-old feud until one of them appears to resolve the issue permanently. Follow it up with rumors to add more fuel to fire." He winced. "Oops, sorry."

"They did spring up pretty fast, didn't they?"

"Tarnish the family reputation and erode their business. Make them pariahs. Eventually the company either collapses or they simply close it. Same end result whether or not there's an indictment." He slapped Goldstein lightly on the arm. "I think you nailed it, partner. Let's get back to the station. We need to relook at everything."

Lundgren practically jumped into the passenger side of the car. He was already keying his hand comp on when his partner slid beneath the steering wheel.

Goldstein cleared his throat. "How are we going to check on off-world businesses?"

Lundgren thought it over as Goldstein pulled them away from the curb. "Maybe the Feds could help with that. As tight as that FBI agent and the Stohlass family have become, what do you want to bet his beating is somehow connected to all this?"

Goldstein glanced over. "I'll take that bet."

CHAPTER 31

They reconvened in the library two hours after the last Enforcer left. Thane was brooding in Nicholas's usual position at the window.

"This is a mess," Gwen said unhappily, her chair still smelling of a fragrant cleaner.

"The warrant went out on all security networks," Nicholas said, standing in front of Gordon's desk. "It also lists her as person of interest in those other events they mentioned. I sent men to Half Moon with Wilmont's picture. The desk clerk remembered her. Not just for her eyes, either. The cabin she rented was destroyed in a mysterious electrical fire same day as the Branson fire. They are currently canvassing all the port hotels and transit dorms for any additional information."

"The evidence they presented is rather damning. Both here and elsewhere," Twobears said neutrally.

Thane felt the silent questions boring into his back. He turned around slowly. Worried gazes met his. He locked eyes with his grandfather: he was the one to convince.

"Just how much do you trust her, son?"

"Enough to stake my life on it," Thane said. Several heartbeats later, his grandfather nodded his acceptance.

"If everything is still just circumstantial, why go for the warrant?" Reyna asked.

"Because everything lines up," Gordon said. "I'm willing to bet they've got something more concrete. Either from their anonymous source or something the imposter deliberately left behind."

"They assume Wilmont is capable of killing." Nicholas flicked Thane a glance. "I'm pretty sure they suspect the knife was hers, here and on Pappia."

"Stealthy and deadly. Which is why the warrant has the a-and-d clause," Twobears said.

"Armed and dangerous?" Thane backhanded the bookcase next to him. Great. Just great. "Everyone's going to be hunting her and not all of them will be carrying stunners."

Twobears nodded. "Given the severity of the accusations, every local and federal Enforcer not committed elsewhere will be searching, along with Trackers and anyone else wanting to make a name for themselves. Knowing her preference for Port Circles, they'll be saturated with patrols. Even professional criminals will hunt and turn her in so they can resume their normal business."

"They'll run her to ground like some animal." Thane sunk into a chair. "Why did he do it, Granddad? He has to be the anonymous tipster. Instead of keeping her a deep dark secret for whatever he's planning, she's been thrust into a nova-sized spotlight with all the rumors and circumstantial lies."

"It was actually a smart move on his part." Gordon weathered several stormy looks. "She can't evade the Republic-wide search forever. She'll either be captured—alive let's hope—or she has to turn to him for sanctuary to stay out of prison."

"Some sanctuary," Reyna muttered.

"This move boxes her in and reduces her freedom of movement, which severely hinders any investigation she's doing on our behalf. Last, but by no means least, Kurzvall has made himself one of her victims. There's the investment loss of the lab and anything else he's given them. Those bits of truth add weight to everything else. If we try to point a finger at him now, no one would believe us."

"Everything seems to be working in his favor." Reyna rose and paced angrily. Whipping around, she stalked back to stand next to Nicholas. "What can we do? How can we help? And don't tell me we won't! This is so...so...not right."

"We help by continuing to do as we've been doing." Gordon tapped his desk several times for emphasis. "We find proof, hard proof, of Kurzvall's activities. We need to prove the woman running around Midgard for those weeks wasn't Jem. We prove the woman we know is not a psychopathic murderer. Otherwise, the circumstantial case they're building will stand. Thane, if you've got information from Sagious and those other places that will help offset her current image, we need to hear it."

"I already have it," Nicholas said. "I'll make the file available to any family member."

"Even if we do eventually stop Kurzvall and expose the imposter," Gwen said, her voice troubled, "will it put a stop to the hounds? Will Jem ever be free of the taint?"

"No."

* * * * *

All eyes shifted to the Federal agent.

"Even if we get her cleared of the Branson Fire," Twobears continued, "there are too many other uncertainties surrounding her. Some of which she may actually be guilty of. Maybe there are even others unknown to us. What do we really know about her? In fact, why is there so little known about her? We still have just her word about what happened on Earth. Unless there's more?" he asked, looking at Thane.

Thane pressed his lips together and shook his head.

"There will always be suspicious whispers," Twobears said, giving Thane a cold look. He'd bet his badge there was more. "There will always be some Law Enforcer or Tracker looking to enhance his fortune and career by exposing a known criminal who's eluded justice."

He paused, let his gaze rove over them. "Those who help her or defend her will be included in those whispers. Are you prepared?"

"Of course."

"You're sure?" He gave Thane's mother an unreadable look. Slowly, he turned the same look on the others. "You've all seen how rumors and speculation can affect a person's life. Personally. Socially. Professionally."

Awareness grew and heads nodded in acknowledgement.

"It's already started." Thane stood. "To us as well as Jem." He stalked out.

Gordon looked around the room. "We need a plan and to make arrangements."

Twobears leaned back, listening as they batted ideas back and forth. The more he learned about this family, the more impressed he became. Most people would have distanced themselves from Wilmont, as much from the rumors as from the charges.

He had his own reservations about Wilmont. The woman could be both an ally and an assassin. How much of her reputation was real? How much of it was rumor or deliberate misinformation? What was Baron holding back and why?

CHAPTER 32

Too many hours and cups of coffee later, Lundgren leaned back in his chair and pinched his nose. He'd pulled his senior detectives into a conference room as soon as he and Goldstein got back. Their theory about a psycho competitor was initially met with skepticism. But as the hours passed, he'd sensed a change in their attitudes. They'd scrutinized all the available data on the fire, six months of Stohlass incident reports, and what little they had on Jem Wilmont. Twice at least, he estimated wearily. While they now had a motive—might, maybe, hopefully—they were no closer to solving it.

"Anyone got anything else to add?" he asked, looking around the table.

Patricia Wheeler tilted her head. "The latest rumors are connecting the Stohlass family—Thane Baron specifically—to Wilmont. How many knew that?"

A good point. "Which supports our manipulate-and-ruin theory," Lundgren said.

"The family certainly isn't helping things," Jason Bono said, yawning. "Baron and his grandfather both should know who and what she is. Yet not only have they invited her into their home, they're adamant Wilmont isn't involved. They trust her."

Bono's partner lifted her head off the table. "She saved their butts. Twice for Baron, since we're pretty sure she's the one who helped him on Pappia," Rita Seymour said.

Lundgren grunted. "Yes. Very convenient."

Goldstein shot him a quick look. "Think Pappia was staged?"

"Possibly, especially if we're moving the family from suspect to scapegoat. Only, there's no sense in going that far out just to make contact. She could've arranged to run into him in any Port Circle."

"Hmmm. How about a dual purpose, Lieutenant?" Wheeler tapped her chin. "Wilmont takes a job on Pappia—the mine explosion. She certainly didn't need the EMC pay. Baron is lured there under some pretense. Most likely a job, right? That far out and her already working there, who'd suspect a setup? His assault would've been a nice bonus. It gives Wilmont an excuse for showing up with or without a formal invite to his grateful family."

Seymour straightened, struck a pose, and waved her hand negligently. "Hi. Just drifting through the sector and thought I'd drop in and see how things are going."

Lundgren mulled it over. "She arrives on Midgard, conveniently saving the day." Was that why she was shadowing Dougson? "Then she agrees to help out, giving her an excuse for popping in and out...all the while setting up the Branson Fire. It would mean this had been planned for a year or more."

"How far ahead do we plan vacations and hope we get to go? My wife is still pissed we had to cancel the last one," Bono said, pulling on his ear.

Lundgren winced, empathizing. Yeah, nothing like a week's worth of cold shoulder. His wife planned on taking the next one, with or without him. At the rate this investigation was going, it'd be the without.

"With something this big, she'd need time to get everything in place. Like chess," Goldstein said. "Or maybe Pappia was coincidence and the kidnapping-assault was the opening act."

"I like the sound of that better. Still...if everything's been so meticulously planned...who screwed up with the vehicle assault?" Lundgren looked around at the shaking heads. "Wilmont certainly didn't plan it. Witnesses said their vehicle was still turning cartwheels when it went sailing over the cliff. Both women were lucky to be thrown clear. No way to plan a reliable exit from that."

Silence. Seymour decided to ponder with her head down again. Lundgren squinted at the clock. Yeah, it was frigging late.

"Somebody else taking advantage?" Wheeler offered.

Lundgren rubbed his neck. "It's possible. Miss Williams was a regular Tuesday-morning shopper on Trade Street. Or maybe the local troublemaker didn't get word in time to pull his strike. Wilmont was unexpected, having just popped in for a visit. Or something."

"Without a frigging trail," came a muted mutter. Seymour lifted her head. "Slipping in and out like she does? That's spooky, Lieutenant. How can anyone be sure where she is or isn't? Or has been?"

Lundgren sighed loudly. "Which brings up that very good point Stohlass made."

"The one about an assassin not wanting to be found near the scene of her crime?" Goldstein was slouched in his chair, chin propped in his hand.

"Yeah, that one. If she's so good, why slip up now?" Lundgren said.

Bono drummed his fingers on the table. "Not knowing about the backups, she could have assumed there wouldn't be anything left to connect her to it."

Lundgren shook his head. "A risky assumption for someone in her profession. A worker would probably remember those eyes making multiple visits. A smart crook would've hidden something so distinctive. Wilmont isn't dumb so…why didn't she?"

Wheeler yawned, stretched. "How about we save that headache for another day, Lieutenant? My bladder's processing an overload of coffee, my butt's numb and Rita *really* needs her beauty sleep."

They laughed as the maligned woman simultaneous gave a yawn and a feather. Wheeler evidently hadn't earned the whole bird, since Seymour only extended her smallest finger instead of its big sister.

"Remind me again why you don't have a partner?" Lundgren said, still chuckling.

He and Goldstein were the last to leave. The walk to their personal vehicles was silent. Pausing beside Goldstein's car, he said, "I'm pretty sure Baron knows how to contact Wilmont. He twitched when his grandfather said they didn't."

Goldstein unlocked his door before looking over. "Interesting. Wonder why he's keeping it from the others. The family seems pretty tight on everything else."

"Something definitely going on there. It has to tie in with why Wilmont was watching Dougson, and why Dougson specifically targeted Baron. It wasn't a kidnapping; they were going to torture Mr. Stohlass. He wanted something." Lundgren rubbed his stomach. "My guts don't like it. They're rumbling all kinds of warnings."

Goldstein nodded slowly, thoughtfully. "You get the feeling we're being led around?"

"By the nose hairs, partner. By the nose hairs."

CHAPTER 33

As usual, her friend's social engagement was well attended. Sofia Weaver's living room was standing room only as they waited for the call to dinner. Reyna tuned out the conversations circling around her. They were just more of the same she'd heard for weeks. One couldn't attend a social function, dine at a restaurant, or simply stand in a line anywhere without the same subject coming up. Where was the assassin? Who hired her? Why? Would she strike again before the Enforcers caught her?

My God, can't people just get on with their lives?

"Well, the Branson Fire certainly proved to be a stroke of luck for your family."

The haughty statement hauled Reyna back to her current surroundings. She gripped her glass tighter and turned to face the woman delivering it.

Medium height, medium build, medium intelligence. In fact, medium everything except for a mouth that should be registered as a lethal weapon. Molly Grinnell loomed over everyone else when it came to gossip and innuendoes. The woman had gleefully destroyed relationships and reputations with a well-placed sneer.

"Would you care to explain your remark?" Reyna asked with forced politeness.

Conversations died. Heads turned.

"I don't believe I need to," Molly replied smugly.

"I believe you do. After all, things have a way of getting distorted as the information careens around that vacuous cavern between your ears as it hunts for a couple of synapses to latch onto." That wiped the smile off the detestable woman's face. "I do not consider the deaths of hundreds of people as a stroke of luck. Anyone who does is as sick as the ones who did it."

"Everyone knows Stohlass Enterprises and Branson Hotels were facing another expansion war," Molly snapped. "Now, you're taking over most of Branson's assets plus expanding without any major competition."

Finally. There it was, out in the open. *Thank Odin.* It was impossible to fight shadows and innuendoes. Like any festering wound, this needed to be opened and purged.

The whispers Twobears warned them about had started before the hotel's last embers cooled, but they'd recently grown nasty. Speculative stares bored into her shoulder blades. Calls had been unreturned. Invitations failed to arrive for two functions she or her parents normally attended. Juanita Anderson had all but spit on her when they passed on Trade Street yesterday.

"Yes, our plans on expanding were no secret. Why should they be?" Reyna's eyebrow arched. "Stohlass Enterprises is simply taking the next step in its growth and it was in the planning stages long before the tragedy. Nor are we taking over their holdings. We're *supporting* BH&E, trying to keep it from falling apart and its employees employed while they search for any remaining heirs. We have no plans of keeping it."

"Is that why Law Enforcement has been investigating you?"

Reyna's eyes flashed at the smear attempt. "You've been misinformed. The authorities spoke with us, just as they have with numerous others as part of their investigation. They're following all possible avenues and we were a logical side street. If they hadn't, I'm sure some nasty gossip-addicted...person would be whispering about money, power and buyoffs. They still don't know who or—"

"Yes, they do, and your son brought her here."

I hate this. I absolutely hate this.

Hated having to defend her family in a room full of close-minded people. Half of them probably had side bets on whether or not her family would fall. The other half was just waiting to scoop up the remains.

"If you're referring to Jem Wilmont, Thane invited her to visit us after she saved his life when he was on a job." Her father had already fielded several inquiries from Pappia. Reyna rolled her eyes at Molly's *Oh, really?* No one did sarcastic sneers better than Molly Grinnell.

"Is that why your son left Midgard suddenly, right after the Enforcers paid you a visit last week? Was he afraid they would prove he hired her?"

Who did she bribe for that? And to hell with this. Sorry, Mom.

She cast off the reins she'd kept on her temper these past weeks.

"My family, my *son* did not hire Jem Wilmont nor did she do us a favor, as I've heard in more than a few whispers. If Law Enforcement had anything more than the vicious, unfounded rumors and gossip currently circulating, Thane would have been ordered to stay on Midgard. Or arrested. Do you see any warrants with his name on it? Has *any* member of our family been denied travel or dragged down to the Law Enforcement Center for questioning?" she asked the entire room as her furious gaze raked over everyone.

"As for being luck?" Reyna spat out, returning to the obnoxious bitch that had started it, "It certainly was yours, wasn't it? For years, you have grumbled about your in-laws' tight-fisted control over the family's finances. How Richard's yearly allotment isn't nearly enough to support you as you should be. 'As benefits your position' I believe was your tacky phrase."

The object of her wrath went white.

"Tsk, I believe the two of you only managed *three* cruises last year, one of them even to Earth. Since the fire and he inherited everything, you've both gone on a spending spree that has greatly boosted this quarter's earnings for several businesses. Did you really buy the entire line of Cecilia's fall ensemble?"

"How dare you...you..." Molly screeched, indignation returning bright color to her face.

Reyna's contemptuous "Why the hell not?" had the woman sputtering like one of her nephew's toy boats. "You've no qualms about insinuating my family may be the worse criminals since Jamison's pirates rampaged through the Republic."

Reyna shifted her attention to the woman standing beside Molly.

Mavis Journey was of the same ilk as Molly, and the two women had been an inseparable collective-pain in her rear since college. She'd even taken to thinking of them as Molvis. "Mavis, I heard your parents had forbidden you unsupervised entry in their home. They also took control of your trust fund for reasons we can only speculate. Be hard to keep up with Molly without the credits. There's no problem now, is there?"

"I will sue your family for every credit they have for slander."

"Perfect. I can't express how delighted my father will be to get you in court. You do realize, don't you, accusations of slander will fail when truth stands up in defense?" Reyna's smile held no warmth. *Do it and you bitches are toast.*

She looked over at a snickering young male. Another hypocrite.

"Scott Winter, your family and the Swatch family shared an equal loathing for at least two generations. Never have heard why. You decide to end it?" His face went stony. Reyna scanned the room. Hostile faces outnumbered the sympathetic ones. "In fact, I would say a fair number of you in this room profited, directly or indirectly, from that fire. Did a number of you get together and form a committee to investigate the potential of resolving your individual inheritance issues?"

Several shocked gasps and a few pithy comments drifted over the crowd. With perfect synchronization, Molly and Mavis splattered their glass contents on the front of her dress.

There were more gasps, several snickers, and one *ooooooo!*

Their hostess stepped forward. "Both of you, out of my home. Now!" Sofia ordered. "Anyone else who believes the Stohlass family had anything to do with the fire can also leave."

Reyna wasn't surprised to see a third of them set down glasses and leave. She was surprised by the hurt it caused.

"I'm so sorry, Reyna." Sofia squeezed her arm sympathetically and drew her out onto the terrace. "It's natural for people to want to blame someone for a tragedy like this. If they can take advantage and use it to their benefit, all the better."

"I'm the one who should apologize for bringing this into your home." Reyna managed a wan smile. "At least not all your guests left."

Sofia waved her hand dismissively. "Don't be. I have never liked that spiteful woman, and she came primed to cause trouble. I only let her rant as long as she did because you deserved the opportunity to defend your family. I'm truly sorry about your dress."

"It was worth it, getting everything out. Can't fight whispers." She grasped the railing tightly. "Lord, I don't know when I've enjoyed losing my temper that much."

"I should have removed her from my guest list as soon as her mother-in-law was gone, which was the only reason she was on it in the first place. Whether it's guts or stupidity, at least you know where they stand." Sofia looked back over her shoulder contemptuously. "Half of *them* only stayed to keep the social and business contacts they're afraid of losing."

Reyna glanced back. People huddled in small groups. Some glances shied away when she caught their gaze. Others nodded in a simple gesture of support, including Maria Jorgenson. Her mother would be glad to hear her friend of thirty years believed in them.

"I can't believe so many would believe we'd do something so...so...heinous doesn't even do it justice, Sofia. Most of them have known or worked with our family for decades. The Cortlands and LeBlancs even attended our last family reunion."

"That's precisely why, my dear. When a family grows in size and influence as yours has, so does the envy and resentment among those who couldn't quite keep up. Between your family's various careers and all of your indomitable personalities, political and social enemies were inevitable. Whether or not they actually believe your family is responsible for the fire, it's a weapon they'll use to tear you down. Don't worry about the lawsuits. There isn't a lawyer out there who can best your father, and they know it. You just need to watch out for all the knives pointed at your family's back."

"Naturally," Reyna snorted, "since they're too cowardly to come at us from the front."

Sofia laughed. "Shall I have your driver bring around your car?"

"No." Reyna lifted her chin; Sofia arched an eyebrow. "They can stare at my chest—well, at the stain on my chest all they want. I will not desert the battlefield."

"I rest my case," Sofia smiled widely, "and add stubborn to that list of traits. Let's go wring out the worse of your wound and get this dinner over with. You and I need to sit down for a private chat."

Reyna looked at her questioningly.

"I've never felt your family was in any way responsible. I am curious, though, as to why you're so certain this Jem Wilmont isn't. I'm also worried."

"We can handle the gossip and the idiots."

Sofia waved a hand at a stand of trees. "I sincerely doubt those security guards are lurking around because of gossip and idiots. Your family had troubles even before the fire."

Reyna looked into the woman's shrewd eyes. Only a few years older than her, there wasn't anyone she respected more than Sofia Lutz Weaver. Her friend could be trusted, but… "There are some things I'm not free to divulge."

Sofia nodded. "Understood. Tell me what you can and how I can help. Paste on a smile, my dear. It's feeding time around the campfire and the barbarians are getting restless."

Reyna laughed and followed her hostess. No pasting required. It was a genuine smile that stretched from ear to ear.

CHAPTER 34

The *Lone Tracker* had never looked so good.

Propped against a building's rough brick façade, Thane stared hungrily at his ship. Safety lay at the top of those steps and behind the reinforced hatch waiting for them on the open tarmac. He took a deep breath. *Patience.* There was nothing between it and them except danger and death. They'd be a target as soon as they stepped out of the shadows they huddled in.

"Want to bet there's snipers in case the thugs failed?" Boyd said.

Thane glanced over, but it was Milhann who answered the question.

"No doubt," the man said, examining the area immediately around their side of the port. Like most up-and-coming colonies without much traffic, the space-port doubled as an airport. "I see two, three places where they could set up without drawing attention."

He should know, Thane thought sourly, flicking blood away from his eye. After all, the geo-engineer side-lined his skills as an 'accident generator.' What a ridiculous term. An assassin was an assassin, even if the method used was a rock slide or an avalanche. It was the rumors of the man's association—and fallout—with Kurzvall that had brought him and Boyd to Magnus.

Milhann turned to Boyd. "You up for it, bonehead?"

Boyd's eyes narrowed at the heavy-worlder insult. It implied one had a smaller, less cognitive brain due to gravity-thickened skulls. "How about I just toss you out there as a test?"

Thane grunted. "Don't need that now." Milhann was being an ass. Yes, Boyd's home was higher at three Earth gravities, but Magnus pulled a full two E-gs itself. Which is the frigging reason he'd talked Boyd into coming with him after learning about Milhann's planet.

"Fine. Which one you want me to take?" Boyd said.

Milhann pointed out the most likely spot on their left, about halfway between them and the main concourse. He slipped off to check the ones to their right. The deep-throated roar of an atmospheric craft swelled then quickly diminished in the distance.

Boyd looked at Thane. "Think he'll come back?"

Thane spat out blood. "He's come this far. He's as much a target now as we are."

Boyd gave the area a careful look-see before sliding cautiously out of their hiding place.

Thane leaned back against the wall, not daring to let his body slide down like it really, really wanted to. He had to keep watch. As if he'd be much good if they're found. He carefully felt his left side, unable to stop a hiss of pain. Two broken ribs at least, maybe a cracked jaw. He'd nearly bit his tongue in half from the blow. The cut above his right eye was an annoying drip. His left arm was still useless, even after Milhann had wrenched it back into place.

He was either out of shape or this planet's gravity was underrated. The locally hired thugs had delivered their devastating blows at a speed he'd struggled to block. He swiped blood away again, spit out even more. Boyd had fared the best. Besides the gravity advantage, he'd evidently done some serious brawling prior to slinging supply crates for a living. He and Milhann were the only two reasons they had survived the trap.

A well-planned trap.

He glanced worriedly at Jem, slumped near his feet with her arms wrapped around herself. The bastards had damn near killed her. Guess they weren't aware of her value to certain parties.

Relief had been his dominate emotion when she'd appeared behind their attackers, forcing them to disarm. Then horror, when one of the bastards had spotted Jem's sluggishness and knocked the stunner from her hand, breaking her wrist and kicking off the vicious brawl that followed. Her left eye was turning black and swelling. Blood ran down her face from a gash in her hairline. How many of her ribs were broken? He'd heard the cracks when those vicious blows landed and again when she slammed into the wall behind him. No telling what kind of internal injuries she had.

"Jem? If someone other than Boyd or Milhann comes around that corner, ghost out of here. You're in no shape to fight."

"Like you are?"

"Ghost. Shift. Whatever you need to do."

Jem raised her head slowly, her breathing shallow. She blinked several times before her good eye finally focused on him. "I don't think I can," she admitted.

Thane cursed silently. Those thugs would've picked themselves up by now. They'd come searching, either for revenge or to ensure payment for whatever bargain they'd made. He swiped more blood away and evaluated their hiding spot.

No external doors on the two buildings they were sandwiched between. Unless their attackers could scale the two-story wall connecting them, a rear attack was out. He carefully maneuvered his left arm around his waist and tucked his useless hand into his waistband. Painfully, teeth clenched together, he drew his weapon from its holster and turned sideways. Shoulder braced against the wall, right arm braced on his left, he faced the vulnerable opening.

CHAPTER 35

Goldstein watched his lieutenant stalk into the room. Uh-oh. The meeting with the Captain hadn't gone well. Maybe now wasn't a good time to bring up his theory.

Lundgren kicked his desk. Two junior detectives decided to be elsewhere. Nope, he'd wait until—

"You're staring like you got something to say," Lundgren snapped.

Goldstein gulped. "Well, uh…it sounds kind of crazy wild."

"Just spit it out."

Goldstein gave him a tentative smile. "The last couple of weeks…the discussions about Wilmont? You know, no disguise or anything?" So far, the favorite theory was that the Branson Fire would be her final job and she'd be retiring with a new face and identity. Assuming she didn't have one already. "I've been thinking about that and…*weeelllll*…if the Stohlass family is being set up, could Wilmont be too?"

Lundgren snorted. "You're right. That is wild, even for you."

Goldstein's voice turned earnest. "Think about it, LT. Wilmont is supposedly this super saboteur-slash-assassin phantom nobody knew about, much less track. Until now. There's no attempt to hide her distinctive features as she wanders around the Branson hotel or buys a large quantity of kerosene. If all criminals were that helpful, we'd be out of a job. Then she rents *one* place for *two* weeks instead of bouncing around like before. Three men—an experienced Tracker, a renowned lawyer and a savvy security expert—trust Wilmont completely. Well, the security guy might be a bit leery about her. But they all insist she is not involved in the fire. Not to mention, she's nearly killed in the attack on Miss Williams."

Lundgren crossed his arms. "You're talking impersonation."

Great. He was listening. "And what about her Earth account, LT? Would *anyone* leave that much behind? It should have already been emptied, moved before disappearing behind another identity. Shifting even a single credit now will set off a shit-storm of flags."

Lundgren leaned against Goldstein's desk and pinned him with a stare. "Wilmont and her history would make a great patsy."

Goldstein continued quickly, slightly unnerved by his partner's unwavering gaze. *If he agrees, why give me the stink eye?* "Granted, she could be a phantom who knows how to sabotage engines. Regardless of what she's done elsewhere, it doesn't mean she's guilty of what's happened here. Baron's crack about us relooking at her history means there's more out there than what that message provided. He did list some specific places."

"Interesting theory," Lundgren said, lips pursed. "Especially since it kind of supports what came up in the meeting with the Captain. I got to watch an interesting vid-message from the Tallon Enforcer Commander on Tardon—one of the places Baron named. The Commander basically told us to get off our asses and find the real criminals."

Goldstein winced. No wonder the meeting had gone badly.

"Oh, he was a little more tactful about it. He categorially denies Jem Wilmont would have done what the warrants say, while simultaneously saying he can't tell us why. Captain Kelding is not amused and demands to know where we stand on solving this."

"Well, hell," Goldstein said and rubbed his nose. "Did we just shine a huge spotlight on a deep undercover FLEA?"

A horrified expression flashed across Lundgren's face. "God, I hope not. But Feds would have the resources for alternate identities and transports to make it appear like she vanishes. Let's skip rafting that river until we have to and assume your setup scenario is the most likely."

And the safest, Goldstein thought glumly. Could they be that unlucky?

Lundgren paced to his desk and back, lips pursed, brow scrunched. "Assume the Stohlass and Branson families are being watched, their activities tracked as our psycho looks for a way to muscle into their territory. He learns about Wilmont. Probably from events on Pappia. *Bam*! A plan is born, complete with scapegoats. Now he has to finagle getting her to Midgard," he said thoughtfully. "Get her on your chessboard and set the stage."

"Like the bungled kidnapping-assault?"

Lundgren shot him a surprised look. "That works. The sniper shot was convenient, wasn't it? Setting up Dougson wouldn't even be a second thought to our psycho."

"Sounds plausible. But the psycho and the shooter can't be the same. People with money don't get their hands dirty."

"Some bastard just as sick as our psycho was hired to captain the operation here," Lundgren agreed, disgusted. "He sets the stage. He hires someone with the same basic features and provides contact lenses and a long wig. Those features are what people will see and remember the most."

"Pop the contacts out and pull the wig." Goldstein mimicked a yanking motion. "The imposter fades into the crowd and we get an anonymous message pointing us at Wilmont."

"*If* there is an impersonator. Have the analysts pull Wilmont's EMC records and do an in-depth comparison between their employee picture and the hotel security tapes. We need verification." Lundgren rubbed both temples. "Is Wilmont responsible for the Branson Fire or not? Is she being set up? Is she working with the Stohlass family, a psycho, the Feds, or on her own? Are there multiple fingers in our pie? I'm getting a frigging headache."

Goldstein's head bobbed in sympathy. "We've never had a case with so many who-what if-maybe possibilities. The Captain isn't going to like it, especially about the Fed possibility."

"We'll flip to see who tells her."

"Nope. You're senior."

Lundgren shot him a sour look. "If Wilmont isn't involved, we're back to square one. Let's hope it doesn't turn out to be the undercover scenario."

Goldstein grimaced. "We could end up on permanent Circle duty. At night. Think they'll hear from Wilmont?"

"I'm counting on it." Lundgren scratched his ear. "Assuming they're right and she's not guilty—of our fire—she'll take a vested interest in finding who did it and who pointed a finger at her. She might even know which of her peers is capable of doing something like this. As a friend of the family, she'll also want whoever paid for it."

"But will she turn them over to Law Enforcement?"

"Oh, yeah. Wilmont will ensure all their names are cleared. Whether or not they're still breathing when she dumps them on our deck?" Lundgren shrugged.

Goldstein doubted it would bother anyone if they weren't.

CHAPTER 36

They stumbled aboard the *Lone Tracker*. Milhann slammed both hatches closed behind them, spinning the manual locks. "Thor, secure the ship," Thane ordered hoarsely. Several loud *clunks* sounded as additional locks snapped into place. Even with the two snipers successfully taken out, he'd never felt so exposed and helpless crossing the open expanse to his ship. Wondering with each step if they'd missed one.

The soft moan from Boyd's arms sent a flutter of worry down his nerves.

"Bring ion engines to standby and contact Port Control," Thane ordered as he stepped on the lift. "Tell them we're leaving immediately." They were lucky Magnus didn't have separate in-out transit times. The small cargo lift smoothly deposited him outside the med-room.

"Sensors indicate immediate medical attention required by you and the female. Unknown male is carrying multiple weapons."

"Weapons authorized," Thane said. Milhann was, for now, an ally. He sent the lift back down for Boyd and Jem. Grabbing a handful of pain pills from the medical cabinet, he gulped them down as he hurried toward the command area. He was easing himself into the pilot's chair when Milhann bounced out of the stairwell, apparently unhindered by the laser burn across his right bicep.

"Neutralize ship's internal gravity to zero-point eight E-gs." While he'd done it more for Jem, Thane appreciated the immediate relief on his own body.

"Internal gravity at zero-point eight Earth gravity," Thor confirmed. "Engines reaching standby. Port Control denying request."

"It wasn't a request," he said. "Tell them we're leaving. Calculate closest transit point to Midgard." He winced as his left arm let him know it was coming alive.

There was a pause before Thor's voice came back. "Port Control reports a Hold Order against the *Lone Tracker*. We are instructed to power down engines or face arrest and impoundment. No notice of such action has been recorded in ship records."

"In case the others failed," Milhann said, dropping into one of the kitchen seats. Gingerly wiping blood from his lip he added, "Which means there'll also be a backup plan."

"Connect me with the Port Master. Emergency override of any protocols," Thane ordered.

The startled image of a middle-aged man came onscreen several seconds later. "What? Who are—what's happened?" the man sputtered, his eyes widening at Thane's bloodied image.

"Thane Stohlass Baron, on the *Lone Tracker*. I have an emergency situation and need to leave immediately." Thane watched the man's eyes flick to the side, verifying his information on another screen.

"Your ship has a Hold against it and you obviously need medical attention. I'll send—"

"Did you place the Hold Order?"

His brow wrinkled. "Well, no, but—"

"Was there a recent shift change?"

"Well, no, but—"

"Hold Orders can only be placed by the Port Master on duty and the affected ship notified. You didn't do it and neither I nor my ship's comp brain has received notice of said Hold. That's against several protocols."

"You're a fine one to be talking about protocols. You…you…" The Port Master's sputter was abruptly replaced with a frown as he stared at something off to the side. "Where did those ships come from? There aren't any flights scheduled over the western territory today."

Why was the guy asking him?

There was a muttering in the video background. The Port Master's head whipped around to whoever was offscreen. "No ID broadcasts? None?"

"Thor!" Thane all but yelled. "Identify ships entering western sensor range."

"Three XTF-13A fighters," Thor announced, eliciting shocked gasps over the video link. "Trajectory and velocity indicate arrival in fourteen point three minutes."

Space capable and able to follow them up. Dammit, they'd planned for everything. Boyd materialized beside him. "Jem?" Thane asked quickly.

"Medicated and strapped down in the med-bed. Her entire rib cage is either broken or fractured. She's got a punctured lung." Worry underscored the seriousness of his words.

"What is going on?" squawked the Port Master, leaning into his terminal screen.

"How bad is the puncture?" Thane's worry matched Boyd's.

"Your comp brain rates the seepage at approximately one point zero seven percent."

Minimum. For now. Thane turned back to the viewscreen.

"My friends and I have been attacked and damn near killed. The Hold is a bogus attempt to keep us here so those fighters can finish the job. They won't care about collateral damage to your port. We're leaving, with or without your clearance. Send your complaint to Wotan Two."

"*Lone Tracker* cleared for immediate takeoff. Use full nav-control as inbound ships may not be able to clear in time." Rage had replaced the Port Master's shock. "Full investigation to follow," he snapped. With a slashing motion the screen went blank.

"Emergency broadcast on all frequencies," Thor reported. "Civilian ships beginning to vector away from immediate airspace. Emergency protocols engaged; safety restraints required."

"Engage engines, fastest safe thrust—get us out of here."

The deck plating's vibration intensified as the engines' roar increased. Thane fumbled one-handed at his harness. Boyd grabbed it and yanked it over him before dropping down opposite Milhann, the other man already dragging straps from his chair's pockets. Boyd was still snapping his into place when they launched upward with an injury-screaming jolt.

"Climbing at seventy-four percent thrust. Hull temperature entering safety margin."

The *Lone Tracker* veered to miss an inbound ship, flinging them sideways in their straps. More grunts and groans accompanied a second abrupt motion despite the reduced gravity.

"Activate main viewscreen, radar mode. Show all ships in relation to us," Thane said, gritting his teeth against the throbbing pain.

The large screen over the main control console switched to a dark purple background. *Lone Tracker* was a solid blue dot in the center. Civilian ships were white dots angling away from them in several directions. The three 13As were red dots moving in on the left side. Four more red dots came into view from two different directions.

Curses started.

The four new Reds changed to Greens.

Curses stopped.

"Four ships entering range identified as STF-15Ds, Magnus security forces. Vectoring and communications indicate intent to engage enemy ships identified as rogues. *Lone Tracker* passing seventy kilometers, hull temperature dropping; thrust increasing to ninety percent." The screen's background gradually shifted to solid black.

Two of the Reds changed direction as they left the atmosphere behind, swinging toward the Greens arrowing toward them. "Lasers engaged," Thor reported. The third Red continued to chase after them. A red circle appeared, centered on their blue dot. "Enemy ship approaching its firing range in two minutes, fifty-three seconds."

Two of the Greens flared in quick succession and were gone. Then a Red flared. The second Red and a Green battled on the screen's lower center. The remaining Green raced toward the one aiming for them. It wouldn't make it in time.

"If they want you alive, they'll only take out the engines."

"Assuming that's what's wanted," Boyd shot back at Milhann.

Oh, yeah. They wanted. "I'm about to disappoint them. Thor, activate dome laser—authorization on my voice print." Thane ignored the questions and comments behind him. He kept his eyes on the screen as a section on his control's flat counter top slid sideways, revealing several rows of switches and buttons. A hidden panel on top of the ship would also be sliding open as the cannon lifted into position. A gold circle indicating their own fire zone was added to the screen image. It was a short distance outside the red one.

Excellent. They would be able to fire first. "Track and lock," Thane commanded.

As the enemy crossed the gold line, a gold targeting circle surrounded it. He pressed the firing button, unwilling to give its pilot a chance. They'd taken out two defense fighters too easily. The Red flared then disappeared. Their blue and two green dots were the only ones left.

"Commander Devlin requesting contact," Thor announced.

"Connect communication. Visual on main screen, lower right quadrant." Thane rubbed his tingling left arm as a helmeted head popped into view. The eyes were hidden, but he bet they were as cold and furious as the feminine voice coming in over the mic-speaker.

"What the bloody hell is going on, *Lone Tracker*?"

Thane smiled tiredly. "Thanks for the assist, Commander."

"'Thanks for the assist?' she parroted. "I just lost two good officers. I want answers and I want to see the license for that laser cannon you just fired."

"Certainly. I'll send the regis—" Thane sucked in a sharp breath at the new information displayed in the top right quadrant.

Two ships were coming out of the asteroid field that used to be Magnus's third moon. One each of Class II and III Frigates, according to the tags Thor helpfully posted next to each dot. At one hundred and two hundred meters in length, these ships were the Republic's primary military workhorse. They were deadly, outfitted with any number of swarm fighters and weapons. Thor colored them red.

"Well, that explains the 13As," Thane said.

"Why are those military ships here?" Devlin demanded.

"I doubt the Republic is invading your system," Thane said. This was bad. "Have they contacted you or your Port Master, yet? Have they identified themselves or stated why they're here?" Lip movement without sound said the commander was asking those same questions on a secured channel.

"Thugs, snipers, fighters, and now frigates. They must want you pretty bad," Milhann said dryly. "Just drop me off at the next moon."

"Not me. Jem," Thane told him grimly, eyes locked on the red images.

"Wilmont? Jem Wilmont?" Milhann said, surprised. "She's the woman everyone's looking for?"

"They don't know she's with us," Boyd said, frowning.

"They do. The Port Master wasn't the only one who heard our conversation about Jem. They were monitoring the port frequency. It's how they knew when to send in the fighters they'd prepositioned somewhere."

Two more identical ships slid smoothly out of the same asteroid field. Thane stared in disbelief. Four ships? Milhann was making a choking sound.

"Head back down, *Lone Tracker*," Devlin ordered, switching back to standard frequency. A babble of background voices could be heard over her comm link. "Planetary defenses are scrambling."

A fifth and very large blip popped onto the screen. Mouths fell open, shocked by the 'Class V Battleship' tag next to it. Complete silence fell across all the communication links.

"Milhann? Does Cameroon have a Class Five Defender?" Thane asked softly. Too large to travel any distance in a timely manner, system defense was their primary function. Normally.

"No," Milhann replied, just as softly.

"That big sucker would've needed months to get here from—hell, from anywhere." Boyd said.

"Verify the battleship designation, Thor."

"Large vessel is an unknown configuration but well within Class Five modification parameters," Thor said. "Class Fives are extremely dangerous with an extended firing range." The red circle snapped into position again, only now it was well outside their golden one. "Interaction discouraged."

"*No shit*," echoed dual voices behind him.

"Devlin, is Magnus set up to handle a rogue fleet?" He was momentarily distracted by her reply. He'd have to remember that one. "We'll make a run for it, draw some of them away."

The Commander hesitated, but their options were limited. "Good luck, *Lone Tracker*." The two fighters turned back at full burn.

"Thor, plot best vector away from the battleship and go to full power. Recalculate transition point." Thane eyed the five red dots. "End radar mode. Project all ship locations relative to planetary positions."

He leaned back, wincing. Those pills could kick in anytime now. He kept his left arm tucked firmly against his ribcage, supporting it. Last thing he needed was a punctured lung.

The viewscreen changed to a star field. Magnus's mass was in the lower left, one of its four remaining moons slowly sliding across the bottom as their blue dot moved farther above the orbital plane. Three Reds closed in on Magnus from the right. The remaining two—the Class V and a Class II—changed trajectory, angling toward them. Another red ring appeared between the battleship's and their gold one: the frigate's firing range. As if that one mattered.

"How soon before engaging O-drive?" Thane asked his ship.

"Thirty-nine minutes, seventeen seconds to updated transition point."

That was the closest? Right. Magnus's four-plus-debris moons. They extended its gravity field farther out. "Time for the Class Five to reach its firing zone?"

"Twenty-two minutes, six seconds."

"Guess I should have updated my will," Boyd said to no one in particular.

There was a bright flare on the screen, followed by two more in quick succession.

"Planetary communication and navigation satellites destroyed," Thor said into the heavy silence. A spray of small red dots flowed from both Class IIIs. "Fighter swarms launched."

Milhann launched into a low-voiced stream of curses.

Thane added a few of his own silently. This wasn't just a well-planned trap. It was a demonstration of power.

The swarms disappeared into the atmospheric envelope. The enemy ships crept closer.

"Time to transit point?" Thane asked.

"Thirty minutes, ten seconds," was the reply.

"And for the Class Five to reach maximum firing range?"

"Thirteen minutes, forty-one seconds."

"We'll be spaced," Milhann grumbled, "as soon as they get the woman. Tell them we've suited her up and dropped her off with a beacon."

There was a loud *thump* behind him. Boyd expressing both their opinions about that?

"Not actually do it," Milhann said with a loud snarl. "Just dump the beacon in a suit to give us time."

"The battleship wouldn't stop, *bonehead*. The frigate would," Boyd said.

"And then it won't be aiming for our engines," Thane added. "Thor, plot a new transit point at fifty-five percent safety."

"Not recommended," Thor replied.

Otanak engines didn't work well in gravity fields. The stronger the field, the more likely—and violently—an engine would explode on activation. Experimentation had determined the minimum field strength for safe operation, although most pilots applied a safety factor past it when setting their transition points.

"Noted. Verbal override under emergency conditions."

"Blown up or spaced," Milhann said, his voice resigned. "Such a great ending."

"Got another option?" Thane said, watching the red dots move closer. "Let's hear it."

"Odds are still in our favor," Boyd said drily. "He could have gone fifty-fifty."

"How soon to engaging O-drive at the new point?" Thane asked. The dots were closing in on the red line.

"Seven minutes, ten seconds." Then Thor added, "Class Five accelerating and will reach range in approximately four minutes, thirty-one seconds."

Boyd grunted. "Bastard probably guessed we'd risk a closer transit."

Thane deactivated the cannon, the gold circle disappearing and all panels sliding smoothly back into place. "Bring all auxiliaries up on standby," he said, a calmness settling over him. He flashed the viewscreen a smug grin at Boyd's startled yelp behind him. His ship still had one surprise behind its hatch.

"This thing has more engines?" Milhann thumped the table top. "A thousand credits if we make it."

"Your boneheaded ass is only worth a hundred dollars?"

"Fine, basalt scrunched gnome. One thousand *dollars*."

Thane ignored the squabbling kids as a green indicator lit up on a side panel. The auxiliaries were ready. He focused on the screen. Waiting. He had to take them by surprise.

The battleship nosed into its firing line.

"Engage all auxiliaries, full power."

The *Lone Tracker* surged forward, the laser beam behind them falling short of its target.

"Class Five continuing to accelerate," Thor announced. "Transit in fifty-one seconds."

It was a race.

All eyes locked on the screen. The distance shrunk steadily between death and its bloody line.

"Transitioning."

The ions cut off and the O-drive engaged. Milhann let out a loud whoop when the screen went black with no accompanying *boom*.

Thane sagged in his chair. *Owww*. He straightened back up. "How close was the Class Five to firing?"

"Four point one seconds."

So. Plenty of time. Releasing the safety locks, he twisted his seat around. "Basalt scrunched gnome?"

CHAPTER 37

Lundgren walked in with two coffees and a steaming rich aroma.

One deep inhale had Goldstein closing his file with two keystrokes. He accepted his cup with another deep breath. "This did not come from the cafeteria."

"Nope. Stopped in at Lana's on my way in. Sorry I couldn't make it in sooner."

"You didn't miss anything. How's the wife doing?" Goldstein took a cautious sip. Lana's Café was a favorite lunchtime spot for the South-Central office workers. Their coffee was usually just short of boiling.

"She's doing great. The cast will be coming off her leg in a couple of more days. Can't wait for the doctor to clear Ella for driving again. She can deal with a master manipulator with big blue eyes," he said to Goldstein's grin. "The reasons Sarah comes up with for not going to school are getting outrageous."

"My younger brother tried similar tactics. Dwayne's headless ghost tale was my favorite. What'd she come up with today?"

"Spiffy and Stripe needed a good scrubbing."

Goldstein's coffee halted in mid-air. "Wait…aren't those her reef fish?"

"Uh-huh. And if they didn't get it—now, today—they'll die."

"Okay, how do you scrub fish that's not going in a pan?" Goldstein asked, biting the inside of his cheek.

Goldstein's cup was sitting safely on his desk by the time Lundgren finished recounting his daughter's extensive instructions. He shook with laughter. Wiping his eyes, he asked, "What was Ella doing?"

"Same thing you are. She damn near rolled off the couch. I can just see the doctor's face if I haul her in there with something else broken. Bone regen does *not* work well with her." At least her grumpy cast-stomping about the house was almost over.

"Good Lord, Lieutenant. You are in so much trouble when she hits her teens."

"Don't we know it." Lundgren flashed his partner a smug smile. "Which is why we're investing in a future reconnaissance expert." Goldstein gave him a blank look. "Otherwise known as a tattletaling, won't-leave-me-alone younger sibling. Be about another six and a half months before arrival."

Goldstein managed to get his congratulations out around more laughter.

"Besides, every seven-year-old needs someone to torture besides her parents. And if they're driving each other crazy, maybe we'll get a break."

"Sarah will be eight by then," Goldstein pointed out.

"An excellent diaper changing age. The analysis of the two images?"

"Not back yet," Goldstein said, reaching for his ringing phone.

Lundgren sipped his coffee as he walked over to what he privately called the Wall of Frustration. Photos of the Branson Hotel Complex—before and after—along with primary victims and suspects were posted on the wall. Unfortunately, there weren't many of the latter.

He reviewed it every morning, staring into two sets of heterochromia eyes as his questions only grew. Was it one woman? Two? Dammit. They needed that analysis. Were they doing it pixel-by-frigging-pixel? Even when they did get the results, it wouldn't answer all their questions. *Who are you, Jem Seaborne Wilmont?* Assassin? Drifter? Undercover agent? Pain in my ass?

"Think we've got something."

Lundgren wheeled around. "They found Wilmont?"

"I wish. Wheeler found a second, recently opened bank account for one of the hotel's maintenance staff. Records show twenty-five thousand dollars deposited five days before the fire. Part of Leonard Fontana's duties included overseeing the fire suppression system," Goldstein said in a clipped tone.

"What's the address," Lundgren said, striding over quickly.

"The bastard was killed in a still unsolved hit-and-run the day *before* the fire."

"*Damn it.*" Lundgren kicked Goldstein's desk.

"Wheeler is heading to his home to see if she can salvage something. If we're lucky, Fontana's s family just boxed his stuff up instead of disposing it."

He kicked the desk again, his frustration boiling over. "Another dead end. Just like the explosive supplier."

An importer in New Holland City on Stockholm had sold a large shipment to a private company approximately two weeks pre-fire. He died two days later. They'd found said purchasing company to be nonexistent and the warehouse holding only dust. The man's sig-ner of twenty-three years and their children swore, venomously, he would never have committed suicide. The woman turned over all her partner's records and his picture was posted next to the hotel surveillance shots.

Goldstein leaned back, linking his hands behind his head. "I don't think we're going to find anyone alive who was a local player for this job, LT. This was professional all the way."

Lundgren plopped his rear on the corner of Goldstein's desk. It took several deep breaths to calm himself. "Yeah. No finger pointing, no deals, no loose ends. Unless we've bred a bunch of psychos, I'm going to guess Fontana and any others were told it was an insurance scam of some kind and would go off late at night when the wing was empty."

Goldstein scratched his head. "Which supports the idea of someone else manipulating things. Eliminating them ensures no accidental slip of information that could cast doubt on either the Stohlass family or Wilmont as the perpetrators."

"We're no closer now than when we started," Lundgren said, frustration threatening to climb again. "There has to be a crack, a mistake, an oversight—*something*—somewhere."

"Well, the impersonator definitely made a mistake."

"An impersonator has not been confirmed." It came out sharper than he intended.

Goldstein crossed his arms and gave him a defiant look. "Why else would the cabin be burned other than to eliminate DNA? When she didn't hide her identity or anything else?"

"Sorry." Lundgren rubbed his neck. "You're right, but we need official confirmation. This has me all wound up."

"Want to kick my desk again?"

"No." That habit was what he needed to kick. "What mistake?"

"Wilmont's hotel habits. Everywhere else we've traced her to, she's remained—more or less—in one place. Weeks to a couple of months. Except here, on Midgard. They weren't aware of the difference."

"Or didn't think it was worth the effort," Lundgren said thoughtfully. "Which brings up a very interesting question. Why was she so skittish here? What is going on with the Stohlass family? What was Dougson really after? Where and how does Agent Twobears fit in with all this?"

"That's four questions."

Lundgren shot him an irritated look. "It'd be nice to get some answers."

"We'll get them, Lieutenant. There have to be other slip-ups out there. The fire was too big, too complex, and too coordinated. Somebody has to know or have seen something, even if they don't realize it."

"Or else they're hiding. Maybe we should check to see who's missing from their usual haunts, especially in the Circle. People who hang there usually have a sixth sense about survival."

Goldstein's eyes lit up. "I'll put some patrol officers on it."

"Put a word in with Narcotics. They might be able to nose out information no one will provide to a uniform. Speaking of, have you heard anything more from your cousin since he confirmed Twobears's identity for us?"

Goldstein nodded. "He's asked a couple of questions that makes me think he isn't sharing information. Last week he wanted a copy of everything we've got for Twobears's Director on Earth. I passed the request to the Captain. Also," his lips pursed, "I paid a visit to an old girlfriend last night. She works in UPMS's port office. According to her, there has been a number of express messages between Twobears and Earth."

Lundgren's scowl grew as his partner spoke. "Those Feds had better not be holding out on us. If they have something and aren't—"

They both turned at a loud knock on the door frame. It was Detective Heimann.

"Lieutenant? There's a port slug here to see you. He says it's important."

"Send him in."

A man walked in around Heimann. Average height, blue eyes, late-twenties, his clothes inexpensive but clean. A little pissed off too, Lundgren gauged, from the look he shot Heimann.

"I can stay," the detective offered, hovering.

"Thanks, but we've got it. Close the door behind you," Lundgren said curtly. Heimann had been maneuvering to get onto the task force since it formed. If he hadn't been sure it was more for a career boost than anything else, he'd have let him. The detective irritated him for some reason. From the look on Heimann's face as he snapped the door shut, it was mutual.

"I am not a port slug," the man stated angrily. "I've worked full-time at Eastport's East Terminal dock for over six years."

"Glad to hear it, and I'll apologize for my coworker. You are...?"

"Marling Medcalf McQuire and yes, my parents have a sense of humor. My siblings are Mason and Meryl."

Both Enforcers chuckled and Lundgren motioned toward the visitor's chair. "You wanted to see us?" he said.

Instead of sitting, the young man wandered over to the picture gallery. He studied Wilmont's official photo closely. The two detectives exchanged glances amid a rising sense of anticipation.

"Do you know her?" Lundgren asked hopefully.

"No." McQuire stepped sideways and stared at the surveillance stills of a bundled-up woman entering the Branson Hotel Complex. He tapped it gently. "But I know her. Lisa White Sloan, my sig-ner. We were planning to sign prenup contracts one day." He turned, his eyes shadowed. "But I haven't heard from her in two months. I'm pretty sure she's dead."

McQuire left fifty-five minutes later.

"Okay, now we're sailing." Lundgren rubbed his hands together. "We've got a timeline and our crack."

"The Captain is either going to jump up and down or out a window."

"Want to—"

"Nope. Senior."

CHAPTER 38

"I'm sorry, sir, but there's an FBI agent at the door who's insistent on seeing Mr. Twobears immediately."

"Insistent?" Gordon repeated, glancing over at Twobears.

"Two security guards worth" was the servant's dry reply.

Gordon set his wine glass down. That did not sound good. "Show him to the library, Van. Ladies, please excuse us."

Both men rose from the table, Twobears popping one last roll in his mouth. They reached the sturdy wood doors at the same time as their guest. Gordon dismissed his security escort, ushered both agents into the room and assumed his normal position of authority. He had a feeling it would be needed.

"Would you care to take a seat?" Gordon politely asked both men.

The two men preferred to eye each other.

"What's so important you felt it was worth pushing into my home, Agent...?"

"Reis. Rafael Goldstein Reis. I'm tired of being served bullshit."

Curious, Gordon asked if he was related to a detective who paid them a visit earlier.

"My cousin. I verified Twobears's credentials for him." He locked eyes with the Earth agent. "Which came as a surprise since you didn't check in with the local office as per normal procedure."

Twobears shrugged. "I'm on sabbatical."

Reis stepped closer to Twobears. "More bullshit. I want to know what you're doing here, what you're working on, and I want to know *now*." A storm swirled in Reis's eyes.

"Gentlemen, would you both sit down?" Gordon said. After a brief pause, he added in a sharper tone "It wasn't a request, *Agents*."

Gordon folded his hands on his desktop and waited until they grudgingly complied. "Now, Agent Reis, which bullshit would you like me to address? I have several piles on my plate at the moment."

"What do either of you know about my cousin's investigation? And don't give me a puzzled what-the-hell-are-you-talking-about look," Reis snapped, glaring at Twobears.

"Tough, it's all I've got to give." Twobears glowered back at him. "I don't know anything about the local authorities' investigation into the Branson Fire other than what I've followed in the news."

"I assure you, Agent Reis," Gordon said, "we've nothing to do with their investigation, nor are we trying to hinder it in any way. Our only contact was when they searched the house and interviewed everyone in residence. In fact, we are trying to assist them by pursuing a similar line, privately, in an attempt to dispel the silly-ass malicious gossip running rampant and remove the suspicious cloud hanging over us and the woman they're currently—and incorrectly—blaming for the fire."

"Convenient." Reis ignored Gordon's irritated look and locked his gaze on his counterpart from Earth. "I'm interested in Twobears's case and how it ties into my cousin's."

"No case. Sabbatical, remember?"

Reis's lip curled in anger; the storm got wilder. He held up a finger. "You've sidestepped several protocols since your arrival on Baron's private ship and in a badly beat-up condition." Another finger went up. "Your request— actually a firmly stated intent—for a year-long sabbatical was no-notice and, given the timeline, delivered to your office after receiving said beating." A third finger joined the others. "Shortly after I received confirmation of your identity, I received a request from an Agent Flowers in your Earth office to observe and report on all *your* activities."

Gordon's eyes flashed to Twobears's in a tense, unspoken question. Saw the worried answer there. Flowers was a high-placed problem. Returning his attention to Reis, he inwardly groaned at the man's narrow-eyed watchfulness. The agent hadn't missed their exchange.

After a moment, the finger count went to four. "Several days after *that*, I got another request, from your Director Thaxton no less, for copies of those same reports with explicit instructions to not inform Flowers or anyone else I'm providing duplicates."

His thumb made for a full spread. "Last week Thaxton requested a full accounting of my cousin's current case on the Branson Fire, copies of any related documents or reports to said case, and copies of any communique to or from Agent Flowers." Reis's hand closed into a tight fist. "This morning, we received word Director Thaxton was killed three days ago and his home burned to the ground in what *appears* to have been a home burglary since several expensive items identified by his ex-wife are missing."

Twobears jerked forward, his eyes going wide. "Thaxton is dead?"

"He's incinerated and my cousin is in pieces," Reis snarled. "Literally. Someone blew up their car. Lieutenant Lundgren is in surgery."

Shock reverberated through Gordon. Twobears's head rotated slowly toward him. "He wouldn't, would he?"

"He who?" Reis demanded of Twobears.

"I can't tell you."

The storm broke.

"You damn well will!" Reis roared, catapulting out of his chair. Fisting his hand in Twobears's shirt, he yanked the other man to his feet.

"Agent Reis, release him. Restrain yourself or I'll have security do it for you."

Reis forced his eyes away from Twobears. The brusque voice and steel gaze left no doubt the man standing behind the desk would do as he said.

"Reis." Gordon's voice turned sympathetic. "This will not help anything, much less your cousin."

Reis spit out several obscenities before shoving Twobears away hard enough it took him several steps to catch his balance.

Gordon's intercom beeped. He hit the button. "What?"

There was a moment of startled silence before Van's apologetic voice responded. "Sir. There are two Azusa Law Enforcers demanding to see you. A Captain Kelding and a Detective Wheeler."

Gordon sank back down into his chair and propped his head in his hands. "Send them in. Nicholas, too, please. Have him bring a couple of aspirins."

The two LE officers were escorted in. The tall, curvaceous captain's gaze shot to Reis. "I know you...one of Goldstein's cousins. FBI." He nodded. "And now you're here. Why?"

"I have something to discuss."

She folded her hands onto her hips. "What a coincidence. So do I."

The door opened again, admitting Stuart. Gwen and Reyna followed hard on his heels. The determined looks in both women's faces told Gordon they weren't leaving. Just as well. He'd have briefed them anyway.

"Nicholas is currently unavailable," Stuart said to Gordon's questioning look. His eyes slid to the Enforcers then back to Gordon. "He's been informed of our visitors and is returning as quickly as possible."

It has something to do with either Thane or Jem. Downing the aspirin Gwen handed him, Gordon brought the new arrivals up to date with a few terse sentences.

Gwen walked up to Reis and lightly touched his arm. "I'm truly sorry about Detective Goldstein. If there's anything we can do to help?"

"Start by telling the truth," he replied brusquely, pulling his arm away. He returned to his seat, stone faced and silent.

"I agree," Captain Kelding said. "There's been too much mystery swirling around this case, and your family seems to be dead center of it." She paused, her lips pressing into a tight line. "Sorry. Bad phrasing."

Gordon asked everyone to take a seat. "Please? I have a feeling this may take a while."

Reyna hesitated before choosing the small sofa to the right and behind Twobears. Stuart leaned back against the library doors, his arms crossed and eyes watchful.

"Captain, Detective?"

Kelding looked at Wheeler and they both turned to stare at Stuart. The two seats Gordon indicated would put his security guard behind them.

Stuart gave a heavy sigh and moved across the room to prop his butt on the end of the sofa opposite Reyna. "Better, ladies?"

"Captain."

"Detective."

"Touchy," he murmured.

Gordon shot Stuart a warning look then barked "*Sit!*" Kelding's eyes flashed, but they complied. He took a deep breath. *What a frigging mess.* Two Azusa LE on his right, two Federal LE on his left. Dueling at ten paces in ten minutes if this wasn't defused.

"We've already discussed Reis's reasons for being here, Captain. I'm assuming you're here because of your two men, which Reis just told us about. Please accept our condolences. As we've told Reis, we have nothing to do with his cousin's investigation other than to prove, independently, Miss Wilmont isn't involved."

"I'd like to hear what the previous discussion was about," Kelding said, looking over at the Federal Agent.

"That depends on what you came to discuss," Reis said.

"Azusa LE business."

"Sorry. FBI business."

Reyna rolled her eyes. "Oh, please. This is the inter-department cooperation both your PR offices always brag about? Why don't we just play 'I Spy?' No, wait. We can't. It requires the maturity level of eight-year-olds who actually know how to provide useful clues."

Twobears shot a grin over his shoulder.

"You all want—*demand*—cooperation and information from others, especially us *civilians*, but won't do so yourself, not even with each other. We're up against something so vast—"

"Reyna!" Twobears and Gordon said in unison.

"We're running out of time, Dad, especially if everything is connected." She looked at him, half pleading. "It's going to take all of us working together to stop it."

"That will be a *family* decision," Gordon said angrily. "It will impact—"

The curse Reyna spat out shocked her father and had four sets of Enforcer eyebrows swinging upward. "Hiring extra guards? Limiting personal activities? Triple checking cars and homes while waiting for the next strike? That's not an impact? When was the last time you needed aspirin?" She flung her hand out. "This isn't some nasty legal case being fought with words and documents and precedents in an organized courtroom under strict protocols and civilized rules."

She surged to her feet. "It's a *war*, Dad."

The three Midgard Enforcers wore shocked expressions. Twobears twisted around to face her.

"A war fought in shadows behind masks and locked doors. No protocols, no rules, and the bodies are piling up. Who's next? You? Mom? One of the kids? Thane? My *son* is out there now facing who knows what, God knows where. We've heard nothing for weeks. *Nothing*! Is he even still alive?" Her voice broke.

Twobears pushed out of his chair and pulled Reyna into his arms. She buried her head in his shoulder. Thick, anticipatory *what's next* silence filled the room.

Gordon glanced over at Stuart and frowned at his slight head shake. What was going on? He looked at his daughter and her lover. His concerns about their quiet change in status melted under the tender compassion in the face over Reyna's shoulder. His gaze lingered on her. Where was the controlled, coolly-in-charge woman? Had this truly been such a strain on her? He glanced down as Gwen's hand slipped into his. Looking up, he was surprised at the hint of tears.

"Don't you see what's happening around you?" his wife whispered softly.

Time turned backward.

Gordon was twenty-four again, a restless rogue gazing up at the black-haired, dripping-wet goddess who had knocked him on his ass. *"Don't you see what's happening around you?"* He sat mesmerized as she thoroughly and excruciatingly dressed him down, unaware she was slicing deeper into his heart with each indignant syllable. Accidently knocking her off the pier had been the best thing to happen to him. She'd become his anchor, chaining him solidly to life. She was his life. When he thought he'd lost her…

The others watched as Gordon lifted her hand. Gwen's lips curled. He kissed her wrist gently, then her palm before laying her hand briefly along his cheek. Just as he had that first time on that long-ago magical day.

Gordon looked back at his daughter and thought of the long days and endless nights of worry and planning. The reports, the research, the bomb— found in time, thank God. Katrina, attacked at her college library, the assailant's poison-filled syringe knocked from his hand by a screaming classmate. Tactics meant to harass, to divert their energies and resources from an enemy now aware he was being stalked.

He gave his wife a soft smile. As usual, she was right. Focused on the cause of their problems, he had totally missed the strain emanating from them. Gordon turned back to the Enforcers, clarity and resolve flowing into him from the hand laying firmly in his.

"If you can show us how this is connected with what we're working on, then we'll tell you—not everything, but what we can."

"Take what you can, Captain," Twobears warned when the woman's mouth opened. He tugged Reyna down on the sofa, keeping his arm around her.

Kelding's lips pursed. Her gaze shifted, locked with Reis's. Gordon saw the unspoken agreement flash between them. She turned back to the group.

"Shortly after oh-nine hundred this morning, Marling McQuire entered our office and asked to speak to the ones in charge of the Branson Fire investigation. He spent approximately sixty minutes with them, after which Lt. Lundgren contacted me by phone. I was in Odinheim for a meeting. Based on what he told me, I instructed him to take Mr. McQuire into protective custody and to a safe site. They were unable to reconnect with Mr. McQuire until approximately sixteen hundred, upon which they then did as ordered.

"They entered a safe house in the Tesaurus district at approximately sixteen thirty along with two other detectives. Lundgren and Goldstein remained for several hours, reviewing the man's testimony and trying to identify any other useful information he might possess. They were to meet with me and the rest of the task force at the station for a full debrief at twenty one hundred. As we all know" she pulled out her buzzing phone "they never arrived."

Her eyes closed for a second after reading the text. "We lost Lundgren."

She put her phone away slowly. Wheeler blinked at the ceiling several times.

"You're right. The bodies are piling up," Kelding resumed, her voice even harder than before. "We've just come from the Tesaurus site. Detective Rita Seymour and Officer Steven Abboud—he was assigned perimeter patrol—were lasered at close range, their weapons still holstered. Detective Jason Bono, Seymour's partner, had enough time to draw his weapon but not to fire it. McQuire got it in the back with a second shot up close and in the head. All electronic devices at the site are destroyed or missing."

My, God. Gordon looked slowly around the room. Gwen's eyes were closed, her hand gripped tight in his. He probably wore the same shocked-resigned look as Twobears, who still had Reyna's head buried in his shoulder. Reis was staring at his feet. Stuart was slipping his phone out of his pocket.

Twobears broke the silence first. "Captain, what information did McQuire have that precipitated these events?"

"He was sig-ner to a Lisa White Sloan, who he claimed received minor plastic surgery, a large payment, and a pair of bi-colored contacts."

Reyna's head shot up. "The impersonator! Where is she?"

"Dammit, he would've proved Jem's innocence."

"Thane and Jem will be extremely happy to hear this."

"Any salvageable notes? Recordings?"

"Where did Stuart just bolt off to?"

"*Why is this Jem Wilmont so damn important?*" bellowed Reis.

"Now," Kelding said coldly after several seconds of startled silence, "it's your turn. I believe Agent Reis's question seems to have hit the central point of this whole conversation. Who *exactly* is Jem Wilmont? What *exactly* is going on that involves her, the FBI offices of two systems, my Azusa Enforcers and a mountain of dead bodies, including my parents, my husband, and our two children."

"I am so, so sorry."

The door swung fully open. They turned, surging to their feet at the sight of the ragged group in the doorway. Nicholas supported a heavily leaning Thane while a shorter, older man with the squat powerhouse-frame of a heavy-worlder carried a nearly unrecognizable Jem. A broad middle-aged man stood behind them, his cold gaze assessing them.

"Oh, my God. Thane." Reyna rushed to her son's side. She drew back when he flinched.

"I've already contacted the hospital. Stuart will escort them in." Nicholas's grim tone conveyed more than his words. His eyes sheared to the enforcers. "You need to hear what they have to say."

Boyd walked over and carefully laid Jem on the small couch Reyna and Twobears had vacated. Thane sat gingerly on its arm.

"I'm so sorry," Jem repeated, closing her single eye in weariness. "The fire was something we didn't expect. No sane person would."

Kelding jerked forward, only to be stopped when the heavy-worlder swung out a warning arm. "What *did* you expect and from whom?"

Thane shook his head, pressing a hand against his temple. Nicholas gripped his shoulder when he swayed. "Later. It's a long story. Right now, you need to get someone to the Cameroon system. The colony was under attack when we left." Questions flew at him. "No, I don't know about damages," he said, raising his voice over the babble. "We barely made it out ourselves."

"Hello, Honey. May I to speak with Sergi? It's important."

Reis was speaking into his phone. The various stares and glares had him hastening to explain. "Honey Hamilton. Wife to General Sergi Kowalski, Planetary Defense. He's—Sergi, hello. Yes, critical in fact and needs to be kept quiet. How soon can you get a scout to the Cameroon System? In stealth mode?" he added, running his gaze over Thane's group. "I'm dead serious, Sergi. I've just been told the colony on..." he looked over.

"Cameroon Two, Magnus. Three days ago." the hard-eyed, middle-aged man supplied.

"Cameroon Two was attacked three days ago." Reis paused. "Rogues, I'm assuming. What kind of ship?" he asked, looking over at the group.

Thane's reply sent his listeners into stunned shock.

Reis's phone was demanding an answer. "Sorry, I'm...it's..." He cleared his throat. "Unknown assailants and ships—yes, plural." His raised eyebrow asked Thane if he was sure. Taking the miniscule nod as an affirmative signal, he took a deep breath and said, "Two each of Class Two and Three Frigates and—yes sir, very creditable source—and one," he swallowed, "one Class Five Battleship. Can you—Sergi?"

Reis slipped his phone back into his pocket. "Sergi is either ordering the scout or my commitment."

Stuart burst into the room, followed by several people carrying medical cases and a grav-gurney. The paramedics surrounded Thane's group and began triage. Medical babble replaced the room's quiet.

Kelding scrutinized Jem closely as she was lifted onto the gurney and they sped from the room. Detective Wheeler stayed hard on their heels at her signal.

A burly medic pulled Thane up gently, his arm positioned around the man's shoulders. Starting to walk him out slowly, Kelding stepped in front of them. "He's not going anywhere just yet. I have quest—" Yanked sideways and around, she managed to halt her automatic defensive move before striking Reyna's furious face.

Reyna jerked her head at the medic for him to continue.

"You'll get your explanations, Captain Kelding," Reyna spat out. "But only after everyone has been seen to. You've already sicced Detective Wheeler on Jem."

Kelding jerked her arm free. "You expect me to just let a woman we've been searching months for get away?"

The senior medic halted with a derisive laugh, motioning the last medic to continue on with the middle-aged man. "I don't know what's happened, but I haven't seen injuries like theirs since my last shuttle crash. The woman's collarbone is broken. Her ribcage is a broken mess and by some miracle the only thing punctured is one lung. She'd be dead if the hemorrhaging into her pleural cavity wasn't such a slow seep. She also has a deep laceration in the scalp, a broken wrist, a fractured cheekbone, and a concussion. I won't bother listing the minor stuff. The younger man isn't in much better shape."

With a final "They're not going anywhere," the medic followed Stuart out.

Reyna stared blankly at the door. Pale, frozen, she appeared unaware of anything until Twobears put his arms around her. She stared up at him. "My God, Lee, frigates and a battleship? What's happening?"

Twobears rubbed her arm, gently comforting her as he assessed the heavy-worlder over her head. "Maybe he can tell us. You don't need to go with the medics?"

Boyd stuck his hands in his pockets. "I'm okay. Mostly just bruises and a few cuts."

Gwen stood. "Why don't we first let the man sit down and we all introduce ourselves?" she said firmly. "He could probably use a drink."

"I'd appreciate one," Boyd said. He glanced sideways and up, way up, at the giant beside him. He sat down in the chair the behemoth pointed at.

"I'm Gwendolyn Holms Williams, Thane's grandmother," she said, handing him a glass of brandy. "My husband, Gordon Larrs Stohlass, is planted behind the desk. Reyna Williams Stohlass is our daughter and Thane's mother. Agent Leroy Jamison Twobears is FBI, Earth Division, on sabbatical. The tall guy, Nicholas Delvarias O'Daniel, is head of our security. Agent Rafael Goldstein Reis is also FBI, local office, and Captain Kelding—I'm sorry, I don't know your full name—is Azusa Law Enforcement."

Boyd silently studied each person as they were introduced. Then, "I'm Boyd Perez Papagiannopoulos." He took a sip. "I just go by Boyd," he said into the stillness.

There were a couple of male coughs.

"Pleased to meet you, Mr. Papagiannopoulos," Gwen said serenely. Boyd's smile flashed at her correct pronunciation. "Can you tell us how you came to be with my grandson and Jem, as well as what happened to them?"

"Baron asked me to go with him to Magnus to pick up Milhann. He was the guy with the laser-clipped arm. I'm from Brisbane, Anatolia Three, which pulls three-point two Earth gravities. Magnus only pulls two and Baron knew he would need help if something went wrong." Boyd took a sip, then followed it with a larger swallow.

"What happened?" Reyna asked.

"An ambush," he replied flatly. "A local assault team attacked us on the way back to the ship. Baron put up a good fight but was out of his league in that gravity. Jem? She never had a chance. We fought them off, then dealt with some snipers between us and the ship. We blasted off but the bastards had some 13As waiting in reserve."

Kelding's stony gaze didn't change, but the two agents' eyes widened as he spoke.

"Planetary defense fighters, alerted by Port Control, took out two of them. Cost them two of their own. Then," he stopped, stared off for a moment. "The rogue ships came out of a debris field. We took off at full burn with two of them after us, one being the battleship." He paused again, then continued quietly. "The rest vectored toward Magnus. We saw them take out all the satellites and launch two swarms. We went into O-drive as soon as we could."

Boyd stared into his glass for a long moment. "We utilized the ship's medical supplies and cleaned up as much as possible. I wrapped their ribs and treated Milhann's burn. Sorry about the bloody clothes. We were too afraid of making Jem's internal injuries worse and no one had anything that would fit Milhann."

"Who is Milhann?" Kelding demanded brusquely, as Stuart slipped back in. "Why was Baron picking him up and when did he reconnect with Wilmont? I should have him arrested for withholding information, maybe even as an after-the-fact accessory."

Boyd gave the Captain a hard look. "Daniel Rocca Milhann. Baron heard he had information about an individual his family's been investigating. Jem found us. Her showing up unexpectedly threw the ambushers off or we wouldn't be here. You should be more worried about the damage Magnus took," Boyd told her coldly. "You don't launch *two* swarms against a mostly defenseless target unless you intend on doing massive damage, ma'am."

"It's Captain."

"Then act like one."

Gordon wasn't the only one smirking at the woman's open-mouthed affront. Kelding was being an ass and the pissed off heavy-worlder had just called her on it. It also sounded like he had a military background.

"Who survived, who didn't?" Boyd continued. "Commander Devlin? The Port Master? The freckle-faced salesman?" He drained his glass in one gulp. "I still have the candy the kid wheedled me into buying." The glass shattered in his hand.

Gwen was instantly there with a cloth she'd grabbed from somewhere.

"Sorry," Boyd muttered as he carefully scraped glass into the cloth.

"It's understandable," she returned gently. "Looks like you've only a few nicks."

"Hands are tough," he said, wiping his hand across his pants. He stood. "Thanks. Could I trouble someone for a ride to the nearest transit dorm?"

Reyna stood. "That won't be necessary, Mister…Boyd. We have plenty of room here." She walked over and gripped his arm, giving him a light kiss on the cheek. "Thank you for keeping Thane alive and bringing him home."

"Your son's ship had a lot to do with it." He flashed her a tired smile. "It has some unexpected features. We wouldn't have made it to the transition point without the acceleration boost from the extra set of engines."

Reyna smiled warmly. "My son and his ship are full of surprises. If you will follow me, I'll take you to a room. Close your mouth, lady, not another word," Reyna snapped as she walked past Kelding. Flashing eyes and a pointed finger punctuated her warning.

* * * * *

Kelding glowered at the two figures disappearing out the door. "Just who did the bitch think she was?" She turned to find five hostile faces and Reis shaking his head. She'd deal with the Federal Agent later.

"Mr. O'Daniel, when did—" She jerked to a stop when Gwen Williams stepped in front of the tall man.

"Captain Kelding, I realize you may not be working at your usual competent level," she said, her voice in the sub-zero range, "due to the strain of losing your family. I was willing to allow some leeway on your behavior. You have just used it all up. You may leave now."

Another one. Guess bitchiness is inheritable. "I'm not going anywhere until—"

"Any warrants? No? Nicholas, will you and Stuart please escort the captain out?" Stohlass said, his tone matching his wife's. "Make sure she gets out the gate."

"I'm an Azusa Law Enforcement Captain. I'm investigating multiple murders, including those of several law enforcement agents," Kelding ground out as the two security guards moved to flank her.

"No, you're looking for revenge and don't care who you trample over or how you go about doing it. You have lost your objectivity, Captain, and your respectability is dangling precariously from those bridges you're burning. I suggest you do as my wife says before you also forfeit your dignity."

Pale, hands fisted at her side, Kelding spun around and marched toward the exit. Humiliation burned long after the gates closed behind her vehicle. They were right.

CHAPTER 39

Milhann groped blindly for the chair behind him. Missed. He hit the floor with a thud. It didn't hurt. His ass was numb. His whole body was numb. Reis and Twobears remained silent as he pulled himself up, sliding boneless into the seat. He used his knees to support his elbows, which he needed to brace his head. He had known when they asked to speak to him privately it wasn't going to be good. But this? His mind reeled. *Delgados. They used Delgados.*

Reis cleared his throat before continuing. "Swarms took out the defenses. They dropped three of them: Magnus City, New Adrens and the spaceport."

Named for the first colony wiped out with them, the destructive weapons had been created almost a century ago by a rogue genius with pirate tendencies. What the initial explosion didn't wipe out, the devastating firestorm it generated would. In the airlessness of space, the largest battle cruisers were annihilated in an incandescent nova of death and destruction.

Samuel Costello Jamison and his pirates held entire systems hostage with them, forcing huge payments and concessions until finally defeated by a large military force. Now three of the most destructive devices known to mankind had been used on a planet with an oil-based flora ecosystem.

"The firestorms ignited the surrounding vegetation in fast-moving conflagrations. They...grew. Merged." Reis made a helpless gesture. "Just kept...growing." He paused, took a steadying breath. "I'm sorry, Milhann. Everything east of the Mangel Divide is gone."

Milhann raised his head to stare at the two agents. "That *was* everything," he grated out hoarsely.

His planet had been settled for just under a century. He was third generation. The colonists had spread across the land situated between the east coast and the slash nearly ripping the single continent apart. He'd been to all seven trading and industrial hubs sitting strategically along the coast. Most of his people were farmers and ranchers living in small towns and family conclaves. His sister's family had a small bush-beaver farm a couple of miles east of—his mind sheared away.

All gone. Everything from the Divide to the coast was ash. Charcoal.

"There are survivors. On boats, in caves along the far northern ridge or in a few other places. A few of the defense fighters who crashed on the western side." Twobears gave his shoulder a sympathetic squeeze. "Rescue and medical personnel are already mobilizing from here. You can count on additional ones from other systems once the news spreads. They're setting up shelters on the west side."

"West," Milhann repeated tonelessly. "A few outposts. Licensed trappers and some science stations. There's a small inland sea two thirds up the Divide. They're planning a ferry service." He was rambling. He never rambled. "My nephew was on the committee drawing up the plans for a new city anchoring the western edge. They were going to call it Port Royal."

Milhann's head fell back into his hands. The two agents silently left the room.

CHAPTER 40

Two and a half weeks in an induced coma? Jem was stunned.

"You were already dangerously weakened," Reyna told her. "The doctors didn't want to take additional chances with the stress the forced-accelerated growth would put on your system. Your ribs...were a mess."

Yes, there were fuzzy memories of doctors speaking in medical tongue. Sounds. Equipment of some kind. Pain. More pain. Then nothing, until waking in a bedroom here in Thane's home. What had happened during those weeks? On Magnus? With the Law Enforcers she remembered speaking to?

Reyna brushed away her questions. Later, she said.

Laughter and conversation remained light after she was wheeled in and parked next to Thane. Her initial wariness gradually dissipated as everyone acted as if her inclusion was the most natural thing. His uncle had even gotten the back of his head bopped by his neighbor for some remark she didn't quite hear. To tell the truth, the two bowls of thick broth laced with hearty chunks of vegetables meant more than the conversations around her.

Reyna again brushed off her questions while helping her back into a comfy bed. She evidently wasn't under arrest. *Maybe I am* Jem thought sleepily. House arrest. She certainly wasn't going anywhere anytime soon. Tomorrow... questions. Tomorrow...

* * * * *

"How is she?" Gordon asked when Reyna rejoined them at the table.

"Exhausted. Weak. She's probably sound asleep by now, especially with Meryl's soup in her stomach. She's stiff and sore, nothing unexpected," Reyna added. "She needs at least a week of real sleep and food before she even thinks about getting out of that wheelchair."

"Can we hold off the others that long?" Erik asked. "Captain Kelding would have been notified when she left the hospital."

Thane frowned. "I sent word to Milhann as soon as the doctors scheduled her removal from the burn bed." Its specialized gel was used to support her battered body while she healed. "No word yet when he'll be here."

"And from Lee's message, it'll be three or four days before he can make it back." Reyna's lips pursed. "That woman can just wait. Tell her Jem's not up to a lengthy interrogation and key individuals are currently off-planet. Have her make an appointment in, say, three months."

Gordon shot his daughter an amused look. "Not hardly. But the appointment is a good idea since it keeps control in our court. We can't stall them too long or they'll claim obstruction or collusion." He shifted his focus to his grandson. "How much *do* we tell them?"

"I don't know, Granddad," he said tiredly. "Jem was either unconscious or sedated on the trip back, so we don't know what she's learned. But she must have found something. How else would she have shown up on Magnus when she did?"

"Family huddle," Gwen announced.

"Not now," Thane protested. "Jem has to be included. We need her information."

"Naturally. She's the one most affected by this mess. She also needs to know what's occurred here. We can do it over several days, gradually and stopping when she needs to rest."

"I'll keep her entertained in between."

"Really, Clint? Like your *welcome back to the land of consciousness* quip?"

"Seemed apropos to me."

His wife sighed, then bopped him again. Harder.

CHAPTER 41

The table was a beautiful reddish-gold, the clear finish polished to a warm glow. The natural grain swirled in a mesmerizing pattern. Eighteen burnt-gold chairs went well with the wood. They looked comfortable. Not that she'd get to find out. She shot an annoyed glare downward. This wheelchair was gone just as soon as she got back to the house. She'd humored Reyna, but eight days was more than enough.

A male huddle conversed quietly between her and the huge multi-pane windows lining the wall behind her. What could they possibly have left to discuss after days of non-stop planning? She glanced at the clock hanging above the door: 1340. Her stomach clinched. Twenty more minutes.

The door opened, admitting Milhann.

He had arrived late last night, looking older than she remembered. No wonder. The man was helping to rebuild a world. He was only here now to give his testimony. It was critical in proving to the Midgard Enforcers they weren't spitting bullshit. That Kurzvall's public image was a false façade hiding the real man. Catching his attention with a raised hand, she got only a hello-nod before Thane pulled him into the group huddle. Men.

1342.

1343.

1344. The door opened again. The murmurs behind her broke off as Law Enforcers filed in silently. Twobears moved to meet the newcomers, his silent hand motion indicating the seats opposite her. Her breath hitched. *No turning back now.*

Gordon took the seat at the table's head as the rest arranged themselves around her. Twobears sat on Gordon's right. While it put him sitting with the other Enforcers, everyone knew which side he was really on.

The two groups eyed each other.

"Well," Jem murmured, "we're off to a good start. No yelling or shooting."

"Yet."

Jem locked gazes with the hard-eyed woman who had shifted another person so she could sit directly across from her. It was a face she knew well from the media shots. Even with the warrant for her arrest rescinded, she was positive the Azusa Captain had wanted to drag her down to the Enforcement Center. Surprising all of them, she hadn't tried. *Yet.*

The door opened a third time, admitting two military men. The general—if she read the insignia right—dipped his chin in greeting to Gordon before taking the next seat beside the Enforcers. The other one took the seat next to her and across from the general. Curious, Jem leaned forward slightly. Why—*ah!* Both military men's chairs were angled to easily see the entire table. Their eyes watchful, shoulders tense. Expecting a physical assault, were they?

Gordon cleared his throat. "It's not quite 1400 but it looks like everyone is here so we'll go ahead and get started. This meeting will be recorded and a non-transferable copy will be provided upon request to those attending. Any other devices are to be kept off. Otherwise, they will be confiscated and you may be evicted. We have three lawyers here to oversee this, including myself."

The agent sitting next to Twobears curled his lip. "I intend to have my own *unedited* recording. You have no authority over me."

"No, but Federal Judge William Stanton Meyer does," Seth Sullivan said. "This is a closed meeting concerning critical Planetary and Federal issues. As such, all activities and/or information revealed here will be classified at the highest Federal level."

Gordon and Seth stared at the scowling Earth agent. After several seconds, so was everyone else. He finally jabbed a switch on his hand comp and tossed it on the table. Gordon motioned for Seth to continue.

"Any confidential notes you make concerning what you learn here after we've adjourned are to be considered an extension of this meeting. Same classification and must be transcribed on non-copyable media. Information may be shared, but only *as* needed, to whom *does* need it, and *only* with the agreement, in writing, of the inherited conditions. Even to other Law Enforcement personnel. Anyone who cannot agree to these stipulations, for any reason, needs to leave now."

No one moved. No one said a word. All the Enforcers, minus Twobears, frowned.

Gordon raised a finger. "Judge Meyer has also authorized immunity from prosecution for anything *explicitly* revealed here."

"What?" "Impossible!" exclaimed several listeners.

"A copy of his order will be provided with each recording or upon request."

"You can't be serious," Kelding said hotly.

"Would you like to bet your career on it, Captain?" Gordon asked, his voice a razor-sharp whip. "Anyone?" He looked around the table. "You'll be happy to hear that anything tied to that explicit item, but not referenced directly, may still be freely acted on in an appropriate manner. Does everyone understand the distinction?"

The silence held glares and a couple of head nods this time.

"Excellent," Seth said. "As for immunity, the only thing that will negate the clause is lying." He deliberately met each person's gaze across the table. "We are not here to share ambiguities, half-ass truths, or outright lies. Refusal to answer a question or reveal related information is your right, but it may bite you in the ass later."

"If anyone wants to say something off the record, please do so now," Gordon said. More silence. He flipped a switch.

"My name is Gordon Larrs Stohlass, President of Stohlass Enterprises and fully empowered lawyer for said company. I'll be mediating. The purpose of this meeting is to share information related to several cases both Midgard and Federal Law Enforcement are working on. Location is the Southeast Conference Room at Stohlass Enterprises. Time is 1412 on June 20, 2817, Midgard. Starting on my right, we'll go around the table and have everyone state their name and affiliation, if any."

"Agent Leroy Jamison Twobears, Earth, Sol System. FBI."

"Agent Adam Carlson Stallwood, Earth, Sol System. FBI."

"Agent Rafael Goldstein Reis, Midgard, Wotan System. FBI."

"Agent Jennifer Holden Gaines, Midgard, Wotan System. FBI."

"Captain Anna Fritzpatrick Kelding, Midgard, Wotan System. Azusa Law Enforcement and Commander of the Branson Complex Fire task force."

"Detective Patricia Martin Wheeler, Midgard, Wotan System. Azusa Law Enforcement and Task Lead of the Branson Complex Fire task force."

"General Sergi Harmon Kowalski, Midgard, Wotan System. Commander of Planetary Defense."

"Major Elijah Drummond Markowitz, Vangeline, Tardis System. Marines, Special Forces, temporarily attached to Midgard Planetary Defense."

"Daniel Rocca Milhann, Magnus, Cameroon System. Consultant, retired."

"Jem Seaborne Wilmont, Earth, Sol System. Umm, bartender."

"Thane Stohlass Baron, Midgard, Wotan System. Tracker."

"Bethlynn Sullivan Masters, Midgard, Wotan System. Legal Assistant."

"Seth Stohlass Sullivan, Midgard, Wotan System. Legal Advisor to Stohlass Enterprises."

"Erik Williams Stohlass, Midgard, Wotan System. CEO of Stohlass Enterprises."

"Thank you," Gordon said. "General Kowalski, you asked to say something first?"

"Yes, thank you. We believe the Branson Complex Fire was a first strike by the same individual responsible for the attack on Magnus. Someone who has zero regard for human life. Major Markowitz and I are hoping to learn something here that might give us a lead as your family appears to have some knowledge of the intertwining events."

"Intertwining," Reis retorted. "That's one way to put it."

Kelding waggled a finger at those across the table from her. "I keep getting told they're not involved. If so, why do they need immunity?"

"The immunity refers to everyone at this table," Gordon said.

"You can't be serious," Agent Gaines burst out. "For one of *us*?"

"As General Kowalski stated, there are a lot of intertwining factors in the events we're about to discuss," Gordon said, addressing the whole table. "We need complete informational transparency. Withholding something because of possible legalities or turf wars is not in our best interest. There's no telling what will be revealed. Or by whom."

Jem watched the exchange of wary glances. Yep, the implication was huge.

"Where do we start?" Detective Wheeler asked. "Do we pull it apart or put it together?"

"Why don't we start with the largest elephant in the room," Jem said quietly, placing her linked hands on the table. "Which is in some ways connected to everything else. Captain Kelding, I believe you have a number of questions for me?"

Kelding studied her for a moment. "We've had to piecemeal information about you and from a lot of different places. You've gotten around quite a lot in the last few years."

Jem nodded. "Curiosity is my vice. I like to travel, to see different places and people. I like to see what they've done and what kind of world they've created."

"Things seem to happen when you're in the area."

"Things are always happening, Captain, especially in the Port Circles."

"Have you ever killed?"

"In defense of myself or others, yes."

At Kelding's motion, Wheeler pulled out a picture from the folder in front of them and pushed it across the table.

Jem's eyebrows scrunched at the slightly blurred image. It looked like her but... "Where was this taken? I don't recognize the background."

"Branson Hotel Complex, the evening before the fire."

Jem shook her head. "I've never been there." She'd been warned about the imposter.

"Do you know a Lisa White Sloan?"

"No."

"Do you know why Sloan would go to a medical facility in the Tamarian System seven weeks pre-fire and have facial plastic surgery done?"

"If it was to look like this," Jem tapped the picture, "the obvious reason is to frame me. To make it appear I was directly involved in the fire's planning. I understand she also received specialized contacts."

"The frame worked, didn't it?" Thane said. "You issued a Republic-wide search and arrest."

Reis held up a hand. "Based on the evidence at the time, any Law Enforcement office would have done so. Her's simply beat ours to it."

"I was off-planet at the time of the fire in the Palmyra System. I remember seeing the news about it." She still saw flashes of the stark video in her nightmares. "I left Midgard two—no, three—days after the vehicular attack on Thane's grandmother and me."

"About that." Kelding leaned forward and folded her arms on the table. "Your arrival on Palmyra Two is confirmed by port records, various surveillance feeds, and a report from a Port Security officer who spoke with you. You obviously wanted everyone to know you were there. Then you disappeared— which *is* your normal mode—until checking into a rental cabin outside Azusa. Several employees remember seeing you, usually late in the evening coming or going."

"I did not return to Midgard until about three weeks ago, and then I had to be carried in. It had to have been Sloan." She tapped the picture again. "She needed to establish my 'presence' and start the impersonation."

"What were you doing on Palmyra Two? How do you travel undetected between systems?" Gaines asked.

"I had been investigating problems the Stohlass family were experiencing," Jem said, switching attention to the enforcer beside Kelding. "Rumors led me to a mercenary group based there—or they had been. The entire group is missing. As to your other question? Let's just say I have a talent for going unnoticed."

Kelding gave her a hard look. "Which means slipping back and forth wouldn't be a problem. You're seen in various security recordings at the Branson Complex for over a week prior to the fire. There's no further sightings after it."

Jem let her irritation show and tapped the picture a third time. "Again, not me."

"Do you actually believe that after giving herself an iron-clad alibi—off-planet no less—she snuck back and then conveniently leaves a trail basically screaming *I did it?*"

Markowitz's sarcasm had Kelding shooting him a dirty look. "I'm trying to get more information than what is being carefully dribbled out to us," she waved her hand, "by everyone on that side of the table." She shot Jem a frustrated glare, huffed out a breath, and sat back in her chair. "Yes, we've verified Sloan's surgery. Extensive analysis of comp graphics has also verified the woman in the Branson security images is Sloan, not Wilmont. The warrant was canceled."

"You don't need to sound so disappointed," Jem said tartly.

"Where's Sloan?" Markowitz asked.

"Unknown," Kelding said. "Her sig-ner, who brought her to our attention, indicated she was most likely dead. He's dead now too, along with five of my people. Any information they might have gained was lost. All we have is his initial interview with Lundgren and Goldstein at the Enforcement Center."

"Why go to so much trouble to implicate Miss Wilmont?" Reis asked. "Why was the Branson Complex targeted?" His eyes trailed across the faces opposite from him. "And why does this all seem to center around the Stohlass family?"

"Manipulation," Gordon replied, "and long-term planning. We believe the entire sequence of events was set up to look like an escalating feud. We were not responsible for Branson's problems and we're sure they weren't responsible for our troubles. Mostly," he added with a shrug. "Some of the vandalism on either side could have been the work of young hot-heads. The Branson Fire was meant to look like our final resolution in response to the attack against my wife. Between rumors, suspicions and maybe a few arrests, our family was supposed to be ruined, socially and financially. The method chosen was…brutal."

"You want us to believe all of your troubles, all those deaths, all the manipulations were just to ruin your family?" Kelding asked, disbelief in both voice and face.

"That was just a bonus," Jem said. She stared down at her hands. So many dead. "The Stohlass family was to be the scapegoat and punished for helping me. The main purpose was to kick off a massive manhunt utilizing Republic-wide assets." She raised her eyes. "For me."

"Why?" Kelding said bluntly.

"Because I have something someone wants very badly. Given the atrocity of the crime, he ensured the focus would be very, very strong. Once captured, he would move to reacquire me through his agents."

"Reacquire you?"

"What do you mean, 'through his agents'?"

"Who's this psycho?"

"Just what the hell do you have?" Kelding demanded.

"I hold the key to unlocking an encrypted hand computer containing all the information from Earth's Myerstone Research Lab."

Stallwood leaned forward, his eyes narrowing. "The Myerstone Lab was destroyed and its entire science team killed in an explosion about four years ago. It was never fully resolved. You were cleared during the initial investigation. The evidence, and your status, has been re-evaluated recently in light of these other events."

He tapped his hand comp, glanced over at Gordon. "Ah, retrieval only." Drawing up the information he quickly scanned it.

"Wilmont's statement, taken two days after the explosion, claims she'd quit the lab and was in town looking for a new job." He looked up and around. "On review, we've found a memo—never followed up on for some reason—identifying an individual who was positive he saw her outside the Myerstone estate shortly before the explosion. Unfortunately, the individual cannot be found for confirmation after this length of time."

"When and who ordered the review?" Reis asked.

Stallwood checked through the file. Scowled. "A little over two months ago. No record of who, though."

"An unsubstantiated memo conveniently comes to light on Earth about the same time Law Enforcement here receives an anonymous message about a highly identifiable but completely unknown assassin. No record of who ordered the review finding said memo. Hmm. Anyone else buying it?" Twobears asked, reaching over and taking possession of the hand comp. He smiled; Stallwood glared.

"This is getting outrageous," Gaines said. "You're talking about major manipulation of events both here and on Earth. Everything from the murder of Law Enforcement agents to illegally tampering with their files. What's next?"

"War." Kelding's voice was barely above a whisper, but it froze the entire table.

"Captain? Would you care to explain that, please?" Kowalski asked, leaning forward to peer around Wheeler and give her his full attention.

Kelding was staring at Gordon. "That night…there in your library, your daughter called it a war. A war fought in shadows and behind masks. I thought she just meant something here, on Midgard. A power struggle of some kind. But all that's been happening here, on Earth, on Magnus…it's all connected. Isn't it?"

All eyes shifted to the end of the table. There were several sharp inhales on seeing Gordon's slow nod.

Kowalski's hard voice was firmly in military mode. "And now we have a rogue fleet and a scorched planet. I think, Mr. Stohlass, you need to start at the beginning. Regardless of how far back it might be."

"Jem," Gordon said, "I believe that would be you." Eyes shifted again.

Jem pressed her lips together. It was time to tell a carefully worded story which told no lies but omitted her secrets. It counted heavily on her listeners making a lot of assumptions. Starting with her hiring on as general maintenance, she told them of Myerstone's true agenda. About the disagreements and the fallout.

Jem bit her lip. Now for the tricky part.

"Their lab's security system had locked up one day. They couldn't get back in to reset it, so I did it for them." It was the only time Dr. L had asked her to use her ability for them.

Stallwood gave a contemptuous snort. "Ridiculous. They had a level six system."

Why, thank you. The snotty Earth Agent just provided more credence to her story. "I can get past most security systems, including level seven." She ignored the shocked looks. "That was a mistake. Once Kurzvall learned about it, he began pressuring me to work for him. I refused."

She paused. The room waited for her to continue.

"I left Myerstone, having stayed longer than I normally do. By that time, the fallout was in full swing. Drs. Lammstein and Bluethon had terminated their agreement with Kurzvall, and he demanded copies of all their data. They refused. But Kurzvall was determined to have the data. And me."

She closed her eyes. Thane squeezed her arm lightly. She took a deep breath and looked around the table. Sympathy. Skepticism. Watchfulness. Curiosity.

"Grathen, a lab tech Kurzvall had bribed, lured me back one night with a text message using Dr. Bluethon's phone. He incapacitated me with a quick-acting drug he'd already used on the others. Dougson, Kurzvall's enforcer, and his men were waiting for him outside. They took me and all the data Grathen had stolen. I'm guessing they incapacitated him in some manner before throwing him back inside with the others. He had set the generators to overload to cover the theft."

"So, you were there. You lied in your statement."

"Yes." She met Stallwood's glare with a steady gaze. "Do you think anyone would have believed a part-time drifter over the rich and powerful head of Kurzvall Industries? Especially about afterwards, where I was taken to his apartment and he personally threatened me with dire consequences—including bodily harm—if I refused to work for him?"

Stallwood made a strangled noise. "You expect us to believe a respected citizen of Mr. Kurzvall's standing—"

"You have just demonstrated exactly why she lied. *Then*." Gordon fixed him with a hard look. "As for today, I remind you of the conditions on this meeting."

No lies. Stallwood's expression soured.

"Dougson." Reis leaned forward. "Isn't he the one who orchestrated the attack here on you and Baron?"

"Yes." Gordon gave a curt nod. "He was Kurzvall's right hand man up until, according to Kurzvall's office, two weeks before the attack on us. They state he was released for substandard performance and didn't know why he was on Midgard. Oddly enough, my investigator spoke with several in his organization and they were quite surprised to hear he'd been fired."

"Guess they hadn't gotten the memo" was Twobears's sarcastic comment.

"But he was still a recognized employee at the time of Myerstone?" Reis said flatly.

"Most definitely. Mr. Milhann also had dealings with Dougson." Several curious glances were cast the heavy-worlder's way. "Which we'll get to later," Gordon added smoothly. "Let Jem finish."

"The rest is pretty straightforward. I escaped, taking Grathen's backpack with me." Jem described finding the data, realizing why she couldn't keep it, and secretly returning it to Kurzvall encrypted and passcoded.

Thane took up his part of the narrative, describing Kurzvall's lies and skimming briefly over his search." His face hardened when he got to Jem's capture. "I was expecting LEs with a warrant. Instead, he sent Dougson and a mercenary named Branigan to Pappia."

"Obidah Ross Branigan of Granden? One of the Palmyra mercenaries?" Markowitz asked, leaning forward and staring down the table intently.

"Yeah."

"He's been on our radar for some time."

"No doubt. He was one of the most twisted, vengeful people I've crossed paths with."

"Was?" Markowitz said, eyeing Thane. "We could never link anything to him. People who came to us with information had a tendency to die. Violently. Then he disappeared about a year and a half ago. We assumed he was dead but could never find out how or where."

"They tried to kill Thane," Jem told him as Thane only shrugged. "Realizing he'd been lied to, he rescued me. They attacked us and almost succeeded. Show them the scar." He scowled at her. "Show the scar," she repeated.

Thane pulled back his hair. "From Branigan." He let it fall back into place.

"We researched Wilmont thoroughly after she came to our attention." Gaines said. "There was no report of an extra body on Pappia. Even unidentifiable."

257

"It was quick and at night; they lost, we won. Branigan's body went into an acid wash," Thane said. Irritation flashed on all the Enforcers' faces. "We sent Dougson back to Kurzvall with a message to leave Jem alone. And no, we didn't report it for several reasons, especially after Jem's explanation of events."

Thane quickly resumed his narrative, forestalling more questions. He briefly summed up his meeting and rescuing Twobears on Belladona Two. He finished with the failed attack on him and his grandfather.

"We have no idea who took over as Kurzvall's new enforcer. Whoever the guy is, he's a top-notch planner and completely amoral," Thane said, disgusted. "We believe he was the maestro orchestrating everything leading up to and including the Branson Fire after their first plan failed. He was probably behind our trap and the attack on Magnus. He's lowered psychopathy to a new level."

The Enforcers bombarded Thane with questions but Gordon held up a hand. "We're not done yet. Lee, I think this is where you need to come in."

Twobears nodded. "I went to the Belladona System to hire Baron since I needed someone outside Law Enforcement I could trust." By the time he finished his story, Stallwood was red with fury.

"This is for real?" he sputtered. "A conspiracy of political deaths, including Federal Senators? You believe Director Carl Thaxton's death was arranged from *inside* the FBI? And you didn't even give me a hint?" His voice was several notches higher by the end of his tirade.

"Why should I? To say I don't trust you is a serious understatement," Twobears retorted, swiveling his chair to face him. "You've never truly cared about the job. All you care about is getting up that next rung and whatever it takes to get there. Your six-star ass-kissing has gotten you promoted over agents with longer, better service records and more commendations. If someone could buy you a couple of those rungs, you'd take it."

Stallwood's eyes blazed. "How...how dare you."

Twobears wasn't done. "You're only here now because a couple of those kissed asses forced you on me. Are you hoping the notoriety of this case puts you in the—now fortuitously open—director's office?"

Stallwood went sheet-white, then back to red. His mouth opened, closed. "I had nothing to do with Director Thaxton's death."

"But you have no trouble sharing confidential data outside the department, do you?" Twobears's smile turned predatory and he leaned forward. "Go ahead. Deny it. *Lie.*"

Stallwood's eyes darted around the table. He swallowed. "I've shared nothing of any consequence or that would have adversely affected an investigation."

"What did you give Kurzvall?" Gaines asked, angling around Reis to pin him with a disgusted look.

"He only wanted information about Federal Senators, their family or staff."

"Who is Agent Flowers?" Reis asked, eyes narrowed.

"Jason Brabec Flowers? He was Director Thaxton's assistant and is—" Stallwood broke off and went white again.

"The current acting Director," Twobears finished, his eyebrows forming an angry V.

"I suggest this line of questioning be dropped," Gordon said quickly, "before something gets *protected,* we'd prefer not be."

"Damn straight."

Jem saw the gleam in Reis's eyes. She bet the agent planned to investigate Flowers, looking for any connection to his cousin's death.

A quiet knock at the door preceded Nicholas's entry. Gordon's face registered first shock, then anger at whatever was being whispered in his ear. "Tell him we'll meet later."

"He said now or never."

"Fine. We have a late entry into our meeting," Gordon said, biting each word off.

Nicholas returned, escorting an average-looking, well-dressed man.

The man paused, assessed the table's occupants, and then arrogantly strode to take the seat opposite Gordon. Nicholas leaned against the wall behind him. Placing a briefcase at his feet, the man sent a condescending smile winging its way down to the other end.

Gordon met and held his gaze. "Allow me to provide the introductions. The tall gentleman at the back of the room is Nicholas Delvarias O'Daniel, of Midgard and Chief of Stohlass Security. The other individual joining us is

Reginald Salazar Kurzvall of Hebros, Hermes Four. Owner and CEO of Kurzvall Industries."

CHAPTER 42

Kurzvall gave everyone what he considered a benign smile. Even Baron and the bitch.

"Mr. Kurzvall has *graciously* offered to impart important information concerning several events of interest to this meeting, including the rogue fleet," Gordon said coldly, "as long as he gets to do it *now*."

"I wish to clear up some misunderstandings that seem to be getting spread about." Kurzvall looked pointedly at Wilmont and Baron. "And this is the best time since all parties are represented here. And yes, I know about the immunity clause currently active."

"Naturally, it wasn't a consideration." Gordon's comment was loaded with sarcasm.

"It wasn't," he said, raising a number of eyebrows. "But it does keep future dealings simple." Now the eyebrows drew down over speculative gazes. *Yes, they should be wary.*

"Introductions evidently aren't necessary since you're aware all parties are represented," Gordon said stiffly.

True, Kurzvall thought, except for the heavy-worlder sitting next to Jem. No mention of him in the report he'd paid for. Must be the one Baron recruited from Pappia.

"What do you know about the rogues?" Kowalski demanded.

"I prefer to go over misconceptions first. So, Ms. Wilmont, what version about me have you spouted this time?"

Jem raised her chin and remained silent.

"You seem to be working under your own misconceptions, Mr. Kurzvall," Gordon said, hands folded and smile razor sharp. "Your preferences have no standing here. You are here on my sufferance and I will gladly have you removed if you fail to cooperate."

Twobears's smile was not pleasant. "Then I will have the extreme pleasure of arresting you as an accessory to—oh, we'll start with a Republic-wide terroristic conspiracy."

"And I'll provide your new quarters. It'll be military standard, not a cushy civilian one," added General Kowalski. He didn't bother with any type of smile. "Now. The rogue fleet?"

Only the slowly whitening of his knuckles betrayed Kurzvall's inner fury. A minute passed. Two.

"Nicholas—"

"Beckett," he spit out. "The leader's name is Joseph Kawan Beckett. The ships he's using were stolen from my shipyard."

"Who is he? Anyone know?" Kowalski threw out to the whole room.

Markowitz reached for his comp but yanked his hand back in time.

Kurzvall let them mutter among themselves before finally enlightening them. "He's a mercenary. I've hired his group a couple of times for…odds and ends."

Thane leaned forward. "Out of the Palmyra System? Last leader was Branigan?" His lips twisted at Kurzvall's nod. "Well, now we know where the mercenaries went. Did you—"

The general's hand flew up, forcing Thane to a sudden halt. "That can wait. What kind of ships and how many went missing?"

"All the ones that attacked Magnus: two each of Class Two and Three frigates and one Class Five battleship. They only had standard lasers and kinetics when they were stolen. I don't know where Beckett acquired the Delgados."

"Taurus Naval Armory," Markowitz said, tapping on the table. "An emergency inventory ordered after the Magnus attack revealed nine empty Delgado crates there. An investigation is underway to determine how, when, and what moron decided to help."

"That would've been nice to share," Kowalski said, a cheek muscle twitching.

Markowitz shot him an apologetic look. "My chain of command is a bit touchy about it."

"The maniac spent a third of his most powerful weapons in a senseless act?" Agent Gaines said.

"Deliberate act," Markowitz corrected. "He just cowed ninety-five percent of the Republic. The inventories are still ongoing so he might even have more." He turned back to Kurzvall. "How long ago did it happen?"

"At the most, three Earth-standard weeks before the attack on Magnus."

"Impossible," Markowitz said. "Especially for the Class Five."

"Everything was normal when a supply ship left the shipyard about three weeks prior to the attack. As soon as the news broke, I sent a courier to Avery— it's a barren planetoid in an uninhabited system on the edge of Sector Three— and he reported back what he found. Rather, what he didn't find. Figure four or five days to ransack the place and load all the ships. The battleship would only have required nine days transit time to the Cameroon System from Avery," Kurzvall said smugly, enjoying the shocked expressions around him. "Then just sit and wait."

Markowitz's shock turned into horror. "You built a battleship with the transfer time of a Class Two frigate?"

"You've solved the TVS problem." Kowalski sounded dazed.

"No. Just a way around it."

"My ship's comp brain said the Class Five was an unknown configuration," Thane said.

"You have the battleship schematics with you?" Markowitz said.

"Why not a cargo or passenger ship?" Erik said. "It would make more sense financially."

Kurzvall reached into his briefcase. "Not feasible. As I'm sure you'll understand once you've seen the schematics." He tossed a T-drive to the major. "That's propriety information that I expect you to protect." Which wouldn't do much good. Others would be coming up with their own designs once the information leaked out.

Markowitz shoved to his feet. "I need to leave. Please forward a recording of the full meeting to me as soon as possible." He practically raced around the table.

Kowalski made the same request as he rose to join Markowitz. Stopping at the door, he turned and favored Kurzvall with a look holding as much disgust as it did anger. "Do not leave Midgard without my authorization or you'll see that cell," he promised before striding out.

"I have additional information I believe the others would like to hear," Kurzvall said haughtily, as Stohlass attempted to end the meeting. Yes, immunity would prove handy.

Gordon paused, then ungraciously motioned for him to continue.

"So, Wilmont, back to my first question: what story are you telling?" Kurzvall settled back in his seat. "I ordered Myerstone destroyed? Everyone killed? Now why would I do that?"

"Because you're an all-around bastard. Because you're a greedy psychopath willing to kill for the exclusivity to their research. To protect your material and financial positions."

"Sociopath. There's a difference." He ignored the muttered *not by much* from his left. "As the primary source of the lab's funding, I was entitled to any data they produced."

"Their charter disagreed. I've read it," Erik said. "You evidently didn't."

"I was denied what I paid for."

"Pesky legal rules don't apply to you, right?" Thane said, his tone contemptuous. "You took what you wanted."

Kurzvall shot him a cold look. "Yes, I paid Grathen to spy and then copy their data for another lab I was establishing elsewhere. I financed their work for several years and was therefore entitled to it. I did *not* instruct him in any way to destroy the lab or kill anyone. I intended to revisit their lab—occasionally—in the future."

Shocked suffused Jem's face. "You planned to keep stealing from them?"

"They were the best. Dr. Lammstein and his group stood a better chance of succeeding than others. But even geniuses need years—decades—to resolve the universe's riddles. If ever. Even then I anticipate it'll function only on a small, planetary scale. Kurzvall Industries would remain unaffected for, oh, forever. And I did *not* pay him to kidnap you."

Although bringing Wilmont under his control was in his plans.

"There were *two* cash cards in the backpack. Yes?" He got a wary nod. "Only one was mine. I assume the other one was from whomever Grathen did sell you and your skills to. That person was also most likely the source of the drug he used. While it's possible they might also have given the kill order, I believe that's on Grathen himself. His feelings toward the scientists ranged from despise to hate. They were smarter than him and, frankly, he couldn't handle it. According to several rants I endured, Grathen believed they were holding him back and robbing him of his proper recognition."

"'Doubly rich.'" Jem said slowly. "There in the lab...right before Grathen drugged me. It's what he said I was making him."

Kurzvall bristled. "Which means your vendetta against me and Kurzvall Industries is completely unfounded, especially your tampering of the Hermes Ion Engines."

"Tampering?" Jem said blandly.

"I believe the source of contamination was found at the production facility," Gaines said. "The experts agree it's impossible—"

"Your so-called experts are close-minded idiots refusing to accept anything contrary to established dogma. They don't know how it could be done, ergo it can't be. Those engines *were* sabotaged," Kurzvall retorted. "Just like all the others."

"Okay," Gaines said skeptically, "then tell us how she did it."

"I don't know how, and it's beside the point. She *is* responsible." Kurzvall gritted his teeth at the derisive comments that followed. "She can waltz through security systems and disappear without a trace, too. Isn't everyone curious about that?"

"Yes, but it's totally irrelevant for this meeting's focus." Gordon met Kurzvall's glare with one of his own.

"Admit it," Kurzvall said, jabbing a finger at Jem. "You sabotaged all those engines."

Jem glared back. "Fine. Yes. I did."

"I demand public acknowledgement for your tampering and an apology."

"When the Core dies."

"You owe me."

"I don't owe you squat!"

"You little—"

"Enough," Gordon said firmly, then he grinned. Broadly. "Kurzvall, you've tied your own hands. You can't force her admission about the engines—which is no longer prosecutable—without violating the terms of this meeting. I doubt any Federal Judge will rule in your favor." He paused. "Unless you happen to have one in your…employ?"

He shot Stohlass a baleful glare. He wasn't about to admit that, even here.

Jem swung her gaze over the Enforcers. "I wanted to cause as many problems as possible for him," she yanked a thumb in Kurzvall's direction, "financially, reputation-wise or otherwise. I sought no profit and intended no harm to anyone. I only targeted multiengine craft and always left them with enough engines for safe operation."

"How?" Gaines asked. All she received was a shrug-smile combo.

"Any kind of tampering is a huge risk," Reis said.

"That became evident on Folsum," Jem admitted. "It never occurred to me another engine would fail simultaneously with the ones I had messed with."

"You were lucky."

"Yes sir, I was. Those pilots earned their bonus and vacations. If it's any consolation, I swore to never touch another one." She flashed a happy smile at the end of the table. "Then I learned I didn't need to."

Gordon held up a hand. "We've gotten off track. Now, Kurzvall, you were telling us about Grathen and stealing data."

It took several breaths for Kurzvall to compose himself. "When my men met Grathen outside the lab—"

"And killed him."

"—and rescued Wilmont—"

"And kidnapped her."

"And rescued Wilmont," Kurzvall repeated, ignoring Baron's barbs. "I saw no reason to not take advantage of the situation. Her skill set is quite unique."

"The perfect spy and thief," Gaines said.

"The perfect assassin," Kelding added, making Jem's eyes roll. The captain pinned Kurzvall with a cold look. "Why didn't your men stop the overload or save the others?"

"Not enough time. They barely made it to the edge of the blast zone before it exploded."

"But they had time to argue with Grathen, incapacitate him, strip him of his stolen goods, and toss him back *inside the lab* with the others before running away." Thane voice was heavily infused with sarcasm.

Kurzvall ignored the angry mutters. "Yes, I wanted Wilmont to work for me. She refused and left with Grathen's pack. She eventually returned the hand comp with the data locked, but kept the cash cards." Which he'd used to substantiate his story to Baron. "After months of trying to find her, I decided it wasn't worth the trouble or my time." He waved a hand. "I hired others."

"Like Baron, Branigan, and Beckett? Huh," snorted Reis, "your B plan." He got several snorts and a smack on the arm from Gaines.

The Azusa Captain was almost vibrating with tension, her focus completely on Kurzvall. "You and Beckett are behind everything leading up to and including the Branson Complex Fire."

"Beckett is solely responsible. His orders were to get every resource possible engaged in hunting Wilmont. Framing her for blowing up a Branson board meeting would have been sufficient. He didn't keep me appraised of his plans. I was unaware he'd changed both target and location once he learned of their upcoming reunion. And no, I don't know why he did."

"Yes," Gordon said sarcastically, "a dozen deaths would've been less messy. And the attacks on my family?"

"Besides providing the foundation for the frame? Punishment for sticking your noses in my business."

The two men glared at each other.

Kelding rose. "You are complicit in the deaths of hundreds of people. You're under—"

"Captain?" Seth cleared his throat. "Immunity clause."

She stared uncomprehending at the young lawyer for a moment. "You're serious?" She waved her hand toward the end of the table. "He's…he's…he can't…" She sank back down. Her head shook slowly at whatever Wheeler was whispering in a low murmur.

"Can we continue without the melodramatics?" Really, could these people be any more pathetic?

"I believe we've established who was behind the events on Midgard, on Magnus, and how the rogue fleet came to be. Anything else you'd like to confess—sorry—admit to while you can't be prosecuted for it?" Gordon said.

Contempt weighed heavy in the look Kurzvall aimed at the opposite end of the table. Why not? "Yes, Dougson was acting on my orders on Pappia and here although, again, things went further than I anticipated." But not far enough. Dougson should have just killed the old bastard.

Ignoring the disbelieving looks, he folded his hands on the table and said, "I have—for personal reasons—been monitoring Earth's politics. Director Thaxton's death occurred not because I ordered it but because certain individuals who were associated with me acted on their own initiative and/or to protect them-selves." He glanced at Stallwood, "Thaxton must have been close to exposing someone."

Stallwood turned white again. "Not me!"

Kurzvall looked at the Azusa enforcers. "I have no knowledge of who Beckett was working with here."

He switched his attention to Baron. "Your problems on Random Two? I was intrigued enough to look into it. From all indications it was engineered by a pissed off, albeit anonymous woman." He gave Jem a speculative look.

Jem raised an eyebrow and echoed Stallwood. "Not me."

Thane shot Kurzvall an amused smile. "Expect me to believe that?"

"Besides not caring whether you do or not? No lies." Kurzvall felt a keen sense of satisfaction as the Stohlass men exchanged glances. Who was it then? That should keep Baron looking over his shoulder. *Hmmm.* Maybe he should look more into it himself.

The heavy-worlder who had sat silently throughout the meeting stirred. "What of Tylander and Sys-Senator Roberto Stevenson's death?"

Kurzvall froze. That was getting too close to things he wasn't ready to reveal. And this from the one person in the room he didn't know. "Who are you?"

"Daniel Rocca Milhann."

Kurzvall's eyes widened. *The engineer.*

"Just what kind of consulting do you provide?" Gaines asked.

"Did. Retired now," Milhann corrected without taking his eyes off Kurzvall. "I'm a Geo-Engineer. I'm an expert at redistributing geological formations in a manner that renders the resulting area useful or permanently removes a problem."

"How does moving rocks around pertain to this meeting?" Kelding said impatiently, having regained her composure.

Milhann studied her for several annoyed seconds. Then he flashed a toothy smile. "I moved the rocks that pushed Senator Stevenson's car into a ravine."

Kurzvall sat silent. The Enforcers' eyes shifted between Milhann and him several times. Postures and facial expressions indicated Baron's group already knew it. At least he couldn't be prosecuted for it now, he thought sourly.

"You're telling us," Reis said carefully, "you were hired for, and successfully carried out, the assassination of a System Senator and his family?"

"Just the Senator." Milhann's jaw line was rigid. "I was told he always traveled to the city alone, his family taking a separate vehicle due to recent threats he'd received. It was a *lie*."

His furious gaze flashed around the table. "Think of me what you will, but I have my standards. I've refused jobs—good paying jobs—because children were likely to be included in the fatalities. I even eliminated one bastard who was seeking to have his four young cousins removed from the inheritance pot."

"Did you arrange Fed-Senator Rawlins's death?" Twobears said sharply.

"No, someone else did. Over the last six years, I've been hired for several jobs by an anonymous individual calling himself Jonston. We never met face-to-face and he always paid by cash card delivered to a pre-paid rental locker somewhere. I went after him when I heard the news about Stevenson's family. Took a couple of weeks, called in some favors, but I finally got a name." He fixed his gaze on Kurzvall. "Artemis Stein Dougson."

"I'm not accountable for whatever information Dougson may or may not have provided."

Milhann's eyes glittered and his cold smile could only be called mercenary. "Obviously just hired help himself, I wanted to know who his boss was. He was killed before I could ask him. Wasn't hard to find out then since all the FLEAs knew who Dougson was. I paid a visit to Hebros only to find your security unbelievably tight. Because of Wilmont, no doubt.

"I went home to Magnus and made plans." He glanced over at a small noise. "Yes, Agent Gaines, plans to kill. Shocked? I was an assassin. Kurzvall became aware of my interest and burned two problems with one flamethrower. My world was both trap and punishment." Bitterly he added, "I will grant the firestorm was probably unexpected."

"I am not accountable for Magnus either. Yes, it was a trap for Baron. I intended to use him to force Wilmont out of hiding. Rumors were seeded about your connection to me and carefully routed in a manner Baron wouldn't suspect. Beckett was supposed to only use local help and some XTF fighters from the shipyard for backup. He again modified plans after stealing my ships and acquiring the Delgados."

"Another fine example of employee initiative?" Seth said.

"*Ex-employee*," Kurzvall said testily. "It was probably his idea of a coming-out declaration similar to the one the pirates used a century ago."

"So. You're not *responsible* for the Myerstone explosion. You're not *responsible* for the Branson fire. You're not *accountable* for Magnus and the Stevenson family's deaths." Disgust filled every one of Gordon's words. "Just what should we hold you responsible for then?"

"All of it." Kelding's voice was frost. "Your drive has been behind everything."

"For what purpose are you ordering assassinations?" Reis demanded.

Kurzvall sat stone-faced and silent.

"I heard the rumors, too," Jem said, breaking the tense silence. "That's what took me to Magnus. I'd already spent two uncomfortable days watching Mr. Milhann before Thane and Boyd showed up." She faced Milhann. "I saw the others watching you and decided to wait and see what was going on. I'm sorry.

If I had contacted you, let you know, maybe…" She trailed off as his head shook slowly.

"No, Beckett was set on dropping those Delgados. I have to agree with the bastard here on that."

Seth looked down the table. "Does Beckett know why you want Jem so badly? Is he likely to keep trying for her himself?"

"I hope to hell not," Reis said with feeling. "He doesn't need a sneak specialist."

"He knows, to an extent," Kurzvall said, watching Wilmont tug on her braid. A nervous habit he'd noticed back at the lab. "But like most people, he's not aware of her skillset's full range." He noted the curious glances in her direction. Let them wonder. "I have no idea what he's planning now."

"If there's nothing else?" Gordon glanced around the table. No one responded. "Then this meeting is over. I remind everyone of the conditions existing on the information disclosed here." Gordon looked at the man sitting opposite him. "Despite any urges to act upon them."

People began drifting out. The hostile glances and mutterings didn't bother Kurzvall. The cold promise in Milhann's smile did.

"Wilmont," he called out before Thane could roll her out the door. "I want the passcode and encryption key now that you know I wasn't behind the lab's destruction."

Jem stared at him. "You just don't know how to ask for anything, do you. You have it with you?" Her eyes dropped to the hand comp he removed from his briefcase, rose to meet his again. "I'll think about it." She stared straight ahead as Thane wheeled her out.

Anger washed through Kurzvall. *That little bitch.* He shoved the hand comp back into his briefcase and slammed it closed.

Nicholas pushed away from the wall. "I'll escort you out."

Kurzvall spotted several huddles at the end of the hallway. Conversations stopped. Their gazes drilled into his back as he and his giant shadow walked toward the elevators.

Kelding slid in just before the elevator doors snapped shut. "Allow me to assist."

Midgard has been nothing but one humiliation after another, Kurzvall fumed. Escorted out of the building like a common interloper. His ship refused permission to land at the small port outside Azusa and forcing him into a three-hour shuttle flight. Treated with contempt, even threatened with *incarceration*, at a meeting which had not gone as he'd planned. Goals, years in the planning, now at risk of exposure due to that…that moralistic back-world assassin. Now more humiliation as he waited for his chauffeured car to arrive.

At the curb. In a fog-drizzle.

Enduring curious stares caused by the two on-guard stances behind him.

The car was still rolling to a stop when the giant politely opened the door for him. He just as politely closed it hard enough to rock the vehicle.

"Airport," he snapped to the startled driver.

Water dripped from his hair onto his ruined suit. He wanted off this condescending affront of a planet. His ship was on standby to leave as soon as he boarded. Now that had been ruined by order of a pompous ass. The vein in his neck throbbed.

And still no passcode.

CHAPTER 43

The family gathering was Jem's favorite part of the day. Whoever wanted company would drift in and out. Conversations, discussions, anecdotes: it flowed around her and occasionally swept her in. Tonight, she could do it in a comfortable chair which boasted not a single wheel.

Head back, eyes closed, Jem enjoyed the sheer pleasure of relaxing in front of dancing flames after another scrumptious meal. She missed the terrace with its breeze and night sky, but a thick rainy fog had settled in earlier. Again. Thane hadn't been exaggerating. According to her hosts, this was the predominant weather until spring, about mid-February.

Reyna and Lee Twobears were on a two-seater off to her left, wrapped so tight a skinny third could have squeezed in. Thane, Seth and Gordon were sipping drinks and conversing quietly behind her. From the overheard snippets, Kurzvall's revelations about Thane's frame bothered them. It sure bothered her. If not him, then who? And why? Would she try again?

She looked over as Gwen laughed boisterously. Seth's wife was relating the recent antics of their five-year old. Jem chuckled along with her as Gina then described the budding lawyer's attempt to talk himself out of punishment.

Milhann had already excused himself and retired for the night, but not before sharing welcome news from Magnus. The new capital of Port Royal and the Magnus Spaceport were growing at a slow but steady pace with help and donations pouring in from systems Republic-wide. The new spaceport sat on the ashes of the old. The remaining charred land would be left to nature and memories for now.

The best news of all? Milhann had unexpectedly found family. His nephew had been on the western side of the Divide overseeing final construction plans.

He had spoken only briefly about the young man and that they were living together. How do you relate to someone who watched a towering wall of flame devour everything they knew? Everyone they loved? Hopefully the two men would lean on each other when needed. She knew all about nightmares.

Jem took advantage of a lull in the conversations. "Has anyone found out anything more about Lisa Sloan? Who she was?" Other than another of Beckett's victims.

Seth nodded. "LE provided Lee with her file and McQuire's interview information. She was a teenage petty thief who went clean when she hit her twenties and entered a sig-ner relationship with McQuire. Then someone waved a lot of money under her nose. McQuire only saw the man once and at a distance. The description he gave isn't Beckett."

"Well, da—arn," Gwen said, glancing sideways at a small pair of inquisitive eyes. "Was it another local dupe or one of Beckett's rogues?"

"Who knows?" Gordon said dismissively. "If it's the first, he's probably dead like all the others. If it's the second, he's probably long gone."

"I'm thinking it was Beckett's man," Lee said. "Most likely one of his lieutenants, or whatever he calls his inner circle. Something that critical to their plans wouldn't be left to chance. I bet he was also the one doing all the cleanup."

Reyna lifted her head from his shoulder. "Cleanup? You mean murder."

"McQuire didn't know what she was hired to do?" Jem said.

Seth shook his head. "According to his statement, she refused to tell him anything other than the money was for them—for their future. Yeah, how many times have we heard that? McQuire even threatened to end their relationship. Then he lost contact with her."

"Timeline would put it around the time the impersonation began," Gordon said. "When the warrant went out for Jem, when he saw the description, he didn't know what to do. He waited, hoping she'd contact him and explain things. He finally accepted a very hard truth and came forward."

"The poor man," Gina said, lifting her son onto her lap. "What he must have felt, thinking someone he cared for could be a part of something so terrible."

Footsteps preceded one of the family servants into the room. "Miss Wilmont? There is a call for you on the house comm."

She stood slowly, a bit unsteady. Thane rose and took her arm.

"I'll take her, Van. I need to go get rid of some dinner anyway."

"Thane!" Reyna admonished, then shot an irritated look at her chuckling menfolk.

Luckily, the alcove wasn't very far. Sinking down into a chair, she debated who on a short list would be calling her. Unless…yep, it was the bastard's face popping into focus when she activated the screen.

"Have you thought about it?"

Wasn't that a sour tone. Was it due to their earlier meeting or Kowalski's later message? Gordon had gleefully passed on the news about Kurzvall being ordered to meet with a military team at his ransacked shipyard.

"Good evening. How are you? I'm doing great. Having a great time here. How about you?" An irritated look whizzed across his face. *Hah!*

"Is that supposed to mean something?"

"It means I'm sitting around with friends and no one's tried drugging, kidnapping, assaulting, or otherwise abusing me. Quite refreshing."

"Do you expect it to last?"

"Planning to send someone else after me?"

"No. Recent events have forced me to change several plans. It doesn't mean someone else won't. Others are now aware, somewhat, of your capabilities. You can thank the FLEAs for that. Their description of an individual with high-level stealth and security skills has stirred interest in a number of circles."

Shit, damn, crap. While her picture and information hadn't been released to the general public, every Federal office and port facility had been plastered with it. One wouldn't have to look too hard to find it.

"I'm willing to pay premium for use of those skills, especially since I know what they don't."

The sly smile on her screen got Granny's favorite response. "I am not working for you. Ever. Will you be sharing that premium information?"

"Not at this time," he said, the smile growing brighter. "I consider it my trump card and, as such, should be saved for the most opportune time. For me."

Jem wanted to reach across and smack that arrogant, self-satisfied smirk off his face. He was going to hold the threat over her head like the sword of…of someone. She leaned forward and asked, "What's to keep me from eliminating your trump card?"

"The same asinine morals that have kept you from doing it already or becoming the galaxy's best thief. They are extremely restrictive."

They glared at each other…and an epiphany burst like a supernova over Jem, pushing her back in her seat. She wasn't afraid of him. She wasn't afraid of the what-ifs and maybes. The frightened girl who fled Earth was gone. She had a life. She had friends. And if she wanted to keep both, she needed to face reality. It was time to face forward and accept who and what she was. *Unique.*

Tardon. It was the turning point. For the first time, she'd deliberately worked with her ability. Used it as it could be—as *she* wanted. Resolution followed hard on those realizations. Her secret couldn't keep forever and, yeah, there'd be problems. But they could be minimized. Management and control: those would be the keys. Starting with the current king-sized problem.

Her glare had gradually changed to a smile as she worked through her thoughts. Kurzvall's had changed to wariness.

"Go ahead. Make your grand announcement. I don't care," she told him.

"You think I won't?"

"I don't care," she repeated. "I'm done with running and hiding. My life is going to be as normal as I can make it. And if a situation arises that warrants it, I'll help as needed. *As needed.* Yes, it means others will gradually become aware of my full capabilities, but it's bound to happen sooner or later anyway. I'll deal with the consequences. So," she waved her hand, "trumpet your secret to the universe. Sell it to some manipulative-minded SOB with grandiose plans. But if you do," her voice turned hard, "you might want to also share this warning."

"Warning?"

"Anyone using or abusing my friends—even by proxy—to get at me will severely regret it. Maybe even find themselves an exception to those *asinine morals.*" She watched his brows pull down. Uh-huh, this tool just became a threat. That triggered another thought. "Did you ever find out who gave Grathen the second cash card?"

"No."

She chewed the inside of her lip. That was going to bite her. Sometime, somewhere. Well, nothing she could do about it for now. "You really didn't order their deaths or Myerstone's destruction?"

"I did not."

"What made you investigate Thane's frame on Random Two?"

"Curiosity and the possibility of an ally with information or resources I could use."

Right. Ask a stupid question. Despite a few misgivings, she came to a decision she'd been chewing on all evening. Boyd was right: a locked-up legacy was no legacy. "The original hand comp stays with me," Jem said, crossing her arms. "You'll receive a copy of everything on it except the last six months." Management and control. Yep, that was her new mantra.

His expression turned predatory. "Those months are crucial. Keep your secrets but give me all the data."

"No."

"I want those six months."

"No, and it's non-negotiable." Her voice lowered, became charged with emotion. "I know *exactly* why you want it. Their work will not be turned into a weapon. I'll destroy it first."

Jem's head swiveled at movement in the corner of her vision. It was Thane, heading back to the others. He gave a brief nod in passing.

How much had he heard? She turned back. Kurzvall was glaring at her. "Push it and you won't get anything. In exchange, I want a copy of all the information you gave the Major."

Glaring turned to surprise which turned into understanding. He tilted forward.

"One million credits if you can locate and return the Class Five in a reusable and relatively undamaged condition."

"Cheapskate. Twenty million *dollars*."

"Five."

"Twenty. Half up front."

The screen went blank.

Thane looked over as she rejoined the group. "Everything okay?" he asked. He turned back to his conversation when she nodded.

She put her head back and relaxed. Everything was okay. He hadn't heard her.

Three days later, Jem glowered at the items spread out in front of her. There were two hand computers, one still in its wrappings, and a T-drive that should contain the Class Five specs. She had signed the courier's log for Kurzvall's package about fifteen minutes earlier. Thane walked up and laid down the last item from the package: a credit account card.

"Account is at Wotan National Bank, in your name. Balance is ten million and one dollars. Verified. Twice." he said neutrally.

One dollar? Was that Kurzvall's idea of a finger?

"I wanted the information to help destroy the frigging thing," she snapped. "Not rescue it. I want it in twenty million pieces. Which is why I threw out such a huge number after he made that ridiculous offer."

Thane tapped the credit card. "He accepted your terms. You've been hired."

"*I have not!*" She yanked hard on her braid. "It's in my name, yes. But it's a reward for whoever brings in his frigging ship."

Thane shook his head. "He made an offer specifically to *you*, you counter-bid. After negotiations—yes, even five seconds count—he accepted." He pointed at the table. "The items you just signed for match your upfront requirements. You can bet he not only has a recording of your conversation, but has formalized it. The damn thing may get blown up in the course of events, but you've been hired to retrieve it if possible."

Thane's voice turned wry. "Sonofabitch, Jem. He finally got you working for him."

"Shit, damn, *crap*."

"Yep. That pretty much covers it." He angled his head. "Where'd you pick that up, anyway? I've heard you use it a number of times."

Jem rubbed her nose. "Mom did not like cursing. While Dad did it some-times just to rile her, I wasn't quite as brave. But like any budding teenager, I wanted to rebel. So," she shrugged "I started saying them in my head."

Thane burst out laughing. "And stringing several together was being really rebellious."

The formal contract Thane suspected arrived an hour later. After reviewing the file with his newly acquired client, Gordon sent it back with amendments calculated to get it withdrawn.

The term "ship" was replaced with "Primary Control Section (PCS)" as the entire construct was comprised of individual ships linked together. The phrase "reusable and relatively undamaged condition" was changed to "operational condition." It would also pertain only to damage received during recovery as Jem could not be held liable for any damages caused while in the possession of unauthorized squatters. If the PCS became unattainable, either destroyed or lost somewhere in space, the contract became null and void.

A paragraph was added stating any additional ship units recovered in the same agreed-on conditions would be billed at an additional five million dollars per unit. Last but not least, all monies advanced were non-refundable.

It was returned one hour later. Digitally signed.

Jem threw her arms out. "Why is the bastard throwing away millions of dollars?"

* * * * *

Thane scratched his laser scar. He understood her frustration. "Besides the satisfaction of pissing you off? He has gazillions and can afford it, especially if it gets him what he wants."

He rocked back on his heels. "Jem, it's not like you're a fulltime employee. Think of it this way. You're a specialist hired for a job by someone you don't like personally. Granddad's done it. I've done it—and not counting Kurzvall. Just deal with it and hope the Marines do blow it up."

"Nothing says I can't lead them to it."

Thane studied the fuming woman. "If you're giving him the data, why not all of it?"

Jem's eyes cut to the encrypted hand comp. "He doesn't deserve it. His new lab is already getting a head start. They can work for the rest."

Thane thrust his hands into his pants pockets and bit back a retort. While that might be true, it wasn't the truth. Another lie without lying. He thought back to that overheard snippet: *I'll destroy it first.* He couldn't decide if it was the words or the vicious tone they were delivered with that troubled him the most. It'd taken a lot of self-control to keep walking and pretend he hadn't heard it. Then there was the hostility she'd displayed when Boyd pressed her to give up the data or destroy it.

What the frigging hell was on that computer? Which was the real drive behind Kurzvall's search? Jem or Myerstone's data?

CHAPTER 44

Death permeated the base. It was a miasma clinging to the walls, thickening the air and chilling the skin. It dulled the mind and drained the body of strength, of warmth. Bodies lay where they last drew breath. Forgotten. Unclaimed.

Kurzvall stood in what had once been the Operations Control room of his nascent fleet. It was now a wrecked shell, stripped of anything useful. It matched the rest of the shipyard and the two abandoned frigates drifting forlornly. What hadn't been taken, they'd destroyed.

A vein pulsed in his neck. *His* ships, *his* property, *his* money—used by others for *their* purposes. It was intolerable. Goals he and his partners had been working toward for years—*years*—in jeopardy because of one man.

One traitorous, ambitious man.

Kurzvall was forced to admit he hadn't realized how dangerous Beckett had become. He had admired the way the man assessed and eliminated problems, including removing his predecessor upon his capture. Another spoiled plan he could chalk up to Baron and Wilmont. Dougson's body should be drifting toward some star. He'd planned on his ex-employee being the focus of the ensuing search while his new one continued unimpeded.

He had chosen to keep his new enforcer in the shadows. What a mistake that had been. It had given the man too much autonomy and too much authority. *And how*, he fumed silently, *did the bastard reward him?* By betraying him. By taking what was his.

The hotel fire on Midgard was a warning he should have heeded. Not only was it extreme, Beckett had abandoned their original plan without his knowledge or approval. He had wanted a quiet Republic-wide search for

Wilmont. Instead, it became a Republic-wide frenzy with highly recognizable and informative flyers slapped in all the major spaceports and FLEA offices.

Kurzvall rolled his shoulders. More plans ruined.

He glared at the two naval officers monitoring the on-going activity. This fiasco was squarely Beckett's fault, too. Forcing the exposure of more secrets, of key elements in his plans before he was ready. Forced to tell the authorities about the shipyard and his fleet. Forced to reveal *everything* about his Class Five.

* * * * *

Naval Task Force Commander Admiral Gleason stood in front of the transparent viewing portal, listening to the information coming in over his earpiece. Maintenance was reporting the atmospheric plant up and running. Good. Air quality should improve, though he doubted it would completely remove all the stench. He shot a contemptuous look in Kurzvall's direction. There hadn't been any effort to reclaim or clean up the place. Not even the bodies.

"It looks like they took control of the ships first, then punched several holes in the habitat dome with their lasers," Lt. Commander Johnson said quietly. "Took out over half of the personnel in one swoop."

Gleason nodded in agreement. "Then they just went through and mopped up the rest."

"Beckett was in charge of the hiring. Evidently he filled it with his type of scum."

Kurzvall's sneering comment had Gleason's back molars grinding together. Three hours in this disgusting person's presence had been two hours and fifty-nine minutes too many. Thank God the man had arrived on his own transport. He turned.

"Can you verify he is the base commander?" Gleason asked, nodding toward a closed door and the remains it hid from view. "Otherwise, we'll need DNA to identify the bloody mess."

"Name's Anderson," Kurzvall snapped. "Captain of the *New Beginnings*. Base commander is one of the bodies out in the hall. His name's Cheng."

"Ah, yes, the battleship," the Admiral said stonily. "They probably wanted the command and firing codes."

"Which the bastard evidently gave them." Kurzvall shot the door an annoyed look.

Gleason caught the flash of disgust on the guards' faces. He barely managed to keep it off his own. This man's callousness was unprecedented.

"You have yet to explain, exactly, why you felt you needed so much firepower for what is supposed to only be a system defense." The Admiral rocked back on his heels. "Which isn't even being established in the system it's supposed to be defending." Full of unnamed rocks and planetoids, the system was barely on the edge of Sector Three.

"And why," Gleason continued stiffly, "in the bloody hell did you feel the need to design a Class Five Battleship with a transit time only slightly longer than a Class Two Frigate?"

"I think the military would appreciate such a maneuverable weapon."

"The military does not appreciate a weapon designed to facilitate war."

"Then it's a good thing a system will be able to defend itself."

Gleason's eyes narrowed. "Are you expecting trouble?"

"I'm expecting you to deal harshly and definitively with the bastards who stole my property and with as minimum damage to that property as possible,"

Gleason raised a hand to stop whatever his aide was about to spit out. "We'll handle them with extreme care." He didn't bother to hide his feelings.

Kurzvall's jaw tightened. "Do what you want with the debris here." He turned and strode purposefully toward the exit. The two Marine guards shifted to block him. "Stand aside," he ordered, stalking forward. "I said—" He froze when their hands dropped to their side arms. He wheeled around to aim smoldering daggers at the Admiral.

Gleason matched them with his own. "Why all the fire power?"

The locked glares spiraled the room's tension upward. Finally, Gleason motioned for the guards to let him pass. Lip curled in disgust, he watched Kurzvall storm out of the room, the huddled entourage of ass-kissers and lawyers hard on his heels. Gleason would get his answers later. For now, he just wanted the sonofabitch out of his sight.

Johnson exploded. "He has no right to talk to you like that, sir. He showed no respect."

"I doubt he even knows how."

"The battleship. Does he know what he's done?"

"He knows."

Gleason had to admit the design was ingenious. Designed into five individually self-contained sections slightly larger than a standard Class Two frigate, each one was capable of transporting itself to their destination and then reassembling there. With the TVS limitation bypassed, how long would it take before greed and ambition sent massive destruction speeding across the Republic?

"Cold, obnoxious, arrogant bastard," Johnson muttered. "Sorry, sir," he added.

"Don't be. I happen to agree with you. Especially since I believe he's lumping the bodies in as part of the debris."

"What?" Johnson sputtered. "They're his people. How does he expect anyone to—*hell*, he is." His hand rose to his ear, absorbing the report coming across their main communication band. "The bastard has boarded his ship and the captain is requesting to undock."

The Admiral silently added a few colorful adjectives of his own.

"Shall I refuse clearance?"

"Lord, no. I'm already practicing severe restraint by withholding an order to fire." His aide grinned. "Have the men start collecting the bodies and move them to the *Ice Maiden*." The ship, designed for handling frozen cargo, had been brought for just that purpose.

Johnson passed the clearance and orders on. "We going to return them to that—?" he paused, apparently unable to come up with a suitably disgusting adjective.

"Why?" Gleason snorted. "So he can dump them in a hole or out an airlock?" Kurzvall was the universe's worst asshole, a man who evidently believed loyalty was something he bought from others and sold none himself. "No. We'll locate and return them to their families."

"Sir. What they did to Anderson? Do you think he really held out that long? Or did they just…have fun." They both glanced toward the office.

"Bit of both, I believe," Gleason said somberly. "It sends a warning. 'Mess with us, fight us, this is what you can expect.' Intimidation, Johnson, pure and simple. Just like Magnus was meant to be."

Johnson nodded. "I'll get a body bag for him."

Gleason stopped him with a hand motion. "One of ours with the naval seal on it," he said quietly. "He deserves it." He felt sure the man had protected his people for as long as he could. Gleason saw no disgrace in the man's breaking. Everyone broke. Eventually.

He turned back to the window and contemplated the planetoid turning beneath them. *Why all the firepower?*

* * * * *

Kurzvall seethed at the shipyard's receding image. The whole situation was intolerable.

The Midgard upstarts and humiliations. Beckett's betrayal. Now this…this *Admiral* deigned to treat him as if he was nobody? Who had every intention of destroying his battleship?

He was done with them.

He was done letting others run over him. He was done with stupid rules and controls that had no business being put on him.

Kurzvall's lips curled. Very well. Their plans had already been turned upside down and critical parts exposed. Time to begin implementation. Time for the Consortium to show the Republic it wasn't the only option.

CHAPTER 45

Beckett's rogues soon surpassed Jamison's pirates.

His ships captured cargo and supply ships near their transition points. The crews were put off in lifeboats if they were lucky, jettisoned out hatches if they weren't. Colony and Rim planets were also targeted, their limited defenses eliminated by fighter swarms before the raiders landed. They left behind a legacy exceeding the original.

Bank accounts drained into cash cards.

Stores and homes looted. Burned.

Beatings. Rapes. Deaths.

People missing: the young and good-looking of both sexes.

But no battleship.

Everyone's worst fear hadn't been seen since Magnus. It was only a matter of time before it and its Delgados were used against a more established, heavily defended system. Was it even now traveling through O-space toward a rich target?

Marine and Naval forces were stretched thin. To bolster them, the senior classes of all academies, regardless of time left, were graduated without ceremony and spread among the experienced. Their training had become hands-on.

The Federal Senate dusted off the Emergency Protocols drafted after Jamison's defeat. Admiral Anton StClair Gleason became the first Supreme Military Commander in the Republic's history. He would be responsible for directing and coordinating all the military branches, as well as planetary system defenses as needed.

The Republic had declared war.

CHAPTER 46

The weather was being cooperative tonight. Jem settled happily into her favorite chair on the fog-free veranda. Her eyes were on the stars, her ears on the buzzing conversations. The biggest topic was the surprising discovery of a Branson heir, the unexpected visitors having materializing just after breakfast this morning.

Sadie Feltman Ash was the nanny to Charles Branson's granddaughter, Charo Branson Vandyke. She had stepped away from the family gathering with the fretting infant and was on the other side of the hotel when the explosions occurred. She'd hidden them at her parent's home outside Azusa, first in shock and then in fear when the rumors about the Stohlass family started. Now that it was known to be an act by the pirates, she'd come to them for help and guidance.

"I know you would have preferred the guardianship," Gwen said to Reyna, "but you made an excellent choice in calling Sofia Weaver."

"Sofia will make sure Charo doesn't become a spoil of war," Reyna said. Getting several puzzled looks, she waved her hand. "Never mind. Inside joke. With the danger currently swirling around us, it just wasn't practical. Not to mention, it would have just set the tongues wagging even harder about us taking over the hotel chain."

"Sofia can handle the Branson board and ensure Charo has something to inherit. On that note, I need to have her paperwork ready for filing in the morning." Gordon left after giving his wife a peck on top of her hair, only to return minutes later with Nicholas and Major Markowitz.

The major settled into a chair, politely refusing an offered drink. "I apologize for coming so late in the evening."

"What can we help you with?" Gordon asked, lowering back into his seat.

"Actually, I'm here to speak with Miss Wilmont," Markowitz said, switching his attention to Jem. "I'm interested in knowing how you managed to avoid capture after the fire. Everyone, from all levels of Law Enforcement to, uh, interested civilians, was searching for you. The military was even alerted. Ports and their circles were plastered with your picture. Despite it all, you still managed to pop up here, there and, finally, on Magnus. With nothing in between."

"Shouldn't you have more important things to worry about?" Jem asked.

"Maybe, maybe not."

"It was discussed at the meeting but you left before we got to that part."

"I've reviewed my copy of the recording several times. It was barely mentioned and doesn't cover *how* you do whatever you do."

Jem blinked, smiled politely.

"Yeah, that was your response then, too," he said dryly. "I received an interesting vid-message this morning from Mr. Kurzvall. He insists the battleship be returned to him with little to no damage. He actually insisted I work *for* you." Annoyance colored his words.

"*Ouch*," muttered Thane.

"According to him, you, Miss Wilmont, are the only one who can do it. Which is why," he said, "it appears he's already hired you to do so."

"Not by choice. I was out-maneuvered."

"My team and I have been studying the battleship's technical information he provided. It's groundbreaking. The best and most creative design I've ever seen. We've yet to find a way to breach its defensives that doesn't include, at minimum, ninety percent casualties."

He studied her in the ensuing silence. "How is it he believes you can—supposedly—do something the Republic's best commando teams can't?"

Jem's gaze fell to her hands in her lap. *Ninety percent-plus.* They would have torn the schematics apart. Looked at every circuit, ever panel, every possible avenue.

"I don't know what to believe, but you've certainly proved you're stealthy. If it'll save lives..." He blew out a breath. "If we can locate the damn thing, can you help get my team in? You'd only be responsible for getting us past electronic and mechanical security measures. We'll handle any live guards."

"I would think the military would prefer to just aim and fire," Gwen said tartly.

"Having all the technical information does eliminate the need to keep it," Gordon added.

"Believe me, that is our first preference. Unfortunately, per one already ransomed individual, members of prominent families taken are kept on board. Since they will be released after payment received, taking them to the pirate base—wherever that is—risks someone figuring it out and alerting authorities. They're also insurance against us doing the aim and fire."

Ninety percent-plus. No way could she let them go in without her. To paraphrase an old Earth saying: *Damn the consequences, full speed ahead.* She met the Major's gaze.

"One person infiltrating is simple, Major. A whole team?" His face went blank, probably expecting a refusal. "When and if it becomes necessary, I will get your men into where they need to go. But you and all those involved must first meet three conditions."

Markowitz tilted his head. "Which are?"

"Jem," Thane said softly, "you know what this would mean."

"Yes." She knew he was worried about the reactions of others. He had also promised to support her decision and help with any arising issues. This would be the first test.

"The first condition, Major, is a complete and total non-disclosure agreement on anything anyone learns about me and my, ah, methods."

"Which I guarantee will be binding." Gordon gave him a pointed look.

"Agreed. I can understand wanting to limit specific knowledge from those not as conscientious as you. Beckett only knows in general, right?"

"That's the theory. But he had plenty of time to observe Kurzvall's security and come to a few conclusions on his own." Hopefully, not the correct ones. "My second condition is keeping the number of participating individuals as limited as possible and you as my primary contact."

"Also agreeable, since it'll be me and my team you'll be working with. The third?"

"If I say it's a no-go, at any point, at any time and for whatever reason, it's a no-go," she said firmly. "For the whole team, which includes you."

"I can't put you in charge."

"Not in charge of the team, Major, just this one security decision. I realize it'll be hard to back off if we're close, regardless of the risk. You're asking for my expertise. Don't ignore it when it becomes inconvenient or you think you know better. Don't sacrifice your team for ego."

Everyone waited in silence for his answer. They could see his struggle.

Finally, "I'll agree only if you can *prove* you're as good as it appears and it's not just some sleight of hand."

"That's fair. Will sneaking into your commando headquarters be sufficient?"

"You're kidding."

Nicholas laughed. "I still haven't found how she gets past my security. Even adding dogs hasn't stopped her."

Markowitz gave him an appraising look then turned back. "Hell, yeah. If you can get past my guys, you're on."

Jem turned to Gordon. "Is the building where Douglas ambushed you still empty?"

"I need to check, but I think so. If not, I can find a similar one."

"Jem, you're still healing," Reyna protested.

True, but two weeks of good food and rest had made a difference. "Don't worry, Reyna. It's a sneak job, not a fist fight. I should be more than ready in, say...two weeks? The major's team will need to establish themselves at whatever address Gordon provides."

The major's expression became offended. "We don't need two weeks."

Jem shrugged. "Recon. Set traps. Whatever. Two weeks to prep. Then I come calling." Her own prep would be exercising to get herself built back up.

The major's eyes grew thoughtful. "How realistic?"

"Whatever you'd normally do in a hostile zone. Making it easy defeats the purpose of the exercise."

"Hold on, now. Let's not get too realistic." Thane scowled at her, then turned it on the major. "Use dyes and stunners…nothing that will cause serious or permanent damage."

Her lips twitched. *If he only knew.* "How do you expect me to prove—"

"Agreed," Markowitz interjected. "Deadline for penetration after the two weeks? Waiting for weeks is out of the question."

"One week." She didn't want to dent their egos too badly.

"One week?" Markowitz repeated, his jaw hanging open. "You think you can infiltrate the defensives my team can set up in a *week*?"

Jem couldn't help laughing; their responses were almost comical. The Major was flabbergasted. Thane was smirking. Nicholas's expression was speculative while Gordon's was fascinated. The women simply looked contemplative.

"Didn't you say I had to prove myself? And I won't even peek while you're setting up. Promise."

Markowitz addressed Gordon without taking his eyes off Jem. "How long to verify a site?"

"I'll have something for you by the end of tomorrow."

"Then the clock starts the day after tomorrow. One week, huh? This is going to be interesting. Until then." Markowitz stood to leave.

"Major?"

He gave Thane a questioning look.

"Out of curiosity, who are the five percent Beckett didn't cower?"

Markowitz showed his teeth. "All of us military members, of course." Giving everyone a polite nod, he made his exit.

* * * * *

"We going to give her any additional days, Major?"

"Hell, no," Markowitz said. "She said one week, that's all she gets. Tonight is her last shot."

Lieutenant Blakely made a snorting sound as they stopped outside the room Markowitz had commandeered as his office. "We did set a pretty heavy perimeter, sir. And those new sensors you got us? Wow."

Markowitz unlocked his door.

"The guys are taking bets on how far *they'd* get through them. It's unrealistic to expect a civilian to—Major?"

Blakely bumped into his commander's back when he froze halfway through the door. A look over Markowitz's shoulder had him gaping in disbelief.

Wilmont. Sitting at Markowitz's desk, wearing a dark outfit and a broad smile. A small black backpack leaned against the wall behind her.

She cocked her head. "You were saying, Lieutenant?"

"*Shhhhhiiit.*"

CHAPTER 47

Two months passed in a happy blur.

Jem's body acclimated to Midgard's gravity, her bones and muscles knitting thicker and stronger. She worked out with the Stohlass security people, learning new moves and even teaching them a few. The family took her on tours to various sites around Azusa and Oslo, including their small vacation home located in a chain of islands off the west coast.

The Spine Islands were the tops of a long undersea mountain range stretching hundreds of miles toward the equator. The other end didn't stop at the continental shelf but marched right up it. The Spine Mountains wrapped a jagged wall around Oslo's western edge like, well, a spine. While the numerous fjords and bays among it were smaller cousins to Earth's Norway, their rugged beauty was breathtaking.

Spine Ridge Fjord, where the two halves met, was incredibly beautiful...and Thane's favorite spot. *The Fjord is this wild, untamed place. Untouched. You're sailing into the primordial...as if no one else exists but you.* Laughing at his horrified expression after he realized what he'd just spouted only added to his embarrassment.

Her favorite spot was Trade Street.

A colony's startup was usually short on credits. Swapping homemade goods, produce, livestock and one's muscles would be the norm for the first decade or three. Trade Street was the dusty lane in Azusa where they'd come to barter and gossip. The area had grown and matured with the city while remaining true to its purpose.

Traditionally limited to three stories, buildings hugged streets or encircled courtyards tucked here and there. The variety of merchandise offered ran the gamut of Republic-wide imports to native products and crafts. Purchases and exhausted toddlers were pushed in carts throughout it, as only emergency vehicles were allowed in.

Was it the goods or the people or the sense of history that drew her? A combination, maybe?

She had wandered through streets meandering without design, as they had when stalls and carts were set up on any open spot. Slipped through narrow alleys providing shortcuts to yet another loop. She'd relaxed on one of the many benches, sipping a drink and watching a river of life flow past her in a multitude of ages, dress and mannerisms. One day, as she studied a display of Earth goods, she came to a deep-seated realization.

Earth no longer called her. She was home.

CHAPTER 48

Nothing, Jem groaned silently, had prepared her for this kind of torture. Shopping. With Andi.

The woman was taking advantage of the winter season's rare sunny day to pick out a wedding present for Nicholas. For what totally and completely insane reason had she agreed to go with her? Must have been boredom. Yeah, that was it.

No word yet on the battleship or pirate base. Thane had left two weeks ago for a repeat client who couldn't seem to keep track of his kids. Personally, she thought it'd become a game of hide-and-seek, with each kid trying to see who could go the longest before being found. Maybe if the parents started deducting Thane's expenses from their allowances, they'd rethink the game.

"Andi?" Jem stopped in front of a shop displaying various fishing equipment. "How about this? Could he use some new gear or gizmo?" What did you get a seven-foot giant whose main pastime was studying security techniques and martial arts?

Andi shook her head. "He doesn't like to fish. I know, I know," she added when Jem gave her a wide-eye look. "Don't tell anyone. Trade Street is just a block over. Let's try there."

"Andi, it's been over *three* hours."

"I know for a fact you've spent a whole day wandering through Trade."

"That's different," Jem muttered, following her laughing friend. They emerged onto the busy street, Jem immediately dodging a fast-moving toddler. The laughing kid was snagged moments later by a red-faced, not-amused woman.

"Looks like the sun brought everybody out today," Jem noted dryly. "Where to?"

"I don't know, Jem." She let out a deep sigh and started down the sidewalk, glancing into display windows. "I just want something special. Something different."

Jem paused in mid-step. "Nicholas's family are foresters, right? Like Gordon's?"

"Yes, the Achilles Archipelago is—*what?*"

Jem grabbed her arm and dragged the taller woman past four stores, two restaurants, one squalling infant, and into Courtyard Three. The store she remembered was tucked into the left-hand corner. Breaking to a stop in front of its window, Jem motioned toward the items on display. "Maybe a wood carving?"

Ten minutes of browsing put them in front of a beautifully carved Midgard river hawk. Jem stared, entranced. That was not here before. No way could she have missed it.

The hawk stood almost as tall as her, not counting the limb it perched on with deadly talons longer than her fingers. The polished single piece of blue-black wood was done in such exquisite detail, Jem almost expected the bird to snap its beak in annoyance and take off. The head was cocked slightly to the left with a slight downward tilt, as if scanning for its next meal. From the slightly unfurled wings, it might have just spotted it.

"Oh, Jem. It's perfect."

"Is that actually life-size?" she asked, mouth slightly agape at the attached card.

"Hmm? Probably. Sea hawks can get larger."

Jem did a double take at Andi, but the woman was studying it too intently to be joking.

Thirty minutes later, Jem collapsed onto one of the benches set around the courtyard's central fountain, politely declining when Andi wanted to continue. "I'll come up with something later. We need to get back. Security needs to know about the delivery and to sneak it past Nicholas."

Jem gave the woman staring from the other side of the fountain a polite smile. The woman's eyes got bigger. Bundling her kid into a carrier, she all but ran out of the courtyard. Jem gave the sky an irritated *grrrrr*, the growing overcast matching her mood.

Her new life was off to a bumpy start. The local news had reported the retraction of her involvement in the Branson Fire, but merely flirted with the assassin rumors. They had listed some of her suspected activities and added in a few speculations from other places. She didn't even know where the Lucian System was. Several members of Thane's family had fired off complaints to the editor.

The response? *"She's news. Care to make a comment?"*

Jem doubted he appreciated the one Thane sent. Reyna's had doubled her over with laughter. Neither comment had been used.

A casually dressed man rose from an adjoining bench and stopped in front of them. "Could I ask a question?"

"As long as it doesn't have anything to do with assassins," Jem replied tartly.

"Unfortunately, Miss Wilmont, it does. How would you like to keep your redheaded friend, among others, alive?" The words jarred against the nonchalant manner with which they were delivered.

Andi took a step backward as Jem shot to her feet.

"Un-un. Run, scream, or sock me and your friend is forfeit."

"Unless it's in his boots, I don't see a weapon," Andi countered, running her eyes down his frame. She grinned. "No bulges anywhere."

He flicked her an annoyed glance. "I have men positioned…somewhere. This place has lots of trees and low roof tops. Plenty of hiding spots and targets to choose from. They'll start shooting when I give the word or if either of you causes a scene."

"Think he's bluffing, Jem?" Andi asked, one eyebrow raised.

"Possibly. The shopping trip wasn't planned. We've covered a lot of territory and moved randomly. Even with resources readily available, by the time he threw something together we would have moved on."

"True. It would've been smarter to lay in wait somewhere on our route back." Andi's lips twisted in a grimace. "But we've been here for almost an hour. Time enough to set something up if a team's waiting."

The man actually rolled his eyes. "Am I supposed to be impressed by your blasé?"

Jem's lips curled in disgust. "You're one of Beckett's mercenaries, from his original group." A well-trained, nasty bunch.

Andi stepped up beside Jem. "Did you help set up the fire?"

The man pulled out his phone and dialed. "Sound off," he snapped. He held the phone out for them to hear the responses.

"Snipe One. I'm locked on the redheaded flame, three feet front and to your left."

"Snipe Three. I've got a mouthy bitch in my sights I don't think anyone will miss."

"Snipe Two. I've got a moron on a bench just cloud watching."

He pulled the phone back. "Standby." Pocketing it, he pulled a small mobile unit out and fixed it over his ear. "Well?"

"What did Beckett do? Post a sign: psychos wanted?" Andi's fists bunched. "Nicholas is going to kill me for not taking guards."

The guy smirked. "Unless I do it first."

"Okay, the voices were different but not proof they have weapons attached. Where's Snipe One?"

"How about I tell him to fire?"

"That will be your last order." She shifted her body weight, her gaze drilling into his.

He hesitated, then said, "Yarn shop behind and to the right."

"Andi? Spot anything?" Jem kept her eyes locked on him.

There was a pause. "Yep. On the roof. Hat, scope and a finger."

"Flame, you're going to sit and admire the fountain and flowers. If Wilmont doesn't give me any trouble, you can go home in three hours. If she does, you won't know it. Take a seat. Keep your eyes off the roof and don't give him a reason to shoot. Oh, hand me your phone."

"Psychos need a reason?" Andi handed her phone over.

Jem looked at her friend as he pocketed it. "No heroics, Andi."

* * * * *

"Time starts now at…fourteen seventeen. Enjoy the rest of your day, Flame."

Hands clenched, Andi watched as they moved toward the street. Jem jerked her arm away when he tried to take it. They disappeared around a corner. She walked around the fountain twice before sitting and facing the yarn shop. If he was going to shoot her, he could damn well look her in the face. She checked the decorative clock over the courtyard entrance. Fourteen twenty-six.

Raising her eyes to the roof line, she carefully and distinctively mouthed *Bastard!*

The finger made a brief reappearance.

CHAPTER 49

Light. Voices. Hands lifting her, turning her.

"My wife doesn't do well in enclosed spaces...pill to help her relax."

Her foot slipped off a step and several hands grabbed her.

"Looks like she took two, sir." Laughter. *"Or three."*

Solid. Her knees bent. Fumbled. More hands.

"Darrin, I need your help getting her...one way to do this boss...umm umm..."

Jem felt herself lifted, flying, then the world turned upside down. She tried to focus but the legs kept shifting in and out. Legs? Oh, yeah. She'd done this before. She'd even told him he had a nice ass.

Sudden burst of laughter. Loud. *"...won't tell if you don..."*

The world shifted again and she was lying flat. Vibration. Ship. In a ship. Need to send a message. What message? Need to plan. To think. A blurry form leaned over her. There was a sharp prick in her arm. Later, she thought, sliding back under.

CHAPTER 50

The quiet was eerie. No ships blasting off, no ships landing. General Sergi Kowalski had locked the entire planet down as soon as the Stohlass family had given him the alert. Ships were searched, their crews and passengers verified. Nothing.

Two squadrons of fighters circled in orbit, the rest waited on full alert. Hastily recruited volunteers patrolled the inner system. Frigates held position in the most likely corridors of approach. If that bastardized battleship showed up, hopefully they'd spot it and blow the thing into a few more pieces before it could link up. It didn't need to use Delgados. Its firepower alone would be devastating.

His jaw tightened. Beckett's pirates. Here.

Impossible, he'd thought. Then Miss Sullivan picked Daryl Newton Richardson out from the salvaged shipyard records. The man also matched McQuire's description of his sig-ner's mysterious benefactor. Commander Cheng had neither liked nor trusted the man he'd identified as Beckett's second. It had to be a small, covert team. Four at least, according to Miss Sullivan. His jaw clenched. Twenty-nine hours and still no sign. Where the hell were they?

Azusa's small spaceport was private, authorized use only. Eastport was the only other port just barely within the three-hour limit. Unfortunately for them—*and lucky for us*—it'd been in the middle of an inbound window. No exits for another ninety minutes, which gave them time for those verifications. *Why three hours?* He'd been puzzling over that all day. It wouldn't have bothered Beckett's psycho second to have Miss Sullivan quietly disposed of somewhere, giving him time to make the next exit window.

The Port Circle had been searched twice by officials, then scoured again by its inhabitants. Hotels and dorms canvassed. The "no exception" stance had generated a flurry of complaints from a bunch of self-important, overblown civilians. That halted abruptly after arresting several for interference or obstruction. One fed-up Enforcer's report simply stated *for being extremely mouthy.* About the only thing they hadn't done was a house-to-house search.

Or island-to-island.

Kowalski rubbed his jaw tiredly. That's where he'd be, just from the sheer number available. Many of the smaller ones weren't even cataloged. With sufficient pre-positioned supplies they could squat down on one of those dots until things loosened up. Midgard couldn't be locked down indefinitely. They'd be able to choose their time for sneaking her off-planet.

At least, that's what everyone was assuming. But what if it wasn't? What if something was planned for here on Midgard? With her skills, they were screwed.

"We are so screwed."

Kowalski looked over at his aide, amused their thoughts had aligned. Tired of listening to the man's grousing about the 'unreasonably intense focus,' he'd given him Major Markowitz's classified report to read. It detailed their extensive security defensives and their ineffectiveness with regard to Jem Wilmont.

"If the pirates force her to work for them..."

Kowalski nodded. "Potentially, nothing and no one is safe. She could render our most critical systems impotent." Motioning his aide aside, he retook his seat. Best get the search started. This being the heaviest part of fog season was going to make it painfully slow.

"Contact Commander Long, Sea Patrol. Have her start canvassing—"

A chime from his computer signaled an incoming vid-call. Switching over, Kowalski found himself facing a worried looking executive.

"Mr. Poole, I understand Port Authority would like to get things moving again, but we cannot afford to let them off-planet with their captive."

"Yes, yes, I understand. Everyone's being quite philosophical about it. Well, not everyone. Several businessmen have—never mind. UPMS has requested an exemption for Eastport, General. It's their auxiliary terminal on Oslo. After all, they are just mail pods. None's left since yesterday and the impact is quite extensive—"

"I'll speak personally with them."

Kowalski's *oh shit* radar had just pinged. Four minutes later he was questioning the main comptroller for UPMS. "And when was this courier lease requested?"

"Yesterday, at thirteen fifteen," the woman replied, checking another screen. "Both compartments configured for humans. Destination was Cygna Three with a scheduled exit of seventeen hundred. Yes, I know," she said when Kowalski's mouth opened, "that was during a transit-in period. However, the request included an emergency medical exemption filing. We authorized a narrow flight path below standard orbits and posted an alert to all inbound ships."

"Did they make their launch time?" A ship's exit window had a plus-or-minus leeway of five minutes.

"Yes, sir. Seventeen three."

"From Eastport? Thank you." He closed the connection, then his eyes.

Ohhh, the sneaky bastard. They'd left before the search even started. He'd never even thought about reconfigured UPMS pods. Medical exemptions? What medical exemptions? How did they know that when he didn't?

Kowalski rubbed his face tiredly. "Remind me to never, ever, underestimate anyone."

"But, sir, wouldn't UPMS have notified us about them? Or one of the services? We've been broadcasting their pictures since yesterday."

"Richardson undoubtedly had them assume disguises." *Damn. Damn. Damn.*

The aide frowned. "Why? They didn't need them. They were leaving ahead of the search."

Kowalski made a mental note to review the list of available aides. Lt. Shaw was just not working out. "It made us think they were still here." That was the purpose of the three-hour tease. "We wasted a day turning the entire planet upside down. It gave them time to meet their connection at Cygna Three because you can bet your next promotion they didn't stay there."

"Oh. Uh, what do we do about this?" Shaw waved his hand toward the window.

Kowalski took a deep breath, released it. Took a second one. "Take the photos of Richardson and Wilmont to the UPMS auxiliary terminal at Eastport. Find the ones who strapped them into those compartments and enhance the pictures with the descriptions they provide. Inform me immediately, matching or not." He wouldn't issue the stand down until he was sure.

He stared at his aide's disappearing back. Shook his head. "We are so screwed."

CHAPTER 51

This was not how she'd envisioned it.

She would break into the pirate's base with a well-armed and massive force. Not dragged to an abandoned Survey camp in a drugged daze. Richardson had very sneakily injected the first one while pretending to give her a loving peck on the cheek. She was out before the UPMS workers snapped the seal into place. How many days had she lost?

Beckett's pirates had found a barren rock not even worth mining and simply moved in. Inactive Survey bases were left intact: it was cheaper and reusable. They served as emergency shelters, training sites, and quick reactivation if needed. Pirate base was a new addendum.

At least Beckett didn't know everything about her. She'd have been kept drugged otherwise. Thinking she was safely locked up—*hah!*—she had ghosted past guards and other late-night roamers for the past eight days. Her first discovery? Where all those missing people were kept. It hurt that she couldn't help them for now. But one particularly sadistic rapist wouldn't be revisiting them for a while. He was currently nursing two broken legs in the infirmary. A heavy cargo pallet had broken loose somehow and fallen on him.

Accidents do happen. Such a pity, too, with no regen boosters available.

Beckett was a wily tactician and effective leader, despite what else she'd like to call him. They weren't the disorganized, don't-give-a-shit mob Jem had unconsciously pictured. She found a disgustingly well-organized and cohesive group, undoubtedly due to Beckett's influence and hard fist. Security was tight; paranoia rampant. Cameras watched critical areas, backed by additional guards roaming in pairs throughout the complex. She'd verified her living quarters were camera-free with a quick peek over shoulders in the monitoring room.

Richardson had taken her reputation seriously. Two men delivered her meals and physically sat with her whenever a shuttle was prepped and launched. One always remained outside physical attack range.

Roaming had also discovered a large amount of hidden unrest.

Not everyone was happy being a pirate, or had chosen it of their own free will. Which could also explain the tight security. A small number had been coerced from Kurzvall's shipyard—pilots and battleship maintenance mostly. Beckett's original mercenaries liked the booty they were collecting, but didn't have anywhere to spend it. They and others she could only think of as port trash—*spash*—wanted to go after richer prizes.

We've got a battleship for fuck's sake. What good is it just hanging up there? When's he planning on using it?

She revised her strategy. Created a backup plan using that unrest and watched it leave on a raid. She studied security boards, watched codes entered into security panels, and located critical wiring junctions. That well-armed force she was returning with would be well prepped.

Just one problem. Getting the hell out of here.

Make that two problems. Beckett was back from his mayhem and plundering.

Kurzvall was right: he was only a sociopath. Richardson was the psychopath. This? This was worse. What sat on the other side of the table only appeared to be human.

The self-proclaimed pirate king had no eye-catching scars or other distinguishing marks. He would pass unnoticed, blending into any crowd. Until you looked into those cold, empty eyes. No soul. Nothing human looked out. No wonder he could do what he did on Midgard and Magnus.

She tossed any idea of trying to play up to or manipulate him. Drawing on her Port Circle education of never showing fear or weakness, she gave him an annoyed scowl.

"About time. I was getting bored. So, how much are you asking from Kurzvall?"

There was a slight pause before he answered. "None. You'll be working for me."

Not good, not good. "You need a bartender?"

"Don't pretend stupidity."

Jem hid the double thump in her chest with a bored, "What, exactly, would I be doing?"

"Teaching my people how to breach security others can't."

"Nope." Didn't seem to bother him.

"Then you'll do the work yourself."

"Nope." This time Beckett's head tipped slightly at her flat response. She wondered how long it had been since he'd been told that.

"I can make life painful for you. For others."

Jem leaned back and crossed her legs under the table. "I'm sure you can, and maybe I'll eventually concede. Do you want someone working for you who will either sabotage your operation or sever your balls at the first opportunity? Maybe both?"

The two guards propping the wall up behind him goggled.

"As for others, I'm assuming you mean the Stohlass family." *Show no fear, show no weakness.* "Unfortunately for you and them, saving Andi's life by cooperating with Richardson repaid my debt. I didn't count on being drugged."

Beckett sat perfectly still, studying her. The guards watched her warily, one of them nervously fingering his weapon.

"With a simple message, one of them will die. Maybe even Thane Baron."

"That's how Richardson pulled a team together so fast—you've got the Stohlass family under surveillance. You that worried about them?" She pretended amusement, letting an eyebrow drift slowly upward. How many were still there? Was he bluffing? "If they haven't gone on high security after my snatch then they deserve what comes."

Her calm façade hid painfully clenched stomach muscles. Hopefully her backup plan came through before she was forced to do something drastic, like going invisible in front of a bunch of frigging pirates.

* * * * *

Beckett's study of the woman across from him found tension but no fear. Could Wilmont have overpowered or otherwise escaped Richardson? Maybe. He had the impression she was ready to launch out of her chair right now. Attacking, not running.

Interesting. Not the usual reaction he engendered.

Wilmont crossed her arms. "I'm sure you researched me, plus whatever info Kurzvall gave you. Did you find any friends? I make acquaintances, not vulnerabilities. It's one of the first things you learn in the Circles. Sure, I might shed a tear if one of them is killed. They're a nice family and, sure, I kind of like tall, dark and brooding. Thane is interesting. But," she pursed her lips, "not enough to compromise myself. Would you?"

"You don't care at all about them? Do you expect me to believe that?"

Her lip curled slightly. "Don't care what you believe."

Could she be bluffing? With him? "Refusing to cooperate is not in your best interest."

"Forcing me to cooperate is not in *your* best interest. I don't like being drugged or kidnapped." She leaned forward. "And I don't. Like. You." She leaned back.

He blinked. Defiance. Unbelievable. "So, we're at an impasse?"

"You might want to rethink the ransom option. Kurzvall's been after me for several years and I doubt you give a damn about his balls."

One of the guards snickered.

"I find that interesting. He can afford to buy or compromise most security systems or personnel. Yet he's spent over a million dollars hunting you. Why?"

"That much? How about obsessed? And I think the key word there is *most*. If, for obvious reasons, you want to avoid your former boss, you could try the Stohlass family. They would pay something out of gratitude. Probably not as much as Kurzvall, though."

Beckett let the silence stretch as he pondered the intriguing mystery sitting in front of him, adding it to everything else he knew about her.

"It has to be something unique you can do." More silence.

"It has to be something intrinsic to you that's difficult to teach. If at all."

Dismay flickered so quickly in the woman's eyes he almost missed it. He knew Kurzvall hadn't told him everything. "It's also probably what allows you to sabotage supposedly tamper-proof engines."

"Don't know what you're talking about."

Motioning the guards forward, he ordered her returned to her quarters. "I have other things requiring my attention at the moment. We'll continue this conversation later."

Jerking her arm away from the guard's grasp, Wilmont pushed herself up. Leaning her weight forward on the table, she gave Beckett a conspiratorial smile.

His eyes widened slightly.

"There's an old Earth saying," she told him, "that what goes around, comes around." She ambled unhurriedly out of the room.

Beckett waited until the door closed before activating his voice mic. "Richardson, have a camera installed in the hallway outside Wilmont's quarters." She'd find and render it unusable if he had it installed inside.

For the first time in a long time, Beckett was unsure how to proceed. Fearful cooperation was the usual reaction for someone under his control. Wilmont wasn't afraid. She refused to cooperate. Not only did she refuse, the woman threw it back in his face. She'd insulted, even threatened him. *Challenged* him.

For the first time in a long time, interest stirred. Who was this fascinating woman?

CHAPTER 52

Thane met Boyd at the door. The only surprise he felt was it'd taken fifteen days for the man to appear at their gate. Boyd and Jem's relationship was closer to father-daughter than either one wanted to admit.

Boyd scowled. "No word?" He followed Thane into a small den.

"None," Thane said grimly. "Except from Kurzvall reminding us he's had nothing to do with Beckett and his plans for months."

"Can we believe him?"

"Yes. Kurzvall is as pissed at Beckett as the military and Feds are with him."

Thane stalked over and stared out a window. At least they now knew Jem was alive. General Kowalski had verified their departure in a courier pod and backtracked to the pilot who had unwittingly flown the disguised couple there in an express shuttle.

His jaw tightened. Furious and worried. That described both his and the family's current state. Worry for Jem. Fury for Andi. For three hours his cousin had waited, wondering if she'd be alive at the end of it. She'd walked into Nicholas's arms and stayed there for a half hour. The lack of expression on the tall man's face had said plenty. Richardson's future included a long stay in a med-bed. If he was lucky.

"This is not good. How much does Beckett know?" Boyd asked.

"About Jem? Enough to know she'd be very useful. But Kurzvall assured me Beckett was unaware of her ghosting ability." Restless, Thane turned toward a small bar built into one side of the room. "Can I get you something to drink?"

"I'll take a whisky. Pour another one for yourself. You'll need it."

Thane pivoted on his toes. "Why?"

A servant materialized in the doorway. "Major Markowitz is at the gate. He says his presence was, uh, requested."

"Let him in," Boyd ordered. His hard gaze met Thane's. "I called him. Told him to get his ass here. Best pour three glasses."

Thane shot the heavy-worlder a guarded look before giving the servant a sharp nod. He melted away. "What the hell, Boyd?"

"Wait."

Thane brought out three blue-tinted glasses. Given Boyd's habit of flexing his hands when agitated, he'd ordered some Jaguide-reinforced ones. He'd also gotten a set for his ship.

Markowitz rode his irritation into the room. His fury landed on Boyd. "Who do you think you are, *ordering* me here?"

Thane winced and continued pouring whisky.

Picking up two glasses, Boyd walked over and thrust one into the Major's hand. "I don't know where the pirate base is," he announced, "but I know how to find it."

CHAPTER 53

"Sorry to disappoint you but, really? Drugging me *again*?" Jem said as Beckett studied her untouched supper tray.

She snuggled back into the couch corner and tucked her hands under her arms. Wary, worried. Where were the two guards he normally had? Didn't think they were needed because of her drugged food? It'd been a triple dumb move, challenging him like she had yesterday. She still didn't know what made her do it.

"The individuals who brought it should be grateful I'm positive they were unaware. How did you know?"

"Sensitive taste buds." And a ghostly peep.

He settled in the seat opposite her. "You wouldn't have been incapacitated, simply more responsive to questions."

And he didn't want the guards to hear the answers.

"I'm interested in the Jaguide System."

"Not surprised." Jem feigned disinterest despite a sinking feeling. It was every crook's dream heist. "I hear they're looking at deposits on a fourth planet."

The system's ten planets were rich with assorted gems. Mines on three of them had been operational for two hundred years. More valuable than the commonly found diamonds or emeralds were the unique crystals named for their system.

The majority of Jaguide crystals were flawed or broken shards. Ground into powder and blended with other components, the resulting bond was many times the original item's strength. Blast glass was as strong as steel. Treated steel became nearly indestructible. Light and four times stronger than regular steel, jagtin—Jaguide enhanced tin—was now the workhorse of the construction industry, especially in spaceship construction.

The unflawed crystals were the single most critical component of any laser. Polished and precisely cut, their amplification factor made laser tools and weapons practical. The largest and most expensive crystals powered the military's destructive weapons.

"You do know," Jem continued," the system has more defenses than Sol, including two battleship defenders?"

Beckett didn't even blink. "The Repository is in Regent City on Jaguide Three. It collects and processes all gems mined from the various sites and sits a hundred feet down. Crystals are stored in a quantum-titanium vault three feet thick with a single entrance from the processing room. The processing room has three entrances: one for the workers and two large lifts for the gem containers. Workers arrive and leave by elevator through an intermediate entry room. No stairway. Multiple sensors, multiple safety-checks, multiple everything."

The knot in her stomach tightened even further.

"At the first indication of an intrusion or attack, warning sirens go off and all security protocols engaged. Elevators and cargo lifts are frozen and their controls locked. People in the vault and entry areas have ninety seconds to make it into the processing room before doors to both are sealed by seamless Q-T panels lowered from the ceiling. Anyone still in the vault will eventually suffocate. Those still in the entry will be blasted by automatic lasers targeting anything that moves. Lockdown will last a full Jaguide day unless an override code is received, or extended if more attempts are detected.

"Basically, Miss Wilmont, the vault was designed one hundred and eighty-eight years ago by a genius who envisioned the impossible and counteracted it. By all human standards, the vault is impregnable."

"I take it you can't get the codes or the override."

"No."

That annoyed the hell out of him. "No one to terrorize or torture to convince them smuggling is a good career?"

He gave her a blank look. "Elevator sensors would detect any crystals being smuggled out, even if the person swallowed it."

Yuck. "I take it you expect me to help you rob the bank." Yep, that would've perked the guards' attention.

"You appear willing to sacrifice the Stohlass family—in whole or in part—to keep your secrets, Miss Wilmont. How many more? Azusa's population is over three hundred thousand. You will get me Jaguide crystals or I will level the city with a Delgado."

Jem's face went white. She stared into those empty eyes. "What if I can't breach the security? What if I trigger it? You said it was impregnable."

"By human standards." He studied her for a moment. "I think you are more."

"That's…ridiculous."

"Doesn't matter. No Jaguide crystals, no Azusa. If you double-cross me, run or alert anyone, I'll take out something else. My choice of targets, planets, systems. You won't know where I will hit until it's burning."

Jem stared at the monster masquerading as a human. He'd do it. Magnus proved it. She rose slowly, deliberately. He matched her movements. Beckett would be a charcoaled cinder if rage and contempt had a physical presence.

"I'll need full schematics and operational protocols," she ground out.

Beckett reached into his pocket, pulled out a T-drive and tossed it on the small side table. "Do not reveal this to anyone. You leave in two days," he said. Pausing at the door, he looked back. "Your food will be clean. I wouldn't want to interfere with your studies."

Hours later Jem dropped her head into hands he had very efficiently tied. The monster was gone. Safe aboard his battleship. Had he read the promise in her eyes? Guessed what she intended to do, even if uncertain how she'd do it? It didn't matter now. Raising her head, she stared helplessly up at the stars from the deep shadows hiding her.

CHAPTER 54

I'll deal with the consequences.

Jem stared stonily at Westmore's image from high orbit. She'd faced Kurzvall down with that bravado, but how many times would she be forced into something she didn't want to do? Who would they hurt to do it? Had her boast been naive or foolish? Foolish naiveté? She was here, at Jaguide Three, and three hundred thousand lives hung in the balance.

She glanced at the T-drive beside her. She'd studied the files until she knew them by heart. The guy who designed the system had been a paranoid genius.

Anything capable of breaching the vault—like a military super-grade tactical bomb—would destroy the contents. Ultra-sensitive sensor arrays saturated the entire complex, both above and below ground. DNA-specific badges controlled access, eliminating the possibility of impersonations. The security comp brain monitoring everything was isolated from all external sources and had its own power supply. All input, especially those critical DNA profiles, was performed on-site by a DNA-identified manager whose changes had to be approved by two other DNA-identified supervisors.

Those were just the publicly available protections.

A memo several months old had indicated an upgrade for the vault was under review. What or how or when was unknown. Close inspection of the schematics had led to the discovery of what could only be large gas cylinders with conduits leading to all open areas surrounding the above-ground facility and the processing cavern. She'd bet there were additional, undocumented security measures known only to the Keepers.

The T-drive had dedicated several pages to them.

The Keepers were the last hidden layer, their identities unknown. They had the ability to override and even shut down the entire security system if necessary. Five individuals of unquestionable honor were entrusted to hold those critical codes. The original members were personally selected by the designer himself. Phrases such as 'mum as a Keeper' and 'private as a Keeper' had worked their way into the local idiom.

On death or retirement, a new Keeper would be carefully vetted by the remaining members. No one outside their circle could know their identities. Anonymity was the only thing protecting them from sadists willing to torture entire families to gain their secrets.

Monsters like Beckett and Richardson.

The T-drive had recounted the only instance a Keeper's identity became known.

Two back-to-back massive solar flares had wreaked havoc across the system sixty-one years ago, including the repository's protocols. Many were trapped within, the controls overloaded and shorted out. Then an elderly woman arrived and calmly shut down all the protections. Half the planet's air and ground forces stood alert while technicians worked furiously to repair or replace the damaged components. Sipping a whisky and tea concoction she'd brought with her, the woman waited patiently to reset the systems.

Her duty finished, Cecilia Gundersen Nau was escorted home by three battalions. They stood guard while she spent the day quietly surrounded by family and friends…and just as quietly died during night. Miss Nau was never prominent in politics, academia or society. She lived a simple life as a small business owner and busy mother of four. In an emotional statement to the public, her family said they had no idea when she joined the Keepers.

Jem had read the final passage several times, its poignancy touching something deep inside. *Honor and integrity were the foundations of my wife's character. Our family is honored to know she was a trusted Keeper, but it is the woman she was we will miss: wife, mother, grandmother.*

The planet's image was larger now, one side sliding completely off the viewscreen. They were inbound. The door opened after a single sharp knock. "We've received clearance to land."

Jem hadn't been surprised to find her leash once again held by Richardson. Nor was she surprised to find herself on a ship licensed as a specialized cargo hauler. They had to have some way of slipping in and out of ports when necessary. The *Hidden Trove* was a Class Five Drone, its Cargo sub-designation and basic shape inherited from the workhorse of its ancestors. It was also the largest of its class certified for both space and atmospheric use. The crew was apparently augmented with whatever skills were needed for a particular trip of mayhem and theft.

"Doesn't it bother you...what Beckett's threatening?"

"Why should it? They'll die sooner or later anyway."

Jem gave him an appalled look. "That's your justification? It's going to happen someday so it doesn't matter if you help them along? Young people planning a future. Elders enjoying another day."

Mild vibration signaled they'd entered the atmosphere.

"Children, Richardson. Children who won't have the opportunity to *live*. All their possibilities killed. Who knows, some ten-year old playing on a swing set may one day solve the Otanak TVS riddle or cure the common cold."

"Or plan his parents' and siblings' deaths so he inherits everything."

"Is that what you did?"

"Wasn't worth it, though."

"I certainly hope not."

"The bitch had already lost the bulk of it. Mom sank it into some business venture on Aquarious, which then proceeded to do just that. Those oceans define the term bottomless. After taxes and lawyer fees, I ended up with only a few properties. I sold them and used the money to go adventuring for a few years. Hunting."

Jem snapped her jaw shut. "Dare I ask for what?"

A low rumble announced the landing gear locking into place.

"A rich female, of course. Preferably one without a large or close family."

Of course, Jem thought disgustedly. "And just how long would she live?"

Richardson shrugged. "A few years at least. It would depend on what else came with her. Partying in High Society gets boring after a while." He made a throwing-away motion. "Instead, I met a man who offered me adventure and wealth and, as they say, the rest is history."

"Oh, yeah. You're definitely making history."

Vibrations had been steadily increasing, and now a brief double thud announced their landing. A slight swaying motion replaced the vibrations. Several minutes later, all motion ceased and the engines cut off.

She followed Richardson out into the corridor and past a gauntlet of closed doors. The conversation between the kitchen's two occupants stopped in mid-word as they passed through to the lounge. The door to the flight deck was open, the pilot busy over his control panel.

"Any problems?" Richardson called out.

"No," the pilot replied. "Unless you count two queries about cargo space."

"Tell them we're under a pre-arranged contract and will contact them if there's room left."

Jem headed toward the stairwell until a hand gripped her arm painfully. Unable to shake it off, she was forced to ride the lift down to the plazo with Richardson. He pulled her to the access hatch, its stairs already extended.

A waiting crewmember handed Richardson a backpack. He passed it to her, describing the pre-assembled contents she'd requested. The energy bars were all she actually needed; the rest was misdirection. He pulled a key out of his pocket and unlocked the thin tracking bracelet he'd attached to her left wrist when she boarded.

"The Repository has been closed all week for some stupid holiday. That gives you an advantage. The disadvantage? Security protocols are fully engaged until it resumes operations in approximately twenty hours."

She hid her dismay. She'd planned on hitchhiking on the elevator.

Reaching into his pocket again, he removed two counters. He handed one to her and held the other up. They both read *22:18*.

"These are plastic, old-fashioned wind-up, so there's no electronic signature or metal to detect. In twenty-two hours and—he glanced down—seventeen minutes I send a message. You determine its contents." He smirked. "And results."

***

Jem clicked her flashlight on. The vault was enormous, with crates and bins stacked on all sides and in aisles through the center. Polished crystals of all sizes winked back at her. Rough, dingy raw stones in the three shipping crates next to the closed entrance didn't wink: they absorbed her light.

She was filthy, sweaty, exhausted. Her right arm was numb from forcing her way through an unexpected electromagnetic field outside the vault. It had to be the upgrade mentioned in the memo. Bet scientists would love to learn they were right: elemental particles can exist across dimensional boundaries. She'd been forced to shift farther into the grayness than ever before to breach the field.

She checked the counter: *3:23.*

Good thing dayshift started in an hour. No way could she work her way back up in time. Most of the night had been spent making her way down to the vault, finding hidey-holes to rest in between shifts, which had grown progressively shorter. *Note to self: practice.* Right now, she couldn't shift if her life depended on it.

Jem looked up. *That wasn't a challenge,* she told the Universe.

Walking down the aisles, she stuffed crystals of all sizes into her backpack. Going back to the entrance, she finished filling her bag with raw stones from the nearest shipping crate. Sinking down, she leaned back against it and cut off her light. She took a deep breath, testing the air. Still good. As large as this place was, it should last longer than she needed.

2:00.

Where are they? Oh God, they didn't extend the closure, did they?

1: 22.

She shifted as the vault door opened. Even with two hour's rest, it still took gritted teeth and willpower to hold it while the elevator ascended for the next batch of workers and then stagger out of the facility to a nearby building. Collapsing behind it, shift released, she endured nausea she hadn't felt in a long time. Over-extended. She pulled the last energy bar from the pack's side pocket.

1: 14.

She slung the straps across her good shoulder, a slight jiggle settled the heavy pack into place. Another glance at the counter.

1: 12.

Head down, she joined the growing crowds on the sidewalk. Just another worker headed for work in the growing light.

Richardson was waiting just inside the hatch when she arrived. All six crewmembers clustered behind him.

Jem wavered to a stop in front of him. Their eyes locked.

She slid her pack off. It dropped at his feet with a loud *chunk*. The look on his face was priceless. He really hadn't thought she'd succeed. Holding the counter up for all to see—*0:11*—she let it fall on top of the pack. She stepped around him. The crew parted to let her pass. No whispering. No *how the hell?*

The silence was worse.

She took the lift to the upper level. Walking straight into the bathroom, she stripped and stepped under the hot streaming water. Face raised and eyes closed, she simply stood while the grime and sweat swirled down the drain. Finally, reluctantly, she cut the water off. Her arm was still numb, but she wrung her hair out and wrapped it in a towel as best she could. Another towel covered her from breasts to thighs.

The engines fired up.

Jem's upper lip curled. Richardson must have scheduled an exit window whether or not she returned on time. He'd be releasing the ship's small messenger pod—*where did they steal that from*—before the *Hidden Trove* itself transitioned to O-space. It'd beat them back by days and stay Beckett's plans. Until the next time.

The Delgado threat was a noose around her neck. After this, it'd be even tighter. He knew her weakness now.

Leaving her clothes where they dropped, she stepped out to find Richardson waiting. Jem couldn't even dredge up a glare as he locked the tracker around her wrist again. At least it didn't contain drugs. On legs nearly as numb as her arm, she stumbled toward her room at the far end of the corridor.

His stare burned into her back.

CHAPTER 55

Jem stepped outside her room as the last chime faded. The door next to hers at the corridor's end stood ajar. Curious, she pushed the normally locked door open.

Boxes and equipment were netted in neat piles on the floor. Shelves lined the walls, their contents also netted or enclosed. To the left was a maintenance airlock, the locker next to it holding suits of several sizes. To the right…one scowling mercenary standing in front of an open tool cabinet.

Only an inch or so taller than her, the Kid's strawberry blond hair curled around a face the same light color as hers. He was the youngest of Richardson's crew—of all Beckett's pirates, as far as she could tell. Thin, wiry, talkative as a monk, probably not even twenty, and his eyes...

"What turned someone so young, into a mercenary as cold and hard as the oldest?"

The Kid's eyes turned from cold blue chips to icebergs.

Oops. Maybe she shouldn't have said that.

"This area is off limits. Close the door behind you."

"You do realize you're all dead after we meet up with Beckett, right?"

The icebergs got a little bit colder.

"Fine," she said, backing out. She cocked her head, listening to voices drifting from the other end of the corridor. Less than thirty minutes to transit now.

She gave Richardson's door a sideways glance in passing. The man had rarely come out of his quarters since leaving Westmore and then only at odd hours to eat or issue curt orders. *Afraid the bag of crystals might prove too tempting?* From the looks she'd spotted aimed in his direction, he might not be wrong. Persuasion tactics to open the safe wouldn't be pleasant.

Her lips curled upward as she entered the kitchen. Paranoia and greed. A highly combustible mix and she was about to strike a match. Selecting a drink from the cooler, she popped it open and leaned back against the counter to study the four men sitting at the narrow table. The bearded guy on the end was Bowshur, the crew's unofficial sub-leader from what she'd observed. He was intelligent, ruthlessly self-controlled, and highly ambitious. And probably the one Richardson was most wary of.

Manx. Hard-eyed and volatile, any idiot who made fun of his stutter became a bloody mess someone had to dispose of. *Hmm. Holloway's perpetual scowl is deeper than usual.* The man had about as much patience as there was hair on his shiny dome. Tank lived up to his nickname, occupying a space almost equal to the two across from him. If it weren't for his height, she'd have thought the massively built man was a heavy-worlder.

They ignored her. Typical.

"You know you're all dead, right?" she said again, interrupting Bowshur's nauseating description of his last visit to the rape house.

Bowshur looked over his shoulder. "Raids always lose a man or two. And fights are inevitable over stuff but…" His gaze lingered for a couple of seconds before turning to fully face her. "But I don't think it's what you meant."

Jem glanced at the clock hanging over the lounge entrance. "I'm referring to the next twenty minutes or so."

"W-what makes you say th-that?"

"Would you walk into a room—much less an entire base—of thieves and killers with a whole *bag* of Jaguide crystals? Would you want word to get out on how you got them?" She waved her drink. "Beckett's not going to want to share that piece of information."

"Because anyone could grab you to do likewise," the Kid said, now propped against the corridor entrance. "He intends to keep your skills for his own personal use."

"Exactly," Jem said. "Beckett's known for eliminating risks. In this, Richardson might even be one too many. How many of your, uh, co-workers know what you left to do?" They exchanged frowns. "Okay, how many of you even knew before takeoff?" No response. "So, to state the obvious, this little jaunt was kept top secret from everyone."

Low mutters broke out. "…back to base…yeah, they'll want to know…"

"Who says we're going back?" Their glares curled her toes. "It took us just under six days to get to Jaguide Three. We've now been traveling close to seven."

Tank bolted up from the table and out through the lounge.

Jem blinked. Wow. Never underestimate a man's speed based on his size. After several seconds and a surprised yell, Tank shoved the profusely cussing pilot into the room.

Bowshur stood. "Hopkins, you want to tell us why we haven't reached base yet?"

"Richardson gave me new co-ordinates to enter and stayed on the flight deck until we transitioned. And, no, I don't know where we're going."

"Got an idea?"

"Somewhere on the rim. Maybe slightly out past it."

"W-why d-didn't you say someth-thing?"

"I don't see any of you questioning Richardson's orders."

"Let's see." Jem paused to take a sip. "Secret mission followed by unknown destination to coordinates he ensured weren't changed. What would—"

The Kid slid sideways, his back pressed against the wall. Richardson stood where he had been, watching her with cold speculation. "Inciting mutiny?"

"Inciting survival."

"No, we're not heading directly back to base." His gaze flicked over them. "We had a pre-arranged rendezvous if she succeeded because, yeah, it'd be stupid to show up there with the crystals. Just the looks from you six have kept me in my quarters with a ready weapon."

"And a means of listening to conversations," Jem added.

Richardson ignored her. "We'll be rendezvousing with Beckett in a safe area."

"Safe for who?" Bowshur asked, stroking his beard and eyeing Richardson intently. "When and how do you plan on divvying up the crystals?"

"We don't need Beckett for that."

"Give us our share now." They were all on their feet.

Holloway moved forward. "Now. Right now. We divvy the cr—" He dropped to the deck, the smell of charred flesh and insulation filling the air. The others whipped around to check for structural damage. Fortunately, it was only a smoldering black spot on an interior wall.

The potential of catastrophic damage to critical components or walls made laser weapons universally forbidden on spaceships. Even the toughest crews wouldn't risk breaching their hulls. Space stations and other environmentally enclosed structures usually banned them for the same reasons. But Richardson had drawn and fired without hesitation through Holloway's head.

"Dammit," Bowshur snarled at Richardson. "You could've hit something important."

Jem dragged her gaze from the body to gape at Bowshur. *I'm surrounded by psychos.*

"Low setting." Richardson motioned the Kid to join the others. "Now, anyone else want to argue about waiting for Beckett? Good. Wilmont, return to your quarters and stay there."

"No." She straightened her shoulders.

"Go to your room. *Now.*"

"No. And shooting me could be suicidal."

"I don't think I'll miss from this distance."

"I was referring to yours, courtesy of Beckett."

"A shoulder shot won't kill you."

"Damaged. Mobility limited? Unable to do whatever he's got planned next? Perhaps permanently?" She shook her head. "Tsk, tsk. What will your boss say?"

Richardson's expression told her he'd love to pull the trigger regardless. She finished off her drink, setting the empty can on the counter. Looked at the clock. Only minutes left. Avoiding Holloway's body, she took several steps toward Richardson.

He sidestepped away from the corridor. "Your room or a shoulder shot."

"Choices," she said thoughtfully. "Options. Life's full of them. Beckett gave me one. Now it's your turn."

"What are you blabbering about?" Richardson said.

The others had spread out around her. "You can all slip away and survive—maybe even see old age. Or you can stupidly continue down Beckett's suicidal path, which will end sooner than later. Oh, you have another option: killing me before I kill you."

"You're not a killer."

"No," Jem agreed somberly, "but I have done so when necessary. Today, tomorrow. First chance I get, I will take you and Beckett out as ruthlessly as you plan on taking out these men."

"I think you'll find me a lot harder than—" He froze, realizing his admission.

So did the others.

"Harder?" the Kid sneered from her right. "She breached the Jaguide Repository."

"Decide," Jem said. "Whatever plan you two had isn't going to work now. Do you really trust Beckett to share those crystals with you?"

She could almost hear his brain whirling, calculating odds in the tense silence. Did he think he could take all of them out before someone got him? Would he risk critical ship damage? Jem felt the shift in the O-engine. Time had run out.

Hopkins bolted for the flight deck as the double chime marking transition back into normal space sounded.

"What guarantee do I have someone doesn't shoot me the first chance they get?"

"Guys? Can you work with Richardson? At least long enough to—"

"*Got a problem,*" Hopkins shouted. *"Visual on lounge screen!"*

Tank stepped around the corner. His expletive had the others racing in. Jem and Richardson watched each other warily until she finally turned and joined them. Richardson slid in behind her, maintaining a cautious distance from everyone.

A small scout ship hung in the middle of the screen. Magnified for maximum view, it was almost split in half by two gaping slices. One cut a hole through two opposing sides, the other ripped the ship diagonally from just behind the flight deck to the engine compartment.

"Incoming signal!" Hopkins directed it again to the large screen.

It was Beckett. He was suited up except for a helmet. The flight deck was intact.

"What the hell happened?" Richardson said.

"The base was attacked in mass. They must have used half the military fleet."

Gasps, mutters, and curses filled the room.

Richardson ran a hand through his hair. "How many got out?"

"None. They were englobed, and I spotted landers being launched. I only made it because I was already outbound. As you can see, it was just barely. They probably think I'm dead or as good as, floating in a useless hunk of metal. I'll jet over when you get closer. See you then," he said, giving Richardson a terse nod. The screen returned to displaying the ruined craft.

"Wow, their deaths and/or capture really tore him up," Jem said. They'd meant nothing to him. Tools thrown away.

The silence lasted two full minutes.

"They think he's dead," Bowshur said grimly.

"Only one w-way t-to stay th-that w-way."

"Yeah. There's no one alive to tell them differently," the Kid said in a flat voice.

"To make a deal? You bet I'd turn him in." Bowshur scowled. "Any of us would."

Richardson nodded. "We're all liabilities now." He looked at Jem. "Looks like you win."

* * * * *

Richardson met Beckett at the plazo airlock, gas mask dangling from his hand.

"How'd it go?" Beckett asked as soon as his helmet was off.

"As planned." *Jet over* had been the signal. "The gas took them out before they knew anything was wrong. Gave them each a stun shot so they stayed that way. Gave Tank two. Gas just finished purging." He tossed his mask down.

Beckett removed the last of his suit and dropped it on the floor next to it. They moved toward the lift. "Wilmont?"

"Out, in my quarters. She thought she could seduce me to her side," Richardson added at Beckett's sideways look. "I enjoyed her trying."

They rode the lift upward. Richardson watched carefully as Beckett walked around, studying the men sprawled around the lounge. Bowshur and Manx were slouched in chairs. Hopkins could be seen slumped over the flight deck's console.

"Where are the others?"

"Kitchen."

Richardson trailed behind him. Tank was belly-down on the floor, an unopened drink canister in his hand. The Kid looked to have slid down the wall, his head hanging down on his chest. "Holloway got impatient about divvying up the crystals," he said. The body on the floor was coming in handy.

"Always knew that trait would get him killed someday. Why are Bowshur and Manx wearing stunners?"

"Not sure if they were planning on backing up Holloway or had plans of their own. Especially Bowshur. He was watching me too closely."

Beckett nodded, walked back into the lounge. "Crystals in the vault?"

"Yes." Richardson's muscles tensed, even as his face and voice remained neutral. This double checking everything was more than just being careful. "I stayed in my room. Armed. They were definitely thinking greedy thoughts."

Beckett turned, pulling his stunner as he did. "Given her potential and your ambition, I'm wondering if you haven't also."

Perfect. Beckett faced toward the rear. Now, if he could just keep from getting shot. Any movement toward his weapon would have Beckett firing.

"Me, the ship, the crystals...we're here," he said stiffly. "As planned. Are we going to space them or not? Am I going out the hatch with them or not?"

"Yes, to both. You I hadn't planned to, at least not right away. The attack has changed things. It was only a matter of time before they found the base anyway." Beckett's tone was conversational, murder simply a minor matter to him. "I'll fund my new lifestyle somewhere on my own."

"The crystals will fund two," Richardson ground out. *You bastard. The woman had been right.*

"Consider me greedy. Unfortunately for you—and Wilmont now—I can't run the risk of being exposed as alive and well. They'll never stop looking. Any false ID, no matter how good, will eventually crumble under that level of scrutiny."

Hopkins's rise had been stealthy, his hidden stunner held ready. Richardson kept his eyes on Beckett, but some instinct must have warned him.

Beckett stepped sideways and looked back. "Hopkins!"

"Now!" Richardson shouted.

Beckett stared as bodies began standing and pulling weapons from holsters. Tank stepped into the room.

"Drop the stunner," Richardson ordered.

Beckett looked around him before complying. Grabbing Richardson in a swift move, he yanked the man's laz-gun free. Arm around his neck, weapon at Richardson's head, Beckett kept him positioned in front and began backing toward the stairwell.

"Go ahead, blast him," Bowshur growled. "We don't care. The bastard was planning on killing us."

Beckett scanned the room. "Where's the Kid?" He shot a quick glance over his shoulder. Changing direction, he backed until he came up against a wall. Sliding sideways, he found himself cornered. Literally.

* * * * *

Jem walked into the lounge. "You're outnumbered and there's nowhere to go. They've agreed to help me turn you over to Law Enforcement in exchange for letting them disappear with the crystals." Even Richardson, which stung the most. Enough she almost hadn't made the deal.

"That's no bargain."

"You'll be alive. Considering what you had planned for them, you should count yourself lucky."

"I have another idea. I'll split the crystals, fifty-fifty, with the last man standing."

Jem stared at him. "You want them to fight each other?"

"They're thinking about it. Thinking about how rich they'll be."

Jem rotated slowly. They were eyeing each other, evaluating. Her hands clenched. *Damn him!*

"Are you going to hand him the advantage?"

Jem whipped around. The Kid was hanging on a stair rung.

Stepping to the deck, he gazed at each man in turn. "Eliminate each other and it only leaves one for him to take out. Did you not hear what he said to Richardson? The only thing he'll split is your skull." He nodded toward Jem. "She'll keep her promise. We stick to the deal."

"Agreed." Bowshur said, glancing around at the others. "Besides," he continued, face lighting with vicious glee, "I like the idea of him rotting on a Fed-Pen planet while we enjoy life's luxuries." Several other smiles now matched his.

Beckett took in their unyielding faces. After a moment, he shoved Richardson away and tossed the gun to him. "I still have the advantage. You won't get those crystals without my co-operation. I'm the only one who can access the vault."

Richardson raised an eyebrow. "I set the security code."

"Check the log. You'll find a transmission from me to the ship after I terminated our conversation."

Hopkins dashed onto the flight deck. He returned quickly, his face set. "He's correct."

"*Ship comp on*," Beckett said, activating the computer's audio input. "Identify last transmission received."

"Transmission received from Master Controller," stated a flat, metallic voice. "Identity Beckett, Tarsus five nine—"

"Stop," Beckett commanded. "Identify transmission content."

"Command to activate Beckett passcode Three-Exclusive and arm protection devices."

"Comp off. Any further questions?"

"Protection devices?" Richardson asked warily.

"Explosives built into the vault's walls. All of them. Any tampering," this said with a look toward Jem, "will result in a very big hole and a lot of expensive space dust."

"Doesn't the pilot have a Master override?" Bowshur asked Hopkins.

"Normally, yes. Someone in the command crew has to know how to reset the command in case the current Master becomes incapacitated. Or dead," he added, glaring at Beckett. "But he never gave it to me."

"Or me," Richardson said, disgust in his voice. "He probably didn't even set one."

"Do we deal, or do you think you can convince Wilmont to get more? Sorry, I don't have any Delgados with me."

"Can we set down somewhere, then let it blow?" Tank asked.

"The crystals will still be destroyed," came a derisive retort.

Jem rubbed her ear thoughtfully. "How big is the safe?"

"It's actually a small cargo vault, about four by three meters," Richardson replied. "It's designed for holding smaller items, either valuable cargo or passengers' personal effects. Those charges would destroy most of that deck section. Cargo area and external bulkheads will be breached. Probably the deck area above it, too."

The area from the plazo in the nose to the back wall dividing the main ship area from the cargo area would be compromised if not outright destroyed. Food and water storage. Oxygen recycling. How much would be damaged on the first deck? Would enough be left to survive making it to a port somewhere?

Jem gazed at Beckett. Arrogant and so sure of himself. She ought to walk up and knee the SOB. "Does 'tampering' include trying various combinations?" *Sure did,* she thought when he just shrugged.

"The passcode could be anything."

"You can't mess w-with it!"

"There's nothing we can do."

She watched the appraising looks around her. Great. They were back to thinking about Beckett's deal. "Why don't you let me evaluate it before you make any decisions?"

"She'll get us all killed. You can't let—*z-ping*." Beckett crumpled to the deck.

The Kid holstered his stunner. "I've been wanting to do that for some time. What do we do with him?"

"Lock him up in one of the rooms. Tie him down."

"He'll need to be gagged or he'll order the computer to do something." Richardson scowled down at Beckett. "No telling what commands he's pro-grammed in."

"T-tie him in a chair. Stun him w-whenever he w-wakes."

"I'm not playing babysitter." Bowshur scratched his beard. "Be simpler to just disable all audio and computer components in his room."

Everyone nodded in agreement.

"Remember, I need him alive," Jem said. The way the unconscious man was being eyed, would it even be possible? If not, a body would still end speculation even if questions couldn't be asked.

Tank quickly had him wrapped in a cocoon he'd probably need to be cut out of.

"I need to study the vault." Jem told them.

"It's just outside the internal cargo entrance, port side. Hopkins, set a course for the Euphrates System. It's big enough for us to slip away, no matter which deal we take." Richardson met her eyes squarely. "I intend to leave with crystals."

The others echoed his claim.

Jem took the stairwell rungs down to the lower deck. Her or Beckett, they didn't care which. With the pirate life gone, only wealth and survival mattered to them now. Did she expect anything different?

She turned down the narrow corridor. After a short passage, it turned sharply to the right and she entered a small open area. The wide hatch in the wall to her left would open into the lower cargo hold. She stopped in front of the small door, the corridor continuing on past it, turning sharply again toward the front.

The vault was flush against the ship's outer hull and formed the short leg of the L-shaped alcove. The arrangement simplified moving items between the two storage areas. A keyboard rested on a small shelf below a text panel displaying 'PASSCODE REQUIRED' in bright red letters.

"Can you do it?"

She looked over her shoulder. Richardson and Bowshur's eyes swiveled between her and the vault a couple of times. Greed burned in their depths. *Would these be enough for them or would they try and force her hand again at some future date?* Jem chewed her lip. Seven men of questionable ethics. Would giving them the same warning as Kurzvall even matter to them?

"I believe so," she finally said. "How long to Euphrates?"

"Nine days," Richardson said.

"I'll retrieve the crystals shortly before we arrive." Their gazes turned suspicious. "I don't want to be stepping over bodies as you each decide you'd like a bigger share. Manage Beckett however you like. I don't care if he's tied, gagged or hung upside down."

She was halfway back to her room when the O-engines engaged.

CHAPTER 56

Bodies accumulated anyway.

Tank insisted twisting Manx's body into a pretzel was self-defense. Richardson claimed the same thing two days later. When Jem looked up from the charred hole above Bowshur's ear, Richardson shrugged, saying the man turned to run after realizing he was armed. Really? Beckett was the only one not armed on this frigging ship.

They were gathered now in the lounge, watching each other with furtive glances. Tank even managed to do it while eating a sandwich. Beckett was safely tied in a chair.

"Well, where is she?" Beckett demanded.

"Here." Jem stepped in cautiously. The tension was strong enough to cut with a knife. Good thing Richardson returned hers, albeit reluctantly.

"You have the crystals?" Richardson asked.

Beckett snorted derisively. "You actually believe she got into the vault? The woman is leading you on, hoping to get off at Euphrates before anyone can stop her. She'll turn you over to the Enforcers. She hates your guts."

"No, just you and Richardson," the Kid countered. "And I trust her more than I trust any of you." His hand rested lightly on his stunner.

"What's the plan on divvying them?" Jem asked.

"Split them as equally as possible. Flip for any extras."

Jem gave Richardson a disgusted look. "Any extras are going to Magnus to help them rebuild. Now, everyone put their weapons over on the table next to the wall, especially your laz-gun."

"Told you," Beckett said in a bored voice. "She's going to turn us over to Law Enforcement. Not a problem for me. I'll make a good bargain with the crystals. I won't end up as rich as I'd planned, but you fools will be the ones in a Fed-Pen cell. Assuming they don't straight up kill you. My offer still stands."

Tension increased. Hands made small movements toward weapons.

"No. No more deaths," Jem said firmly. "Those crystals have caused enough."

"Let's see you get those crystals before we decide anything further." Richardson's even tone belied his guarded eyes.

Jem knew, without a doubt, Richardson didn't plan on sharing with anyone. He'd do whatever was needed to terminate the rest, then re-partner with Beckett. A partnership that would last only until one of them killed the other. What would a battle between two monsters look like? She reached into her pocket and pulled out a dull, roughly egg-shaped stone. Holding up the palm-size item for all to see she said, "I already have."

All eyes zeroed in on the gem. Greed replaced every other expression except Beckett's. His was shock. *Hah! Not so arrogant now.*

"I know it doesn't look like much in its raw form, so how about this one?" She pulled a second one from her other pocket. Careful polishing had given it a deep blueish-green glow. She held them side-by-side and said conversationally, "Hard to believe they're the same, isn't it? I picked up some of both. Now, before I bring out the others," she nodded toward the table, "weapons down, please."

They drifted toward the table, distrustful glances bouncing between them.

"There is no way you could have guessed the passcode," Beckett said.

"No. But there was one other who knew it," she replied, pointing up. They'd think she hacked *Hidden Trove's* computer. His stare didn't waver.

The men began laying down their weapons. Richardson's laz-gun was down. Good. Tank, Hopkins and the Kid had disarmed and stepped back. Richardson pulled his stunner out and placed it next to his laz-gun.

The next few seconds were a blur.

The laz-gun was in Richardson's hand, boring a hole through Tank and a wall before anyone could move. Whipping around as Hopkins dived to the side, Richardson stumbled, a knife hilt protruding from his chest. He stared downward, as if confused on how it got there. He sank slowly to the floor, staring wide-eyed at the Kid.

"I knew you were going to pull something." The Kid reached down and picked up the laz-gun. Hopkins rose slowly from the floor, his hands out to the side.

"I only want to live quietly. Somewhere," Hopkins said. Deep lines etched his tired face. "Someday have a wife, maybe children. Hope to God they never learn what I got into."

The Kid tossed the gun on the table. "Where are we heading?" he asked, reclaiming and holstering his stunner. Reaching down, he gave the knife a swipe on Richardson's shirt before it disappeared up a sleeve.

"McCutcheon Space Port on Euphrates Three. It's a major cargo port, so we won't attract any interest. We've docked there before." Hopkins headed forward, his weapon untouched.

Jem looked at the bodies. She had no sorrow for them, especially Richardson. Captain Kelding might have shot her on the spot after learning she let him go free. This tied up things so much better. The bow on top? She turned to Beckett, who had remained silent throughout the whole mess. Still staring at her.

"Nothing to say? Not surprised, since you no longer have anything to bargain with."

Walking back toward the kitchen, she reached down and behind the divider to lift the backpack into view. He didn't even glance at it. She met his gaze. Worry sneaked its way along her nerves. There was something scary going on behind those unreadable eyes.

***

Hidden Trove joined the line of ships inbound for Tigres, Euphrates Three. Three and a half hours later they were sitting at the kitchen table in a short-term parking slot. Jem sat at one end. Beckett sat at the other, wrapped snuggly to his chair. Hopkins and the Kid sat on either side of her.

Jem carefully emptied the backpack contents on the table in front of her.

Jaguide crystals. A whole pile of them. Of varying sizes, they represented unbelievable wealth. And greed. And so much death. She set them, one by one, in front of the two men, balancing each pile with polished and unpolished stones as much as possible. She slid the last stone toward herself. Its polished wealth would go a long way in helping Magnus.

"You each have twenty-three." She looked at first one, then the other. "May your choices be better in the new lives you build," she said quietly.

Hopkins looked at his pile of stones, then down the table at Beckett. "When you gave me an ultimatum at the shipyard...I was afraid. Anything was better than dying, right?" He turned haunted eyes to Jem. "I swear, if I had known then what I'd witness...what I have to live with now..." His head shook slowly side to side. Selecting the largest polished crystal, Hopkins slid the remaining stones in front of Jem. "For Magnus. For Midgard." His somber gaze held hers. "For anyone who needs it. Promise me."

"I promise."

Nodding, he left to pack his few belongings.

"He's an idiot."

"No, he's a man with honor and a conscience," Jem told the monster. "Two things you will never understand."

She began loading crystals back into her pack. The Kid slid his stones into his own pack, gave her a nod and headed for his quarters. Jem smiled at the three raw stones left sitting on the table. Whatever had hardened the Kid, the past days had shown her there was still some good inside. At the bottom of a deep crevasse perhaps, but there.

An hour later, firetrucks raced toward a fiercely burning cargo ship. An unexpected sight standing a safe distance from the flames sent a call to the local Law Enforcement. After a quick assessment, the Enforcers called the Federal LEs, who contacted the military. The news quickly leaked, spreading as far and fast as small couriers could be found to take it.

There were tears, hugs, and back-pounding as the entire Republic breathed sighs of relief. The nightmare was finally, truly, over.

CHAPTER 57

Jem watched herself being whisked into the local Judiciary building. The video was replayed a lot less often now, eight days after the real thing. The bodies had been taken away and their identities confirmed. Beckett was sitting in a maximum cell, armed guards just waiting for him to do something stupid.

Stupid wasn't one of the many things he was being called.

Formal questioning had started two days later.

She couldn't remember how many times she'd repeated her story. Of how they fought and killed each other. How their distrust and fear exploded in panic after learning about the raid on their base. The toughest part to get the authorities to swallow was the rogues' agreement to let her live, when it would have been much simpler to kill her. Less risk.

Jem told them she played to their basic natures of survival and revenge. She'd convinced them the authorities would forgo hunting the small fish if they got the big bad shark. With all DNA evidence destroyed in the fire, they'd be able to blend anonymously back into society. Their revenge? Knowing Beckett was locked up and they weren't.

Her presence on the ship? *I was being taken to meet Beckett.* Could she identify the two who escaped? *No, they used only last names or nicknames.* The descriptions she gave would fit a million people. Yes, Beckett and Richardson orchestrated the Branson Fire on Midgard. No, Richardson only hired local thugs to assist in her kidnapping.

Yesterday, after a tense confrontation, she'd had enough.

"I've been grilled for days as if I was Beckett's right hand instead of another victim. I can't help it if you don't like my answers."

She remained silent for the remainder of the session, even after the others kicked the aggressive FLEA out of the room. Then she walked out, flanked by her bodyguards—Thane and Boyd—while Markowitz and his team formed a protective cordon around them.

Seth Sullivan, acting as her lawyer, joined them in the waiting vehicles after announcing sharply his client was done. "You can reference the recordings from now on. They have everything—several times over."

The three had arrived on the *Lone Tracker* two days ago. Markowitz's team was right behind them on a small military transport. They immediately took over—*Thank God!*—moving her from a hounded hotel room to a secured private residence big enough for them all. Seth responded rarely to inquiries and ignored demands.

She needed time to think. Lord, there was so much. Where did she start? Trying to keep her face hidden had been a wasted effort once her name came out. Her school and EMC records were easy to find. Not to mention all those old FLEA flyers. Where would she go? What could she do? What about Kurzvall? They still didn't know what the Consortium was planning.

Last she'd heard, his ships were still impounded and he was threatening all sorts of things if they weren't released. From the growing number of newscasts about dissatisfaction and unrest coming from all four Consortium systems, things might be falling apart for all of them. Should she do more snooping? There had to be something tangible the Enforcers could pin Kurzvall with. Something not brought up at the immunity-free meeting. Another assassination maybe?

No, Kurzvall could wait. There was a hidden bag of crystals to deal with first.

Question was: How to get them to Magnus without raising a lot of interest? Yes, they were stolen. And if—no, when it leaked out, what then? Three men knew what she'd done. One of them was a snake biding his time. Beckett's silence was worrisome: he should have relished making things difficult for her. Someday he'd strike, using the information to make a deal. The 'under duress' excuse should keep her out of prison. Unfortunately, the Jaguide authorities wouldn't rest until they knew how she breached their security.

She let her head fall back. Tired. Dejected.

Her future was sliding further and further out of control. She'd hoped to have one that resembled *some* normalcy, even if she never could be. Thane and Boyd had accepted the ghosting, but what would happen when they learned the truth? The whole truth? That she didn't do something as mundane as rendering herself invisible? Un-un. Like the O-field that had cursed her, she shifted out-of-phase to the rest of the universe.

Bitterness swamped her. Could anyone handle knowing she walked between the atoms of their reality? She was a freak. She was an anomaly. *I'm something that couldn't, shouldn't, exist.* She took several deep breaths, holding each for a moment before releasing it slowly. Yes, issues would rise, as she'd so arrogantly stated, but she hadn't expected to get slapped in the face with them right off. Or this extreme. She needed to regain control. She needed a secure position from which to handle the next slap. *Management and control, remember?*

Jem turned off the comp and stared unseeing at the blank screen.

CHAPTER 58

Seth sighed inwardly as his cousin stalked into the room, Boyd only a few steps behind him. Couldn't they have waited until he got his second cup of coffee down? He stifled a yawn. His system, still on Midgard time, was wanting to go to sleep, not trying to wake up.

Thane stopped in front of his desk. Boyd chose to slouch against a wall.

Seth held up a hand, forestalling the obvious question. "I don't know where Jem went."

Thane scowled at him. "You're her lawyer."

"No, Granddad is. I'm merely an associate appointed to represent him." The way things were shaping up, Jem was going to need a whole team. Maybe he could finally talk them into establishing a family law firm.

Thane sighed, frustrated. "Dammit. There was no need for her to go slipping off."

Really? Seth shot him a surprised look over his cup. He took a much-needed swallow before setting it aside. "The woman went from a quiet, under-the-radar life to universal recognition and celebrant, Thane. She's not handling it well."

Boyd gave a snort. "She abhors it."

"I got the same message you did," Seth said, folding his hands on the desktop. "She's correct. There are decisions to make, some of which will be crucial. How does she structure her new life? What does she do with the remnants from her old one? She can't make rational decisions from the bottom of a pressurized cosmic fish bowl. When she's ready, she'll be in contact." Though when that'd be was anybody's guess.

"So," Thane said scowling, "we just go home? Get on with our lives?"

"Inasmuch as it's possible," Seth replied quietly.

Thane gave him a wary look. "Why?"

"Our family, for good *and* bad, is now linked with her. In general, there'll be the constant and annoying questions. Do you know where she is? Have you heard from her? What do you think about blah, blah, blah? There'll be the loss of social and business connections of those distancing themselves from her... reputation. There'll also be the reverse, a gain in both as they try to wiggle their way into Jem's orbit. You, specifically, can count on a lot of attention as her," he coughed, "friend."

"And what," Thane duplicated the cough, "was *that* for?"

"I don't believe he's seen that particular piece of news yet," Boyd said dryly.

Seth's eyes twinkled. "You've been linked romantically with Jem."

"Well, we aren't." Thane shoved his hands in his pockets. "Yes, I kissed her. Once. In a euphoric adrenaline state due to my and Granddad's timely rescue."

Seth blinked. "Euphoric adrenaline state?"

"Timely rescue?" Boyd said, then started coughing.

Thane shot them both a dirty look. "We're just friends."

"People *might* believe that," Seth said, giving his cousin a huge smirk, "until they learn you're the beneficiary on Jem's ten million credit account."

Thane cringed. "I didn't even know about it until you told me. I don't know why she did it. Certainly not because of some idiot's claim of romance."

"Who else could she leave it to?" Boyd said, shrugging. "Not like she has family."

* * * * *

"Could have left it to you," Thane grumbled and stomped over to the open door. He slumped against its frame and stared blankly into the next room. Voices filtered in from where Markowitz's men were packing up their gear. Their lively debate on how she had once again sneaked past them held equal parts irritation and admiration.

"Has Markowitz found out who helped steal the Delgados?" Thane asked, glancing back.

"No," his cousin said. "Beckett is uncooperative on all subjects. I've filed a claim with Kurzvall Industries requesting the balance of Jem's payment paid into her Midgard account, plus the additional thirty-five million owed. Five each for the other ship units," he clarified, seeing their puzzled looks.

"Last time I checked, four times five equaled twenty," Boyd said.

"The other fifteen is for the three frigates also recovered." Seth grinned wickedly. "I quote: *any additional ship units recovered in the same agreed on conditions would be billed at an additional five million per unit.* End quote. Any. Nothing about it specifically limits the terms just to the battleship components."

"He'll protest it." Boyd's grin matched Seth's.

"Let him," Seth replied confidently. "She convinced one of Beckett's shipyard draftees to come to you with enough information to identify the Survey base they took over."

"Why did she have him go to you?" Thane asked Boyd, puzzled and more than a little bit hurt. Once again, she had turned to the heavy-worlder for help.

"She was afraid you and your family were still being watched."

Okay, that made sense. Some of the hurt dissipated.

"Anyway," Seth continued, "the military was able to attack it with a sufficient and overwhelming force. One Class Two tried to fight its way out and promptly got blown up. Kurzvall isn't complaining because most of Beckett's original mercenaries were on it. The remaining ships, including all the battleship's parts, were captured with hardly any damage."

Thane gave a short, sharp laugh. "Because they gave up."

"Irrelevant. Her actions led directly to its recovery in the desired condition and is therefore entitled to her specified fees." His smile was all legal shark. "If he does contest it, we'll get another ten, twenty million out of the SOB for breach of contract. In the meantime, she has authorized a payment of a hundred thousand dollars to the man in recognition of the risk he took deserting during the attack on Stanlov Two."

Testimonies from surviving rogue members had provided gruesome details of examples made for disloyal behavior. He'd known what to expect if he didn't get safely away.

Seth cleared his throat. "Do either of you know what she meant? The promise?"

Thane shook his head and looked over at Boyd. He was doing the same.

"I'll bet my diploma it's connected to whatever she did during that missing month."

Thane wheeled around completely. "What *she* did? They kidnapped her."

"They went to a lot of trouble to do so and it wasn't for ransom. Beckett had something specific in mind brute force wouldn't get him. He needed stealth."

The two cousins locked gazes.

"I know it. You know it. The fleas know it. Frustration is what drove Agent Simmon's aggression in that final session. I heard Beckett was even offered a more comfortable cell if he'd tell them what."

"Those assholes!"

Boyd's response wasn't as polite as Thane's.

"Beckett's not talking." Seth continued. "He'll probably use it to broker a deal with the Feds sometime in the future. Jem's not talking. She gives vague non-answers and leaves the rest to assumptions. What exactly is she capable of, Thane? What could she have done?" Seth looked at the two blank-faced statues and pointed at himself. "Lawyer. Confidentiality."

His stare grew hostile when the silence dragged on. "There's something out there just waiting, Thane. I can feel it. We can't protect her if we don't have all the facts."

"Honest, Seth. She hasn't told me anything. The rest…it's not my place to tell."

"Well, *they* knew enough about it to kidnap her," Seth bit out, "and it's now impacting the family. Think about *that*, cousin." Slamming the files closed, he stacked them in a neat pile before turning his attention to the document displayed on his comp screen.

Boyd gave Thane a sympathetic grimace and slid out the door.

Starting to follow, Thane paused in the doorway. Seth looked up briefly, but resumed reading when he remained mute. The set of his jaw told Thane his cousin was well past irritated.

With a final shake of his head, he turned and left. Reaching his room, he stared silently out a window. He didn't see the crowded, sun-drenched sidewalk. He saw the dark, silent alleys of Pappia. After several minutes, he dropped heavily into a chair. Turning the desk comp on, he retrieved the vid-message everyone had awakened to.

He stared at the image. It stared back with quiet dignity.

His eyes roamed her face. When he reached those eyes, he looked into them. In their depths he found sadness. Regret. Guilt? Secrets.

Secrets, he kept telling himself, she was entitled to. But Seth was right. Would any of them affect the family? How? To what extent? He'd hoped those walls would drop—even just a little, and she'd trust him. The painful truth was, she didn't. Not after his family had risked their reputations and business. Not after he had almost been killed. He'd given her several chances to explain, but all he got was vagueness. Or lies.

He gave a resigned sigh. Guess he didn't know Jem Seaborne Wilmont of Sol. "Play vid-message."

She smiled.

"Good morning. To everyone here and elsewhere who has given me help, support, and most of all, friendship, you have my deepest thanks. I would not have made it to this day without you. Obviously, I cannot simply resume my old life. I must find a way to coexist with this new one. I need... She looked off to one side, taking and releasing a deep breath before looking back. *There are things I need to think on. Decide on. I cannot do it in this madhouse. I also have a promise to keep.*

I respectfully ask my current legal team to continue their representation and bill my Midgard account as needed. Stay well. I will see you again."

He watched a wicked grin spread across her face and light up those eyes.

"Even if you don't see me."

Word of mouth is very important to a new author. If you have enjoyed this book, please consider leaving a positive review. Even a few lines will help my readership. Thank you.

.

Made in the USA
Monee, IL
19 December 2021

86451420R00193